The PURSUIT OF PLEASURE

The PURSUIT OF PLEASURE

ELIZABETH ESSEX

BRAVA

KENSINGTON PUBLISHING CORP.

www.kensingtonbooks.com

BRAVA BOOKS are published by

Kensington Publishing Corp.
119 West 40th Street
New York, NY 10018

All Kensington titles, imprints and distributed lines are available at special quantity discounts for bulk purchases for sales promotion, premiums, fund-raising, educational or institutional use.

Special book excerpts or customized printings can also be created to fit specific needs. For details, write or phone the office of the Kensington Special Sales Manager: Kensington Publishing Corp., 119 West 40th Street, New York, NY 10018. Attn. Special Sales Department. Phone: 1-800-221-2647.

Brava and the B logo are Reg. U.S. Pat. & TM Off.

ISBN-13: 978-0-7582-5154-1
ISBN-10: 0-7582-5154-8

First Kensington Trade Paperback Printing: December 2010

10 9 8 7 6 5 4 3 2 1

Printed in the United States of America

*To Judy, for friendship
and for her devotion to romance.*

ACKNOWLEDGMENTS

I would like to thank the members of the Dallas Area Romance Authors for their support, encouragement, and sterling advice, especially Vicki Batman; the members of the Beau Monde who gave this book its first push with their Royal Ascot Contest; my kind and lovely editor, Megan Records and all the staff at Kensington Brava; my hilarious agent, Barbara Poelle of the Irene Goodman Agency; my family for their patience and for making it easy for me to write; Anne Calhoun, for her much needed help with all things spicy; and last, but certainly not least, my brilliant critique partner, Joanne Lockyer, without whose sterling advice this would be a much lesser work.

CHAPTER 1

Dartmouth, England
May 1794

"I do say I'll never marry, but I have always wanted to be a widow."

The young woman's voice, with its droll, self-aware tone, wafted down the length of the assembly room's dimly lit balcony, floated into the darkness beyond, and entwined with the smoke dancing off the hot end of Jameson Marlowe's cigar.

Marlowe clamped down on the cheroot to keep from laughing out loud into the warm night. He didn't need to look around the other side of the column to know who was speaking. He'd spent years away, and still, he knew. She came to his mind as swift and unbidden as a gunshot.

Lizzie. No one else could manage to be so ridiculously charming.

"A widow? You must be joking." Another girl, her voice as young but much less world-weary, sounded scandalized. Her breathy little voice rose higher with each word.

"I'm not. If I were a widow I'd have everything I need. Independence. Social standing. Financial stability." Lizzie blew out a long sigh full of wistfulness. "It would be perfect. A marriage without the man."

"You can't mean it!"

The owner of the breathy little voice didn't know her friend very well, it seemed. Lizzie always meant it. Always. He could picture her impudent, challenging smile as she tossed her opinions off like grenades.

Marlowe grinned, leaned his head back against the column, and took another deep drag from the cigar, his mind whirling like a steel clockwork, ticking away, crystallizing his plans. He had waited a long time for this moment. He would make this work.

Defiant little Lizzie Paxton.

Yes, she would do very well. In fact, she was perfect.

He ground out the cigar with the toe of his boot and stepped out from behind the column. "She always means it, don't you, Lizzie?"

At the sound of his voice, two young women, dressed in fashionable white muslin chemise dresses, turned their heads towards him. But only one of them smiled. Ever so slightly. Lizzie.

A sharp pang lanced through him at the sight of her, like the ache of a long-healed bruise. Despite the years he'd spent away, despite the fact she'd grown up, Marlowe still recognized the girl he'd known inside the beautiful young woman leaning negligently against the balcony railing. The same ginger-tinted hair. The same boneless, feline physicality. The same slightly feral smile. The smile that always led to mischief.

Lizzie slowly straightened from where she lounged against the railing. The pale dress, belted with a sash of bright green satin that matched her eyes, accentuated the liquid grace of her body. On anyone else, it would have looked demure. On Lizzie, it looked like a challenge.

One he was definitely going to accept.

"Is that you, Marlowe?" Her tone was all jaded indifference, but her voice poured over him like whisky, full of warmth and bite. Oh yes, with her, he'd need to keep his wits about him.

"It is indeed, Lizzie."

Her sparkling gaze flicked over him. "Back from the wars, are you?"

"Yes," he acknowledged with a sketch of a bow, "from service in His Majesty's Royal Navy."

"Oh. Well, good for you." She turned back out to the night, but he caught the flash of a smile brewing along her lips.

Ah, perhaps she *wasn't* as indifferent as she wanted him to think. Nor was her companion, who sent her an urgent look. And an unpleasant little jab in the ribs.

"Oh, all right. Celia, may I present Mr. Jameson Raphael Marlowe?" Lizzie flourished a fine-boned wrist in his direction. "Miss Celia Burke."

"*Captain* Marlowe, at your service, ma'am." He bowed over Miss Burke's perfumed hand and graced it with a kiss. The young woman's cheeks colored prettily.

"Come to make moon eyes at the ravishing Celia, have you? You'll have to get in line, even at a backwater assembly such as this." Lizzie's brilliant eyes teased even though she pursed her lips to keep from smiling. He remembered that look, but it was much more effective now that she was all grown up.

"No. Although Miss Burke is indeed ravishing." He straightened and turned to face his childhood friend—and the reason his childhood had ended. "It's you I want to see, Lizzie. I've got a proposition for *you*."

This time her mouth smiled along with her eyes, the apricot lips widening until he could see the shine of her teeth. He remembered them as being particularly sharp.

In contrast, poor Celia Burke gasped at his audacity. Her blue eyes practically popped out of her head. It must be rare for her to witness a gentleman giving Lizzie as good as he got.

"Oh, off you go, Celia." Lizzie gave her friend a gentle nudge towards the door. "I'm safe as houses with dear old Jamie," she drawled.

She made him sound like a senile old uncle. He'd take pleasure in disabusing her of that notion.

"She'll send my mother out," Lizzie surmised as Miss Burke left reluctantly, with a wide-eyed last look over her shoulder at her friend. "We'll have to leg it."

She turned and, without waiting, led the way back into the building and down the narrow, creaking servants' corridor. It was somehow perfectly natural Lizzie should know the hidden ways and back rooms of the local assembly hall as well as she knew her own home. She was just that kind of girl, always had been. The sort of lazily inquisitive child who acted as if she had a perfect right and a perfect reason to be where she oughtn't.

"I couldn't help overhearing your conversation." He wanted to steer their chat to his purpose, but the back of her neck was white and long. He'd never noticed that long slide of skin before, so pale against the vivid color of her locks. He'd gone away before she'd been old enough to put up her hair. And nowadays the fashion seemed to be for masses of loose ringlets covering the neck. Trust Lizzie to still sail against the tide.

"Yes, you could." Her breezy voice broke into his thoughts. "I beg your pardon?"

"Help it. You *could* have helped it, as any polite gentlemen *should*, but you obviously chose not to." She didn't even bother to look back at him as she spoke and walked on, but he heard the teasing in her voice. Such intriguing confidence. He could use it to his purpose. She had always been up for a lark.

He caught her elbow and steered her into an unused parlor. She let him guide her easily, without resisting the intimacy or the presumption of the brief contact of his hand against the soft, vulnerable skin of her inner arm, but once through the door she just seemed to dissolve out of his grasp. His empty fingers prickled from the sudden loss. He let her move away and closed the door.

No lamp or candle branch illuminated the room, only the moonlight streaming through the tall casement windows. Lizzie looked like a pale ghost, weightless and hovering in the strange light. He took a step nearer. He needed her to be real, not an illusion. Over the years she'd become a distant but re-curring dream, a combination of memory and boyish lust, haunting his sleep.

He had thought of her, or at least the idea of her, almost constantly over the years. She had always been there, in his mind, swimming just below the surface. And he had come tonight in search of her. To banish his ghosts.

She took a sliding step back to lean nonchalantly against the arm of a chair, her pose one of sinuous, bored indifference.

"So what are you doing in Dartmouth? Aren't you meant to be messing about with your boats?"

"Ships," he corrected automatically and then smiled at his foolishness for trying to tell Lizzie anything. "The big ones are ships."

"And they let *you* have one of the *big* ones? Aren't you a bit young for that?" She tucked her chin down to subdue her smile and looked up at him from under her gingery brows. Very mischievous. She was warming to him.

If it was worldliness she wanted, he could readily supply it. He mirrored her smile.

"Hard to imagine, isn't it, Lizzie?" He opened his arms wide, presenting himself for her inspection.

Only she didn't inspect him. Her eyes slid away to inven-tory the scant furniture in the darkened room. "No one else calls me that anymore."

"Lizzie? Well, I do. I can't imagine you as anything else. And I like it. I like saying it. Lizzie." The name hummed through his mouth like a honeybee sprinkled with nectar. Like a kiss. He moved closer so he could see the emerald color of her eyes, dimmed by the half light, but still brilliant against the white of her skin. He leaned a fraction too close and whispered, "Lizzie. It always sounds somehow . . . naughty."

She turned quickly. Wariness flickered across her mobile face, as if she were suddenly unsure of both herself and him, before it was just as quickly masked.

And yet, she continued to study him surreptitiously, so he held himself still for her perusal. To see if she would finally notice him as a man. He met her eyes and he felt a kick low in his gut. In that moment plans and strategies became unimportant. The only important thing was for Lizzie to see him. It was essential.

But she kept all expression from her face. He was jolted to realize she didn't want him to read her thoughts or mood. She was trying hard to keep *him* from seeing *her*.

It was an unexpected change. The Lizzie he had known as a child had been so wholly passionate about life, she had thrown herself body and soul into each and every moment, each action and adventure. She had not been covered with this veneer of poised nonchalance.

And yet it was only a veneer. He was sure of it. And he was equally sure he could make his way past it. He drew in a measured breath and sent her a slow, melting smile to show, in the course of the past few minutes, he'd most definitely noticed she was a woman.

She gave no outward reaction, and it took Marlowe a long moment to recognize her response: she looked careful. It was a quality he'd never seen in her before.

Finally, after what felt like an infinity, she broke the moment. "You didn't answer. Why are you here? After all these years?"

He chose the most convenient truth. "A funeral. Two weeks ago." A bleak, rain-soaked funeral that couldn't be forgotten. The downpour that April day had chilled him to his very marrow. He went cold just thinking about it, unable to shake the horrible feeling sitting like a lump of cold porridge in his belly. It was wrong, all wrong. Frank couldn't be dead. He shouldn't be dead. And yet he was. They'd found his body, pale and lifeless, washed up cold and unseeing upon the banks of the Dart. Drowned.

At least that was what the local authorities said. But Marlowe knew better. Frank was murdered. And he would prove it.

Lizzie's murmur brought him back. "My condolences, for what they're worth." She ran her palm up and down her other forearm as if she were chilled. Lizzie had never been at ease with open emotion. "Anyone I knew?"

"Lieutenant Francis Palmer."

"Frankie Palmer?" For a moment she was truly affected. Her full lips dropped open in an exhalation. "From down Stoke Fleming way? Didn't you two go off to sea together, all those years ago?"

"Yes, ten years ago." Ten long years. A lifetime.

"Oh. I am sorry." Her voice lost its languid bite.

He looked back and met her eyes. Such sincerity had never been one of Lizzie's strong suits. No, that was wrong. She'd always been sincere, or at least truthful—painfully so as he recalled—but she rarely let her true feelings show.

"Thank you, Lizzie. But I didn't lure you into a temptingly darkened room to bore you with dreary news."

"No, you came to proposition me." The mischievous little smile crept back. Lizzie was never the sort to be intimidated for long. She had always loved to be doing things she ought not.

A heated image of her sinuous white body temptingly entwined in another man's arms rose unbidden in his brain. Good God, what other things had Lizzie been doing over the past few years that she ought not? And with whom?

Marlowe quickly jettisoned the irrational spurt of jealousy. Her more recent past hardly mattered. In fact, some experience on her part might better suit his plans.

"Yes, my proposition. I can give you what you want. A marriage without the man."

For the longest moment she went unnaturally still, then she slid off the chair arm and glided closer to him. So close, he almost backed up. So close, her rose petal of a mouth came but a hairsbreadth from his own. Then she lifted her inquisitive nose and took a bold, suspicious whiff of his breath.

"You've been drinking."

"I have," he admitted without a qualm.

"How much?"

"More than enough for the purpose. And you?"

"Clearly not enough. Not that they'd let me." She turned and walked away. Sauntered really. She was very definitely a saunterer, all loose joints and limbs, as if she'd never paid the least attention to deportment. Very provocative, although he doubted she meant to be. An image of a bright, agile otter, frolicking unconcerned in the calm green of the river Dart, twisting and rolling in the sunlit water, came to mind.

"Drink or no, I meant what I said."

"Are you proposing? Marriage? To me?" She laughed as if it were a joke. She didn't believe him.

"I am."

She eyed him more closely, her gaze narrowing even as one marmalade eyebrow rose in assessment. "Do you have a fatal disease?"

"No."

"Are you engaged to fight a duel?"

"Again, no."

"Condemned to death?" She straightened with a fluid undulation, her spine lifting her head up in surprise as the thought entered her head, all worldliness temporarily obliterated. "Planning a suicide?"

"No and no." It was so hard not to smile. Such a charming combination of concern and cheek. The cheek won out: she gave him that feral, slightly suspicious smile.

"Then how do you plan to arrange it, the 'without the man' portion of the proceedings? I'll want some sort of guarantee. You can't imagine I'm gullible enough to leave your fate, or my own for that matter, to chance."

A low heat flared within him. By God, she really was considering it.

"And yet, Lizzie, I think you may. I am an officer of His Majesty's Royal Navy and am engaged to captain a convoy of prison ships to the Antipodes. I leave only days from now. The last time I was home, in England, was four and a half years ago and then only for a few months to recoup from a near fatal wound. This trip is slated to take at least eight . . . years."

Her face cleared of all traces of impudence. Oh yes, even Lizzie could be led.

"Storms, accidents, and disease provide most of the risk. Don't forget we're still at war with France and Spain. And the Americans don't think too highly of us either. One stray cannonball could do the job quite nicely."

"Is that what did it last time?"

"Last time? I've never been dead before."

The ends of her ripe mouth nipped up. The heat in his gut sailed higher.

"You said you had recovered from a near fatal wound."

"Ah, yes. Grapeshot, actually. In my chest. Didn't go deep enough to kill me, though afterward, the fever nearly did."

Her gaze skimmed over his coat, curious and maybe a little hungry. The heat spread lower, kindling into a flame.

"Do you want to see?" He was being rash, he knew, but he'd done this for her once before, taken off his shirt on a dare. And he wanted to remind her. He'd lived off the promise of that day for years.

She gave him a saucy smile. "You mean I don't have to dare you this time?"

Marlowe felt his mouth turn up in a grin as he peeled off his cravat, shucked the coat, unbuttoned his waistcoat all the way, and flipped open the close of his shirt at his throat. He tugged the linen open to reveal the motley spray of bullet scars across his otherwise smooth chest. Daring her to look this time.

Oh, but she looked. Her eyes widened in the dark as she leaned forward, inching her inquisitive gaze closer. So curious—always had been. Like a nearly wild barn cat sniffing at a pot of cream. She couldn't seem to help herself.

Ah, but he would help her. He took her right hand and placed it flat against his skin.

A mistake.

Marlowe sucked in a breath through his teeth. Her cool, nimble fingers danced tentatively across his flesh. Sweet God, such open, agile curiosity. It was unbearably erotic. His nipples contracted, and his eyes threatened to buckle shut. Her touch had propelled him from want straight into compulsion. God help him, less than twenty minutes in her presence, and he was desperate to have her, to bury himself in her heat.

He should have known. He should have been prepared for the rush of desire skittering like a hot, searing wind across his exposed flesh. There had always been something about Lizzie, and only Lizzie, that got under his skin. Maybe it was the way she looked at a body, all teasing, insolent dismissal, or the way she smiled behind her eyes. Though it didn't really matter how she did it. It only mattered that she still made his skin prick and his gut clench and his pulse race. It only mattered that his fingers itched to trace the long, white line of her nape and kiss the impudent little smiles from her face.

Please God, let her say yes, and he could finally have her in his bed, beneath him, at least for a few days. Lizzie was bound to be good at that. She was made for hedonism.

Marlowe anchored his hands to his side to keep from pulling her to him. It would put her off to do anything uninvited, but her simple touch was pleasure so painful it was nearly unbearable, and he didn't want the sweet torture to stop. So he endured her featherlight strokes and tried to remember to breathe.

"Well," she whispered at last, "I don't know when I've been more surprised."

It was pure Jamie. She'd always thought him a bit of a bully trap—a boy whose mild, self-effacing manner masked his deeply honorable, courageous soul. Too honest and honorable for his own good. Cheerfully going off to be killed and showing her the probability of his death scattered across his chest.

And it was shockingly nice, his chest. And so unexpected. Smooth and warm and sleekly muscled. Heat seeped off his skin to singe her fingertips. He'd always seemed so slight and unassuming as a boy, but now he was tall and handsomely made. Very, very handsomely made. The years had changed him into a man.

She had tried so hard, so very hard, not to think of him during the past ten years. And she had failed. But she had always thought of him as a boy, as the boy she'd known. Her playmate, her friend, her conscience, and her tormentor. Her companion. To her, he'd been everything she thought good and right with the world, until the day he had left her behind without a backward glance, gone to seek his fortune in that world. The world of men. The one place she could not follow.

And yet she still had missed that boy. Desperately. It was impossible not to want to see if he still remained inside this formidable man.

But perhaps he was not so formidable. She could feel him tremble beneath her palm. Or was it her own hand that trembled? Lizzie stole a peek up at him. His clear gray eyes looked right through her pose, as he always had done, pinning her like a butterfly to the truth.

Her hand quivered in earnest, now. But she didn't stop. She couldn't seem to resist touching his skin. Because he was Jamie. He was like a lodestone, pulling her to him without even seeming to try. She simply couldn't resist him. And she liked the astonishing feel of his chest rising and falling ever so slightly under her hand. His body gave off a crackling tension, like the air before a thunderstorm, as she drew her fingertip from one scar to the next, connecting the dots that littered his chest.

His breath blew out in a rush, a warm breeze against the back of her hand. He smelled like sweet, mellow whisky. And she wanted to taste him. To taste Jamie.

Lizzie snatched back her hand and turned away to cover the piercing stab of attraction. How much did he remember? Good Lord, but she'd been a forward little girl, sure of her secure place in the world.

She wasn't twelve anymore. She gathered her composure like a shield and turned back to face him, armed with her most flippant demeanor. "You've convinced me you're likely to die, but why else should I marry a junior captain? I've no want to be left with your debts."

When he finally spoke, his voice sounded strange and winded. "No debts, I can assure you. You can write up all the settlements yourself, if you like. And there is a lovely house, Glass Cottage. Up along the cliffs above Redlap Cove. With several hundred arable acres. There's a steward to mind that." He shrugged his coat back over his broad shoulders.

"A cottage?"

"A house. Not too big, not too small, with eight principal bedrooms, or so. Lovely view down to the sea. It's nothing to Hightop, but it could be yours."

"And you own it? The rector's son has certainly come up in the world." But she'd never doubted he would.

"Prize money, Lizzie. Didn't anyone tell you? I've made my fortune off the Spanish Dons."

She felt the genuine delight of a conspirator. "How very enterprising of you."

"How very," he agreed with a laugh. "Of course, if you don't marry me, when I do die, the whole thing will go to my useless cousin Jeremy, who as you must recall is a prize prig."

"Wroxham? I thought he'd taken himself off to Oxford or London."

"He did. But he'll either come back here and play lord of the manor, or he'll sell the place, which I can't have. That's my only stipulation, Lizzie. You mustn't sell. No matter what. You can't live there, of course, but neither can you sell the place."

"Rather sentimental of you, isn't it?"

"Perhaps, but then I don't mind being sentimental. I owe it to the blood of the honest, true men who toiled and died winning that money, Lizzie, and I'll be damned if I let a snuff-eating toad like Jeremy Wroxham have any bit of it."

She wrinkled up her nose at the mention of Wroxham. "Bloody Oxford men—think they own the world."

"And that, my dear Lizzie, is why *you* must have it instead. You must see it. It's beautiful and covered with roses that Wroxham hasn't the wit or temperament to appreciate. And I've enough money too. That would be yours as well. You could do anything you wished with it, once I'm dead."

She tossed up her shoulder to show him she'd changed. She wasn't about to count his money to find out how much "enough" was. It had always seemed an unbridgeable gulf between them, money and status. Between Lord Paxton's daughter and the rector's son.

"And what about you? My father has offered an enormously vulgar amount for someone to take me off his hands."

"No takers?"

"No one I'd take. Gorgers, the lot of them."

He laughed at her blunt description at the sort of overfed, self-satisfied young sportsmen who strutted through Dartmouth's version of the marriage mart. "Well, if you married me, your marriage portion would be yours straight away. And when I die, you'll have my entire fortune."

It was all so tempting. Such a perfectly simple and straightforward way to gain true independence. But far too good to be true. She slid another glance over his tall, lean form. So slight and unassuming—that's what she'd always thought. With his brown, tousled hair falling over his pale, open eyes, he still looked younger than his twenty-four years. But she was wrong. There was something more.

There were many men of her acquaintance, even some of the men who had tried to court her, who were far better looking. Not that Jamie was homely. Not at all. He just looked so . . . familiar. Until you got to those eyes. Translucent, pale, sea gray. Stormy. Like a wolf in winter, sleek and persistent. The vivid image of him as a hungry predator took her by surprise. He had changed from that gangly, pale, laughing boy. He was still lean and lanky, but there was now something hard, honed, and tensile, something almost dangerous lurking beneath the easy smile and sly, intelligent humor. He was a man who had been tested.

Her fingertips still tingled from the feel of his chest beneath her hands. "Are you really going to die?"

"More like than not. At the very least, I shall be gone for eight long years." His mouth quirked into a deprecating half-smile, but his eyes looked solemn. For all his dry acceptance, she thought he wasn't quite as ready to die as he pretended.

"Hmm." A sound hummed out of her throat, tight and husky.

"Don't tell me you'd miss me?" His voice teased her.

He wouldn't believe her even if she said so. And she would never say so.

"Not in the least." She winged up a shoulder for emphasis. "I mean, I'd mourn you properly, of course. Wear crepe. Shed a tear or two, because you were a nice enough child, but then your memory would . . . fade. I don't suppose you've had a portrait made I could put over the fireplace to remember what you looked like?"

"No." He laughed. "But perhaps I could arrange for an idealized miniature you could pull out and grow misty over at the proper moment."

"Perfect."

"So, are you going to marry me?"

Was she? The little voice in her head said, why not? It was Jamie, not one of the pot-hunting swells back in the assembly room. But still, she hesitated. Marriage was for life: inexorably, legally binding. Once she said yes, there would be no going back. Not until he died. It seemed so . . . mercenary, so dreadfully cold-blooded, even if it was his idea. Even if he was her Jamie.

It had been one thing to scandalize Celia with the idea of some anonymous, unimagined man making her a widow, but it was quite another thing to contemplate being left by this man. This new Jamie.

"I'll let you know in a few days' time. I'll send round a note." She paused. "Where are you staying?"

"No. I'll call on you. If there's a chance you'll accept, we'll need it to look correct. Or at least plausible." There was that slow, sly smile. It tickled something inside her. Something pleasurable. Something reassuring. But why should she need reassuring? He was taking as big a chance as she. "And I only have a few days' time."

"All right. Come to call, if you like." She gave him one of her patented shrugs.

"Lizzie, you don't sound convinced. Perhaps you need some sort of inducement?"

"Besides your money and your death?"

He just continued to smile at her. She cocked her head and waited. Jamie liked to dole things out slowly, like pieces of candy. Came of being a minister's son.

"How about . . . a little seduction?"

She let out a whoop of laughter to cover her sudden breath-lessness. Not so much like a rector's son after all. He sounded so sure of himself, and those eyes of his—those pale eyes that now gave off an almost incandescent light—they looked right through her, as if he knew the shivery way his words made her body feel.

Heavens above, she would need to be careful.

"You needn't bother." She turned away to cut off his steady probing gaze.

"It's no bother. In fact, it'll be fun. You used to like to have fun, Lizzie. I think you need some convincing. And some kissing."

The tightness in her chest increased. Her breath felt hot and dry. "You're going to convince me with kisses? You'd be better off offering me some of that whisky you've had too much of."

He smiled his Jamie smile, full of light and mirth, as he pulled a slim flask out of his coat pocket.

"Secreting liquor on your person? How delightfully naughty."

"Just your sort of naughty, Lizzie." He pulled out the cork and held it out for her, watching her all the while. Knowing what he did to her. "Ladies first."

She swiped it out of his long fingers and took a tentative sip. It burned pleasantly going down and infused her throat and belly with mellow warmth. Much better than champagne, which went straight to one's head. She took another liberal swallow.

"That's my girl."

She tossed the empty flask back to him. "I'm not your girl."

"You ought to be." His penetrating, laughing gaze dared her. "Come on, Lizzie. Send me to my death happy. Surely you can do it. Or haven't you learned how?"

It was unfair of him to bait her so. She ought to be able to resist a dare by now. But she couldn't, and furthermore, she really didn't want to. And why not? Jamie had come back. Finally. A grown man. A man who wanted her. And soon he was going away again, perhaps forever, perhaps to die.

So Lizzie lowered her chin and gave him her smile, all of it. It made him blink, his pale eyes darkening in anticipation. Then she closed the distance to him and pulled his mouth down to hers.

CHAPTER 2

Oh, yes. Lizzie Paxton had very definitely been doing things she oughtn't. This was not her first kiss.

Not her first *real* kiss anyway. Her first kiss had been down along the riverside that August afternoon when Marlowe had been all of fourteen. She had been so young he was almost embarrassed to think of it.

Tonight, her cool little hand inched up his nape and tangled with the queue in his hair. She pressed her lips into his without hesitation and then moved them ever so slightly in invitation.

But for all that, she went no further.

It was just an act, her pose of jaded indifference. She had no real idea of what she was doing. And no idea of whom she was dealing with. He had more than enough experience, and expertise, for both of them.

The devil deep in his gut smiled. His hands came around to the small of her back to press her closer as he opened his mouth to taste her. Her lips were cool, just like her hands, not yet warmed by his need—his need to taste her, to have her in his arms, under his control, and to finally, finally possess her.

Devil take him. His need was like the roaring of cannon fire in his ears, deafening his better sense. He had to force himself not to grip her, to carefully loosen his hands and pull back before he began doing things *he* oughtn't. She was in over her head, but he'd get nowhere if he tried to control her. With Lizzie, he couldn't press. He couldn't force her to go anywhere she didn't want to go. If it wasn't her own idea, she'd dig in her heels like a balky foal.

So he angled his head and sucked lightly at her bottom lip until she opened her mouth like a flower, slowly unfurling towards the light. Oh God, her lips were soft and sweet and tasted vaguely of cinnamon spice. So soft. So indecently, incongruously, surprisingly soft, when all the rest of her seemed to made up of wickedly sharp angles. She was delicious.

Marlowe lifted his hands to cradle her jaw and stroke his thumbs along her cheeks, encouraging her, slowly feeding his own need. When she began to kiss him back and to taste him with hungry little nips, he sent his tongue out tentatively to dance with hers, waiting, straining his patience until she followed of her own volition.

And she did. Lizzie had always been a fast learner, and now she began licking at him and sucking until he lost his will to resist, until he wanted to devour her. She was like pure sunlight in his arms—she scorched him.

He framed her face in his hands, probing her with his gaze. "My God, Lizzie. Do you have any idea what you do to me? You make me ravenous."

He couldn't stop his arms from hauling her closer still, drawing her body into intimate contact with his. He couldn't stop himself from kissing her hard, as voracious and predatory as he felt, arching her head back and plundering her mouth. Falling into her.

She hesitated a fraction of a moment before she grappled her arms around his neck and wrapped her legs around his, clinging to him as if he were flotsam in a shipwreck. As if her life depended upon him. Above the pounding in his ears, he could hear fabric tear.

A hot explosion of lust fired deep, deep in his gut. Oh, God, yes.

He backed her into the wall, pinning her against the oaken paneling. He knew he shouldn't push her. Shouldn't press into her until he could feel the frighteningly fragile bones of her hips against his belly. Shouldn't plaster his chest against her small, perfectly rounded breasts. My God, he hadn't seen her in ten years and he was all over her like musket fire.

If he tupped her here and now, against the wall like an inn-yard cull, she would think he was trying to force her into this marriage. He couldn't do it that way. She had to choose. He needed her to choose.

Through will alone, he pulled back, leveraging his weight away, letting her breathe. Then he loosened his hands from where they gripped her buttocks and let her feet slide back down to the floor. He allowed himself the one last luxury of nuzzling at her neck and inhaling deeply her scent. Her unique citrus spice. And then he stepped away.

She stood before him without any trace of pretense, completely undone, her eyes glowing like emeralds and her white skin washed silver in the moonlight, her small chest heaving. No trace of indifference now.

"Lizzie." He couldn't think of anything else to say. Actually, he couldn't think at all.

"Well," she said, as her gasping slowly subsided, "haven't you just been full of surprises?"

And then she slipped away, dissolving through the door and into the dark as if she had never been there at all. As if, after all these years, he was still imagining her.

She was still all he could think of when he finally made his way into the grim confines of the Heart of Oak Tavern off Warfleet Row.

God, but he'd waited a long time to finally have Lizzie Paxton. Half his life. There were times when he had wondered if his attraction to her was something he'd made up, a boyish infatuation he'd let run for too long and blown out of proportion in his mind.

No. No mere infatuation would have lasted this long. And no infatuation would have set Lizzie blazing like tinder in his hands.

"Where the hell have you been?" The big blond man in the dim corner at the back of the smoke-filled tavern barely looked up from his ale.

Marlowe hauled his thoughts back into order and put his mind to the work at hand. "And a good evening to you, too. Morning, rather." He kept his voice low as he tossed his slouchy, wool seaman's hat down on the table and slid onto the bench. "I was gracing the local assembly with my presence. One last go, being seen."

"Dancing." Hugh McAlden's upper lip curled back and his voice was laden with scorn. He poured Marlowe a tankard from the pitcher at his elbow.

"Exactly," Marlowe agreed. "Be happy it fell to me."

"I am. Bloody happy it all falls to you. I don't like all this deceit. Goes against the grain."

"I'm not thrilled either. The whole damn scheme promises to become a right mess, but orders are orders. Just be glad you're not the local." He took a long, deep drink of the ale.

His lieutenant and longtime friend remained his usual surly self. "You know I am." McAlden eyed him closely. "Took you long enough."

"I ran into a bit of a complication." That was as neat a description of Lizzie as he could give. "Though I may have found a way to alleviate one of my problems."

"Which one?"

"The house. And my 'estate,' such as it is. I think I've finally come up with a way to get around the Honorable Jeremy Wroxham."

McAlden flashed an unholy smile, curving up one side of

his mouth. "A right couple of Scots bastards, we are. I'm all ears."

Marlowe raised his tankard in a toast. "Wish me happy."

The Squire and Lady Theodora Paxton, Lizzie's parents, resided in a beautiful three-story manor house just north of the town, set high on a hill, overlooking the river Dart. High-top House was a lot like Lizzie: blindingly bright and open to the countryside, its whitewashed stone walls punctuated by a row of lofty, impertinent gables.

Marlowe had gone to a lot of trouble to tog himself out in his best Corinthian rig. His coat of deep blue Bath superfine fitted him like a second skin and, he knew, suited him admirably. He had even gone so far as to try to tame his infernal cowlick, clubbing his hair back ruthlessly, all towards putting in a suitable, suitor-like appearance. He had thought of defying navy custom and his assignment to wear his best dress uniform and sword, but Lizzie was unlikely to be impressed by anything so obvious as braid and silver buttons, however pleasingly it might have aggravated Squire Paxton.

Marlowe swallowed the bitter taste in his mouth. It made him a lesser man to want such a petty revenge upon Lizzie's father for having, quite literally and quite forcefully, cast him to his fate. No matter the Navy had been the making of him. Everything he was, everything he had worked so assiduously to become, his every success, was due to the fact he was an officer in His Majesty's Royal Navy. Yet, the injustice of the Squire's shipping him off, the insufferable presumption of his arranging the lives of lesser mortals still rankled, like a sore that refused to heal.

Perhaps that was why he was unaccountably nervous. Here he was, a man who had faced danger, mortal danger, hundreds of times, yet his insides were clenching themselves up tighter than a Turk's-head knot. He had thought this up as a lark, as a convenient pleasure to have Lizzie and as a small dish of tea and retribution for the squire. But he'd be damn disappointed if she said no. *When* she said no.

Because Lizzie was too sharp to let him get away with it.

Then again, if she had meant to reject him out of hand, she would have said so that night. He was sure of it. Or at least he had been, until he lifted the heavy brass knocker on her father's door and let it fall with an ominous, dull thud.

The door was opened almost immediately, not by the butler, or even a footman, but by Lizzie herself, looking like a scullery maid.

She was wearing an old, out-of-mode work dress made of pale green cotton over a plain white linen fichu and sleeves. She couldn't have looked less the belle, and he could only laugh at his own efforts to play the suitor.

She motioned him over the threshold with an impatient toss of her head, ignoring his sartorial splendor.

"Come on then," she whispered.

"Where's your butler?" He didn't bother to lower his voice. Perhaps they were in tick and the butler let go? That would actually fall in well with his plans.

"Sent on a goose chase. I'd prefer our interview to be private." She kept her voice meaningfully low.

"Ashamed of me, are you, Lizzie?"

"Not yet." She cast him an almost-smile. "But the day is young. . . . You're early."

"My apologies for not waiting until the afternoon to call. I am on a rather restricted schedule."

"Points off for ungallant punctuality—it must come of being a navy man. You've caught me out." She flicked her skirts. "I should say yes, just to punish you."

"Does that mean . . . ?

Lizzie laid a finger across her lips in warning, but it was too late. A quavering voice floated out from behind the drawing room doors.

"Elizabeth, dear, is that you?"

The voice of Lady Theodora—he was sure it could be none other—instantly took him back in time. How many times had he heard her good-natured inquiry after them: "Now, come in and sit and tell me what you two have been up to today."

Lizzie was not at all affected by nostalgia. She rolled her eyes heavenward and scrunched up her nose. She crooked a finger at him and silently headed down the hallway. He ignored her. Just for fun.

"Aren't you going to permit me to pay my respects to your parents, or am I to be dismissed and sent away quietly, like the tradesmen?"

That marmalade eyebrow rose in exasperation.

"Have it your way."

She slid across the hall and opened the door with her back, slouching against the portal, her hands hidden behind her. She simply angled her head to invite him into the room where Squire Paxton and Lady Theodora were quietly engaged, she at her embroidery, and he reading the London papers.

Squire Paxton laid down his newspaper and made to rise along with his eyebrows, but Lizzie sailed on, cutting him out at his mooring.

"Mama, Papa, you remember Jamie Marlowe? Well, he's Captain Jameson Marlowe of His Majesty's Royal Navy now. He's come to propose, so I'm taking him out to the garden so he can do it properly." She cast a saucy glance at his tight, fawn-colored buckskin breeches. "You'll have to mind those kicks on the grass."

And off Lizzie went, unmindful of her mother's strangled protestation at her nearly vulgar, cant mention of his unmentionables. Never mind her cavalier description of his proposal.

Marlowe swallowed his laughter and made a formal bow to her parents, whose mouths were gaping like mackerels. He might have followed their daughter, as he always had done, but those days were over, even if Lizzie hadn't quite realized it yet.

"Good afternoon, Lady Theodora, Squire Paxton."

Lady Theodora Paxton instantly came forward to take his hand. "My dear boy. How wonderful to see you again after all this time."

The lady was as he had remembered: a small, light-haired woman of genial countenance. The daughter of an earl, she had been a great beauty in her day. Time had softened and blurred the edges that were still sharp on her daughter, but Lady Theodora, warm, kind, and generous, was mostly unchanged.

He turned his eyes upon the squire and stood for a long moment, letting him take the full measure of his potential son-in-law. Marlowe was surprised to find the squire diminished, smaller and not at all the intimidating Lord of the Manor of his memory. His gingery hair was liberally streaked with white, and his florid complexion looked strained and tired. Lizzie seemed to have been doing her work rather too well.

Squire Paxton made a very small bow. "How d'ye do, *Captain* Marlowe."

His emphasis was only just short of insulting. How nice to still engender such alarm and bristling hostility after ten years. It had been a long wait.

Marlowe bared his teeth like a smiling dog. It had a wonderful effect upon the squire: his mottled face paled, leaving a spiderweb of purple veins crawling down his nose and cheeks. The years had not been kind to the squire.

"If you will excuse me." Marlowe made a gracious bow, smooth as water, his fine manners well displayed to Lady Theodora. "I have an appointment with your lovely daughter, and I had best not keep the lady waiting."

Another very small bow to Squire Paxton, and Marlowe took himself down the hall after Lizzie.

She was slouched back against French doors leading out to

a terrace, waiting for him with every appearance of nonchalance. Not exactly the picture of the ardent bride-to-be.

"What astonishing cheek, Miss Paxton. Where on earth did you learn such disreputable language?"

"Why, Cap'n Marlowe," she drawled in answer. "There's a big, brawling world out there. Didn't you know?"

He most certainly did. God, she was irresistible. Even in that hideous sack of a gown.

"No wonder they want you off their hands. And no wonder there are no other takers."

She shot him a superior little glance, all narrow eyes and pleated, lush lips.

"Crying off already, are we?"

"Not on your life." No, he was in for as long as she would let him.

"No," she corrected with a sideways glance at him, "not on *your* life."

Once again, she led the way without looking back to see if he followed, her loose-limbed stride taking them out of doors, past a well-tended expanse of lawn and down through the terraced garden set out along the hillside.

As they progressed through the yew hedges, a little flash under her plain gown caught his eye. She wore a pair of very old, but beautifully made, heeled court shoes of the last era, all bejeweled and embroidered, and totally inappropriate for walks out of doors. How like her.

"Don't you think we've gone far enough? You can't put me off forever."

"I've come all this way for privacy. It will take Papa some time to find us here."

Yes, Lizzie always liked to do things on her own time and in her own way. Which brought his eyes back to the beautiful old shoes.

"Aren't they a bit much for a walk?"

"My shoes? Perhaps, but I always feel much better about life when I'm wearing pretty shoes."

"Why?"

"Why? *Because*, that's why. Because I just do. Why do you wear blue coats?"

"Because I'm navy."

"If you're a naval man, why aren't you wearing your uniform? You weren't wearing one at the assembly. Or the other day, in town."

Again, he should have known. Trust Lizzie's sharp little brain to home in on the pertinent details. This was only the second time he'd seen her, but she'd seen him somewhere else. Devil take her. It would be an interesting few days if she took him on.

"Naval custom prohibits me from wearing my uniform while on leave, but I wear fashionable blue coats because my valet insists they match my eyes."

"You don't have a valet."

"No? How would you know such a personal and intimate detail about a man's life? Spying on me, Lizzie?"

"Your boots are scuffed, your hair is disreputable, and your cravat has a tiny little pinprick hole no self-respecting valet would have let you wear in public."

"So very observant, Lizzie."

"Yes, well, I can also observe that you are standing far too close." Her wrist made a disdainful little flick to shoo him back.

He took a step closer. "How else am I to observe you?"

"From a distance." But a blush was spreading up her neck like apricot jam. He wondered how far it spread down.

"But then I wouldn't know you smell of citrus, like sunshine."

"You smell of whisky."

"That's bay rum. Where else did you see me, Lizzie?"

She made another languid flick of her wrist.

"Here or there, about the town, perhaps. With that tall, grave-looking blond fellow. He wore a brown coat."

McAlden. They would have to be more careful.

"But you like blue coats better. Admit it."

"They'll do. I suppose they might match your eyes, though I've always thought they were gray, not blue."

"I'll take it as a compliment you noticed my eyes at all. But tell me, why should you need to make yourself feel better by wearing your shoes? Thought I'd renege?"

"Perhaps you will yet. Perhaps you won't die like you've engaged to?"

"Then you've made up your mind? You'll do it?"

She looked away, gazing out over the fore cliff and across the river for a very long time. His self-control battered itself against the cage of his chest while he forced himself to stand still and wait.

"Why not?" she said at last. "You just might be the antidote I need. Yes, I'll marry you."

The tense heat in his chest expanded into satisfied elation. He swooped in to give her a kiss, but she shied away.

"You'll have to get a special license."

"Special license? They're expensive." He was teasing her. He already had one in his breast coat pocket as insurance. One of the perks of being the son of a rector who was also a Doctor of Theology—he knew all the right people in Doctors' Commons.

"You did say you were leaving in a few days? There simply isn't time for the banns to be read, and I can't be bothered with all the trouble of eloping."

When he laughed, she frowned. "It will never do. I must tell you, I couldn't stand all the silly fuss of an elopement, and besides, I can't abide a closed carriage ride."

"Then you shall have your special license." He handed it to her with a flourish. "Does my lady require anything else?"

"Really?"

He had astonished her. But only for a moment.

"Well, yes. I find I *would* like to see the settlements. Papa will make all sorts of noise about taking them up, but I'd like to begin as I mean to go on. Independently."

He didn't laugh, even at the image of a pampered pet like Lizzie imagining herself independent. While she had always been a self-sufficient little thing, there was a vast difference between her confident expectations and the demands of the world. But she was a clever girl—she would learn soon enough.

"If you like." He pulled out a folded piece of foolscap. "I've taken the liberty of drawing up a draft—time being of the essence. Once you've approved these amounts, all you'll need to do is fill in the amount of your dowry, which, I might add, you'll have control of immediately."

As if on cue at the mention of money, Squire Paxton puffed his way through the yew hedges and across the lawn. He was steaming like a Christmas pudding.

He began before he'd reached them. "Elizabeth, there you are. Now, kindly explain the meaning of all this." His tone was abrupt and the eye he bent on Marlowe sharp and demanding.

"Congratulate me, Papa. I'm going to be married, as soon as can be arranged."

Instead of beaming out his approval, the squire's bushy gray brow beetled. Clearly, he still didn't approve.

"Now, Elizabeth, I've had enough of your radical ideas and newfangled ways of doing things. This is something for your mother and I to decide. We hardly know the young man." He nodded sharply in Marlowe's direction.

"Of course. I'm quite at your service, sir."

Lizzie's curious cat eyes slid back and forth between them.

Incredulity creased her ginger brows. "Goodness, Papa, you've known Jamie, and his family, all his life."

"Of course, we know his father, excellent man, the Reverend Doctor Marlowe," the Squire insisted, "but things must be settled correctly, between gentlemen, without this unseemly haste. You needn't concern yourself, my dear."

"Papa." Her voice held a warning. "You know my feelings. I *shall* concern myself. It is my future we're bartering here, and Jamie and I have already discussed the settlements. I should think you'd approve of our businesslike dealings—we've a draft right here."

"Absolutely not. It just isn't done. Now, I'll just have Captain Marlowe up to the house to have a talk. I insist."

At least he wasn't foolish enough to forbid. Marlowe could only imagine how Lizzie would react to that. She appeared quite put out as it was.

"I'm of age, Papa. You know I'll want to approve those settlements myself, or I'll not marry at all," she replied steadily, though he could see the tension flattening the corners of her mouth. Then she gave her head a little shake and changed her tone. "But by all means let us go up to the house. We'll need your secretary at any rate."

She kissed her father's cheek and walked past, oblivious to the fact that the squire's brow gathered like thunderclouds over the top of his spectacles.

"And we'll need to get down to the rectory as soon as may be," she continued, "if we're to be married today."

"Today?" The squire's face colored like a stewed beet. "On *no* account can it be today."

"Papa, you must understand, Jamie leaves for the Antipodes directly."

Once Lizzie made up her mind about something, neither hell nor highly patronizing father would stop her. She sailed off like a jib. Marlowe followed close in her wake, leaving the squire to trail behind, blowing like a noisy bellows in the rear guard.

She wanted to marry him. Even against parental disapproval. Perhaps even refusal. She wanted him. The feeling was very nearly heady.

She must not know what her father had done, or she would not be so anxious to put herself under his control. And he couldn't imagine Lady Theodora knew either, or she never would have welcomed him so cordially.

"Lizzie," Marlowe called quietly, catching her arm. It was a compulsion, this need he had to touch her. To feel her. To indulge himself in a different kind of triumph. For reasons other than the ones he had concocted at the assembly.

"As flattered as I am by your insistence on haste, perhaps it would be best if we give your parents a bit more time. Tomorrow is soon enough. You father's consent—"

"No." She cut him off, sliding out of his grasp. "I told you, I mean to go on indepen—"

"Independently. Yes, I know. But *you* can't become independent until *he* signs that settlement."

Lizzie closed her eyes and set her mouth. For the first time in his life, he saw an unrestrained look of raw frustration and real anger color her face. A blotch of heat rose on her chest beneath the transparent fabric of the fichu.

"Is it too much to ask to have some say in my own future?" Her voice was low and bitter.

"No. No, it's not too much to ask, Lizzie. All you have to do is ask the right man." It was startling, how little she knew of the world.

"Of course. But then, I still have to ask, don't I?" Her liquid green gaze was resolute and at the same time astonishingly vulnerable. He instinctively reached out to touch her, startled by her intensity.

"We all do, Lizzie. No one in this world can expect to sail on his own tack all his life. No matter what, there are duties and responsibilities, and choices and yes, even loves that dictate what we can and cannot do. You're just too used to getting your own way." He passed over the draft, setting the paper into her clenched hands. "Read it over," he ordered gently, "handsomely now, and I'll make whatever changes you want before it's presented to your father."

She swiped the paper out of his hand, still full of resentment.

"Then why are *you* letting me have my own way? Have such control over your fortune?"

"You can hardly do any worse than I. I'm a sailor, Lizzie, not a cit. And you're a sharp enough lass. You'll do fine." He drew a knuckle along the line of her chin and marveled again at the contrast between the infinite softness of her skin and the sharp line of her jaw.

At his touch a slow smile blossomed across her face, warm and untutored, rising to stretch over the curve of her cheekbones, until it reached the corners of her eyes.

Devil take it, he wanted to kiss her. Here, now, in front of her father and the rest of the world. And she knew it. The marmalade brow slid upwards, daring him. One of these days, soon, very soon, he was going to lick it.

"Why Jamie Marlowe," she whispered as his mouth descended, "you *have* grown sentimental, haven't you?"

Unfortunately, Lady Theodora, trailing a brace of panting, goggle-eyed spaniels, chose that moment to drift out onto the terrace in a cloud of lily-of-the-valley perfume.

"Oh, Elizabeth, at last, there you are! Come in and sit with me so we can make arrangements. I've called for tea. Where are you going?"

"To change my dress, Mama. I'm off to the rectory to get married."

"Married? Right now? Oh, Elizabeth, my dear, no!" A lace handkerchief fluttered out of nowhere. "We must make some preparations. How will it look? I do so hate to see you do something so rash."

Lizzie kissed her mother's cheek fondly.

"Well then, Mama, I'd advise you to close your eyes."

CHAPTER 3

In the end, they prevailed upon her to wait another day. Had she only to consult her own feelings, Lizzie would have proceeded to the rectory without delay. But such haste would have seriously discommoded both Mama and Papa. And despite their philosophical differences, and despite the fact they often exasperated her, Lizzie was too fond of her parents to want that.

She was especially fond of her mother, with all her charming, diverting eccentricities. Lizzie could not find it within her to see Mama made uncomfortable or unhappy by a ceremony that wasn't all it ought to be. And if Jamie was in no great rush to be off to the other side of the world, then she could have no reasonable reason to press for expediency.

Tomorrow would be soon enough. It would even give her an extra day with Jamie. The thought brought an agony of anticipation. Perhaps tomorrow there would be more kissing.

Of course, Papa would insist on things being done properly, between *gentlemen*. He was particularly thunderous in his emphasis, as if he doubted Jamie's right to the epithet. It was terribly, hopelessly old-fashioned, and nothing short of ridiculous. That Jamie was indisputably not only a gentleman, but also an officer of His Majesty's Royal Navy, was obvious to anyone who had eyes and had read a Dartmouth newspaper within the past five years. But Papa chose to remain stubbornly oblivious.

Papa also chose to insist upon speaking to each of them separately. He and Jamie were closeted up in his book room for the longest time, while she was sent away to the morning room with Mama, who went on happily about the necessity of lace and fresh bonnet ribbons for the wedding, glad to have both an occasion and an excuse to fuss.

But Lizzie never could attend to matters of wardrobe with any real enthusiasm. She would much rather know what was being said in the book room. Her ears began to ring with the efforts of straining to hear any word from that direction.

When she was finally called, she ran straight in to the mahogany-paneled room, looking for Jamie, who was nowhere to be seen.

"What did he say? What did you say to him?"

"Sit down, Elizabeth." Her father sounded wearied, but still far from resigned to her marriage.

But Lizzie had learned stubbornness at her father's knee. "I'll not be dissuaded, Papa."

"Now Elizabeth, I don't like it." He shook his head side to side like a stubborn bulldog, refusing to unlock his jaws.

"Why? I thought you'd be pleased." Indeed, this was not their first conversation on the worthiness of a proposed suitor, nor even their second. Papa had very easily entertained, and even promoted, previous offers from gentlemen of far lesser means than Jamie's. She could not understand his objection to Jamie, nor the stubborn vehemence of his dislike, which bristled from him like the wayward strands of orange and white hair escaping in hostile abandon from his queue.

"I don't like it. I don't like it at all," he repeated.

"Is it the money?" She had absolutely no reason to suspect Jamie's fortune, nor his ownership of the house. Such facts were too easy for Squire Paxton to discover. Indeed, she had agreed to delay the wedding in part to allow her father to make his inquiries and put his misgivings to rest.

Papa did not answer.

"What specifically don't you like?" she prompted.

"We don't know the man. We know nothing of his conduct."

"Papa, I've known him all my life."

"Not true a'tall, my girl," he objected. "Haven't heard a thing about him for—what is it? Eight years now?"

"Ten, Papa. Obviously, he's been in the navy. Fighting the wars. Advancing in his profession. He's been promoted all the way to Post Captain at a young age. Surely that speaks for his conduct? Surely the confidence of the Admiralty is recommendation enough?"

"But what of his means of achieving his ends? We know nothing of his conduct, his character."

"Papa." Lizzie could hear exasperation creeping into her voice. "I know you read the newspapers. They were full of how he was cited by his commander for conspicuous bravery at Toulon, among other things. Does that not show he is a man of character?"

He would not meet her eye, but finally, he spoke in so low a voice, she had to lean closer to hear.

"I am simply loath to trust you to him. Your high spirits and pursuit of . . ." He would not permit himself to say the word she longed to hear. He would never acknowledge the truth of her assertions—she ought to be able to live her life as independently as any man. It was simply anathema to his view of the world. "Your temperament calls for a firm hand from a husband. You should have a man who is more than your equal, who can command your respect."

She knew he spoke from fear and love, a father's love for his daughter, but she could not abide it when he began to use words like *command* and *respect*. It meant he was working himself up to his usual lecture about conforming herself to the "natural abilities" of women and forgetting her "unnatural inclinations" for study and independence.

And she would get so frustrated and so angry, she would say truthful but imprudent things, or simply walk out the door, and they would still have no agreements, no marriage settlements, and no wedding.

"Papa." She endeavored to speak with the deep conviction she felt. "You must understand. Jamie *is* worthy of my respect and my trust. Indeed, he has both. I have never been able to even contemplate any other offer of marriage. You must know, I truly think this is what is best for me."

When he made a sound of objection, she cut him off.

"Papa, do my feelings count for nothing?" she asked quietly. "I want to marry him. He is the only man I ever have, or will ever, consider marrying." It was as close to an admission of her private feelings and true emotions as she was ever likely to come with her father.

Thankfully, it had the required effect. He passed his hand over his face and stared into the cold grate of the fireplace for an uncomfortably long time before he finally spoke.

"I cannot give you my blessing, but if you must, you have my consent."

"Those whom God hath joined together, let no man put asunder." The Reverend Marlowe's words echoed through the big, empty stone nave of St. Savior's.

Jamie was her husband, at least temporarily. Until God put them asunder.

"By joining of hands, I pronounce that they be Man and Wife together, In the Name of the Father, and of the Son, and of the Holy Ghost. Amen."

Might as well have said "Man and Chattel together" from her point of view, but all in all, it was for the best, though it had not been the prettiest or most auspicious of weddings.

Gray skies had dripped with rain, and Jamie's father, the

Reverend Doctor Marlowe, had seemed uneasy, anxious almost. He repeatedly lost his place in the well-worn book of prayers he clutched in his knobby, arthritic fingers. He kept darting nervous glances at her, as if he expected her to take flight or bolt down the aisle for the door.

For heaven's sake. It wasn't as if *she* was the one who'd bolted.

Indeed she had been as nervous as a chicken waiting for the ceremony to come. Contrary to her hopes, they'd not been allowed any further time together yesterday. Jamie had been sent away, and she'd been kept at home, busy with preparations, until this morning. Waiting to see if he would indeed come back again.

But Jamie was here now. He had come back, to give her respectability and independence. Yes. She would concentrate on her independence and not think about the inconvenient little flip-flop her stomach made when Jamie turned his penetrating gray eyes to hers.

Her giddy feeling was all due to the astonishing accomplishment of her goal—an independent life. It could have nothing to do with the large, masculine hand pressing warmly into the small of her back as he escorted her to the vestry to sign the registry. Nothing whatsoever.

But all would be right. She knew he was leaving this time. It wouldn't be as bad. She would be prepared. And really, he'd already been gone from her life for so long it hardly mattered.

She had what she needed.

A house. A place to live her life according to her own tastes and the dictates of her education. A place where she could develop her own style of living and thinking. Her happiness was nearly complete.

All that remained was to see the house. Her head was teeming with ideas for it. With ideas for how she would learn to manage it and the land. How she would learn useful skills and truly merit her place in this world. Live a life of purpose and usefulness, not one of idle, pampered indulgence.

Her lady mother's chief skill, other than her exquisite embroidery, was the ability to charm and delight anyone and everyone who came within the warmth of her circle—a pleasant, gracious woman. Celia and any number of young ladies of her acquaintance were content to live their lives as pleasing, decorative ornaments for their suitors, husbands, and society in general. But Lizzie could not. She would not.

She was simply not made for idleness or stillness. She could not sit quietly when she might be out of doors, walking, riding, or sailing. Doing something. Despite the calculated air of indifference she had achieved, she had never been content to lounge about drawing rooms, waiting for life, for experience, to come to her.

Because she did not possess, nor had she been able to cultivate, the happy talent of making men feel pleased with themselves. In fact, she rather made them feel the opposite—edgy and uncomfortable—with her sharp observations and tart tongue.

But now that she had the security of her marriage, she could truly do as she pleased. It was a heady thought.

A small but elegant wedding breakfast, attended only by her parents and Jamie's, was held at Hightop House. Mama's arrangements were, as always, beautiful and charming. Flowers from the gardens graced the tables and their scents filled the moist early summer air with heady perfume. Jamie sat next to her at the long, linen-draped table, looking both very handsome and very pleased with himself, though he spent the meal being wonderfully charming and solicitous of her mother and his own.

"How disappointed I am," her mother was saying, "to find you must leave us so soon, dear Captain."

He was a wonder to watch, this accomplished man, his comportment easy and laughing, his manners fine as French brandy and his clothing tailored to perfection. The very image of the prosperous, happy bridegroom.

It made her wonder if she imagined it, the dark masculine hunger that slid from his eyes when he looked at her from under that errant lock of dark hair as he answered.

"It is unfortunate, Lady Theodora, but duty calls."

No, she hadn't imagined it. For Papa could see it, or sense it. It was the only explanation she could find that would account for his bristling hostility and stubborn objections.

And clearly, her father was still opposed, though the deed was already done. His face remained a study in tense resignation. He sat through the meal as if he were having a tooth pulled: unhappy, uncomfortable, and very nearly in pain.

His brooding silence affected the Reverend Marlowe, who was nothing like his normal, garrulous self. The rector mirrored his host, lapsing into uneasy silence. Without Mama's and Jamie's efforts, the whole affair would likely have been an unmitigated disaster.

"But you will at least spend some time with us before you go. You will of course spend your wedding night here. I've had the blue room prepared so you might have the east wing to yourself."

Lizzie nearly choked on her wine. Wedding night? Here? Mama had never so much as mentioned it to her. Good Lord, what an idea. Whatever Jamie's dark looks held, she was not about to discover it in her childhood home. She needed to begin as she meant to go on. Independently.

"I thank you, my lady, but I had thought to spend the evening more privately. I have taken rooms at the Red Harte." Jamie spoke evenly, in an easy, matter-of-fact tone, but the skin on the back of Lizzie's neck and on her cheeks began to prickle with heat.

How ridiculous. It should be a relief to know Jamie had made such plans to keep the nature of their arrangement private. It was a relief to know the details of their marriage would not be made privy to her parents, nor to every servant in the house.

"You'd be better served to stay here." Papa's voice was rough and dogged. He must have finally imbibed enough wine to make him overcome his stubborn silence.

"Papa," Lizzie tried to appeal to him quietly, to reassure him she was quite safe with Jamie. "I'm sure Jamie's arrangements are more than suitable. I am entirely at my husband's disposal."

Oh, fie. That didn't come out as all as she had intended, and it rather had the opposite effect upon Papa, who was turning an alarming shade of aubergine.

"Take her and be done, then!" Her father's hand slammed down flat on the table, his anger overflowing like the red wine he'd been drinking, spilling over the brim and shocking them all into silence.

"You mark my words. You'll come to regret this wild start, Elizabeth. What's to become of you, I don't know. You're a good enough girl, but wild and headstrong. I've done everything in my power to see you safe. To keep you safe. Even from yourself. But there's nothing more I can do for you now. You've chosen where I would have you not."

He didn't even look at Jamie as he let the words fall like stones from his mouth. Her father's eyes bored into hers, until she closed her own in mortification at his angry, damning denouncements.

"So be it," he went on, oblivious to the shocked silence. "You have made your proverbial bed, and now you must lie upon it. But not under my roof. Take yourself off to the Red Harte and bedamned to you!"

Lizzie could feel her composure crack, humiliation etching its way across her face like hot acid.

She ought to be used to Papa's tirades by now. She ought to be immune to the casual rage that erupted whenever they were at cross-purposes. Which was too often. His careless words, like so many others over the years, made her angry and more than a little sad. They left a sour, unhappy taste in her mouth.

Lizzie faltered for only a moment, long enough for Jamie to rise from his seat and turn to squarely face her father. Oh, no. She refused to let this ridiculous exhibition escalate into a confrontation between Jamie and her father. She couldn't let the day be completely ruined beyond all hope. She could not change her father, though Lord knows she had tried, but she could ignore him. It was her only defense.

She pushed her own shoulders back and quickly rose from her chair, forcing her mouth into a smile and acting as if Papa had never said a word.

"Thank you, Mama, for a lovely breakfast. Mrs. Marlowe, Reverend Marlowe, I thank you. I see Cushing has called for your carriage. Jamie, would you be so kind as to take your mother's arm?"

Her father's butler, Cushing, God bless him, was as used to the Squire's edicts as any man, and was already stationed by the front door, armed with a capacious umbrella to ward off the drizzle.

Lizzie couldn't bring herself to look at Jamie. She wouldn't. It would be too deeply mortifying to see either knowing, laughing superiority, or, God forbid, pity in his eyes. So she just tipped her chin up, smiled as if she couldn't care less about the outburst, and escorted Reverend Marlowe out of the dining room and towards the foyer.

A light touch at the base of her spine, an impression of heat, was all she felt of Jamie, before he came past to escort his mother to the door and the waiting carriage.

Lizzie saw them all to the door but disentangled herself before she was required to give anything but a murmured farewell.

Then she moved quickly, making a break for the stairs. But for all her haste, Jamie was there, behind her, his hands curving around her upper arms to arrest her flight. His long fingers slid up to rest on her shoulders, solid and reassuring.

"Lizzie." His breath blew warm and uneasy against the nape of her neck. "Are you all right?"

She tried to wriggle out from under his hands by taking the first stair, but he was so much taller, his heat still surrounded her. It was all she could do to keep from collapsing back into his sheltering warmth.

She didn't dare. She must remember he would soon be leaving himself.

"Come, Lizzie. You needn't fly off in such a rush." Jamie's low voice probed like a velvet blade.

"Please," she managed. "Please don't fuss." She kept her face averted as she dashed an inconvenient speck of dust from her eye with the back of her hand. She couldn't bear it if he made a fuss. She'd fall to a hundred pieces. "I'm going . . . to change into my habit." To leave as soon as possible—to leave it all behind. All the endless arguments, all the resentment.

"You're going riding? Now? Lizzie." The soft pity in his voice cut her to the bone.

"No." She took a deep breath and turned to face him, mustering every ounce of casual indifference she possessed. "We are going riding. You're going to show me my house."

"*Your* house, Mrs. Marlowe?"

Lizzie squelched the lovely pang at his first use of her new name. He'd made it sound like an endearment. "My house. 'Not too big, not too small, with eight principal bedrooms and a lovely view down to the sea.' You remember. You said I *must* see it, so *you* must show it to me before you leave. Please. I have to . . . go." She gave him one of her enticing smiles, the one where she let her enthusiasm for the scheme show, to cover the cost of such a mortifying admission.

"Even in this weather? How can I refuse you, Lizzie?" His wide gray eyes were clear, but they held the promise of mirth.

His words and his encouraging smile sent a warm feeling stroking up her spine. She shifted her shoulders to shake off the sensation. It wouldn't do to become too attached to him.

"I'll ask Willy to saddle up the chestnut hunter for you. Oh, Lord, you do still ride, don't you? Or have you turned into an arthritic old naval man?" It was so much easier when she was nettling him.

He smiled back, lazy and knowing. "Arthritic? I shall endeavor to show you otherwise," he murmured. "And I definitely still ride."

They were saddled and mounted with the half hour, Jamie on a tall hunter and Lizzie on Serendipity, her leggy, bay Thoroughbred filly. They had a lovely ride in the clearing afternoon, down along the river towards the castle, and then up Weeke Hill and over the headland toward the sea. The rain held off, and the clean wind blew the last remains of the disastrous breakfast from her mood. It was easy to be happy with Jamie. He was kind enough to understand she did not want to talk about her father. Instead he did all he could to be charming and amusing, making her laugh with his witty observations.

They had a relaxed, almost sedate journey: nothing like their pell-mell rides of the past. He looked as well as ever on a horse, perhaps even better. She made a surreptitious survey of his strong, straight shoulders and the long line of his back as it tapered to his waist. Honed like a fencing sword. He hadn't looked like that at fourteen. She swallowed over the queer flutter in her stomach.

"Tell me more about the house."

"It's very houselike. Has a roof and a door."

It was like playing at bowls, the back-and-forth of their conversations, each one tossing off a line. Amazing how quickly they settled back into the playful rhythm of childhood. Although childhood had not been so full of . . . what was it? Tension. Tension that also felt very much like flirtation. He'd become rather adept at it, with his slow smiles and still, penetrating eyes. Gorgeous, dangerous wolf eyes. She'd have to guard herself. He was leaving.

"How long have you lived there?"

"I haven't really. I bought the property some time ago, when I was last in England, recovering, because I couldn't think of anything better to do with my money, and I thought . . . I thought it was pretty."

"Sentimental."

"Yes, well, it's what makes one a gentleman, owning land. And I liked the idea of having something to come home to besides my father's rectory, which, when he retires, he'll have to leave anyway."

Some things were the same. He'd never been one for concealment. So honest and open about his life, his hopes. He didn't pretend to be anything other than himself. He never had. It was something she admired.

Admired, but didn't aspire to. She had no intention of being what she ought. What others so insistently thought she should be.

"And the gardens? You mentioned roses."

"Very well-planted gardens, but very old. I'm afraid they've been rather let go during my tenure. There's no staff to speak of. Only the steward, Mr. Tupper, and his wife, who is the housekeeper. No footmen, or maids, although there are a few . . ." He hesitated, searching for the word. ". . . groundsmen. Gardeners and the like."

"But they've let the gardens go?" That made no sense.

"They've plenty of other duties, keeping the buildings up and such. Jack-of-all-tradesmen, they are, keeping the gutters in good repair. So they've not so much time for the flowers, although the roses seem to do well enough on their own."

"I'm glad the house has been kept up. I can move in straight away."

"No." His voice sounded low and harsh, but she must have mistaken him because when she turned to look at him, he smiled and went on smoothly. "Surely not without maids and all? You'll get lonely all the way out there. I'm sure you'd prefer a house of your own, in town."

"I can't imagine why you should think so." Had she changed so much? "Much as I would prefer, I won't pretend you didn't hear Papa. I may be a 'wild girl,' but I never get lonely or bored, and I don't require maids. I require roses."

"Every lady requires a maid, even you, Lizzie. How else did you manage to look so absolutely fetching in that habit?"

"Why all this empty gallantry? I've already married you—you can stop convincing me. And I don't have a maid. Never have. Mama is forever trying to send one up, but I can't abide anyone fussing about me." She waved her hands back and forth as if clearing out an imaginary room. But she was flattered nonetheless by his notice of how well she looked in her deep green riding habit. It went rather well with the bucolic setting. The habit was perhaps a little old-fashioned in style, but it was superbly cut and fitted her like a glove. Most men were impervious to fashion, but they did like a well-displayed figure.

"How extraordinary you've grown to be, Lizzie."

She let out a little snort. "It's wretched flattery to damn with such faint praise. Am I meant to be so helpless I can't dress myself? You don't have a valet. Does that make you extraordinary?"

"Of course. It is extraordinary I'm so handsomely turned out without one."

Lizzie nearly laughed. It was easy to admire him when he was so charmingly self-deprecating. And she was more than a little ready to do more than admire Jamie.

They turned down a lane lined with low stone walls and hedges laced with wildflowers. The air was sweet with the rising perfumes of late spring.

"This is it then. My land. Nearly six hundred acres."

"Hmm." Like him, the land was enormously picturesque. That was it—concentrate on the land. Best to think of practicalities and not strong shoulders.

"Is there a mortgage?" She had spent as long as possible, in the short time allotted, going over the marriage settlement, fine print and all, but couldn't remember any mention of the mortgage.

"No." He seemed surprised she should ask such a blunt question. His brow lowered, shading his sharp gaze. "Bought and paid for in cash—or bank draught from Hoare's Bank. But it's mine, free and clear."

"How very enterprising of you." Her smile was genuinely admiring. He *would* be enterprising. He would live up to every promise of his boyhood. He would grow up to be a man people would respect and admire. A man she could respect and admire. Quite a bit more than was comfortable. Or advisable.

She repeated her warning again in the privacy of her thoughts. *He was leaving.*

The land stretched down between bands of trees on a gentle slope away toward the sea in the distance. On one side of the lane, pastureland was in use, being grazed with cows, and sheep dotted the fields in the distance.

Practicalities. "Do you keep a dairy?"

"I'm a sailor, Lizzie. I know halyards, not heifers. You'd best put such questions to Mr. Tupper. I'll introduce you. The farms are all tenanted." His gaze focused on her. "May I ask to what purpose are all these questions?"

Would he understand? It had done no good to try to speak to her parents, or anyone else, even Celia, about the need for a useful life and the dignity of work. And it couldn't matter to Jamie what she did with the farm—he'd soon be on the other side of the world. Dying.

"Just taking an interest. After all, it will be my home."

"Lizzie, you can't live here. It's not fit for a lady. I've made plans for repairs, but there is still much work to be done. And even when that's done in some months' time, you'll need to make your own plans, consult with painters, drapers, and such before you could move in. It'll give you something to do besides lounge about assembly rooms looking for trouble."

He thought her a useless fribble. It stung. She'd played the jaded sophisticate far too well, it seemed.

"I've always enjoyed looking for trouble. It seems so much more logical than to wait for it to find me. But you found me, so I must be looking at trouble now."

"You are. But I was only teasing, Lizzie. Feel free to look back upon your fields."

She did so, for her relief as well as his. Every time her eyes had contacted his, a feeling like pressure began to build in her chest, squeezing her breath. She brought her mount to a halt and took a deep inhalation of the fresh, moist air coming in off the sea—the tang of salt mixed with the earthy scents of animal and greening grass. It was heavenly.

"In raptures over fallow fields? Who's sentimental now, Lizzie?"

This time she could hear the teasing note in his voice, as he brought his horse up close beside her. She could also feel the heat of his penetrating scrutiny.

She faced back into the sea breeze to cool her flushed cheeks. "Not sentimental. What you mean is romantic, like the poets. Messers. Coleridge or Blake."

"Romantic then." His gray eyes were warm and laughing at the corners even as they probed.

"Not I. I'm being practical. Why have these fields been let go fallow?"

"I haven't the vaguest. Mr. Tupper again, although he'll probably say something beyond my ken about pastoralism versus agrarianism. You'll probably understand it, my clever girl."

Jamie reached out to stroke the side of her cheek very lightly with the knuckle of his gloved hand. The soft touch sent shivers of lightning shooting every which way inside her body. She felt as if she might jump out of her skin.

She wanted to tell him she wasn't his, or anyone else's clever girl, to combat the spike of yearning that cut into her like a shard of glass, but she stopped. She was. She was anything he wanted her to be. She was his wife. At least for today.

It might expose her to ask, but she had to know.

"Why? Why did you marry me?"

CHAPTER 4

H e didn't pretend not to understand. He was too honest.
"Because I'm drawn to you. I always have been. Surely
you know that?"

She did. She felt an uncomfortable pang of remorse at using
him and his steady devotion to duty as a means to her independence. Even if he'd been the one to suggest it. What had
happened to him in the world to make him too open, too devoted for his own good?

"And you?" His eyes searched steadily even if his tone was
light.

Certainly she was drawn to him as well. She thought him
handsome, but with his strong forehead, clear eyes, high, well-
formed cheekbones, and beautiful lips, so did anyone who had
eyes. But she had always admired him for something more
than mere good looks. For his openness and his mirth. For not
being jaded by the inequities of the world. For the penetra-
tion of his gaze and for not hating her for what he saw in her.

Everything she might say would expose her. Lizzie looked
away and laced her voice with studied, pert carelessness. "Because you promised me arable acres and a house. Where is it?"

He let her get away with her evasion. For now. He smiled

wryly, one corner of his mouth tugging up, and nodded toward the coppice directly ahead. "Tucked down behind those trees."

She moved away from him, urging her mount down the lane at a trot. The big, rangy Thoroughbred covered the ground swiftly and easily, and soon the lane came to the top of a wooded bowl snugged back against the clifftops. There in the middle stood the house.

Oh, it was lovely, even from the back. Surprise pushed the breath from her lungs in a little gasp, until a giddy combination of pleasure and relief let her breathe again. It was a large, two-and-a-half-story edifice of gray stone, the walls of which were dotted with a shining array of glass-paned windows. The tax must be a fortune. There was also a large cottage farther on down the lane to the left and beyond that, a high wall and smaller cottage that must denote the kitchen gardens. Farther along in the opposite direction was a long stable block. Lizzie's hand rose to cover her heartfelt smile. Such a blissful relief. Oh, yes, it would do quite, quite nicely.

Finally. She was home. She'd never have to pretend to be anything other than what she wanted to be again.

"Don't say anything yet." Jamie caught up to her. "The best view is from the front. We'll go along to the stable first."

They took the parting of the lane to the west and moved around the back of the house to the stable block. It was clean and neat enough, an easy task with only one other animal in residence, but no one came to take their horses.

"As I said, there's no staff." He dismounted and came to help her.

"It's fine." She waved him away and slid off without assistance, the way she had when they'd been out adventuring in their youth. The wondrous relief she felt made her feel almost carefree: careless enough to drop her mask. It was so tempting to be herself with him. It had been so long, she'd almost forgotten how. "I know elegant young ladies are supposed to be useless, but I still like to untack and curry my own horse." She led her mare into the cobbled building.

"I don't think you're useless, Lizzie," he said lightly.

She gave him as direct a look as she could manage—she had become rather adept at indirect looks—to see if he meant it. He did.

"Thank you." The relief began to blossom into something more, something altogether too tempting to name.

They turned the animals loose in box stalls and hung the tack nearby.

When she came out onto the yard, he offered his arm, once more all courtly gallantry. "Come, I'll show you the best view."

Despite her temptation to openness, or perhaps because of it, Lizzie felt small, almost overpowered, tucked against his tall side. *He was leaving.* She slid away, no more than a half foot or so, but enough to put space and equanimity between them, as he led her along a graveled drive, past a paved court on the east side of the house and then beyond, onto a sweeping lawn.

"There," he said as he turned her to the front of the house.

Glass Cottage was everything, absolutely everything, she could have hoped and dreamed of in a house. The façade faced the sea and at least half of the ground floor was built with a long row of windows, floor to ceiling, marching like sparkling, silver soldiers west along the front of the house. Above the windows and arching over the doorway were trellises covered with climbing roses, spilling over the stone in an extravagant array of pink and white blooms, their exuberant fragrance perfuming the air. It was thoroughly enchanting.

The house held a sort of fairytale stillness, as if it had been waiting, slumbering quietly in the sun, waiting to be brought back to life.

"What do you think?" There was amused pride in his voice. He really didn't have to ask.

"Oh, Jamie!" Her delight couldn't be contained. She could

only laugh in wondrous pleasure. "I think it's a good thing they don't tax roses as well as windows."

"Well, you'd best go see it. Although I must warn you, don't get your hopes up too high. It is very picturesque and charming, I grant you—the whole reason I bought it—but it's been closed up. I'm afraid it'll be dreadfully damp. It'll take quite a bit of effort, work, and time to put it to rights."

He was trying to put her off the idea.

"And here you were, waxing rhapsodic not two days ago."

"Two days ago you hadn't agreed to marry me."

"Ulterior motives?"

"Perhaps. Perhaps I wanted another kiss."

Lizzie had no plans to test that particular theory, no matter how tempting. *He was leaving.* She let the ridiculous little shiver of wanting subside and ambled across the lawn toward the house.

The front door was opened immediately by a woman who must be the housekeeper: a plain, stern-faced, no-nonsense-looking woman in an unadorned, gray serge gown and white starched cap. Her badge of keys dangled like rosary beads from her waist. She looked a bastion of straitlaced morality.

No doubt they'd be at odds within days. Lizzie was inordinately fond of nonsense.

The bastion spoke first. "Your pardon, Captain Marlowe. I wasn't expecting you till—"

"No matter, Mrs. Tupper, I didn't expect to come myself." He spoke to cover the woman's flusters and indicated Lizzie with a smile. "May I present my wife, Mrs. Marlowe? Lizzie, this is Mrs. Tupper, our housekeeper, wife to Mr. Tupper, our steward."

Mrs. Tupper could not manage to hide her surprise even from her new mistress, but she rallied quickly. "Oh, my! Well, such a surprise you've given me. May I offer my congratulations to you both? You'll want some refreshment, I'll be bound."

Though flustered, her smile was genuine enough.

"Yes, thank you," Lizzie cut in before Jamie could answer for her. She would begin as she meant to go on, independently and in charge. She and Mrs. Tupper should sort themselves out sooner rather than later. She moved through the door and into the wide entry hall, drawing off her supple York tan riding gloves. "Would it be possible to have a dish of tea?"

"My apologies, ma'am." Mrs. Tupper looked to Jamie.

"Lizzie, the Tuppers are but newly arrived here themselves, to begin to set the place to rights. I hired them when I arrived back in Dartmouth less than a fortnight ago. I hadn't progressed to furniture at which to take tea as yet. It seemed a waste, as I'm leaving. I wanted to set the repairs in order first."

Mrs. Tupper nodded in sage agreement as she looked back at Lizzie.

"A very sound plan, I suppose. But I'm here to see to things now." She smiled at both of them. "So why don't you take me through the rest of the house, Mrs. Tupper, so I might see what you've already accomplished?"

There was no mistaking the speaking glance Jamie shot toward Mrs. Tupper, though of what it spoke, Lizzie had no idea. No doubt Jamie's standards of housekeeping were low, what with his having lived necessarily rough on all those ships of his, but she wasn't about to take Mrs. Tupper to task about it. Things would change soon enough.

"Aye, ma'am." Mrs. Tupper held out her arm to lead them across the entry hall.

"Thank you." Lizzie stayed put for the moment, wondering at the space and light. Before her, a half circular stair rose gracefully from the floor of the entry hall like an elegant swan's neck. Her hand rose of its own volition to her throat. It was almost too good to be true.

"Major projects first, ma'am," Mrs. Tupper was reporting. "Roof slates repaired. Then all the windows repaned and sealed. And the floors beneath the windows repaired of water damage."

The herringbone pattern of the parquet floor was in excellent polish. Her shoes made a pleasing patter as she crossed the threshold into a bright reception room.

"The windows here repaned as well, and the doors re-hung."

No, not a reception room—a salon, or better still, a music room. The ceiling was high and there, at the end of the room, before the bay of tall windows, was the perfect spot for a pianoforte.

Yes. Lizzie felt excitement bubble up inside her. Oh, the paint was peeling here and there, off the delicate plaster molding, but it was so very lovely. Though empty, the room was sunny and inviting, redolent with the scent of lemon and beeswax. She hadn't yet caught a whiff of damp.

"Lovely. And in just a fortnight? Well done, Mrs. Tupper. Then the underlying structure was sound?"

This time Jamie answered. "I'd hardly buy a house falling down, Lizzie, no matter how charmingly covered with roses."

"Hmm." The ceiling had some very pleasing plaster decorations as well. "But you've owned the house for over four years, and only just hired competent staff?"

He didn't argue the point. He just winced, scrunching up the right side of his eye and cocking his mouth open to the side. His lips were far too soft for a man. It was disarming.

"I was at sea. My cousin Wroxham was meant to be seeing to it for me."

"Ah, yes, the Honorable Jeremy. What dreadful connections you have, Jamie."

"Not my fault my mother's sister married above herself. I haven't tainted *my* bloodlines with nobility."

He was trying to be amusing, but with the exception of her mother, she happened to agree. Most aristocrats were useless as parasites, good only as ornaments and unfit for the privilege they demanded as their due. But no one wanted to hear such radical, even revolutionary, ideas in the current political climate. The news from France was thoroughly revolting in more ways than one.

"He rather tainted your house with neglect. I hope you didn't forward him funds?"

He didn't respond. That was answer enough. Too honest and open for his own good.

"Dreadful man, your odious cousin. You deserve better."

He smiled at her slowly, one corner of his mouth opening up.

"My dear Lizzie. That was very nearly sentimental."

His words were teasing, but his wide gray eyes saw too much. She turned up her chin and went away up the stairs.

There were two separate hallways, one along the north wing, leading away toward the back of the house, and another in the main body of the house itself. Lizzie strolled down the wing.

"Bedchambers, ma'am," Mrs. Tupper interjected, "with smaller dressing rooms, and then farther on, the schoolroom and nursery, and then servants' quarters. There are only attics above."

Lizzie went no farther, as she could foresee no use for either a nursery or a schoolroom, and the servants' rooms would all be shut up and empty. Though the general state of repair was good, the house still felt deserted and ill-used. Or, more likely, not used at all. It was sad to think of such a lovely house so cold and empty. But she was here now, and things would be different. She would see to it.

"The principal bedchamber is this way, ma'am." Mrs. Tupper led the way to a door at the end of the main hallway. "The other chambers are all very spacious, but none so much as this special room."

"Lovely," Lizzie said as she approached the entrance.

Nothing could have prepared her for what awaited on the other side of the door. The rest of the house, with its broom-swept, vacant rooms, had given no hint of the astonishing splendor beyond. The ceiling rose up in the center of the room to form a beautiful, sky-colored dome. Lizzie tipped her head back, rotating slowly as she gazed above in mute admiration.

"You may not be able to see them now, but there are little gold stars painted across the sky. They glow in candlelight." Jamie's voice came from the doorway. "That's why I didn't put in a tester bed—it would have blocked my view."

But, she noticed with a curious feeling uncomfortably close to alarm, there was indeed a bed, the only piece of furniture in the house, covered in clean cotton sheets and an embroidered, soft blue coverlet of watered silk. A large bed. Jamie's large bed, where he lay and gazed at stars.

"It's why I bought the house really, not the roses."

No, the roses were God's extravagance while this was man's. She wanted nothing more than to throw herself across the bed and stare in giddy wonder, but for the first time in ages, an awkward consciousness held her back.

Jamie had lain here. Maybe even last night as he awaited their wedding.

Had he been alone, naked in his bed, looking up at the stars and thinking of her? The skin on her chest and neck began to singe and her fingers tingled with the remembrance of the smooth skin of his chest beneath her hand. She squeezed her gloves into a ball, shook the uncomfortable, heated image out of her mind, and moved on to examine the rest of the room.

The rim of the dome and the divided panels on the walls were all decorated with a delicate, intricate white plasterwork in the style of Robert Adam, which stood out like lace against the soft green painted walls. Corner cabinets, rimmed with white molding and inlaid with a swirling design of mother of pearl, were built into the walls. The effect was both restrained and ornate. Jamie had been right to buy the house for this chamber. It was simply enchanting.

"This will do quite nicely." What extraordinary fortune, that a house she had gotten quite by chance should be everything she could have desired. She was giddy with happiness and relief. That was it exactly—relief. As if she'd been holding her breath for years and years, waiting and looking for something to happen. For this to happen. Finally.

"You may make up the room for me and have my things put away here when they arrive, Mrs. Tupper."

"You're not staying!" Jamie smiled and frowned at the same time. "Lizzie, you can't. I've bespoken rooms for us at the Red Harte." He sounded rather like her father, when he was working himself into an argument. So she did the only thing she could do. The thing she always did. She turned and walked away.

"Mr. and Mrs. Tupper don't even stay here. They live in the steward's cottage down the lane. The house is completely shut up at night. I've only stayed here a few weeks, but you can't possibly stay here alone. I simply won't allow it."

He regretted the words before they were even out of his mouth. It was absolutely, unequivocally the wrong thing to say to Lizzie. Especially after the travesty of a morning they had endured. And after everything he knew of her, he had still managed to say the one thing guaranteed to send her sailing off into the wind, quietly, ruthlessly determined to have her own way.

But clearly, he was just as used to having his own way. Undoubtedly more so. He'd had years of training with entire ships, lieutenants, masters, and men who jumped to do his bidding at the snap of his fingers. He'd grown more than accustomed—he'd grown to rely upon it.

Damn his eyes. He'd shown more finesse outwitting the

French than he had with Lizzie. She was already sauntering away.

"Don't be such an old woman, Jamie. I'm hardly helpless. I never have been."

There was that negligent flick of the wrist in dismissal as she strolled out of the room. He shouldn't have needed reminding.

"Captain?"

He took a deep, calming breath and turned to the housekeeper. "Not to worry, Mrs. Tupper. Everything will still proceed according to plan. My wife will not be moving into Glass Cottage. But do you think you might manage a pot of tea, or something from your cottage, for us?"

"Yes, sir. Straightaway."

He didn't bother to call Lizzie back. He followed her out, to see where she'd gone to slough off his words.

She had wandered back out the front door, into the garden. He let her roam the flower borders in peace, giving her as much sea room as she wanted. They meandered down toward the cliff top and the viewpoint out over the water, where he turned a weather eye upon the Channel. Experience told him there would be rain again, and soon. Late afternoon clouds were gathering along the edge of the sea, piling up into a threatening blanket of gray. There wasn't even enough time to get back to Dartmouth. They would be trapped at the Cottage by the weather for as long as the storm lasted.

Although he was quite used to being as wet as a fish, he doubted Lizzie was. The flat light threw her pale, fine-boned, porcelain skin and vivid hair into greater relief. She looked like a china ornament, so delicate and fragile, despite all her resolute assurances.

Devil take it, he had no business bringing her out here. He must be getting sentimental, damn it. It had seemed such an easy thing to give her the pleasure of the visit after the casual cruelty of her father's words, but now, as he looked back at the neglected cottage, framed by the blowing trees in the eerie, flat light, he could feel the palpable danger of the place.

A danger he was going to orchestrate.

But he couldn't tell her that, no matter the stray worm of guilt boring its way into his conscience. His duty could not be changed. Nor put off much longer.

He satisfied himself by catching hold of her soft, slender fingers. "Lizzie, truly. I don't like the idea of you being out here all alone in that wreck of a house."

An elegant turn of her wrist, and her fingers slipped away.

"A wreck of a house, is it now? Jamie, really, when day before yesterday it was 'so lovely and covered with roses'? Why did you tell me about it and bring me all the way out here if you didn't want me to stay? You must have known I'd be charmed."

He had wanted her to be charmed by *him* and not just by the bloody house. He'd simply used the means at hand. Even if he hadn't thought about it, he had known deep down she wouldn't be able to resist Glass Cottage—she would do it justice and see its possibilities.

Yet he couldn't push too hard, couldn't insist or she'd dig in her heels as she was doing now. But if there was anything he had learned in the past ten long years it was patience and diligence. He would be both patient and diligent, and he would carry the day with Lizzie.

His beautiful, intelligent, defiant wife.

He came up close behind her. Her hair was fashionably loose and down, a riot of gingery waves cascading over her shoulders, hiding that lovely slide of skin at the back of her neck and the singularly vulnerable tendon that ran down the side. He pushed the heavy locks aside so his breath could whisper along her nape.

"I'm charmed as well. But not by the house."

He drew the backs of his fingertips up along the exquisitely pale side of her neck behind her ear. A shiver skittered along the surface of her skin. Very nice. Very responsive. She leaned her neck to the side, all boneless concession. Until she jumped.

"Jamie, someone's there."

"Where?"

She flung out her arm. "There was a man. Standing below on the path, staring up at us." She started forward to follow.

He drew her firmly away as he looked over the rim of the path. It was McAlden, making his way down to the small beach in the cove where they'd stashed a dory.

"Groundsman, I think. Lizzie." He turned her attention back up to his face. "It's going to rain any moment now. Why don't you go in? I'll just speak to the man about seeing to the horses. You go on back up. Mrs. Tupper will have pulled together a tea, or something, by now."

He pushed her firmly in the direction of the house and headed down the path before she could object. McAlden waited out of sight below.

Hugh McAlden was the kind of friend and comrade one could trust with one's life. Marlowe had done so, on several occasions. Just as McAlden had trusted him with his life.

Perhaps it was their shared Scots heritage that had originally brought them together as midshipmen and later, brother officers and friends. It was about all they had in common— they were opposites in body and in spirit.

Where Marlowe was long and lean, Hugh McAlden was powerfully built. Marlowe was dark-haired and pale, and McAlden was a ruddy-faced blond. And where Marlowe didn't mind sailing by dead reckoning and the feel of the waves, McAlden was a man who liked to plan out every possible ramification of each move and pore over his charts. Together they made a strong team.

"Sorry I broke up your cozy moment. Is it done then?"

"It is. You see before you a happily married man."

McAlden made a guttural sound of disbelief. "Seems an awful lot of trouble to go through just to secure things."

"You only think so because you've nothing to secure."

"Of course I do. Only I keep it safe and sound in the five percents, not lording it about on great big houses."

"Boring. And besides this will work much better for our plans. This way the house is really secure. But you'll have to shift your berth for the time being."

"Shift? What about our plan? What about—"

"Changed for the time being. Today, no more. Needs must . . ."

". . . when the devil drives?" McAlden finished. "And where am I to go? There's a storm blowing in."

"I don't know. There's a loft over the stables with empty rooms for the lads. Take the largest—whatever has a fireplace."

McAlden scoffed. "You'll forgive me for saying you've shite for brains, Captain. There's no fireplace in a stables. It would be like having an oven next to the powder locker on a ship."

"Damn. Hadn't thought of that." He pulled his mouth sideways at the wry admission.

"And that's why you shouldn't be lording it about in great country houses. You're a sailor, not a squire."

"I've got to be both for the time being. Take the gardener's cottage, since that's what you're meant to be anyway. I've told her you're a groundsman."

That got a grudging laugh out of the man. "And me caught out in my smuggler's kit. I'll be sure to get dirt under my fingernails."

Marlowe smiled in return. "You'll do as you are. Just be sure to stay out of sight until we're gone."

"Right," McAlden nodded in concession. "And you?"

"I'm trying to get her back down to the Red Harte, but she's proving fractious."

"Your plan was for the house to be empty."

"As soon as I leave, it will be." Marlowe shoved his hands

through his hair. "Though she's making ridiculous noises about moving out here."

McAlden made a sour face. "I did tell you she'd be nothing but trouble."

"She's not nothing but. Besides, I couldn't take the chance of the place being sold out from under me. The house and estate are protected in the marriage settlement. She can't sell, and I'll take her back into town. All will be well."

Then why did his gut twist into a knot even as he said the words? Glass Cottage was bloody well perfect for what he remembered of Lizzie's sort of solitary pursuits. But surely she hadn't been wandering about in hedgerows for the past ten years? She'd been out in society—she must have gone to dinners and balls. She'd been at the assembly room, hadn't she? Though playing least in sight out the back terrace wasn't exactly social behavior. He squinted up at the darkening sky. "In the meantime, pray for it to rain."

"A howling gale off the channel to scare the stays off her?"

"That'll do. Then I can 'leave,' and we can set to the business in peace, with no one the wiser."

"Not even your little wife?"

"Not even Lizzie."

"You're a coldhearted bastard, Captain. No wonder I like you." McAlden nodded with satisfaction. "Only hard part should be getting you to stick to your plan."

CHAPTER 5

Rain pummeled down upon her. She was as soaking wet as a barnyard mouser and twice as muddy. Her hems were awash in leaf mold and bits of damp moss. All to serve her horribly suspicious mind. *Bloody bother.*

Instinct and pique had prompted her to follow Jamie down the path. She wasn't the kind of person to be set away like a toy he was done playing with. She never had been.

But something else, an almost animal instinct for self-preservation, had her hanging back, hiding low in the shrubbery, out of sight. Unfortunately, distant thunder and the wail of the wind streaking across the water had drowned out most of their words. *Bloody rain.*

But one thing had been certain. They had *not* been talking about horses. And they had *not* gone in the direction of the stables.

They had walked to the east, around toward the lane, and nothing about them, not their posture, gestures, nor tone, had indicated speech between a man and his servant. It had been a conversation among equals.

How awfully curious. How damnably suspicious.

Groundsman? What a bouncer.

Bloody damn. Why did she always expect the worst from

people? Even as a child, she had been suspicious. And curious and sharp-tongued and managing. But mostly suspicious. It was not a comfortable feeling. Never had been.

And it was doubly uncomfortable to find herself suspicious of Jamie. But her instincts were never wrong. She could always sniff out the gorgers like his cousin Wroxham. But not Jamie. The only person in the world she could ever remember trusting was Jamie. That was probably the truth of why she had married him. That and his wonderfully hungry, knowing smile. Yet, all the relief she had felt upon coming to the house evaporated into the clouds, leaving a clammy sense of unease and disappointment.

Lizzie dragged up her sodden hems, thanked providence she was wearing boots, and set herself back through the underbrush towards the cliff top, cultivating the messy mixture of suspicion and disappointment with each mud-slick step.

What on earth did Jamie think he was about?

There had been something familiar about the man, the groundsman, yet she couldn't place him. Dartmouth might be a bustling port, but it was still a small provincial town. She had lived there all her life and thought she knew everyone, from the baker's boy to the Earl's housemaid. But that man was a stranger. He had the rugged, tanned look of a sailor, much more so than Jamie. Perhaps he was one of the rough, itinerant seamen who frequented the Dartmouth waterfront? But such a man would hardly seek work, or be hired, as a groundskeeper.

Only two things could explain their familiarity. One, he was someone Jamie had known from the Navy. And it would be very like Jamie to bring one of the less fortunate or less able of his comrades home to a comfortable job after they'd been cast off by the Navy. Loyal and sentimental, and deeply honorable, her Jamie.

The second explanation was much more likely, especially considering their secluded location along the south coast. The man was a smuggler, one of an invisible network of free traders that ran from the lowest levels of society to the highest. One interfered with the free traders to great peril. Jamie would be a fool, a bloody, blundering, trusting fool, to get involved in any of that.

And Jamie was no fool. If she knew anything about the man he had become over the past ten years, it was that. Open and honest, yes. But not gullible. Oh, no. Not with those eyes of his that prowled and saw everything. He knew what he was doing, but what on earth was he up to? And why, why was he lying to her?

How could he, a captain of His Majesty's Royal Navy, be mixed up in the dirty business of smuggling? The thought overthrew every instinct, every thought she'd ever had of him, of the boy she'd remembered for his honesty and courage, of the man who seemed to speak so openly and honestly. And left her frightened.

What if Papa had been right? What did she really know of him, of Captain Marlowe now? She'd been swayed by his talk of houses and estates and independent fortunes, and convinced by the heat of his kisses. He had told her exactly what she had wanted to hear. Stupid, stupid girl—soaking wet, cold girl.

Her foray into the shrubbery had left her uncomfortably sodden and growing colder by the moment. The big fat raindrops had already soaked through her linen chemisette and were snaking their chilly way down her back by the time she made her way to the edge of the lawn.

"Lizzie? Lizzie!"

She turned at the sound of Jamie's voice. He came across the garden from the direction of the house at a fast, but easy run, laughing at the rain.

"What do you think you're doing out here? Come inside."

"I think I'm getting wet." She told herself she wasn't happy to see him, no matter the sweet curling sensation in the pit of her stomach when he smiled at her like that. She forced her mind back to the cold coil of unease and discontent sliding under her skin.

"Who was that man?"

"A servant."

She didn't know what she had expected, but it wasn't that. It seemed entirely out of character. "A servant? What happened to 'Servants are people'? No, what did you used to say? 'Servants are people and individuals as well, and they do not exist simply to meet your extravagant needs, Lizzie.' "

"Did I say that?"

"You used to do. All the time. And took great pleasure in lecturing me." She turned away to frame her next question. But he had other things on his mind.

"There are other things I'd rather take pleasure in now. You're soaking wet." He stepped closer and thumbed a raindrop off the end of her nose before he shrugged out of his coat and slung it around her shoulders. "Here. You'll do me no good if you catch the ague. I'd rather lecture you on pleasure itself."

Her hands went reflexively to the lapels to pull the coat snugly around her shoulders as the weight of Jamie's large, capable hands settled on her shoulders, holding her still before him. She felt the low melting spiral through her again. The cloth was warm from the heat of his body and redolent with his spice-tinged male scent. Bay rum, he'd said. Yet it was the warmth in his eyes that sent comfort billowing around her as surely as the cloth. She could spend all day trapped in his eyes and forget his suspicious actions when he looked at her like that. It made all her firm resolutions and difficult suspicions melt like toffee in the sun.

But without his coat, he was now the one getting cold and wet. The rain sluiced through his shirtsleeves and under his waistcoat, drenching him. Her gaze fell to his upper arms where the water plastered the fine linen against his skin, making it all but transparent. The elegant swell of his shoulder and upper arm muscle was clearly outlined, wholly masculine and curiously beautiful.

She couldn't seem to help herself. Without thinking, she'd reached out one inquisitive index finger to touch him, tracing the line of his bicep where it curved into his upper arm. Then down the inside to the crook of his elbow. The difference between the long, cool, pale length of his shirtsleeve and the steaming heat coming off his skin was strangely arousing, tipping off a shivery heat low inside her. She gave in to it and let it wash under her skin and wipe away all thought. She closed her eyes and rubbed her face along the slick, silky wet cloth. Beneath her cheek, his muscles were long, sleek, hard, and warm.

A sound very much like a growl rumbled out of him. And then his hands were there, tipping up her lips as his mouth descended towards hers slowly. All the while he watched her, daring her with his knowing eyes to back away.

But she'd always loved a dare. She loved the little anticipatory rush of naughty pleasure.

Yet there was nothing naughty or flirtatious in his kiss. His mouth covered hers and immediately she felt his strength, his physical dominance of her body. His hand slid around to her nape, solid and strong—immovable. The warmth of his palm blotted out the chill of the rain trickling through her hair. He gathered her into him, against his chest and into the hot insistence of his lips and teeth as he kissed and nipped, torturing her mouth open with his honest greed.

His other hand fanned along her cheek, angling her face and tipping back her head so she had no choice, no thought, but to open before him.

No thought but to give over and let the wave of sensation drown her reservations. She was all sensation—the touch of his hands holding her intent before him, the slide of his skin, rougher where his whiskers hid just beneath the surface of his smooth-shaven skin and softer where his lips pressed insistently into hers. The sound of animal satisfaction that wound out of his chest when her mouth opened and the surprisingly sweet tang of his mouth as his tongue swept in to entwine with hers.

Heat and something she recognized as need flashed under her skin, pebbling her body with gooseflesh and abrading her nipples against the cold fabric of her damp shift.

She made her own sound then, one of needy desperation and surrender. It stopped her cold. She wasn't made for surrender.

She pulled her mouth closed and turned away.

He pulled back abruptly. "What is it?" His voice was low and raspy.

She closed her eyes to the probe of his and shook her head. He leaned his forehead down against hers, close and confining, refusing to let her turn away or gather her thoughts.

"Lizzie." His breath blew warm across her face, an uneasy contrast with the chill of the rain. "You're shaking. God, you're freezing. Come."

He took up her hand and set off at a dead run across the lawn. She went, pulled along by his momentum, the rain and wet grass flying by in a gray blur. They raced towards the house like the children they once were, tumbling breathlessly through the front door into puddles of their own making.

But Jamie was done with childhood. Once through the door he kicked it closed and crowded her back against the polished oak of the portal. Without a word he grabbed her upper arms and covered her mouth with his.

The kiss was hard and demanding. He surrounded her, dominating her with his hands, his body, and his mouth. His skin was damp with chill rain, and his lips tasted like the spring shower, cool, fresh, and earthy. He put his thumbs along the edge of her jaw and exerted just enough pressure to open her so he could taste. His tongue swept in and tangled with hers, knotting up all her senses.

She caught at him for balance, gripping his arms and pulling closer to the warmth rising like steam from his body.

"My God, Lizzie." He traced a torturous line with his tongue down into the hollow of her throat. "First we're going to get you out of these wet clothes and then we're going to consummate this marriage. Immediately."

His words prowled like a wolf across her skin, insistent and hungry for her. Her breathing grew hectic and her nipples tightened within her damp shift. She couldn't think.

"I thought this was a marriage of convenience, a straw marriage?" She tried to grasp at her own straws, to buy enough time to sort out her confused thoughts and feelings. She wanted the old Jamie, the Jamie she thought she knew. Not this man she didn't know if she could trust. Not this man with his relentless, driving determination.

She tried to slip away, to slide around the fortress of his chest. To find a chink in his armor of self-assurance. He let her twist and undulate beneath his hands, but he wouldn't let her go. His hands spanned her waist and his thumbs brushed back and forth against her midriff as she moved. He scooped his chin around to nuzzle at her neck.

"Maybe," he whispered against her ear, "but there's no reason we can't make hay. At least for a day. The house is empty."

"No. I must think. I don't want—"

"Don't lie to me, Lizzie. You do want. You can't kiss me like that and tell me you're indifferent. That you don't want my touch as much as I want yours. Admit it. You know it as well as I do. You did from the moment you kissed me at the assembly room. We're inevitable, you and I." His gaze poured over her like heated steel, sharp and dark with something like anguish. It was almost painful to look at him. Too painful to lie.

"Yes." Whatever he was, whatever he had become, he was still hers. Her Jamie. Always. Inevitable.

He pressed his advantage, kissing along her neck and down onto the thin skin over her collarbone. She felt the insistent warmth of his lips inside her bones, all the way to her knees. And somehow she could feel his lips were curved in a smile.

"I'm a desperate man, Lizzie," he teased in his low, smooth, wolf voice. "About to forsake hearth and home for the passage to the grave. And I want you. I want *you*, Lizzie. No one else will do. No one else ever has."

She all but stopped breathing. There was heat and even pain that became pleasure in her chest where his words pierced through her. Her lips came apart, trembling on the shaky rush of her breath. He kissed them into stillness.

"Let me love you."

Words of unbearable, irresistible sweetness. How long had she waited to hear them? She had no defense to such openness.

Her eyes tipped shut and her legs seemed to dissolve out from under her. He took her weight in his arms, kneading the length of her spine, urging her forward into his chest and into his kiss. It was more than she could bear. It was everything she wanted.

Lizzie gave herself to his mouth, sending her tongue out to swirl and dance with his, sucking lightly at his lower lip. Her chest felt tight, as if her breath were bound within her and only he could set it free. She ran her hands up the corded tendons at the back of his neck and into his soft hair, disrupting his queue, fisting it in her hands and pulling him closer. He smelled intoxicating, a potent combination of rain and leather and man.

He unwrapped himself just enough to pick her up without breaking the kiss.

"Come," he breathed against her lips as he gathered her into his arms. "Let me take you to bed."

Oh, yes. She wrapped her arms around his neck and pulled his weight into her, soothing the tight ache that gnawed at her inside. Jamie took the stairs two at a time, carrying her against his chest as if she weighed nothing. She curled into his heat, turning to nuzzle against his neck. She could feel the strong, steady beat of the pulse under his skin. Her own felt weak and hectic.

Once he'd gained the bedchamber, he set her down and turned to light the fire in the grate. "You need to be warm."

The abrupt loss of his heat reminded her why she was cold and uncomfortable in her sodden riding habit. The chill returned her to some semblance of her senses. The doubts she'd so easily pushed aside came back, insistent and demanding. She needed to put distance between them, emotional as well as physical, even as she edged closer to the kindling fire. She needed to understand *this* Jamie, this complicated, confusing man, before she could lie with him.

"I'm not going to just let you sweep me off my feet." She firmed her voice. "You're leaving." She wasn't sure if she said it to remind herself or him.

"Too late. I already have. And here we are." He gave her another of those slow, unfairly intelligent smiles of his, while his gaze roamed her face. Looking at her as if he wanted to memorize her like a line of poetry.

"You're leaving." Such a paltry defense, but it was all she could say. It was the only thing that made sense.

"Yes, Lizzie. But I want you. Now. Fiercely. We will give each other pleasure while we can," he coaxed. "Enough to last a lifetime."

Would it be enough to fill a lifetime? The pleasure he'd already given her had left her shaking and nearly incoherent with want. Ready to abandon her scruples just to feel him and taste him. What more would it feel like to have Jamie, his beautiful, long, lean naked body next to hers? His strong, clever fingers discovering the secret places of pleasure locked away inside her?

"I promise. There's power and freedom in pleasure, Lizzie. Just waiting for you. I'll teach you everything you need to know." His quiet, low-voiced appeal vibrated through her, insinuating its way through her armor.

"Everything?" She let out a gasping breath. "And who'll teach you?"

"Lizzie." His gray eyes changed, the dark, intent gray slowly warming at the corners, until they crinkled completely. "Don't you know? There's a big, wide world out there."

"You said . . . no one else had ever . . ." But of course he had. He was a man now. A man who had lived in that wide world, who had crossed seas and seen other continents. She had never been so far as London. She probably never would.

And he was leaving. She'd never have another chance again.

"I rather meant marriage, Lizzie. I never wanted to marry anyone else but you."

Jamie rubbed his chin against the side of her neck, while his hands roamed lower. "I'll tell you what else I want." His breath fanned alongside her ear, his voice low and insistent. "I want to lay you out in the middle of that bed and strip every last inch of clothing from your very well hidden little body until you are quite, quite naked, and then I want to explore every last, hidden inch of your skin. Because believe it or not, I *have* done this before. And despite your attempts at worldliness, I don't believe for a moment *you* have."

His gray eyes pierced her defenses, stripping her soul bare. As if he knew. Knew that despite the fact that she hadn't done this before, she'd wanted to. She'd lain awake at night, feeling the pulsating hum and rhythm of her body, and longing for a lover's touch. For his touch.

Heat blazed across her cheeks and down her chest. She turned her head away, but that merely gave him unimpeded access to her neck. He ran his teeth along the tendon. A sharp stab of pleasure serrated the last of her defenses. Oh, most assuredly, he had done this before.

He pushed his damp coat off her shoulders and yanked her tight-fitting jacket down off her arms, exposing the translucent fabric of her chemisette and shift. He ran his hand up the sides of her stays.

His low voice was inexorable. "But I'll tell you what, Lizzie. I promise to make your wait, very, very much worth your while." He nipped at her earlobe and took it gently between his teeth as he circumscribed her linen-covered breasts with his hand.

Another shock of heat and desire bolted through her. Her eyelids slid down as her head fell back and her body arched helplessly into his palms.

"Oh, yes." He raised her hands over her head and leaned gently into her, pressing his weight against her. She could feel the heat and power of his body. "Very, very worth your while."

A high keening cry of surrender flew from her mouth as he dragged her chemisette open. With his other hand he yanked loose the tie of her shift and tugged the edges down to expose the swell of her breasts above the molded confines of her stays. His gaze alone brought her nipples into tight, nearly painful peaks.

"Shall I touch them, Lizzie?"

"Lord, yes." She watched in fascination as his fingers brushed lightly across first one tip and then the other. Sensation blossomed, rippling along her skin and down, deep into her core. She pressed into his palms, wanting more of the delicious contact, wanting more of his attention. And he gave it to her, lowering his head to lightly lick and suck each pink nipple until she was overwhelmed by need and gasping for air.

Lizzie felt her knees dissolve beneath her. Jamie caught her up and did exactly as he had said. He laid her down across the bed and began to strip off her remaining clothes. His fingers were swift and adept at the side buttons for her riding skirt.

"You really don't have a maid." His lazy grin skimmed down the front lacing of her stays.

"And you really don't have a valet."

"No," he agreed conspiratorially. "You'll have to help."

Oh, yes. Her fingers itched to feel the smooth warmth of his skin again.

She reached up to untie his soggy cravat as he stripped off her full riding skirt and petticoats. He looked down to see her shod in full-length, gentlemen's riding boots.

"So naughty," he murmured.

Lizzie felt some of the awful tension ebb. This was the Jamie she knew, laughing and teasing. "Just your sort of naughty, Jamie."

His grin spread across his face and up to his eyes, but in another moment he was intent again. He yanked the boots off and tossed them over his shoulder, and his hands, when they slid up her thighs to untie her garters, were rough and urgent. Her flesh quivered against his fingertips as he peeled down her stockings.

Her breath bottled up in her chest when his hands returned to her knees, kneading and pressing them ever so slightly apart. She resisted. If he touched her there, now, she would fly into a thousand pieces.

"What about you?" she asked instead.

"It seems only fair." His smile was slow and knowing, his piercing, gray gaze never leaving her face. He reached up and stripped his shirt over his head. From where she lay, his chest seemed even broader and more defined than before. She wanted to touch him.

A little gasp of pleasure escaped her as she fanned her hands across the gleaming contours of his chest, marveling at the strength and beauty of his body.

"Lizzie? I've taken my shirt off for you before." He smiled like a hungry wolf, all teeth and gray eyes. "As have you."

She was sure he could see her nipples' swift contraction beneath the thin cotton shift, but only she could feel the blissful convulsion deep in her womb. Need pulsed outward from the center of her body.

"You went first."

"So I did." He stepped closer and his hands went to the close of his breeches.

"No."

He stopped, dropping his hands and stepping back a fraction, though the effort cost him something. His hands fisted by his side, the knuckles going white with tension.

"Lizzie?" His voice was both surprised and full of thwarted intent. Full of power he had leashed because she had asked. Power she wanted to fully experience.

She wanted to see him and touch him and feel the loose electricity of his body running under her hands. She wanted him to see her and touch her and make heat and cold pour through her like a sun shower.

But slowly, so slowly she would be able to recall each and every moment like the tastes of a sumptuous meal.

"Well, Lizzie? What's it going to be?" He stayed there, standing before her with his hands loosely at his side, waiting, like a silent, patient wolf, a pale, half-naked, graven image brought to life. Waiting for her to choose.

The silver-white light of the stormy sky skimmed across his broad shoulders, turning him into a marble sculpture. But he wasn't made of cold stone. No, he was flesh and blood. He reached out his warm hand and ran a finger lightly along the outer edge of her forearm. A simple touch as intense as his kiss.

"Lizzie?" His low voice hummed through her.

Her throat seemed dry and tight. The words came out on a whisper. "I want to."

He knew exactly what she meant.

He took a step forward until he was close enough for her to touch. And then she set her hands to the smooth polished buttons, easing them through the buttonholes slowly. And every time she undid another one, the sculpted muscles of his flat stomach jumped in anticipation and impatience. She did that to him. That was her power, the power to give him pleasure just as he gave it to her, freely, openly. She felt a surge of joy, a low heat that began in her chest and flushed out across her skin as she dipped her hands into the waistband and began to slide both his breeches and smallclothes down over his hips, until he was naked before her.

He stepped back and let her look her fill. He was a study in supple tension. Her gaze skimmed over his long, lean, beautiful body and down to his rampant erection. He looked so intent, so potent, so overwhelmingly male.

She blurted out the only thing that came to mind. "I don't want a baby."

CHAPTER 6

"Hush, I'll take care of that. There are ways . . ." Marlowe found himself laughing to cover the savage, possessive thrill in his gut at the thought of putting his seed within her. He reached for her, to bring her back within the persuasive circle of his arms and give her a reassuring smile. He felt surer of himself when he was touching her.

Lizzie was having none of it, damn her eyes. Stubborn, provocative chit. She somehow kept herself just beyond his reach.

"What ways?" Her look was a combination of ardent curiosity, skepticism, and trust. She was relying upon him to act like a gentleman. She always had.

He had acted the gentleman at fourteen. Barely. He'd been too frightened by the power of his own monstrous need for her to do anything else. But what would have happened to them, to Lizzie, if that hadn't been the end of it? What if the squire hadn't sent him away? They had been inevitable, he'd told her. What if they had gone on the way they'd begun? By sixteen there would have been nothing, no conscience strong enough, no punishment harsh enough, to have kept him from taking and using what she so trustingly offered.

Inexperienced and overeager, he would have made a hash of it.

For all his ruthless interference, the squire had been right to ship him off to the Royal Navy. Without his profession, Marlowe never would have become the man he was now, the man who could do more than just tempt Lizzie Paxton. He was the man who could, and would, keep her.

And so he would be a gentleman again. He had already waited nearly half his life to have her. He would steel himself to resist the temptations of her lush little body for a least a few more minutes. A very few. Because he could barely wait another moment to have her. To taste her. To feel the exquisite softness of her pearly skin against his mouth. To see her naked and writhing in ecstasy beneath him.

Instead, here he was, as hard as a keel and aching for her touch, while she waited impatiently for him to explain his intimate knowledge of contraception. It was going to kill him, letting her choose.

It was also taking every ounce of self-restraint he possessed. Because he wanted. He wanted her so much it set his teeth on edge. He wanted to kiss her and love her and command her to need him and love him and lie down on that bloody bed and open her endlessly long, lithe legs and let him sheath his aching cock inside her sweet, tight . . .

God help him.

Marlowe took a deep, fortifying breath.

That would never work. Not with her. Virgins, especially eager, curious, clever girls who ought not still be virgins, like Lizzie Paxton, couldn't be ordered. She needed to choose. And he needed to know she had chosen him.

She would need to remember that, sometime in the future.

Even though, as far as she was concerned, there was no future. He would leave and that would be an end to it. His Majesty's Navy would see to that.

So in the meantime, honor demanded he grant this one request. It was only fair. It wouldn't be fair to leave her alone with a brat. She was hardly more than a brat herself. A brat with lovely, pale breasts and deliciously long legs.

Marlowe moved to kiss the sweet, soft corner of her mouth. "I'll take care of you."

"I don't need you to take care of me." She reached for her shift. "I'm perfectly—"

"No." He stayed her hand. He liked her naked. Besides the fact that she was startlingly beautiful, it gave him an advantage. And he needed all the advantage he could get with Lizzie. "I meant I know what to do."

But he was not, as it were, prepared. He had French letters in his trunk at the Red Harte, but he didn't want to admit to Lizzie her new husband had such supplies as part of his normal kit. It seemed, at best, unflattering to his character. So he closed his eyes to the disheveled beauty before him and yanked his breeches back on over his rampant cock.

"Stay right here. I'll be right back." He padded out the door and down the stairs on bare feet, hoping to God that Mrs. Tupper, if she was still about downstairs, was still enough of a navy wife not to have a fit at his appearance.

He must be mad. He must love her if he was running around an empty house, half dressed, with what felt like a loaded pistol shoved down his pants, looking for contraception.

The startling thought yanked him to an abrupt halt in the middle of the stairway. Did he love Lizzie Paxton?

It was hard to say. He couldn't remember a time when he didn't feel . . . well, what he felt, for Lizzie Paxton. And he admired her, this newly grown woman, from a purely aesthetic point of view, of course, with her sinuous curves and her vivid colors. He liked her, even. She was amusing and never, ever boring. And he loved being with her and watching her doing what only she could do—collect the world to her with her always curious, watchful eyes. As a child, she was always observing and thinking, soaking in experiences and opinions. Holding it all behind those green cat eyes until she made something new, something entirely her own. She was unique, his Lizzie.

And she was his, wasn't she? For better or for worse. Poor girl. He'd have to remind her of that later too, no doubt.

But they had unfinished business between them, he and Lizzie Paxton. And he was going to do whatever it took to bring it to a satisfying conclusion, even if it meant hunting up something in the way of a vinegar-soaked sponge.

Ah, the stillroom. Bound to be some vinegar there.

The housekeeper's stillroom was tucked between the empty larder and the laundry at the back of the kitchen wing. A few neglected bunches of dried flowers still hung from hooks and racks hanging from the rafters, and the room still held a lingering scent of once pungent herbs. But Mrs. Tupper had been busy. Though there was no current housewifery on display, the counters and tabletops were all free from dust and debris.

Marlowe began to pull the corks out of the few remaining bottles clustered in the cabinet, muttering vile imprecations against demanding, provocative, lovely ginger-haired women under his breath.

"What are you doing?"

Lizzie nearly startled him out of his pants. Except what was in his pants got even bigger at the sight of her. She'd retrieved his damp coat jacket and wore it over her nearly transparent shift. She'd taken off her stays, and her ripe little breasts were just barely hidden beneath the edge of the fabric. Sweet God above, give him fortitude.

"God, Lizzie." He didn't care if it sounded like a groan. She was far too provoking a creature. She seemed to have no earthly idea of how beautiful she appeared, or how she affected him. How the sight of her pale, apricot tinged skin made him ravenous with want.

But before he cast his gun loose, he needed to solve the dilemma at hand. Please God, let him find what he needed. Quickly.

He hunkered down in front of a cabinet to ease the tightness in his breeches. "Looking for vinegar. I told you, I'll take care of it."

"I told you, I'm not useless. I want to help. Is this what you want?" She hauled up a labeled earthenware jug from under a counter.

"Bravo, Lizzie." He should have known she'd never stay where he put her, but she was nicely useful, as well as easy on the eye. He rummaged through a cabinet and found a mortar and pestle. He took out the pestle and filled the bowl with vinegar.

"And now we need something to absorb the vinegar, like a rag or a sponge."

"Like for cleaning?" She was nosing in close behind him, watching his preparations with all of her natural curiosity on display.

He took advantage of her closeness and dropped a kiss on her nose. And when she didn't protest or pull away, he had to slide his fingers through her soft hair and inhale her light, citrusy fragrance. And kiss her on her soft, jam-colored mouth, and run a finger down the sweet valley between her breasts. Oh God, she was heaven.

"More like for bathing." The thought of that—having Lizzie pink and wet, steam whispering off her delicately glistening body—blanked his mind. His lungs felt tight and full at the same time. His only recourse was to share the erotic thought with her, to see if it could affect her in the same way. "Think of that, Lizzie," he breathed into her ear, "of all the things we can do. I'd like to bathe you. Draw a damp cloth all over your lovely, warm, wet body."

He could see her eyes widen and her nostrils flutter as he wove his hands into her hair, drawing the ginger silk back over her shoulder and tugged gently, just enough to nudge her head back. The curls leapt and tangled around his hand like a vine, as if even this part of Lizzie could not remain still. He ran the backs of his fingers lightly down the curve of her exposed neck to the delicate hollow where he could feel the hectic beating of her pulse. The contrast between the porcelain fragility of her body and the formidable strength of her will was endlessly fascinating.

"So many things to do with you." He made the words low and soft, the complete opposite of the tense coil of need spiraling through his groin. No one was going to stop him this time. He would explore her to his heart's delight and learn every last secret of her body. He could at long last replace fantasy with reality.

She moved a little apart, out from under his hands, aroused now, but still unsettled. He let her go, forcing his desultory attention to return to the cupboards. He had made her a promise. This one at least, he could and would keep.

Lizzie pulled a slatted basket off a shelf. "What about sea sponges? Collected from the beach, I suppose. Will they do?" Was there a hint of urgency in her voice?

"Perfect." He picked out a small damson-sized sponge and held it up for her edification. "There you have it, Lizzie—the means to your seduction."

"That? Seduction?" She tried to steady and shield herself with that veneer of worldliness. "You'd be better off with your little flask of whisky."

Ah, now they were in familiar seas. He set his hands about her waist and lifted her up onto the table. She weighed nothing, a bare handful of a woman. Her apricot-ripe mouth came almost level to his, as did several other, more pertinent parts. Perfect.

"Is that what you'd like?" He reached slowly into the inner pocket of his coat as it hung off her shoulders, making sure the back of his hand brushed lightly against the flutter of fabric covering the peak of her breast. He drew the flask out and uncorked it. "Then by all means, have a wee dram."

He had meant to arouse her, and judging by the flush heating her neck, he had, but the feel of her soft, warm skin through the insignificant barrier of fabric left him scorched, dazed and thirsty for her.

She had to tip her head back to drink and he feasted first his eyes, and then his hands, on the long slide of her neck leading down to the ripe swell of her breasts. He ran the backs of his fingers lightly along the top edge of her shift, toying with her nipples and reloosening the tie. He had to see her.

As Marlowe carefully peeled back the fabric to reveal the luscious pink tips, he felt Lizzie's breath shiver out on a shaky, uneven sigh of pleasure. So responsive, his Lizzie. So beautiful, so vivid and fresh. Her nipples were the same pale pink as the inside of a strawberry, and suddenly he was thirsty for more than just the taste of whisky on her lips.

He moved to stand between her legs, pressing her knees wider and pulling her heat to the edge of the table. His erection strained against the confines of his breeches, and he eased himself for just a moment by pressing his restless cock into her belly and mound.

God, it felt good. So good. Heat poured out of her core. He was nearly wild to yank up the hem of her shift and show her all, here and now.

No. Virgins needed to be wooed gently, in a soft bed, not taken by flyer or initiated into coition on a stillroom counter. And this was Lizzie. No matter their history, no matter what experience she had, or hadn't had, she needed proper handling. Because he wanted more from her than a quick tupping.

He wanted nothing less than her complete and total surrender.

Marlowe heard the words echo around in his brain: seduction and surrender. They were tied up together in his mind. He could not pursue one without the other.

It took an effort to ease his cock away from her heat, but he was compensated for the loss by the erotic sight she presented. She was a delectable gamine, wearing his dark, masculine clothes: all tumbled ginger hair and soft luminous skin, her breasts framed by the rumpled, translucent shift, which barely veiled the riot of darker curls there, lower, where her waist slid in and then flared back out over her slim hips and long, God they were endless, legs. So perfect, he could not have conjured such a vision even from his deepest, darkest dreams.

"God. Look at you." He put his hands on her knees and spread them infinitesimally wider, and then flipped up the hem of the shift so it rucked up over the junction of her soft white thighs.

She clamped her hands down on top of his to stop him, her knuckles white with shock and thwarted, suppressed need. Trying so hard to keep control of her curious, inexperienced body. She opened her mouth to speak but no words came, only the tense, almost ravaged sound of her breathing.

He smiled, in sympathy or perhaps encouragement, and watched the play of conflicting emotions scatter across her mobile, expressive face. Such a study in contrasts: she looked both vulnerable and avid. Needing to be convinced.

"I want to look at you Lizzie, all of you."

Her breathing became shallower in reaction, her shoulders up in anticipation and confusion. "Why?"

"Because you're beautiful. Everywhere. Because we were talking of seduction. Seduction and surrender. All you have to do is surrender to your desires."

She tried again to cover her shock of arousal with worldliness, though her words were nothing but a breathy little whisper. "I'm going to need more whisky for that."

"No more whisky, love. I want you lucid. I want you to feel and understand and remember everything." He held the sponge up between them. "I want you to show me how it feels when I take this cool, wet sponge and press it up inside the heat of you."

He lowered his hand and pressed it gently against her mound, over the gauzy layer of her shift. She gasped, and he felt the ripple of her desire undulate through her body.

This time, when her hand came down on his, it was as an accomplice, a co-conspirator in her seduction. She closed her eyes and guided his hand over her, letting the ripples of desire lap against the edge of her need until she began to move and sway, slightly at first, tentatively, testing the way it made her feel to appease the want growing within her.

And then in the next moment, she fisted up the material and raised it, baring herself for him.

"Lizzie." Her name whispered from his lips: both a benediction and prayer.

His hand was on her mouth, his thumb tugging at her lower lip, opening her mouth for a rough kiss. He kissed her hard. He kissed her the way he'd always wanted to: with nothing but need and want between them. No barriers or pretensions, no rank, no prohibitions to correct behavior. There was ten years of waiting and wanting in that kiss.

He cupped her face in his hands, staring into her fathomless eyes.

"Do you know, I think I've gone about this all wrong. Here I've been thinking you need all sorts of consideration because you're a virgin, but you don't really want to be a virgin, do you Lizzie? You, so quick and curious, so eager. Your maidenhead must be rather a burden to you at this point. And since you don't want to be a virgin, I rather think you don't want to be treated like a virgin. Certainly a virgin wouldn't ask her lover, or God forbid, her husband, for a precaution. Only a woman with experience, a woman who knew what it was like," he leaned in beside her ear and whispered, "for a man to come between her legs and fuck her, would do that. And I think that's what you really want."

The coarse, improper word shot through her like an arrow tipped in lust, unleashing a flood of dark, forbidden thoughts and sensations. The low cadence of his voice was as evocative and effective as a touch. Each word, each deep vibration of his low tone, hummed through her.

And other words as well, the ones he had said before: *I promise to make it worth your wait.*

And she had waited. Impatiently, it was true, but she had waited. He had left her hovering on the brink of something dangerous. Wanting more. But she had waited out her curiosity and frustration. For him. For Jamie. For *this*. For the dark pleasure he brewed in her like strong, almost bitter chocolate, flowing and swirling through her veins.

And she was lost when he looked at her with those eyes, those pale, gray, all-seeing eyes. Did he not know there was nothing she would not do when he looked at her like that? As if nothing else mattered to him but her. As if he could see into the depths of her soul and he loved her anyway.

"Surrender, Lizzie," he whispered.

Did he not see she already had? She was trapped by her need, pinned by his icy hot gaze as he put his big hand on her belly and urged her back and down, flat on the counter. *Yes. Oh, yes.*

He followed her down, leaning in to kiss her mouth once more before he whispered, "Surrender, to me."

She watched through half-closed eyes, fascinated and aroused by the sight of him looking at her breasts, at her body. By the exquisite feeling of his dark, masculine hands stroking her pale, white breasts. And by the bliss bursting across the surface of her skin and then diving deep into her belly, when he lowered his mouth to take first one, and then the other breast into his mouth. The pull of his lips on her nipples created a tight, needy heat between her legs.

His hand stayed, pressing his warm palm into her belly, holding her still as he sucked and nipped at her, teaching her body to arch and reach up to him. Teaching her to want more. "Yes," he smiled gently. "Give in to the pleasure. Surrender."

Her hands were on his face, along the strong line of his jaw, brushing into his soft hair. Her fingers burned where they touched him, pain and pleasure running riot under her skin. Lizzie closed her eyes and let go, spreading her arms open wide in invitation and surrender. To him. To the bliss.

She let all thought, all decision, slide away into nothing. She opened her eyes to watch again as he circled his thumbs on the soft, vulnerable skin of her inner thighs, readying her, waiting as the soft rush of sensation broke over her, sending anticipation quivering through her body. She watched as his possessive gaze ran slowly down her body until he came to her open sex.

He stirred the backs of his fingers lazily through her curls, and she felt her body draw taut and ready. Ready for the delight he offered her like a gift.

"Look at you. You want me to touch your breasts again, to kiss you, lick you, don't you? But I'm not going to." His low voice was softly insistent. "I'm going to kiss you *here*. And lick you and suck you *here*."

Yes, she thought again. She had no hesitation, no caution left within her. His words and his hands encouraged and emboldened her.

He parted her folds with his thumbs and blew a soft warm breath across her. "You're wet."

"I'm sorry." Although she had no idea what exactly she apologized for. She just knew she didn't want to disappoint him.

"No." She heard his sly smile in his warm voice. "It's good. I like your wet little quim."

Another thrill of forbidden pleasure at his words. Her skin prickled in anticipation as his sea-roughened hands slid ever closer to the tight heat at the junction of her thighs. There. Her quim, Jamie had called it. Now she knew. He made it sound lush and erotic. And suddenly, she understood him, when the tip of his tongue slid into her and she could hear the soft, hungry sound of pleasure hum out of her throat and the answering murmur from his.

She felt lush and erotic. She felt open and free, flying away on a gust of pleasure.

The warmth of his mouth was both arousing and soothing, lulling her with wave after wave of sweet, gentle delight. Until he drew away for the briefest moment, and then, with one precisely delicate touch, licked her, *there*. In a spot that sent heated shivers coursing outward throughout her body, loosening and tightening the tense, unholy heat within her.

She moaned, a strangled, desperate sound, drowning in her pleasure. But her body told him what she could not.

"Oh, yes, *there*," he answered. She felt the vibration of his mirth somehow from within her.

Jamie did it again, only different, his tongue swirling through her, scattering her thoughts out to the farthest reaches of her nerve endings until she could feel nothing but his mouth, his hands, there.

And then there was something new, and, oh God, he'd slipped his finger inside her, touching her deeply, stroking lightly and powerfully at the same time. A burst of almost painful bliss blossomed out of her chest and radiated deeper, feeding the nameless craving, this desperate yearning for something more. She realized her hips were arching up when she felt the stern pressure of his hand holding her down.

A wordless groan of frustration and want hissed through her teeth, but he heard her and understood. So understanding, so generous with this flaming joy he could ignite within her. Another finger followed the first and she felt full, engorged by the abundance of her desire. Drawn tight, inflamed, and nearly, nearly . . .

His tongue flicked over her one last time and she cast herself off, out into the welcoming oblivion, flying, soaring through her bliss, and then floating back and forth upon the updraft of her desire, to land softly back down, with Jamie.

She opened her eyes to find him waiting above her, watching the pleasure steep into her bones. She felt dazed, surprised even, stunned and boneless with relief. He said nothing, only watched her. The only sound was the frantic rush of her spent, ravaged breathing.

"Jamie." She sounded drunk, and she was, intoxicated by the bliss he had given her. She couldn't keep her joy contained.

He smiled back, his eyes still roving over her body, coming to rest on her lips. The pad of his thumb brushed lightly against her lower lip: a suggestion of a kiss. She drew it into her mouth and bit down slowly, exploring his callused finger with just the tip of her tongue, breathing deep to let the growing pleasure refill her lungs.

"Oh, yes." His mouth followed his hand with a deeper kiss. He was right, she did not want gentle. She wanted the heat and light, she wanted him. She wanted to consume and be consumed by him.

"Please."

Jamie nodded slowly and tightened his hands on her hips, still standing between her open legs. And then his hands were fast at the buttons of his breeches.

"Yes."

Yes. Her body leapt inside her skin in anticipation. Yes, she wanted more. She wanted him. She wanted everything his words, his eyes, and his clever hands had promised.

A bell jangled harshly: an unwelcome intrusion of reality, nearby. The kitchen doorway.

Lizzie's horrified gaze shot to the stillroom door—wide open. If anyone were to walk by they would see her . . .

She jerked her legs up and tried to roll. Jamie's hand came down flat, covering and pressing firmly on her belly to still her.

"Don't move. Don't move so much as an inch, a muscle. Don't say a word." He dropped a kiss on her navel. "I'll take care of this—I'll be right back."

He quickly buttoned his cock back inside his breeches before he walked swiftly to close the door behind him.

Lizzie let herself collapse back in relief against the cool counter for only a few blissful seconds before she recovered. And moved.

CHAPTER 7

God Almighty! His cock strained and shifted in his breeches like a swivel gun. But he was going to keep it there for just a while longer. A very short while. Only until he could deal with this untimely intrusion, get back to Lizzie, and get her as primed and loaded as he felt. His restraint was all but gone.

Yet, as he came to the foot of the kitchen stairs, the sight of a large assortment of baggage, piled haphazardly and blocking the kitchen door, stopped him in his tracks. A collection of trunks, to be exact. Lizzie's. She must have arranged this. The sight brought him crashing back to the deck faster than a bucket of cold seawater.

As did Mrs. Tupper, weaving her way through the piles, bearing the supper tray. Marlowe moved to make an aisle between the trunks so the housekeeper could make her way through and set the heavily laden tray to the deal table.

Mrs. Tupper didn't bat an eye at his disheveled, half-dressed appearance. "Caught out in the rain, were you?" she surmised with a smile. "There should still be enough dry things up—"

"Thank you, Mrs. Tupper," he said in an overly loud voice so Lizzie would know who was here. Though Mrs. Tupper, with her years aboard ships, was not in the least put out by the sight of him half-dressed, doubtless she would have been shocked by Lizzie's state of complete undress. "What have you managed to find for us?"

"A bit of stew, nice and hot, bread, baked fresh this morning, and butter as well. Good cheese and cold ham. Didn't have time to shift anything fancier. And we've no tea, but I brought ale and a bottle of claret."

"The claret will do nicely. You take the ale back to Tupper and . . . the lads."

She nodded her understanding and began bustling about the hearth. "I'll set the supper out here then. And just get a fire going so you can dry out a bit."

"No need. I thank you, but I've already got a fire going upstairs. Why don't you take the tray up and we'll eat there?"

"But there's no table, nor chairs, sir."

"We'll spread out a blanket like for a picnic. Do you think you can find one?"

"Ought to be one in the cupboard in the dressing room."

"Excellent. Come, let me carry it up for you."

"Now, sir, no need for that." Mrs. Tupper led the way up the service stairs and in no time at all, the impromptu picnic was ready. All he needed was his missing bride.

"Shall I come back to get the tray, sir?"

"No need, Mrs. Tupper. We'll see to it ourselves."

They descended the way they had come, down the service stairs into the kitchen entryway.

"Then I'll be off, sir."

"Thank you. Oh, would you have Tupper send Mc—one of the lads—down to the Red Harte and have my sea trunk brought back up here? It appears we shall be spending the night."

"Oh. Of course, sir. Then, are you sure there's nothing else I can get for you? Perhaps the lady might need some help?"

"No, I thank you, Mrs. Tupper. That will be all. Good night."

The door shut behind her with another jangle of the bell, and Marlowe was back through the stillroom door in a flash. But damn it all to bloody hell, it was empty. Where had Lizzie gotten to? Marlowe prowled back towards the warren of rooms beyond the larder and stillroom. At the end of the narrow hall he found the laundry room with its stone floor. His coat was hanging out to dry, along with Lizzie's shift. He fingered the damp material. She must have changed clothes.

"Lizzie?"

"Out here. Was that Mrs. Tupper?"

Marlowe followed her voice back to the kitchen entryway, only to find Lizzie dragging one of the trunks towards the baize hallway door. She had changed into a plain chemise dress.

"Yes, she brought a meal on a tray."

Lizzie paused and looked up. Marlowe followed the direction of her gaze over into the kitchen and answered her question before she could ask it. "It's upstairs before the fire."

"Oh. Let me just get this and then we can eat."

He stopped her with a touch. "Lizzie? Please tell me these aren't your trunks. Please tell me this is a mistake. There are at least eight, possibly more, stacked up here."

"There are twelve, or should be, and I'm sorry, they shouldn't have been brought here."

Thank God for small favors—she wasn't planning to unpack. But there was no way Tupper could heft all these into a wagon by himself, and he'd rather keep McAlden out of sight than risk Lizzie seeing him again. "All right. I'll shift the trunks for you later."

"Oh, thank you. They're heavy, but we should be able to manage together." She had already let go of his hand and was nosing through the stacks. She took up the handle of one of the smaller trunks that was set aside. "This will do me for now—to have a few more dry things to change into."

"Lizzie, leave off. You don't need another trunk just for the night." Marlowe swung the chest she'd originally been dragging up onto his shoulder, resolved to take it back to the pile so McAlden could help Tupper shift them into a cart in the morning. He sagged a bit under the unexpected weight. "Devil take it, Lizzie. What the hell have you got in here?"

"I told you they were heavy. Books."

"Books? An entire trunk of them?"

"They're all full of books. Don't sound so incredulous. I can read, you know." She narrowed her eyes to give him an impish, impudent smile.

"But, don't tell me there are twelve trunks of books?"

"We all have our little vices." She smiled and slipped through the baize door and down the hallway. "They go with the others in the library."

"Others!" But she was already gone, leading the way across the house.

When he arrived at the paneled room tucked into the back corner of the house, he saw she had brought one of the smaller boxes in already.

"More books, Lizzie? Really? Where did they come from?"

"From my rooms at Hightop, of course."

"And do you actually read them?" He tried, and failed, to picture her sitting quietly absorbed, a busy little bluestocking, but honestly, he couldn't imagine her spending so much time indoors, poring over print. She seemed to him to be so totally an active, outdoors sort of girl. Most, if not all, of his memories of their childhood involved tromping about the woods and riverbanks, out in all weathers, impervious to discomfort and oblivious to sodden hems. Much like this afternoon, in fact, when she hadn't taken his advice and come in from the rain. There was that steely purpose of will running under the exquisitely feminine body.

A steely will accompanied by a pert, teasing smile. "Only when it rains."

And this was England. Only place wetter was the bilge on a ship.

He set the trunk down and crossed to the open chest. The books, though bound in caramel- and ruby-colored leathers, were well-read and dog-eared. He was astonished to find, among many others, Paine, Wilberforce, and Mary Wollstonecraft. Good God. The titles were decidedly radical. He had imagined she read nothing more than Fanny Burney, Charlotte Smith, or Ann Radcliffe, but there wasn't a novel in the lot. He could not have been more astonished if she had declared her intention of taking holy orders.

"Mary Wollstonecraft? You, Lizzie, with such deeply radical philosophical treatises?"

She gave him one of her unaccountable smiles, but this time he could identify pride in the mix. She was perversely proud of her little vice. "Mmm. You won't tell anyone, will you? No one will invite me to dinners or teas if they think I'm an *intellectual*." She pronounced the word as if it were a rare species of plant.

"Your secret is safe with me, but you'll want to be careful about these." He dug deeper into the wooden box to find Edmund Burke's *Reflections on the Revolution in France*. Something in direct opposition to Paine and Wollstonecraft, at least. "Does your father know you've read these?" That would account for the Squire's diatribe against radical thinking.

Her smile faded into bland sarcasm. "I am not accountable to my father."

"No, not anymore. But don't you suppose you are now accountable to me? We are married." He tried to say it calmly, to phrase his words as a question, but their effect was electric. Her arch expression flickered on her face for only another moment before it was replaced with horrified astonishment. Two spots of color flashed high on her cheeks.

"How disappointingly paternalistic you've suddenly decided to be." She moved and would probably have swept out of the room, but he stepped across her path, cutting off her preferred method of dealing with opposition to her views.

Her words cut him, not deeply, but still, it was no pleasure to hear her misjudge him so easily. He wasn't her father, and he held none of the squire's views. But he had to make her understand her place in his life. "I'm sorry you see it that way, Lizzie. But no one can expect to sail on their own tack all their lives. We are married now, and what we each do reflects upon the other."

"And I am supposed to 'sail on your tack,' as you put it?" Her flippant tone told him she was still growing angry.

He strove for balance. "Not necessarily, but . . . Lizzie, I have no desire to argue with you about your books. You will of course read as you like. But you must see that your conduct reflects upon me, as mine does upon you. We must let our moral consciences guide our intellectual conduct."

"Am I to be punished now for reading books?"

How like Lizzie to leap precipitously from one conclusion to another. "Don't misunderstand me. I've said nothing of punishment, Lizzie. I've spoken of being guided by your conscience and by the understanding of those with greater experience of the world than you."

"Oh, yes, we poor women must be *guided* in our opinions as we lack the necessary education and experience to form sound opinions of our own. And of course we must also be guided and protected from that very same education. This is a very self-serving, self-fulfilling philosophy and just the sort of thinking we're trying to reform in the London Corresponding Society."

Marlowe felt as if all the air had been suddenly sucked from the room. God could not be so cruel. His voice, when he spoke, sounded as if it came from underwater. "What society?"

"The London Corresponding Society." She repeated it

slowly, as if he were a child. "I'm a member, or at least I'm a contributor. Working for parliamentary reform."

"Please tell me you're joking." He wanted to think she'd said it as a goad, to prod and poke at him for the sake of her argument. But of course she wasn't joking. Of course, out of all the things his new wife might be interested in, she would choose the one thing so completely guaranteed to cause him an inordinate amount of trouble, not to mention grief. "God Almighty, Lizzie. Do you have any idea what you're about?"

"Yes, trying to bring much-needed reform to an outdated system of voting. A rotten, scandal-ridden system of voting. Do you know the House of Commons, which is supposed to, and was founded to, represent the common people, is really controlled by the aristocracy through their ownership of the boroughs?"

"Lizzie, are you just spouting something you've read, or do you truly hold such an opinion?" What was he saying? While she may have gotten some of her more radical ideas from her books—he couldn't imagine them coming from anywhere else—she never would have declared herself if she didn't hold such an opinion.

"Of course I hold my own opinions. What person of feeling could not?" She was in full cry now, giving canvas to all her pent-up frustrations.

"I for one."

"I had no idea you were such a confounded old Tory." Her arch tone was just a shade too cool to be teasing.

"Lizzie, I'm not a Tory. I'm an officer. I don't have party allegiance, I have duty. I can't afford opinions or politics in my profession. And I can't afford you having them either." He knew the words would annoy her—set her off like spark to powder—but she had to know how he felt. Her philosophies and her lack of experience of the world could put his mission in jeopardy. She had to know the truth.

"I can't not have my own opinions, my own thoughts!" she retorted just as vehemently. *"Vindication of the Rights of Man* is well and above the most interesting work of philosophy I have read in a long time. Like Paine, I believe in progress, and I quite detest the overreliance on tradition and custom. Anything that a man wants to get away with is explained by custom or tradition, as if they were vital to the national security and not merely an aspect of its present character. A character that is greatly in need of reform."

"Agreed." He held out a hand to try to allay some of the violence of her feelings and to keep her from launching into a diatribe. If this was any indication of the disagreements they had had, it was no wonder Lizzie and the squire had been at each other's throats. God, yes, Lizzie's arguments were too well-honed to be entirely off the cuff.

"I don't ask that you not form or hold your own opinions. You have every right, by both feeling and education. I only ask that you try, as much as possible, to keep them to yourself."

His deliberately calm and nonjudgmental tone let some of the wind out of her sails. She stood there, hands on her hips, luffing in the breeze as she tried to think up a suitable rejoinder. But she was thinking, weighing him out like an undertaker, all careful calculation. Dangerous calculation. Oh, she held an awful lot in behind those eyes.

"You astonish me," she allowed.

"So do you." He gave it for the compliment it was, and rather than continue the engagement, tried a shift of strategy. "Though, I should not be so shocked to find you so well-read with such clearly formed opinions. You never did do anything by halves, Lizzie."

She almost took the bait. Almost. "My opinions, such as they are, will be, as you advised, kept private and none of your concern."

"Of course they're my concern. You're my wife." Everything about her, from her soft lips to her sharp mind, was his concern. Everything about her fascinated him.

But she chose to remain angry. "In name only, especially once you're gone." She flicked out her wrist, dismissing him already.

He'd be damned if he'd let her. He grabbed her wrist in a gentle but implacable grip. "It wasn't in name only a half an hour ago, was it Lizzie?"

She tried to twist out of his possession, but he held fast. She had to understand. He could not afford to simply let it go.

"I will ask you to just consider this: One man's reform is another man's treason."

"And one *woman's* reform is *always* another man's treason." She pulled away her arm and crossed her arms under her chest. The view of her breasts against the wide scooped muslin neckline did wonders for his equanimity.

"Lizzie, please, stop playing at philosophy. You must understand. The government is cracking down on the Society." He clamped his jaw shut and closed his eyes to keep from saying anything more.

"What do you mean?"

"Just that this is deadly serious, Lizzie." He looked straight at her, trying to make her understand the seriousness of his words. "Some would accuse your society of treason."

"Don't be ridiculous." But her voice wavered slightly. "It is not treason. It's simply change, which all Tories abhor, simply on principle. It's reform, to make our government more responsible. Not to get rid of, or overthrow, the government."

"Some people may not see it like that."

"Who? Most people, if they have any sense, see it the other way round. The world has already changed, Jamie, and we need to catch up. Twenty years ago no one thought *The Rights of Man* could be published at all, let alone read by thinking people. But now there have been two revolutions, two! The old order of the world has changed, and it will continue to change. Once people begin to think and see and feel differently, you can't force them back into the old ways. It won't work. Can't you see that?"

He could see a lot of things. He could see his beautiful Lizzie, her eyes snapping fire and passion, caught in the middle of the wide net of the government's displeasure. The net he was going to cast.

"Please, Lizzie." He made his voice as quiet and calmly implacable as he could. "Please. Promise me you'll stay away from such inflammatory causes and their equally inflammatory texts while I'm away."

"Heavens no, why should I do that?" She turned away and would have sauntered out the door in her usual dismissive manner, but he still had her tethered by her fine-boned wrist.

"Lizzie. This is important. Promise me. If something should happen . . . I won't be able to take care of you."

"I don't need taking care of. I've told you I'm not useless."

"I know that. I see that. But this is important." He tipped up her chin, forcing her to meet his eyes. "I ask you not because I want to guide you, but because I care about you. You must see that."

"Jamie, you're hurting me."

His urgency had traveled all the way to his fingers, digging into the soft skin of her delicate, vulnerable jawline. And there it was in her face for the first time. Fear. He hated that he had put it there, but she had no idea of what she was getting herself into by belonging to the Society.

He instantly loosened his grip to draw her against his chest in an embrace, to show her with his body what he couldn't put into words, that he was trying to protect her.

"Lizzie. Please. I can't take no for an answer." He hated what little time was left to them would be filled with argument. "I'll make it up to you. I'll order you a cart full of novels. From London. Racy ones. Naughty ones. Just your sort of naughty."

She peeked up at him from under her lashes, as she considered his olive branch. "Well, I have thought I might begin to augment my reading with something lighter."

"That's it." He could feel relief flow into his body. "Have you read Fanny Burney?"

"No," she murmured noncommittally, "but I've been thinking I should augment my reading with a new author's work."

"Whom do you desire? I'll have it sent to you."

"Saint Augustine."

"Theology?"

His only warning was the perfectly naughty smile she bestowed upon him before answering.

"*The Advantages of Widowhood.* A great thinker was our Saint Augustine." She only waited to see her salvo hit, before she skipped out and up the stairs.

Damned provocative woman. There was only one way to deal with Lizzie's abominable cheek. And she was already headed in precisely the right direction. To the domed bedchamber.

He followed her slowly, heading back through the house and up the service stairs in order to give her more time: more time in which to settle herself out of their brief row. How funny: ten years away, six hours married, and already they had had their first and, he prayed, only, fight.

He paused at the doorway before he entered. Lizzie presented a charming, rather intimate tableau, standing barefooted and so informally dressed in front of the sitting area's windows. She couldn't have been wearing stays, the way she slouched back against the window casing. Heat and the rekindling of need warmed him far more than the fire. Astonishing how comfortable she was in her own skin. Made him want to strip her down right there on the hard wood floor.

But Lizzie had other things on her clever mind. She was not yet ready to completely forgive him and still stood apart, though she did take a plate of food and even sauntered close enough to take a glass of excellent claret from his hand. He would let her keep her distance. For now.

In a little while, she began with an olive branch of her own. "Tell me about the navy."

Too much to choose from. Marlowe leaned back and took a long taste of the rich claret. "What do you want to know?"

"Oh, anything. Amuse me."

It was a phrase straight out of memory, something she used to say when they were younger. And he had always been anxious to tell her a story to impress her with his worldliness. Now that he was undoubtedly more worldly, most of his stories were hardly fit for a lady's delicate ears. Even Lizzie's.

But, no, she was probably as bloodthirsty as any West Indies buccaneer.

"How did you get to be a captain at your age? Aren't you too young to be made post?"

"Perhaps." He wanted to boast and brag. He wanted to tell her all about Toulon and the fireship and all the bloody reckless things he'd ever done just so he might see admiration light her face like sunrise. But where to begin? Surely not at the beginning, with her father hauling his fourteen-year-old, frightened arse off into the night.

But Lizzie could carry on without him. "Where did you get shot?"

"Here. Here, here, and here. And also here." He pulled his shirt open to demonstrate. He was rewarded with her laugh.

"On the map, not on your body." Her green eyes sparkled and turned up at the corners when she smiled. He loved that impudent grin—that mobile smile that always played at the corners of her mouth and was at once a banner of, and a rampart against, her emotions.

"Svensksund, Gulf of Finland in the Baltic."

"The Gulf of Finland? What on earth were you doing there?"

"Getting rich." He took another swallow of claret. The wine was making him expansive.

"In Finland?"

"We'd been put on half-pay during the peace, but my commander at the time, the renowned Captain Sydney Smith, resigned his commission and went to advise the Swedes in their war against Russia. I went, too. I was Smith's First, his top lieutenant, and when we did well, he saw to it that we got our fair share of the prizes. And there were a lot of prizes."

"Why . . . you were a mercenary!" Her face lit up with a sort of horrified wonder. He couldn't tell whether she was pleased or disgusted.

He shrugged the suggestion off. He was uncomfortable with the label. It wasn't as if he'd done it only for the money. "We were put ashore on half-pay, Lizzie. His Majesty's Navy had no use for us, but the Swedes did. And paid us well for the privilege."

"Who paid you in grapeshot?" Her eyes were back on his chest. It was all he could do not to stretch up his arms behind his head to bask in the heat of her eyes.

"The Russians, naturally."

But now she was up out of her languid slouch and leaning towards him, her hand reaching for the edge of his shirt.

"Is that a . . . ? Is that a tattoo?" She was avid with curiosity, her finger stroking across the dark script on the far left side of his chest, below his heart. "I didn't notice it . . . before. I've never seen one. I mean I've seen them on sailors' arms . . ."

"I'm a sailor."

"So you are. I suppose I was thinking of a rough sort of sailor, not an officer. It says *Fides*."

"Means fidelity."

"I know what it means. But why have you got it?"

"Lost a bet." He wouldn't tell her he had actually won a total of twenty-two pounds, six shillings: a fortune for the poor midshipman he had been at the time. Or that more importantly, he had won the respect of the men in his division. Because she was right—it wasn't something an officer, a gentleman, should have done.

She angled closer, dropping to kneel in front of him on the blanket, her lovely bosom on display. His high opinion of marriage was growing.

"And why *Fides*?" She traced the script with the tip of one cool finger.

"Shorter than *England* and much less risky than *Lizzie*."

She laughed out loud, an exclamation of complete disbelief. "You never thought of me. *Fides*. Very senti—"

"Now what have you got against sentimentality? Are you so afraid of your emotions?"

"No, not afraid, but certainly wary. Sentimentality encourages a total reliance upon one's emotional responses to all things. It is much better to be a creature of rational thought. One may take into account one's likes and dislikes, one's experiences for good or for bad, but one must make decisions with a more rational detachment."

She sounded as if the words came straight out of some radical pamphlet she had memorized, probably just to annoy and nettle her father.

"Rational detachment?" He leaned in and lightly kissed the base of her neck, where that long, sensitive tendon ran down the side. "But you'll forgive me if I failed to notice any rational detachment while you were beneath me a short while ago."

"Oh, well I . . ." She swallowed her words and eased her head over to give him access. Clever girl. Warm, nubile, clever girl.

"Yes?" Her skin was unutterably soft beneath his mouth.

"It's as if my mind becomes detached from my body, so the only thing I can do is feel physical sensation, detached and different." Her voice had gone whisper-light and her breath began to come shallow.

"Pure physical sensation without any rational thought?"

"Absolutely." Her lips brushed against his.

"Or emotion?"

The wrong thing to say to Lizzie. She didn't deign to answer. She slid away, dissolving out of his arms. Trying to hold Lizzie was like trying to catch mercury.

She returned to her place at the window, too uncomfortable with real emotion, even now. She kept her eyes studiously averted from him as she looked out over the water, darkening with the falling of gray twilight, and changed the subject. "And that's where you shall be."

This could at least be the truth. He would definitely be on the sea, this sea, but just not in the way she thought. "Yes."

"And shall I write you?"

He couldn't gauge the tone of her voice. Did she sound tentative?

"If you like."

"I shouldn't like, in general." Ah, there was the teasing note in her voice. "I find writing letters tedious in the extreme, but I was prepared to extend myself for your benefit. But if you are indifferent . . ."

"No. I should very much like you to write me, but you do know they will be received and returned very irregularly?"

"That hardly signifies." And the little flick of the wrist. "Yet, I think it ought to be undertaken. Such a useful occupation for a wife. I shall tell my mother I can not possibly come into town to receive bride calls as I am entirely taken up in writing to my absent, beloved husband."

He noted the order of "absent" and "beloved," the former being necessary to the latter.

"Yes," she continued, "I shall write you every day with all the particulars of your estate and its improvements, and you shall write to me and tell me all your sailor things. All the interesting and exotic sights you see on your way to the other side of the world and back."

I'm not coming back, his conscience shouted, even though his mouth did not. *I'm not even going.*

His mouth could only form platitudes. "It would be lovely to receive letters from you. You can tell me what parties you go to and what you wear and how pretty you look."

The warm, glowing smile faded from her cheeks.

"Is that really what you think I do? Go to parties and soirees and balls all day and night? Do you know me so little?"

"I know you would rather be out tromping around a hedgerow with that wicked fowling piece you pinched from your father. Or rather, that's what I know you used to like when you were twelve. But you're grown up now, a very lovely young lady, out in society." Now he thought on it, he had attended a number of evening parties during the past fortnight and yet had seen her only once, at that fateful public assembly. He had thought she would be at her best in assembled groups, where she could show off her dazzling wit to perfection. "Does the thought of going to parties, assemblies, and musical performances give you no pleasure?"

"I go out to entertainments very rarely, although I do like the occasional musical performance. But unless it is really superior, and the audience comes to actually listen rather than gossip, I much prefer to amuse myself with solitary pursuits."

"And why is that?"

She shrugged away any further explanation.

"Lizzie, come back to me. Come back and tell me what you do, and what interests you. I know," he teased, "you've become a follower of Hannah Moore. You're a hidden religious evangelical, and you spend all your time reading improving tracts."

"Heavens no." She sauntered back towards him, her good humor improving with his lighthearted teasing. "There is nothing so annoying as moralizing. I can't abide an upright character."

He laughed out loud. If only she knew the full truth. Well, she would in time. He had no illusions on that account.

He shot out a hand to tumble her down into his chest so he could nuzzle the soft, scented, side of her neck. Her head slouched over to give him greater access. So sweet, so soft.

"I'm very glad to hear it, Lizzie. Let me see if I can assist in returning you to the horizontal."

CHAPTER 8

He concentrated all of his energy, all of his senses, on the taste and feel and smell of her. On the soft, warm, exquisite slide of her skin along her jaw. On the springy orange curls of hair falling over her shoulders. On the drugging scent rising off her body and on the velvet warmth of her mouth. On Lizzie.

He kissed her, letting her set the pace and have her way with his mouth, while he explored the unmapped horizon of her body. He ran his hands over her pearly curves. Over the delicate knobs of bones at the top of her shoulders and down her arms, his thumbs sliding down the soft, vulnerable skin of her inner arm.

She wasn't idle either. Her hands were touches of curiosity, skimming lightly across his sensitized flesh, until she was stroking his chest and kneading into the muscles of his upper arms and back. Her hands were everywhere, sliding across his shoulders easily, but the force of her touch swept across his body and under his skin, and slammed into him like a gale. The simple contact of her skin against his left him drenched.

His eyes slid shut and he wondered if it would always be like his. If her touch would always bring this overwhelming longing.

The answer clawed at his gut.

Yes. Always.

She was like a wild otter, all smooth, sleek, limber muscle and fierce interest. God, she was exquisite. This was why he had talked his way into this marriage—this crashing wave of need and desperate possessiveness.

This woman.

His Lizzie. His.

"Lizzie." His voice held need and wonder, and it was indeed a wonder that he was there with her, and they were finally alone together, that she was finally letting him, wanting him to, make love to her. His hands stroked up, softly brushing the underside of her breasts. She sighed in pleasure and the sound almost broke his restraint. Almost.

He turned her slightly and pulled her back in against his chest, nestled snugly against him. She was easier to persuade when she was in his arms. And persuaded she must be.

"I don't like the idea of you staying out here alone after I'm gone, Lizzie." He kissed the soft, downy spot on the nape of her neck, his voice low and humming into her ear. "Why don't we go into town in the morning and call on my man of business, Mr. Harris, and see if we can find you a house you'd like. You'll be much happier there."

"*You'll* be much happier if I'm there."

"I own I will. You know now how I feel about this. Promise me you'll go back into town. Promise me."

A long moment passed while his words sunk in, then Lizzie tried to wriggle away. She didn't want to talk about his leaving, nor examine her own bittersweet feelings on the subject. To have the one thing she had for so long desperately wanted—her independence—she had to lose Jamie.

Whom she also wanted with a different kind of desperation altogether.

She hated to lie, but she could not give him what he wanted.

Of all the things he could ask her, it was the one thing she was not prepared to do for him. All the things she wanted for herself, freedom, independence, and purpose, were here at Glass Cottage. Why should she leave?

But she didn't want to argue. She'd had more than enough of that for one day. She didn't want to break the fragile truce between them. So she said nothing and waited for the moment to pass. Perhaps if she kissed him, he'd become distracted.

He wasn't. Tenacious man.

"Lizzie, promise me."

"The house is fine, Jamie, it just needs some repair and how else—"

"No, this is not about the house. This concerns you. You can't be out here alone. It's not safe."

Why was he so insistent? Why didn't he see she'd been taking care of herself for years? It was charmingly male of him, but quite ridiculous. "Jamie—"

He cut her off by tipping her face up to his, holding her still before him with those luminous, all-seeing eyes.

"You promised to love, honor, and obey, Lizzie. You took an oath and you always, always keep your word." His eyes pored over her, into her, holding her to the truth.

There was nothing for it. He was not going to let her be. So, for once in her life she would attempt to do the graceful thing. She would try to accommodate her husband in this request. God knew when, or even if, she'd have another chance.

"I'll go into town."

His chest slowly expanded with a long, deep breath. "Thank you. Thank you." He drew her back against him. "I can leave with some semblance of peace."

Good Lord, so heartfelt. Her heart twisted painfully as if someone were wringing it dry. Next she'd be blubbering into her fichu. She couldn't have that. "Peace, when you are going back to war?"

Jamie smiled a little at her arch tone, the ends of his mouth tipping up briefly, but his eyes had gone dark, and very serious, as they had been the first time he'd told her he was likely to die on this voyage. Trying to resign himself. But the pain he tried to hide made her ache.

"When must you go?"

"Soon."

"How soon?"

"On the morrow."

She tried to quash the little sound of distress that winged its way out of her throat, but she'd given herself away, for he turned her in his arms and gathered her close against his chest. His lovely broad chest that smelled of spices.

"Hush, Lizzie. I didn't think I'd say this, but I very much regret I must leave you. I wanted you to know that." He passed a light hand along the line of her jaw. "I wish . . ."

He didn't finish the thought.

Lizzie all but willed the words into his mouth, and waited. Waited for him to tell her what she longed to hear, so she could speak herself. She felt like a door inside her was being cracked open, spilling light into her from the other side.

This was what it was to love. To feel the light inside. To want to share that light with Jamie.

She should tell him. He was too important for her to let pride come between them.

"What do you wish?" she prompted. She hoped her voice didn't sound as wobbly and off balance as she felt.

"It's strange, but I almost wish I didn't have to leave. I've never *not* wanted to go. Before. But we've just come to know one another again. It seems such a . . . shame to have to leave. But I have a sworn duty and I must go."

"Gotten to know one another" seemed a strange euphemism when they were half undressed and lying in each other's arms. But it was true. They had had only four days to canvass the immense changes ten years had wrought. He was an officer now, a gentleman. A man who had become devoted to his profession, to his duty. Of course he should be anxious to go back to the sea.

Wasn't she just as anxious for his departure as well? Her entire reason for entering into the marriage had hinged and depended upon his absence: she could not be independent if he did not leave.

She stopped her mind at this point, purposefully, willfully ignoring the second half of the original proposition—his death. The idea was abhorrent.

She swallowed down the stupid sob brewing in the back of her throat and turned her face against his shoulder, folding herself into his warmth and strength. How could anyone this strong, this vital, be about to die? It was impossible. Unthinkable.

All she had to do was whisper his name and he was there, his mouth warm and firm. And she would be firm. She would be strong. She would not tremble. So she took his lip carefully between her teeth and worried at it for a long, sweet moment before she bit down. Lightly, so as not to draw blood, but enough so he should know. She wanted him.

It was trite and predictable and oh, so very missish to want to feel his arms around her. But so it was. Confronted with death, she would cling to life. To love. She would love him.

He felt it, too, the compulsion to love. His hand closed around the back of her neck, strong and compelling, full of his will, his need. Jamie pulled her close, holding her still against him. He framed her face carefully and kissed her tenderly. He tasted bittersweet, full of regret.

A helpless little sound fluttered out of her throat, but this kiss felt different. As if he wanted very much to get it just right. As if somehow, it mattered. She mattered.

And then he did the most astonishing thing.

He raised his head and held himself perfectly still, and looked at her. Searching her face, looking for something. He opened his eyes, those beautiful, endless seas of gray, and saw her. He saw her. He looked at her and she knew, as his eyes probed and pressed open the doors to her soul, that he loved her. And she loved him.

Loved him strangely, madly, in spite of herself. Perhaps she always had loved him, right from the first, from that day when she had come across the tall, shy boy fishing in her secret part of the river, the place that had been hers and hers alone. In that moment he had become hers and hers alone as well.

How strange she should think of that sun-dappled bank at this moment, with him poised above her. How strange the simple act of showing her that he saw her should make her love him.

Heat began to prickle behind her eyes. She screwed them shut tight.

In that moment she knew she did not want to be touched gently or with tenderness. It would undo her. The fabric of her heart would unravel, all frayed edges and loose, broken strands of yarn. She needed him fierce and living, laughing and snarling into the face of fate.

She pressed hard into his mouth, sucking and biting as he opened for her, letting her have her way, letting her take as much of him as she wanted. He understood her fierceness, or if he didn't, at least he acted as she wanted, drawing her hard against the length of his body. His large palm moved into the small of her back before lowering to grasp her buttocks. He pulled her tight against him and she could feel his body through the layers of skirt and fabric, feel the length of him jut against her belly.

And she wanted him there. Now, inside her. Easing the ache that welled up from her very soul. But the clothes. They had to go.

She let go of his neck to tear off the scarf at her waist and fling it to the ground. It was an encumbrance, as was the voluminous column of muslin that made up the gown. It had to go. All of it—everything.

Again he seemed to understand without being told. His hands were at the ribbons of her neckline, and then on the close of his breeches. And then she was back at him, her hands burrowing through his thick hair, as she grappled his mouth to hers, each kiss full of promise and desperate surrender.

His hands came up to grasp her face and angle it more to his liking. She obeyed willingly, turning towards his mouth so he could fill her. She was so empty. A vastness had grown within her, an aching void only he could fill.

She launched herself at him, into him, with enough force he lost his footing in the fold of the blanket and went down, taking her with him.

Crockery and glass clinked and rattled as Jamie pushed them away. Just as well. He had turned her against his chest so he took the brunt of the fall and now she was on top of him, straddling his belly.

Yes, this was what she wanted. This contact, skin against skin. Sensation building upon sensation. She ran her hands up and across his bare chest. She loved the look and feel of him, the lean whipcord strength, and hated that his beautiful chest was marred by the shiny dots of scar tissue. Evidence of his mortality.

Her fingers skated across his surface, across the arc of warm muscled topography, across his hills and plains, but it wasn't enough. She wanted to be closer. She wanted to be pressed hard against him, to consume him. To be in him.

Such a strange, almost masculine thought. Perhaps this was what it felt like to be him. To want and need to be in her.

And the emptiness was a dull ache where he was not in her. She groaned from it, a sound of pain and frustration.

He heard her, and somehow he understood. He rolled her over onto her back. His hands and body pressed her down into the hard floor. She welcomed his weight, his force upon her. She could feel him all along the length of her upper side, warm and smooth, just as she felt the solidity of the floor at her back. She wanted to feel it all.

She wanted to be naked beneath him. She wanted him naked as well, pressing into her, making her *feel*, so she wouldn't have to think.

It was in him, too, these feelings. He kissed her hard. It was rough, almost harsh, his possession. And she liked it. She wanted more of it. More of his possession of her body.

And then he moved away. He came up off her, breathing hard. The comfort of his weight was gone and she was bereft, adrift without him anchoring her to the earth. She sat up, to reach for him, to bring him back. But he was reaching for her shift. She peeled it off, over her head as he had done, and let him take it, to lay beneath her.

She was impatient with his care. She had no need of such comfort. It did not matter, so long as she could feel. The press of the hard floor, the press of the fabric—it made no difference.

Then he bore her back down; his mouth, his weight, his hands were everything she needed. Ah, yes. She let out the breath she didn't know she had been holding in a long sigh, wondering at herself: so strange that his constraint of her body should fill her with such comfort and ease. Perverse, that's what she was.

Because she liked it when his hand slid up the soft underside of her arm to intertwine with her fingers and hold her hands still above her head. Hold her open to his mouth, exploring along the side of her neck, and lower, his lips making giddy bursts of pleasure flash under her skin.

She sighed again with the wondrous ease of it, the skill with which he could play her, could pluck her nerves and make this beautiful music between their bodies. He did it now with his tongue and his hands at her breast, wetting her skin. Her flesh felt heated and stretched. So hot, when the night air was so cool.

He eased himself up by parts, as loath as she was to have any space between them. But he had to push off his breeches and kick them away so he was naked at last. His hands twined with hers once more, to hold her pinned and stretched out beneath him. He eased up to look between them, and she did so as well.

So different were their bodies; his sculpted musculature thrown into stark relief by the silver wash of twilight, her smooth, slight curves small beneath him. His hands were so big, so wholly masculine against the pale skin of her breasts. She watched as his hand moved over her nipple, teasing it before he dipped his mouth to suck lightly at the pink flesh. Such bliss. It pulled her body upwards, towards him, into his control. She was arching up, moving, rocking her hip bones almost frantically against him, searching for the sweet pressure.

"Sweet, sweet Lizzie," he murmured at her mouth.

He was wrong of course. She wasn't sweet at all. She was tart and ascetic, all sharp, uncomfortable edges. It was he who was all smoothness and grace. His body, taut and beautiful, covered in smooth muscle, powerful and sure. It was the pleasure he could make between their bodies that was sweet.

She twisted again, her hips moving and searching for him, for that part of him that could ease her ache.

He shifted his position between her legs and she could feel him, the hard, thick length of him, pressed into her belly.

"There." She sounded desperate and impatient. She was. She clutched at his hands, when instead of listening to her and doing what she needed, he pulled away. But then his hand was on her, swift and sure, opening her with merciful efficiency. She was already wet and slippery, her body weeping for release. She bucked up into his palm. It was not enough. It could only begin to fill her emptiness. And then his hand was gone.

Did that sound, that needy groan, come out of her? She was pulling at his shoulders, trying to bring him back down, but he ignored her.

"Hush, Lizzie. Easy."

"Jamie." She heard the plea in her voice and she didn't care. She would beg. "Please!"

"Easy, love. Easy."

His hands were rough at her hip bones, forcing her arching body down, holding her still, pinned against the floor. And then he was there, finally, the blunt head pushing against her flesh. Her quim. Yes, *there*.

He covered her mouth with his own in a nearly savage, biting kiss and plunged swiftly in, straight into her scalding heat, rocking her with the force of his possession.

She made a harsh sound, a sharp exhalation of pain he swallowed into his throat, his mouth on hers, licking, kissing, and his hands tangled with hers over her head. Strung out beneath him.

Yes. There. Finally.

His body inside hers, filling her, pushing into the emptiness. Hard. Once, twice. Once more.

"My God. Lizzie."

And the cold glass inside her shattered like ice, melting, flowing along her veins, down rivers of icy hot pleasure. She floated on it, swept along by the rippling current, swirling softly in eddies of bliss. Finally.

When she opened her eyes, she saw stars, and then Jamie. Above her, watching her as she floated downstream on the pleasure. It was so strange that when she felt so peaceful, he should look so anguished. He frowned, almost winced, as he continued to rock into her. She smiled, to help him, to ease him, and reached for his dear, familiar face, such a poignant contrast to his glorious, naked, unfamiliar body. She ran her hand along the rough edge of his cheek and jaw. He closed his eyes and turned his face into her palm and then out again, rubbing against it. Her flesh prickled from the abrasion of his whiskers, but she liked it. It felt hard and rough and good. Like him.

Her fingers found their way around to the back of his neck, and then up, raking through his hair. She pulled his mouth down to hers, kissing him, sucking his taste, his spice into her.

His skin glistened with a sheen of sweat, and he slid all along the length of her body as he rocked relentlessly against her core. She felt sated, filled with him. His lips brushed against her neck, below her ear, softly and then, not so softly. Rougher still were his teeth nipping at the hollow low on her collarbone. His arm wrapped tight around her neck, holding her close, so close she could no longer feel where she left off and he began.

She clung to him like a lifeline, as if he was the only thing keeping her attached to this world.

She felt his hand between them, reaching down to sweep his fingers across the sensitive nub hidden in her flesh. The feeling was less than a touch, just a suggestion of warmth, yet it reverberated through her until she was lost.

Then when the heat again exploded into flashpoints of molten ecstasy burning from under her skin, she took his lip into her mouth and bit him.

She felt his release pound through him as he spilled himself deep inside her body.

"Lizzie." His voice was a shout, full of wonder and thanks.

He was hers. No matter where he went, no matter how long he was gone, he was hers. He would always be hers. Nothing could take him away from her now. Nothing.

Lust—dark, erotic, and fierce—roared through him at the sweet metallic taste of blood on his lips. He had no idea if it was his or Lizzie's, but at that moment he didn't care. He didn't care about anything but shoving himself deeper and deeper into her, over and over. He was lost to everything but the pull of her body and the chant of her name in his head. Over and over. *Lizzie, Lizzie, Lizzie.*

When she arched beneath him, taut as a sail and flying away on her pleasure, he lost the rhythmic cadence and surged into her, the hot slippery friction of her body drowning out everything else as his release sent spasms through him.

Marlowe didn't know how long it took him to come back to himself. Dark gray-green twilight had come with the end of the storm, blotting out the sun, leaving them adrift in time. At some point he had flung himself off her so he wouldn't crush her, leaving him strung out on his back, staring unseeing up at the darkened ceiling.

He filled his lungs with a deep draft of air and waited for reality to return. Nothing he had thought, nothing he had done, had prepared him for the way he felt. Spent, exhausted, exhilarated. Empty.

Shaken to his core.

His release had felt cataclysmic, but the triumph, the finality he had expected was absent. He had thought he would feel . . . complete. He thought he would have finally come full circle with Lizzie and could move on. Could go back to his duty, to the career he loved.

Instead he felt as if the world had shifted below his feet. As if nothing would ever be the same again. As if what he had done were irrevocable.

And Lizzie. God in heaven, Lizzie. He turned his head and found her fighting to calm her breath, staring at him in glassy-eyed, sated wonder. She smiled slowly, her face lighting with impish delight. Her eyes continued to move over him, cataloging each and every detail of his appearance and anatomy. Collecting him into her memory.

That's what Lizzie did. What made her unique. She collected sights and sounds and experiences the way other people collected botanical specimens or seashells. All he had to do was keep giving her new and interesting experiences to collect.

"Let's do that again."

Oh, God, yes. Lizzie was definitely made for hedonism.

In only a few hours, Marlowe watched the first gray light of early dawn slowly illuminate her features. The time had finally come. But not quite yet. He could still watch her while she slept.

He tried to recall just how many times he had made love to her during the night before she had finally drifted off into spent, contented exhaustion. But he hadn't slept. Not for a long while.

He'd stayed awake, watching her as her breath became shallow and she fell into sleep. In the warm mellow light of the single candle she had slept on, oblivious to his disquiet.

He supposed it had been his first real chance to look at her, really look, without any restraint. And without having to work double time to keep up with her clever little mind and devastatingly witty tongue. Without having her look back.

He could simply enjoy her.

She was like a cat. Not a kitten, all curled up and irresistible, but a cat, long and sleek and comfortable in her own skin. She stretched across the mattress like a sunbeam. No, not a cat after all. The image of that bright otter, lolling on the riverbank, came back to him. That's what she was. Sleek and slippery. Inquisitive and aquatic. Last night, very nearly acrobatic.

He rolled on his elbow to look at her face. It was so strange to see it softened by sleep. She almost didn't look like herself. He'd never seen her without animation, without humor, intelligence, or passion blazing out of those eyes.

What an extraordinary beauty she had become. Not one of your milk-and-water English misses. No, everything about her was vibrant, from her vivid orange hair to the glowing whiteness of her skin and the emerald fire in her eyes. Even her nipples were the saturated coral pink of ripe apricots. God, she was glorious.

Lust poured over him like sunshine.

He'd always preferred his women, well, womanly—all lush curves and pillowed comfort. It was almost indecent, the erotic lust that shot through him at the sight of her sleek, animalistic body.

His Lizzie. He'd never have thought it would feel like this. As if it weren't finished. As if it never could be. As if he'd only just started to get her into, never mind out of, his system. He'd certainly got more than he bargained for in marrying her.

He reached out to move a lock of bright hair back off her forehead.

"Talk about your early risers," she mumbled, eyes still closed.

"Ah, you refer, of course, to my body's stunning reaction to waking up next to you."

She blushed. Lizzie Paxton Marlowe actually blushed, the flood of blood coloring her skin from her chest upwards, until her cheeks were stained with it. It was rather gratifying to know he could make that happen.

He could make other things happen, too. He snugged her back against his chest so she couldn't escape, and so his erection was pressing into the small of her back, just above her luscious bottom. He nosed aside her hair to kiss her lovely neck.

"Blushing, Lizzie?" he teased quietly. "You needn't be embarrassed by your remarkable suitability to conjugal bliss. I, for one, am exceedingly gratified by your charming and enthusiastic reaction to my ministrations." He let his hand wander across the silken skin of her taut belly. "And I would be further gratified if you would do that exquisite little thing you did last night when you bit my lip. I very much liked that."

Her head turned up and she opened her mouth to him, slowly sucking his bottom lip between her teeth and biting down ever so slightly. The remembrance of her doing the same last night, an erotic combination of pain and pleasure, forked through him like lightning. It was bliss. She was bliss.

Exhausted bliss. She stifled a yawn. "What time is it?"

"The sun's only just up."

"Why are you so awake?"

"I have to leave. Soon."

Her eyes snapped open, sharp green against her suddenly pale face. "How soon?"

"As soon as I make love to you one more time."

"Jamie!"

He turned her onto her back and brushed her fiery hair off her face. "Handsomely now, Lizzie," he warned. "I want to take my time with you."

"Sentimental." But her eyes began to soften.

"Yes, very sentimental. I desire to be sentimental all over your breasts." His warm breath blew over the peaks, which tightened. "You see, they're sentimental, too."

"Jamie." She moved, undulating against him, her body already stirring with desire.

"Shh." He covered her with his body and whispered into her ear. "Don't. Lie quiet. Don't do a thing. Don't make a sound."

He coaxed her with quiet words and gentle, firm touches. But she held herself back, trying, he thought, not to break, not to cry. Poor Lizzie. She could let her body go and fly away before her, but not her heart. Not her emotions.

But it was beautiful anyway. She was beautiful. And he was careful and quiet with her, willing to give her that one last gift, letting her hide in peace.

They went on quietly afterwards, when the light in the sky told him he must rise to dress and get on his way.

His uniform coat, fetched up from his trunks, felt strange to him, as tight and foreign as the first time he had put in on years ago. He tugged at the sleeve, easing his shoulders at the seams, putting off the moment when he would have to don his gloves and take her down to the carriage sent from the Admiralty.

Lizzie was brushing her hair before the windows. She had retrieved a stunning bright azure blue carriage dress from one of those trunks of hers. It was the color of the ocean in the Caribbean. Beautiful and exotic and so very lovely. She turned and made a surprised little pout with her mouth.

"Look at yourself." She sounded vaguely put out.

He looked down to check the uniform, to make sure everything was correct: braid and button in place, his sword properly hung on his left hip.

"What's wrong with the way I look?"

She tossed him a smile like a present. "Absolutely nothing. What on earth am I to do with you?"

His laugh filled the room. "You're to kiss me, very sweetly," he leaned down scant inches from her lips, "and then put me from your mind forever."

Her smile wobbled at the edges, but she rallied, determined to put on a brave face.

"The way you look, I suppose I'll have to be obligated to miss you after all."

The offhand compliment warmed him. It was as close to praise as Lizzie was ever likely to come.

"Nonsense. You hadn't missed me before, had you?" As soon as the words were out, something tight and binding twisted in his chest. What prompted that particular piece of stupidity? The past ought to be forgotten and done with. There were troubles enough for the present.

She hid her face with a large straw picture hat, but she answered anyway.

"You never did say good-bye." Her voice was small, but she strengthened it. "But I suppose I must have missed you, else I'd have never married you."

Strange, the idiotic wash of relieved pleasure. Such feeling ought to be reserved for the moments when a cannon had whizzed by, missing by fortunate inches.

But Lizzie was trying very hard to be herself. Too hard. "Well, we must send you off. I can't miss you if you don't actually go."

"Then let us go then, so you can begin forgetting me."

CHAPTER 9

She was not going to be ill. Not all over the beautiful coach sent down from the Admiralty, not all over her best morning gown, and certainly not all over Jamie's spotless dress uniform.

Lord, but she hated a closed carriage. Even with the windows down all the way, there was barely enough air to breathe. They were only halfway into Dartmouth town and she already missed the clean sea breeze. She shifted as close to the window as possible without sticking her head outside like a dog on the back of a farmer's cart.

Lizzie slid a glance across the seat at Jamie, lounging comfortably in the backward seat. Drat him for talking her into taking the carriage. Perhaps he was due the admiration that would surely follow such a splendid vehicle, but she would have thought him above such pettiness. Such aggrandizement didn't square with her knowledge, her intimate knowledge, of the man. But it did keep her mind occupied, and for that alone, she was grateful.

The carriage wound its way through the town, and she diverted herself by noting the commotion their passing caused. The carriage moved slowly enough over the steep, uneven streets for her to hear some of the comments of the passersby. It was almost insulting, their astonishment at her marrying. Good Lord, she was only two and twenty, not so old she'd been ready to lead apes into hell.

Jamie made no notice. Or none she could see. His face was a perfect mask of stern haughteur, almost as if he had donned the persona of "Captain" along with his blue uniform coat and white breeches.

But while he made no comments, he had focused his gaze upon her face for much of the ride. Watching, observing. Probably waiting for her to be sick. She hoped her complexion didn't look as green as she felt. She gritted on a smile and turned back to the moving air.

Eventually the carriage picked its way up the hill and came to a halt in front of the offices of Harris and Company, Brokers. They were there. This was it.

Jamie reached across for the door handle.

"No," she shot out a hand to stop him. "Don't get out. Let's make this quick." She swallowed over the thickness of her throat. "Write me."

"Lizzie, I'm not going to leave you at Harris's door like so much lost baggage."

"Oh, why not? It's as apt a description as any." She took a deep breath and made herself look at him fully, no matter the painful knot of loss that burned in her throat.

The words pounded in her head, over and over like thunder—she might never see him again. Yet, she couldn't bear it if he made a fuss, and it would be even worse if *she* did. She was not going to throw away years of character by becoming, of all things, sentimental. Not in front of Jamie. And especially not in front of an office full of clerks. She didn't want his last sight of her to be red-nosed and weeping.

"Do write. Only witty, entertaining stories, of course. Nothing else will do."

"Lizzie. Of course. Let me walk you inside, at least."

"No. I couldn't. And Mr. Harris expects me, does he not? I'm sure I can conclude my business with him without your assistance." That sounded ungrateful. "I thank you. I'm . . ." She swallowed. "Thank you. Take care of yourself." She clutched the hand he reached out to her.

"And you. Lizzie." He squeezed her fingers gently.

She nodded and tried to pull her hand away. "Well, then. Good-bye." She forced herself to smile while the knot in her throat grew so tight, she felt it would choke her.

He didn't say anything. He reached his hand up and slowly stroked her cheek with the backs of his fingers and watched her with those open gray eyes. She had nowhere to hide. She couldn't pretend. And when his eyes had done their work, he leaned down and kissed her softly.

It was a kiss of such infinite gentleness and longing that she nearly broke, nearly fell to her knees to wrap her arms around his legs and plead for him never to leave. But that was impossible, not to mention entirely mortifying. And his kiss was so soft and sweet—bittersweet. She could not keep herself from kissing him back. She put every ounce of caring she could muster into her kiss and took every last thing she could. Each last taste and feel and smell of him. Bay rum.

As soon as her lips left him she turned, groping blindly for the door. She jumped over the foot step and fled across the few feet of gravel, up the porch stairs and into the relative sanctuary of the office. But once inside, she could only sag back against the closed door and sink to the cold marble floor. Her legs simply would not work.

It was done. She would never see him again.

She closed her eyes to the astonished faces of the clerks and let the horrid heat spill up out of her heart and down her cheeks. Good Lord, they would probably dine out on this for years. No one in Dartmouth had ever seen her weep.

* * *

"Remind me why we volunteered for this mission."

Marlowe watched McAlden pace before the only window in the second floor room.

No trips through the hollowed halls of the Admiralty for them. A small upstairs room in the back of the Portsmouth Naval Yard was necessary to their subterfuge.

"For Frank, Hugh, for Frank," he answered quietly, but then firmed his voice. He could just hear Lizzie teasing him as sentimental. "Because we followed Captain Smith out of the Navy and off to Sweden. Because despite our efforts, we failed at Toulon. Because I know Dartmouth. And because we were asked."

"So if we do this right we might get ourselves promoted back to the real war instead of being becalmed in the backwaters?"

"This is the real war, Hugh."

Footsteps, light and quick, sounded on the stairs. Without a word, he and McAlden came to attention. The door opened and Sir Charles Middleton, one of the Naval Lords of the Admiralty, stepped into the room.

"Gentlemen." He acknowledged each with a small bow and a handshake. "Captain Marlowe. Lieutenant McAlden. Let us set to the business." He gestured to the small round table, where they each took seats.

Middleton was a spry man in his late sixties, with a full head of white hair, a genial, forthright face, and a firm handshake. Marlowe had liked him instantly. He had been influenced toward a favorable impression, no doubt, by the knowledge that Middleton, unlike many of the politicians serving as Naval Lords, had actually been a naval man himself, with over fifty years of devotion to the senior service. In active duty, he had earned a reputation as a fair, honest captain, much admired by his men. It was more than enough for Marlowe.

Middleton did not waste their time. Another mark in his favor.

"To begin, I must tell you I have just come from Whitehall, where it was again impressed upon me how vitally important this mission is to the war with France. Vital. We are determined to stamp out this blight and have at last been allocated the necessary funds and equipment to see it done. We have lost one good man already. We cannot lose more."

"Yes, my lord." Marlowe opened up a dossier and brought out a number of maps and charts. "Our orders charge that the Revolutionary Government of France be deprived of all sustenance—food, goods, services, and especially munitions. The Channel Fleet and the West Indies Squadron are at work cutting off the enemy's supply from the Americas, here and here," he delineated the limits of the fleet's cruising range on the charts. "But there remains a small but significant trade between this island and the northern coast of France centered out of the Devon coast, and most particularly, Dartmouth." He landed a pointed finger hard upon the chart of the English Channel. "And Lieutenant Palmer suspected, Redlap Cove."

Lord Middleton's voice shook with repressed emotion. "It must be stopped. This smuggling has progressed to a greater treason than the mere cheating of the Revenue Service."

"Lieutenant Palmer's last messages indicated he suspected a large cache of weapons was headed across the Channel from Redlap."

"And you will find it." Lord Middleton's tone brooked no failure.

"Our preliminary reconnaissance of the house and grounds have, as yet, yielded no sign of either the suspected shipment, nor evidence of the particular gang working out of that cove. A month's watch of the area has provided no evidence of anything other than the usual brandy and lace. And yet Palmer was sure. And his death is proof enough that he had found the necessary evidence and was killed for it."

Middleton mulled over the map of the property for few moments.

"I have chosen you for this particular task, Captain Marlowe, for two reasons. First because you have made a favorable impression upon us, showing remarkable adaptability and success in the Siege of Toulon. Indeed, if we had had twenty such officers, the final result of that battle might have been different. Be that as it may, such cunning will be necessary in dealing with these smugglers. Second, there is your ownership of the property at Redlap Cove. Our Lordships had originally thought that to simply associate the property publicly with you and the navy would put an end to its use by the smugglers."

He peered over the rim of his steel-framed eyeglasses, his lined, blue eyes sharp and bright. "I will scruple to tell you, Captain Marlowe, when that did not happen, when the smuggling continued, it was suggested that perhaps you had simply gone in league with the smugglers to augment your own income, that indeed such had been your primary object in buying the derelict property."

"My lord, I . . ." Marlowe felt heat color his face. He had no idea his honor had been called into question. The very idea was sickening.

Lord Middleton held up a restraining hand. "Suffice it to say, were I not completely satisfied on that account, you would no longer hold your commission, and we would not be having this conversation."

"Thank you, my lord."

"Do not disappoint me, Captain Marlowe. There is a vast deal at stake for all of us." He fixed Marlowe with a penetrating stare. "I can personally assure you that the successful completion of this undertaking is of utmost importance, not only to the Admiralty, most especially to the First Lord, the Earl of

Chatham, but also," he pronounced the words with grave emphasis, "to his brother, the prime minister, William Pitt, the Younger."

Marlowe exchanged a brief glance of understanding with Hugh, who nodded in confirmation.

"Yes, my lord."

"Good. This whole problem has become far too public. That damned sketcher Gilray's latest satirical cartoon of French agents blithely smuggling war supplies from British shores hangs in the window of every shop from London to Portsmouth and every place in between. It is a damned embarrassment and the government wants it ended. Now. Do I make myself clear?" Middleton's pale face colored with spots high on his cheekbones.

"Very clear, sir."

"Good. You have your agents in place at Redlap?"

Another nod of confirmation from Hugh.

"Yes, and Lieutenant McAlden and I are also in place there, in the guise of men ready to be adopted into the smuggling fraternity. With the house empty and all ties to the navy publicly severed, we hope to lure this gang back to using Redlap, where we will infiltrate, identify the leaders, and then end this ring."

"Good. A sound, if unorthodox, plan. Their lordships of the Admiralty had to be convinced having officers out of uniform was the best and most expedient strategy. While they will adopt any expediency at sea, I had a great deal of trouble convincing them our own form of espionage would yield the necessary results." He shook his head at the Admiralty's obstinacy. "However, our lordships have granted your request for naval support. Though a vessel has been made available out of Plymouth, I'm sorry to say, instead of Portsmouth."

"Very good, sir."

"Good. Then there is nothing left but for me to caution you

to secrecy and to the utmost care in dealing with this nest of traitors. They are a deadly lot, and I do not want to lose another of my officers on English soil."

Marlowe took comfort in his vehemence. "I will make certain Lieutenant Palmer did not die in vain, sir."

"I will take you at your word, Captain Marlowe. We rather have need of all our brightest young officers at the moment." The gaze of his clear eyes swept over the two of them.

"I am honored."

Lord Middleton permitted himself a small smile of thanks. "All is in readiness?"

"Yes, my Lord."

"Then there can be no further impediments to your beginning."

"No, sir. No impediments."

"Good. Then let us proceed."

Joss Tupper had just set himself down to his wife's excellent steak and kidney pie when he saw a fancy curricle bowl down the lane and make the turn towards the main house.

Who could it be at this hour of the afternoon? He hadn't been told to expect visitors. Just the opposite.

Tupper pulled on his coat and made his way sharpish up the lane to the big house. When he got to the west courtyard he found a snooty wisp of a man unloading one of two trunks strapped to the back of the spindly vehicle. The man's gaze flicked over him briefly before he turned away in obvious dismissal. Tupper drew himself up and allowed a hearty laugh to rumble out of his chest. Thirty years in His Majesty's Navy hadn't left him without knowing precisely what to do with this lot.

"May I be of assistance?" he asked in his best boatswain's growl, which meant to make his words mean the total opposite.

The fancy jackanapes in the immaculate wig let his face curve into a sneer. "Not unless you can carry a trunk with one arm."

"Oh aye." Tupper swung it up easily to balance on his shoulder. "But I won't." He let it drop with a heavy crash to the stones. That got the little bastard's attention.

"Now then. I am Mister Josiah Tupper, steward of this estate, and if you know what's good for you, you'll wipe that look off your face and tell me your business right quick before I toss both this equipage and your skinny arse off the cliff."

The man blinked, straightened, and backed up in rapid succession, but somehow managed to hang on to the remnants of his haughty demeanor. "Cowles, valet to Sir Jeremy Wroxham. My master has the use of this house."

"Does he now? We'll soon see about that. 'Sir' Jeremy is it?" Tupper knew full well Captain Marlowe's cousin had no courtesy title. Giving himself airs by giving them to his master. Twit. "Fetch your master down to me."

"Fetch?" The man might have defied him, but Tupper gave him a nasty, encouraging smile and he disappeared through the kitchen door, which was, Tupper noted, now unlocked. Wroxham had a key. Another thing Tupper would have to see to— changing the locks.

Tupper strolled in and took up his position in the entry hall, feet planted wide and braced, as he'd stood on many a ship's deck. He placed his good arm behind his back, thrust up his jaw, and waited.

It didn't take long. In another moment a tall fellow appeared at the top of the stairs, followed by the obsequious valet, who was still filling the man's ear with a whispered account of their encounter.

The man made his way down the stairs at a casual pace, giving Tupper all the time in the world to take his measure. Dressed to impress he was. Brocade togs, immaculately powdered hair—a town dandy. Tupper instantly dismissed him as a concern. They'd be done here in less than a minute.

"What's all this?" the fine fellow asked with a practiced drawl.

"You have no business in this house, sir, and I must ask you to please leave." Tupper's words were polite, but firmly to the point.

"My dear man," Wroxham began to drip hauteur, "do you know who I am?"

"That I do. 'Sir' Jeremy Wroxham, according to your man, but I think 'Honorable' is more to the point."

"Yes." The bastard didn't even have the grace to blush. "Yes, my father, Sir William Wroxham is well known in these parts."

"That so?"

"Yes." The fellow's temper was rising. "And who the devil are you?" Wroxham brought out a quizzing glass to examine Tupper as if he were a specimen of insect. Had to hand it to the man—he had some style. If he'd been his captain on a quarterdeck, Tupper might have admired the man's sangfroid. But as he was nothing but a posing popinjay, overprivileged, overfed, and underexperienced, Tupper didn't give a rat's arse about him.

"I am Captain Marlowe's Steward, Mr. Josiah Tupper, and this house is closed. If you'd come through the front, like a gentlemen, you'd have seen the knocker is down. As there is no staff available, your carriage is still in the kitchen court where you left it. Good day to you, sir." Tupper indicated the door.

"My good fellow, there seems to be a misunderstanding. I am Captain Marlowe's cousin, the nearest thing he has to a brother. And it is understood that I should look after the place for him while he's gone, as I have for quite some time before."

"I see. Then I have you and the rotting attics to thank for my employment. My instruction from Captain Marlowe was quite explicit. Quite. The house is closed."

Wroxham finally did color, but it was tinged with anger rather than embarrassment. "I've had a long trip down from London, Tupper, and would like to take my ease. We can sort this out some other time."

"No, sir. We've to sort this out now."

"How long have you been in Captain Marlowe's employ?"

"I've been in the Captain's exclusive employ for these past six months."

"Then why have I never seen you here before today?"

"The Captain took up residence but recently."

"Did he? Here?" He gestured around at the empty rooms. "No one has lived here, apart from myself, for over twenty years. But I suppose it might suit his rather spartan tastes."

Which begged the question of how a town dandy like Wroxham, accustomed to every creature comfort, was planning on living. Or why he should want to. Probably dodging creditors. That was the most likely story for the son of a minor, country baronet.

"As you say, sir, it's not fit to live in. Not for Captain and Mrs. Marlowe, and not for you."

"Well, well. Captain and Mrs. Marlowe? I had no idea he had married. Hushed-up affair was it? Taken her off to some rented room in Portsmouth, I suppose."

"Mrs. Marlowe has taken residence at the manor house of her parents in Dartmouth while the house is under repair." Tupper's voice had hardened. There was no need for this boil of a man to speak ill of the Captain's marriage.

"Manor house is it? Someone of rank? Just whom did he marry?"

Not that it was anyone's business, but he didn't think the Captain's marriage was to remain a secret. Even from this pretty little jackass.

"Miss Elizabeth Paxton, as was."

"Ho ho," Wroxham crowed. "Taken on the little cat, has he? I should have liked to see that. He's bound to be covered in scratches. Yes, this makes the trouble of the drive worth it. I know exactly what to do now."

CHAPTER 10

It was her mother's finest hour. Lady Paxton held her place on the chaise like a queen on her throne, receiving her due after having made a resounding triumph. She had done the undoable: married off an unmarriageable daughter.

Lizzie let her have her triumph. Bride calls were turning out to be more fun than she had anticipated. Who knew being a married woman put a gel in an entirely different sphere of conversation than she had hitherto been allowed to enjoy? It was like becoming a member of a secret society. The Club of Heretofore Secret Knowledge for Brides. What a lark.

And, truth be told, she liked being social. She couldn't stand subscribing to all the social conventions, but she'd hate to do completely without company. And being out in society was so much more fun now she wasn't on the marriage mart.

And besides, it kept her far too busy to moon about, missing Jamie like a sentimental idiot. She had made good use of her fortnight in Dartmouth at the drapers' and the cabinetmakers' workrooms. She had found a famous deal on some lovely lemony silk fabric that would look gorgeous in the sunny music room. Glass House would be the envy of the town in no time at all. It was marvelous, being an independent woman.

And at the moment, she was the toast of the neighborhood.

Her mother's "at home" was exceptionally well attended. The Reverend Mr. and Mrs. Marlowe had come, along with several people with whom Lizzie was not yet acquainted. But forming new acquaintances was the very purpose of an "at home."

"Elizabeth," her mother said, "may I present to you your new aunt-in-law, Lady Mary Wroxham? My daughter, Mrs. Marlowe."

Lizzie was introduced to a tiny woman with a soft, almost fade-away manner.

"It is a pleasure to meet you, Lady Wroxham." Lizzie could not ever remember having met the tiny, birdlike woman before, but then again, in the past few years she had gone about in Dartmouth society as little as possible. Or as little as her mother would let her get away with. And she definitely would have steered clear of anyone with the name Wroxham.

She was just scanning the room over the lady's head for her unfortunate excuse for a son, when Lady Wroxham's soft, cultured voice recalled her manners.

"It is a very great pleasure to meet you as well, for I have heard so much about you."

Good Lord, if it had been her son who had done the telling, then none of it could have been good. But the Lady gave her a sweet, benign smile and reached out to pat her hand encouragingly.

"Well, I must say my dear, you snatched up the prize of the family, as well as of the county. My nephew is entirely lucky to have you."

Lizzie was surprised into her warmest smile.

"You are too kind, my lady."

"Now, none of that, amongst family. You'll call me Aunt Mary now, won't you?"

"I would be honored." What a lovely surprise that this cultured, soft-spoken creature should be Jeremy Wroxham's mother. What a contrast they made; she so kind and well-spoken and he such an insufferable ass.

But there was her friend, Celia, at the door, looking lovely, dressed in an elegant, fashionable pink ensemble that made the most of her dark hair and porcelain skin. "Celia, you look marvelous!"

Celia's response was restrained. "Mrs. Marlowe." She curtseyed prettily, indeed she did everything prettily, how could she not? But her greeting lacked her usual warmth and affection.

"Dear Celia." Lizzie kissed her cheek and immediately drew her to the side so they might be private. "Are you very angry at me?"

Celia widened her blue eyes reproachfully.

"You ought to have written, Elizabeth, at the very least. You ought to have told me of your marriage, so I didn't have to hear it on the High Street from that awful Anne Winterbourne."

"Oh no, not her! Oh, Celia, that is awful. I am sorry. Can you forgive me? I ought to have made you a bridesmaid, but there simply wasn't time. Captain Marlowe was in an awful rush."

"How sad," Celia breathed, "not to have a proper wedding."

Lizzie had to laugh. "Oh no, not sad. There were, how shall I say it . . . compensations. Come sit by me, and we can talk and be seen sharing confidences. That will put Anne Winterface to rout."

She linked arms and strolled away from the others. "You should say you acted surprised because you were keeping my confidences, but that you were there the very moment Captain Marlowe and I fell in love. Right there on the terrace of the Dartmouth Arms assembly room."

"Did you really fall in love? At the Dartmouth Arms assembly room? Really?"

"Of course not," she said as carelessly as possible. "But it's been a great lark."

"A lark?" Celia's eyes warmed with the hint of the forbidden. Her mother never allowed her larks. She could only live vicariously through Lizzie's. "Never say, when he said he had a proposition for you, it was marriage?"

"It was!"

"Oh my, who could have guessed?"

"Certainly not I."

"Nor I either. That's just famous!"

"Yes. The workings of the male mind continue to be as unfathomable as they are amusing." Lizzie took a moment to look her friend over. "You do look well, Celia. How have you been keeping?"

"Not as well as you, I think." Celia pinked becomingly and gave her a shy smile. "A married woman. And is it true what they say?" she asked on a whisper. "And don't clam up and tell me the topic is unsuitable for my maidenly ears."

"Heavens no, what a bore. Come let's sit and have a good long coze, for I've so much to tell you, you simply won't believe it."

It was such fun to be with Celia again. They talked of all sorts of topics, and Lizzie even began to be seduced out of her resolve to go back to Glass House.

"Oh, Elizabeth, if you take a house in town, think what fun it would be. I could spend my afternoons with you, and you could chaperone me to the dressmakers, for you're an old married woman now. It would be so much pleasanter than with Mama."

It was a delightful idea. She could still be independent in town.

But her attention was called away from Celia and back to the assemblage by her mother. Everyone, it seemed, wanted their turn to congratulate.

"I must say you've surprised us all by becoming Mrs. Marlowe!" Sir Edward Foster had always been jolly and teasing. But she imagined he used his long acquaintance with the Paxtons to say out loud what everyone else merely thought. Lizzie supposed many of her mother's friends must have been privy to her parents' despair as she grew into a veritable ape-leader.

"And where has your Captain Marlowe been dispatched? Back to Toulon?"

So his exploits were more generally known than she thought. It was rather embarrassing to realize she'd been so unaware of things going on around her in the world. Well, that was going to change, wasn't it? No doubt she'd be secretly glued to the newspapers and naval lists to keep up with the latest news of the war.

Yes. She would order the newspapers directly. What fun to be a married woman, able to lead her own life as she pleased. Another benefit of the Secret Society of Brides. Wonderful.

She steered her pleasant thoughts back to the conversation. "The Captain sailed for the Antipodes."

"The Antipodes? Halfway around the world while we're in the middle of a war with the Revolutionaries across the Channel? Where's the sense in that?" Foster barked at her, as if she had been the one making irrational decisions for the Admiralty.

Lizzie slid a shrug down her shoulders. "I find there's little sense to be found in war at all, Sir Edward."

"Not a very patriotic view for someone so recently wed to a decorated naval officer."

Lizzie turned to find herself addressed by none other than the Honorable Jeremy Wroxham, Jamie's obnoxious but handsome cousin. He was, by most standards, more than tolerable to look at, if you liked that overconfident, patronizing type.

Lizzie did not. She had always avoided him and his kind. Too smooth by half in her estimation. But at least half the young ladies in Dartmouth were mad for his poetic good looks, and his handsome face always ensured he was invited to all the best of Dartmouth's drawing rooms.

But he and Lizzie had never got on. Probably because she

had always preferred the company of his younger, poorer cousin, Jamie. And she had made sure Wroxham had known it.

Lizzie made the barest of curtsies.

Wroxham echoed her civility with a brief, shallow bow. At least she knew where she stood.

"Miss Paxton, or should I say, Mrs. Marlowe."

"You should."

Now that she looked, it was easy to see he was related to Jamie. They had the same light colored eyes from their mothers. On Mrs. Marlowe the gray was mousy and on Jamie a bit otherworldly, but with Wroxham the gray eyes were just cold. And he was a shade shorter that Jamie, though it was hard to tell with his elaborately coiffed hair. Such a town dandy. This man definitely had a valet.

He struck a Corinthian pose, hand on one hip, one leg casually placed in front of the other so he could swivel from the hip, surveying the room with his cold, patronizing eye. He was the kind of man who was always sure he was the cleverest person in the room. That was probably the real reason why she disliked him. She was almost always convinced *she* was the cleverest.

"I was informed of your happiness by my esteemed Uncle." He gestured in the Reverend Dr. Marlowe's direction. "My congratulations." His paper dry tone told her he meant anything but congratulations.

Lizzie was having none of it. She was a married woman, a young matron, and she could finally speak as she pleased. She gave him her nastiest smile. "Come all this way up the hill to give me your spleen, Wroxham?"

"I know what's due a bride, however hasty she's been. When can we expect a certain blessed event?"

"Don't be any more obnoxious than you can help, Wroxham. Your cousin and I did not marry because I found myself with child." She pronounced the vulgar words with emphasis, just to watch him recoil with an elaborate show of alarm.

She hated such hypocrisy. He would have it his cleverly veiled barbs were socially acceptable, the norm, while her blunt truths were completely beyond the pale. And she'd have to put up with more conversations like this if she took a house in Dartmouth. The town was rapidly losing its charms.

"Quite. But one can't help but wonder why my cousin should marry, when he knew he was about to leave for active duty."

"We married, Wroxham, because it suited us. It pleased us to be married." She hoped her smile was condescending. "If you'll excuse me, my mother has other guests."

He put out an arm to stay her.

"What are your plans for that house?"

Lizzie disengaged her elbow. "What house?"

"His house. That damp little place out in the middle of nowhere. Perhaps you don't know about it. Glass Cottage."

So that was the root of his spleen. Their marriage had foiled his hopes of inheriting. "Why, live there of course. I am sorry for your disappointed expectations, but 'that damp little place in the middle of nowhere,' as you put it, is actually quite charming, and I am happy to call it my home now."

His only reaction was two spots of color high on his cheeks. "My dear little cousin," he drawled. "It's entirely uninhabitable. The place is a complete wreck."

Lizzie hated being patronized. Nothing was as sure to raise her temper than a show of self-aggrandized, male superiority.

"And you'd know all about being wrecked, wouldn't you, Wroxham. I say, does anyone even let you play cards with them anymore? I understand your vowels are, how shall I say, in decline?"

The lines around the edge of Wroxham's mouth pinched white with suppressed rage.

"You always like to think you're the cleverest girl in the room, don't you? You'll want to mind that. It's rather unattractive."

How funny that she had been thinking the same thing. They were rather alike, she and Wroxham. Perhaps that was why she distrusted him.

A body interposed itself between them, dispersing the tension in the air.

"Elizabeth." Her father cleared his throat. "A message has come for you."

"Of course." Lizzie stepped away from Wroxham with the slowest, shallowest impression of a curtsey.

But Wroxham didn't move away. "What's that?" He gestured to the official-looking packet in her father's hand.

"An express, just come from the Admiralty for Elizabeth. From your Captain Marlowe, I daresay," her father told her.

Lizzie could only laugh and snatch it out of his hand. How romantic. An express! How like her Jamie to be so sentimental.

"It is addressed to you, Elizabeth," her father clarified for Wroxham's sake, for the toad was still hovering about. "Why don't you use my book room?"

"Nonsense. It's just a silly love note or some such," she said with real happiness, though she said it to deliberately aggravate Wroxham. But it would send a very clear message to one and all they had married for love. Although Wroxham had been the only one boorish enough to say it, no doubt others were thinking she had married Jamie so quickly to hush up a scandal. "I can't imagine why he should go to all the trouble of an express for a billet-doux."

Still, she moved toward the window, where the light was better, if only to cool the impatient heat that had blossomed in her cheeks. His first letter. And he'd said he'd never write.

Her hands shook slightly from excitement and happiness as she tore open the seal and let her eyes skim down the paragraph. But the words didn't make sense. It wasn't from Jamie at all.

Dear Madam . . . Sad duty . . . Regret to inform . . .

Lizzie felt the cold settle into her bones even as she read and reread the words, searching, hoping vainly she was mistaken—she had misread the horrifying news.

"No!" The words fell from her lips like drops of poison. "So soon."

The room had gone quiet around her. She looked up to find the company was staring at her. Her knees became jelly and she sat on the floor in an abrupt little heap.

"Not this soon. So very soon." Why did breathing feel so cramped?

"Elizabeth," her father hurried over, "what is it?" He bent over her to assist her.

"I had not thought he would die so soon. He just left." The painful squeezing tunneled down into her chest.

"Who has died? You don't mean . . . ?"

"Jamie. My Jamie. He's gone."

"What?" Her father took the letter out of her useless hands.

"Yes." She felt like winter, bare and exposed for the fraud she was. "I thought it would take . . ."

"You thought what?"

Was it Wroxham who asked? Where was her mother? She wanted her mother.

"I didn't think it would happen so soon."

The burning sensation in her chest expanded and then contracted to a hard knot of icy fire. She could feel the itchy heat sting her eyes. Oh, good Lord, she was crying. She would not. She'd said she wouldn't. She clenched her jaw and willed the tears away, blinking furiously.

But it hurt so much. How could she feel such pain without anything happening to her? She hadn't been shot, she hadn't been poisoned. It only felt like it.

She tried to think, to understand what she was doing and what was happening, but she felt like she was watching the drawing room from underwater. She felt heavy and still, weighed down, as if someone had thrown a wet blanket over her.

Then she saw her mother's face, white with shock and distress as she came to her. Her face was crumpled into folds, but she held Lizzie and shielded her from others' view. Her father had begun to politely usher people out. He must've been saying something, but Lizzie couldn't hear.

The faces of the guests blurred before her, all wide eyes and shocked, chattering mouths. They had barely stopped talking long enough to catch the news. And now they would go and spread it. Jamie was dead.

Only Wroxham resisted the exodus. And only he had the bad taste, or perhaps it was morbid curiosity, to look directly at her face, to pry into her pain. All the other guests had averted their eyes from her, leaving her some semblance of privacy to fall apart. But not Wroxham.

"Get him out." Her voice rose, with a sharp, hysterical edge. She didn't care. "Get him out of my sight."

He looked too much like Jamie.

Jamie. All she could think of was his hand. How he'd laid it across her cheek and then all along her body. How he'd looked so happy. And now he was gone. Totally and completely gone. Just as he'd said.

Soft, careful hands came around her arms and lifted her to the chaise. It was Celia who, along with Mama, came close to comfort her and sit next to her on the chaise. Her knees bumped up hard against Lizzie's. She barely felt it—but the pain in her chest and throat was horrendous.

Celia had an arm around her shoulders and was talking to her quietly.

But all Lizzie could hear was her own coldly mocking voice echoing in her head. *You did say you've always wanted to be a widow.*

CHAPTER 11

One thought, one need, stayed in Lizzie's mind while the world crumbled around her: she must get back to Glass Cottage. If she could just get back there, to the place where she had been so happy with Jamie, everything would be all right.

No, not all right. But better somehow. Her heart would stop racing and starting, and the piercing pain that recurred every time she temporarily forgot and then remembered he was dead, would go away.

Jamie. Thoughts of him crowded her mind. The image of him walking out of the darkness on the assembly room's veranda as if she'd conjured him from her silent yearnings. He had been everything she remembered and nothing she had expected.

Grown so tall and powerful, so handsome. So teasing. So ready to shake the dusty boredom out of her life. God help her, she wasn't bored now. She was wrecked.

Hands steered her up the stairs of her parents' house and into a darkened guest chamber. But it was an impersonal room. She wondered, with one of the distracted thoughts that kept flitting across her mind, why she could not even have her childhood room for comfort.

But of course, her childhood room, the one she had occupied until just a week ago, was another two flights up, on the third floor, in the schoolroom. She'd taken over the whole wing up there, once she'd grown too old and too unruly for governesses.

So they had left her in the first available, empty guest room, at least temporarily while Mama went to find a maid to come to sit with her, so she could go and make one of her famous soothing tisanes. Laudanum with tea and oranges, most likely. But Lizzie didn't want laudanum. Not even opium could dull this pain.

And if she stayed still and quiet, as they all softly advised, the pain would consume her.

It didn't occur to her to change out of her silk morning gown, or to change her lovely shoes for boots. She simply walked down the empty back stairs and out to the stables, saddled her horse, and rode home as fast as the mare could carry her.

The ride was a blur, a series of sharp tableaux passing in sequence. The gate at Hightop. The turn around the high stonewall at the corner. The long lane across the ridge of the hill and the perfect blue of the sky above. The brilliant and delicate wildflowers dancing in the wind.

And then her lane. Her home.

Home.

She had enough presence of mind to do the bare minimum for the mare, pulling off her tack and leaving her in a clean stall with water. Each task gave her something on which to focus, a momentary respite from feeling the immediate pain, before she made her way across the stone-paved yard to the kitchen door.

The house was locked, completely closed up.

Even though she hadn't sent word she was coming, she had rather expected Mrs. Tupper to be up and about the house the way she had been the last time she had come out unannounced. With Jamie.

She pushed thoughts of Jamie, the pain of Jamie, from her mind and headed down the lane toward the steward's cottage, like a dumb animal seeking shelter, the hems of her pretty silk dress trailing in the muddy ruts. Surely Mrs. Tupper was to be found there.

Lizzie tried to occupy her mind with tame observations. She busied her brain with the thought that to call the main house a cottage was a misnomer, a gentleman's affectation, especially as there were two other, large-sized cottages on the property. The steward's cottage was just as charming and rose-covered as the main house, a smaller two-story version of the gray stone building.

Lizzie trudged around to the kitchen door.

"Mrs. Tupper?" she called. Her shoes clicked on the blue slate floor of the passageway. She could hear voices, cheerful and ordinary, as she came by the pantry and larder.

Mrs. Tupper was seated at the deal table in the kitchen taking a dish of tea, bread, and cheese. It looked so homey. So ordinary. Beside her was a weathered, one-armed man, his empty coat sleeve pinned to his lapel. As soon as she entered, he stood up from the table.

"You must be Mr. Tupper. He spoke of you."

"Yes, ma'am. Are you . . . are you all to rights?"

"No. No, not at all to rights." She could feel the tears, cool and wet against her face, and taste the salt that dripped into her mouth. "He's dead." The words hollowed her out inside, leaving her empty of everything but the racking ache that wouldn't subside.

They both stood now, the Tuppers, but stayed where they were and looked at her strangely. They didn't understand.

"Captain Marlowe. They sent me . . . notice." She pulled the crumpled piece of paper out of her pocket, creased and smudged from being too tightly held in her hand, and reached it out to them. Proof.

Mrs. Tupper looked to Mr. Tupper for a long moment.

It was all so strange. How could they just stand there? They shared that long look, and then Mrs. Tupper came forward tentatively, holding on to the back of the chair for stability, or courage, the way one did when approaching a stray dog.

"Ma'am, you've had a shock. A nasty shock."

"God, yes. A horrible shock." A sound halfway between a laugh and a cry came out of her mouth. She covered her face with her hand and looked away, down at the simple slate floor. At her shoes. They were covered with mud. "They're ruined. It's all ruined."

"You poor lamb." Mrs. Tupper took her into her arms, and Lizzie was gently cradled in a warm, lavender-scented embrace. She threw her arms around Mrs. Tupper to stop the shaking that had begun in her hands and had traveled down to her knees.

The monstrous ache in her chest expanded until she couldn't hold it back. Grief poured out in hot, stinging tears and wailing sobs. She was embarrassed to lose such control of herself, but it was too much. It was too horrible.

And it was all her own fault. She had doomed him. She had, by blithely agreeing to his proposition. By laughing and teasing when he said he was likely to be killed. By never telling him she loved him more than any other person or thing here on this beautiful, godforsaken earth.

And no matter what the terms of their agreement had been, she was never, never going to forgive him for leaving her so utterly, completely alone.

Lizzie's first thought when she awoke was that Mrs. Tupper, for all her starch, was as wily as Mama and must have put something in the tea. Her second thought was that in spite of the unpleasant dryness in her mouth, it had turned into a beautiful morning. She was in an attic bedroom, small and homey. Must be the Tuppers' cottage.

And then it hit her, like a hammer between her eyes. The yawning emptiness. The sharp, aching pain.

That was when the shaking began again. It started with her hands as she pulled away the bedcovers and reached for her clothes, and it continued. She made a complete hash of her lacing but was so agitated she couldn't pull her stays back off. She jerked the rest of her clothes on, with no care in their arrangement. It didn't matter. It only mattered that she be up and moving, away from here before her legs gave out beneath her and she was reduced to a pitiful, spineless puddle of silent tears.

She went down the stairs with careful attention to the rail and went straight out the front door without answering Mrs. Tupper's query. She just wanted to walk, to be outside and distracted the way she had been on her ride yesterday.

Was it only yesterday? It felt like forever. It felt as if the earth had changed. And it had.

How strange. Less than two weeks ago, Jameson Marlowe was the furthest thing from her mind. She had not seen him in ten years time. She had not exchanged so much as a word or a letter in all those years.

But now he was all she could think of. She had exactly four days of memories to fill all the emptiness that came before and all the emptiness that would come after. The emptiness that began the moment she had read the damned letter and would stretch endlessly through the rest of her days.

So she walked, pacing, back and forth along the cliff, down along the beach, around into the fields, over and over, trying to wear the pain out of her body. To exhaust the body enough so the mind would finally give up its tenacious hold on the painful truth.

"Ma'am." She turned at the sound of the voice. Mr. Tupper

stood quietly on the path, illuminated by a circle of lantern light. "Mrs. Marlowe, please, ma'am. It's gone dark already. You've no shoes on. You ought to come in."

She turned and looked down the coast to the west, where the last of the sun bled orange onto the horizon. The day had come to an end, and the endless night stretched out ahead of her like a prison sentence. She looked down at her feet. Tupper was right; she had no shoes. She had no right to the comfort of their beauty. Wearing them would have only ruined forever the solace she had once found in wearing them. But her feet were cold.

"Ma'am, you've been out all day, with nothing to eat. Come with us. Mrs. Tupper's got a good dinner for you."

"I . . . can't." She deserved to be cold. As cold as Jamie, sunk somewhere at the bottom of the sea, cold forever.

"Please, ma'am. For Mrs. Tupper. She's that worried, she is."

Lizzie looked at him. Lines of tension and worry creased his face. His accent was as rough as his face, but he held himself with dignity and assurance. He made a short nod, and knuckled his forehead.

Ah, that was a navy gesture.

"May I ask if you were in the navy, Mr. Tupper?"

"Aye, ma'am. Boatswain. 'Bosun' as we say."

Just as she'd thought. Jamie *had* brought home one of the less fortunate of his men.

"How long were you aboard, in His Majesty's service?"

"Near thirty year, ma'am. Until I lost my fin at Toulon."

How like Jamie to have brought the couple here to Glass Cottage when Tupper was made redundant in the Navy. How thoughtful. And how ruinously sentimental, to let a one-armed former boatswain run an estate.

"And that's where you met Captain Marlowe?"

"*Resolute* it was, ma'am, back in eighty-eight."

It somehow gave her relief from her feelings to talk about

Jamie to someone else who knew him and loved him. "He would have been eighteen. So young."

"Aye. Just promoted he was, to Third Lieutenant under Captain Jackman."

"And how long did you sail together?"

"Until Toulon, madame. Through the thick and the thin."

Lizzie heard the feelings hidden behind the bluff words. Yes, she had lost Jamie, but so had Tupper, who had spent much more time with him in the recent past, who knew him as a man, had watched him grow to be that man.

"Yes, he was loyal that way, wasn't he?" He had been loyal to her too, in his own fashion, coming back after all those years to marry her.

"He was, ma'am, and he wouldn't want to see you out here like this. Please, ma'am."

"Well, I daresay you're well out of it, the Navy. It seems a particularly mortal career."

"Yes, ma'am. Don't fret about it anymore." Mr. Tupper put a supporting hand to her elbow. "Let's just get you up to the house to have your dinner."

"Yes, all right." It didn't matter what she did, but she couldn't have Mrs. Tupper fretting, nor Mr. Tupper out looking for her at all hours of the night.

If only the dull ache in her throat would subside, she might feel more inclined to eat. But all she could think and feel was the gaping hole of loss.

The next time, they found her at the overlook on the cliff path. She had been outside, walking, as was her want, since the first faint hint of dawn. The attic bedroom in the Tuppers' cottage had proved to be only a temporary refuge. She hadn't slept in days, it seemed. It had been too hard to sleep, especially at night, when all she could think of was Jamie and the stars above his bed.

"Ma'am?" It was the tall blond man, the man Jamie had

talked to that first day. Why should he want her? She was too tired, too spent, to mind the cold itch of unease that wrapped around her neck at the sight of him standing less than four feet away. She hadn't noticed him coming. But unease felt too much like misery for her to bother.

"What do you want?"

"Mr. Tupper's been out looking for you. We both have. There's someone come to see you at the big house. From the rectory in Dartmouth."

Her father-in-law. She hadn't been back inside the house yet, but she could hardly meet a visitor on the lawn. She trudged back along the cliffs to the house and went through the front door and across the foyer to find the unwanted visitor poking about the mantelpiece in the empty drawing room.

It was the Reverend Marlowe's curate, Mr. Crombie, looking not a day under fifty, though she knew him to be nearer to thirty-five years of age: the very picture of the perpetual curate. He resembled nothing so much as a timid blackbird: all red, runny beak and beady eyes, always pecking tentatively at something. Lizzie wondered why it was her turn to be pecked at.

There were two new pieces of furniture in the drawing room, but as Mrs. Tupper had kept them under Holland covers, Lizzie stood just inside the doorway.

"Yes, Mr. Crombie, what might I do for you?"

Poor Crombie visibly recoiled at the sight of her. She turned and took a slow, detached perusal of herself in the old looking glass hanging on the wall. She did look a fright. Hair unbound and tangled by the wind. Her cheeks reddened by the sun and salt air. Her dress a careless accumulation of random garments, instead of a tasteful ensemble.

And why not? She was bereaved. Why should she not look it?

"The Reverend Doctor Marlowe sent me with word for you, Mrs. Marlowe."

"Yes?"

"They've sent the body down for burial. Arrived this morning. A lovely oak casket, too—" He stopped when Lizzie's look near sliced his tongue off.

"Lovely?" She felt the first strange, familiar stirrings of rage. The sharp anger suited her. It was, at least, better than dull, omnipresent pain. "A . . . casket?" She forced the word out of her mouth. "Who sent it? He died at sea. The letter said so."

"I'm sure I don't know, ma'am."

"Where did the casket come from?"

"From the Admiralty, ma'am, surely. The rector said he had not made any such arrangements, as it was not his place. Unless the late Captain Marlowe had friends in the Navy who might have seen to his remains as a token of their esteem and friendship, it must have been the Admiralty."

Lizzie couldn't think of who such unknown benefactors might be, but Jamie was the type of person who made friends readily. Surely his own generous nature had been known to his colleagues? It made sense there might have been people ready to make an act of charity for him at the last.

But now something would need to be done. "Did Reverend Marlowe make any arrangements or send any instructions?"

"Oh, yes." The curate fished awkwardly in his pockets. "He gave me a letter for you."

At least it was still sealed shut. She wouldn't put it past old Crombie to take a peek at the missive, but she could only imagine he hadn't because he was already appraised of the contents of the letter.

She broke the seal and forced the angled script into focus. Her father-in-law asked her preferences for funeral arrangements. Oh, Lord, a funeral. She'd never thought about an actual funeral, with a body and a coffin and horrible dirges and hymns. She had assumed he'd been buried at sea. For goodness sake, Jamie had been on his way to the Antipodes, not

Plymouth. She'd never thought they'd box him up and ship him back, like a piece of lost baggage. It seemed so small.

And so final. So irrevocable.

"Thank you Mr. Crombie. You may tell the Reverend Doctor Marlowe I will call upon him tomorrow." She might have sent a note telling him the same thing, and telling him to make whatever arrangements he felt were necessary, but it would give her something to do, someplace to go.

And she owed it to Jamie. She was his wife. She should arrange his funeral.

"We'll have to get ready to go in to town," she told Mrs. Tupper, who had hovered in the drawing room doorway like a chaperone. "I haven't any black."

Her last black gown had been for Great Aunt Elizabeth's death nearly four years ago. It wasn't even vaguely fashionable. She thought of Jamie and his fine blue coats. Blue to match his laughing gray eyes. He had looked so irresistible that first night at the assembly, so tall and handsome in his dark coat and buff breeches. So full of light and mirth. She should have had that portrait made after all.

Well, she'd have to mind her dress to do him proud. Lizzie took the curving staircase up and made her way slowly down the hallway to her room. His room. His beautiful domed ceiling, his wide bed.

But the room held no ghosts. It was spotlessly clean and full of morning sunlight streaming through the windows. Lizzie sat in a pool of light that fell across the bed warming the blue silk coverlet. They had been so happy here, in this room, buffered by its comforts from the harsh realities of the world for so very short a time.

She reached absently for the pillow, smoothing her hand across the soft linen. A faint trace of his scent, the spicy smell of bay rum, he had called it, rose up to tease her. Ah, there were ghosts after all. But still she raised the pillow to her face and breathed in deeply, surrounding herself with the last of his essence, before she curled down into it. The blue silk was warm in the patch of sunlight falling across the bed, the bed where she and Jamie had lain together.

She must have finally slept, for Mrs. Tupper woke her some time later, when the sun was much higher in the sky and the patch of sunlight had moved off the bed.

"Mr. Tupper's ready to take you into town, ma'am." The housekeeper had shaken out a carriage dress.

"But I had thought to ride. I don't like a closed carriage."

"We've only got the trap, but it's comfortable enough and open. And if you'll pardon me, ma'am, I don't think you're in any right state to ride all that way alone."

"Oh, no. We'll all go. I mean, I thought . . . I thought you would like to, seeing how long you both knew him, Captain Marlowe. That it would be fitting. There are plenty of rooms at Hightop. We could all be accommodated there."

"Oh, I don't know, ma'am. It's very generous in you, I'm sure."

"I thought . . . Well, I'd like it." And Lizzie did something else she never would have done two weeks ago. She asked for help. "I'd like it very much if you would come with me. Please."

And so the Tuppers did. They stood with her as she rang the bell at the rectory, sober and respectful in their black. It made her feel a little better to see other people's grief. It was one thing to lose a husband of two weeks, and it was quite another thing to lose one's child and only son. The grief etched in Mrs. Marlowe's silent, lined face was unbearable, for Lizzie feared that it was mirrored in her own.

But the hardest thing was the coffin, placed out on trestles in the front room. God Bless Mr. and Mrs. Tupper. She could not have done it without them—her shaking legs might not have held her up. But she would manage. She would do her best to make Jamie proud. She ran her hands over the box, feeling the smooth certainty of the wood, wanting one last time to touch him and feel the liquid tension and heat in his body. Feel his mouth curve in a smile as it came down upon hers.

It was a physical ache, the missing of him. And she did not know how she was going to bear the pain.

He watched. He made himself, though it was painful to see his father's tears as he read through the ceremony at the graveyard, and hear his mother's restrained weeping as the horse-drawn bier made its way from the church across the burial ground.

He clamped his jaw tight as he watched the Admiralty's instructions for a very public, highly visible funeral being followed to the letter.

Damn it to hell and back. It had seemed a necessary evil, originally suggested by himself and approved by Middleton, but he had never considered the cost. He had not considered anything beyond the benefit to their mission. But now he could see the price, the horrible cost to his family, was nearly too much. His parents, who had toasted his marriage with such joy only days ago, now looked unnaturally frail, aged by their grief.

Pray God they would one day understand and forgive him.

But it was Lizzie who concerned him most. He'd thought to find her handling it all with her usual self-possessed aplomb, observing the proceedings with her air of detached amusement.

But she looked anything but amused. She looked bereft.

Hatless, with her sweet, sun-flecked hair left down, tangling in the wind. She stood there alone, as the other mourners, his parents as well as hers, allowed themselves to be led out of the wind and away from the brown mound of dirt poised in the churchyard. But Lizzie stayed. She stood there so still and unmoving as the wind whipped and mangled her skirts.

She looked exquisite—a fragile figurine—the unremitting

black of her clothes only served to highlight the exquisite porcelain translucence of her skin and the vivid red of her uncovered, loose hair. But her face was screwed flat, with a horrible tension, as if she were afraid to move lest she fall into pieces. Mrs. Tupper hovered close behind her. Lizzie held herself upright, stiff and brittle as if she would break.

It killed him to watch her, the pain a tight knot in his chest. He couldn't bear to see her, to watch her crumble with grief. Grief he had knowingly caused. Astonishing grief. He had not thought it would come to this, had not thought it possible. Not from Lizzie. She was unassailable, impenetrable.

He'd had no idea she would be affected so deeply.

What in the hell had he done?

A hot dry hole was burning its way through his windpipe. But he didn't put the telescope down. He owed her at least that much respect after using her so callously.

CHAPTER 12

Lizzie insisted they return to Glass Cottage. Though it seemed every voice was against her, she could not countenance staying away. Even with Mr. and Mrs. Tupper adding their quiet conviction that she would be best off staying at Hightop, or taking a house in Dartmouth, Lizzie could hear none of it. She needed the peace and solitude of her house by the sea and the freedom to come and go as she pleased. It was as necessary as air.

And strangely enough, the necessity of exertion, of having to consider the feelings and needs of others, had brought her a good ways back to herself. While she had no desire for the constant companionship others seemed to think she needed, she did understand she needed the exertion—needed to think and feel about something other than herself.

She would resume her efforts to restore Glass Cottage and to make the estate profitable. There was no better way for her to honor Jamie's legacy to her. She would make him proud.

Yet, no sooner had she ridden up and seen to Serendipity than her peace was interrupted.

Lizzie was astonished into politeness at the courtesy of a condolence call. Not from her parents, nor the Reverend and Mrs. Marlowe, but her aunt-in-law, Lady Mary Wroxham, accompanied by her son, the Honorable Jeremy. They had been at the funeral, as Jamie's near relations, but she had not expected this.

"My dear girl!" Lady Wroxham took Lizzie's hands between her own. "I could not bear to think of you, all alone out here. I knew I must come to you, as my sister, in her grief, could not."

"I thank you, your ladyship," was all Lizzie could think to say.

"Not at all, my dear. One must be able to rely on family in times of difficulty, and I would have you know you may rely upon me. And of course on your cousin Wroxham."

Cousin Wroxham? But for once the gentleman was all correct politeness.

"My dear cousin, I am sorry for your loss," he said with every indication of sincerity.

"Thank you. I would offer you refreshment, but I am chagrined to say we are not as yet set up to receive or entertain visitors."

"No, of course not," Lady Wroxham agreed with a kind smile, as she took in the empty rooms. "How could you be, in such a derelict property? Yes, I don't mind telling you, my nephew, Captain Marlowe, quite astonished us all when he bought the place. I don't know what he was thinking."

"I believe he was thinking it was charming."

"Ah, yes. How like him to be so nonsensical."

Lizzie could feel the corners of her mouth turn up in the beginnings of a smile. "Yes," she agreed. "How very like him."

"But now, of course, you will no doubt be thinking of selling the place and getting something more suitable to a lady's needs."

"But I find it very suitable to my needs. And why does everyone persist in this belief? I have no intention of selling."

"Actually," Wroxham contradicted mildly, "it is rather clever of you to want to keep the property. A landed property will always have value and provide you income, even when you live elsewhere."

"Oh, how clever you are to see that, my dear." Lady Wroxham smiled lovingly at her son.

"But I don't intend to live elsewhere," Lizzie persisted. "Why should I?"

Wroxham astonished her by speaking, not with his usual lacerating sarcasm, but with quiet grace. "Because you are young and beautiful, and despite your recent bereavement, you will remain young and beautiful for quite some time. It is expected at your age and stage of life that you should want to see and experience more of the world than secluded country living should have to offer."

Lizzie did not know whether or not to be flattered by Wroxham's praise. Certainly she was *meant* to be, but to what purpose?

"Yes, now that you have independence, you will want to join society," Lady Wroxham was encouraging. "Oh, I know Dartmouth is nothing compared to town, and a season there of course, but who knows? Perhaps our local amusements might whet your appetite for a London season after all. Really, it is the very thing you need—a change of scene."

"I am but newly bereaved. . . ." It was almost bizarre to hear such a prim excuse come out of her mouth—she who had never cared for propriety or appearances. "You will forgive me, but it hardly seems an appropriate time for gadding about."

"Oh, but you may take advantage of the change of scene without anyone remarking on anything unseemly in your behavior. I know just how it is to be done, for Sir William Wroxham is always to be found in town, and I am very conversant in the ways of London society."

It was more of the same litany she had endured for the past several days and it was more than enough. There was no harm in it, of course, but it was excessively wearying. And it made her long for the peace and silence of an empty home.

Lizzie put on what surely must be a rather wretched face—people had been telling her she looked awful for days—and begged their leave. "I hope you will forgive me. . . ."

Wroxham stepped forward to offer her his hand. "We've tired you."

It was a relief to answer honestly. "Yes, forgive me. I do wish I was able to offer you some hospitality after your long drive out, but I am afraid . . ." She let her words trail off.

He drew her to her feet and gave her his arm to escort her to the stairs.

"It pains me to see you so," he murmured as soon as they were out of earshot of his mother.

"Oh. Well then, don't look."

Wroxham chuckled. "Now, *that* is certainly much more in your normal style."

Lizzie merely shrugged, uneasy that Wroxham should feel confident enough about her to remark upon her normal style of conversation.

"But you know, it cannot be good for you to be out here all alone," he continued in all seriousness. "You had best find accommodations in the town."

"I am hardly alone. I have servants."

"A crippled manservant and his wife? They hardly qualify. I do not even see them about. You have no one to attend to you as you must need."

Lizzie made no response. His opinion of the Tuppers was of no account to her, for she knew their true worth. As had Jamie.

"And what will people think with you insisting on staying all alone?"

Lizzie felt her fragile strength begin to rise along with her temper. Strange, how anger made it all so much easier. Anger focused things right down to what was absolutely necessary. "People will *think*, if they think at all, that I am newly and greatly bereaved."

"Perhaps. But perhaps they will think you stay for the freedom, for the privacy to do as you please. And with whomever you please."

For a moment, he had had her. For a moment she had been taken in by his apparent insight into her feelings, but with every word, Wroxham seemed to be returning to *his* usual style of conversation.

"Perhaps," she said as coolly as she could. She did want the freedom, but not in the vulgar way he implied.

Yet she could detect no sarcasm, no cynicism in his tone or look when he replied.

"I meant what I said. You are a beautiful woman, Elizabeth. Too beautiful to hide yourself out here and bury yourself in widowhood."

She slid her arm from his and would have moved away, but he caught her by the wrist and continued, his voice urgent and low.

"You must know I admire you. You must. I cannot imagine your marriage to Marlowe was a love match, but it gave you what you needed—money, this house. But I can give you standing, a place in society, everything you could want."

His confession jolted Lizzie as nothing else could have. Here was his reason for years of rude behavior? This was his declaration? He had been jealous. He continued to be. Jealous of a dead man. It explained a great deal, but excused very little. Still, his admission smothered her burgeoning rage. She could feel little beyond pity.

"I am sorry, Wroxham," she said as gently as she could. "But what I want is my husband back."

Lizzie was not surprised her would-be suitor and his lady mother left directly. The barouche bowled away down the drive before Tupper could even arrive to shut the door behind them, which he did with some apparent satisfaction.

"I take it you don't approve, Mr. Tupper."

"Captain said the house was to be closed. Knocker's off the door and still they came." He shook his head.

"I'm sure they meant to be kind."

Mr. Tupper was as eloquent as he was blunt. He made a sound of utter disbelief. "Nah. Don't like 'em at all, especially the lady. Like a cat sniffing in the gutters that one is. And her son no better. Glad to see the back of that one."

"Mr. Wroxham? He's harmless." Though she was glad of his departure as well, she was warmed by Tupper's partiality. "Do you not think so?"

"That one? I shouldn't trust his arse with a fart."

It occurred to her, as she retreated to the library, Wroxham and his mother's visit was most likely an early indication of the way her peace was going to be cut up if she did not rouse herself and her staff to take an active part in discouraging visitors.

Which exertion would also give her the added benefit of staying too busy to brood. She didn't have to be happy, but she did need to be active or she would . . . She didn't want to think about what she would be.

"Mr. Tupper," she called, "I should like to see all the household and estate accounts, if you please. And then together, I think we should make an inventory of the rest of the repairs needed. And before I devise a budget for the repairs and even furnishing of the rooms, I think it wisest to consult all the other ledgers concerning the income from the farms and the property as a whole. Don't you agree?" She paused to smile at him, but gave him no time to disagree.

If he was surprised by her request, he hid it with resigned compliance. "Yes, ma'am. But I do think you'll find it best to do as the Captain planned and close the house. Ledgers'll show you how expensive your repairs will be."

"Yes, thank you for your advice." To which she didn't want to listen. Why could she not make anyone understand, she *needed* to be there? She needed to be busy. She needed to feel connected to Jamie. It was the only thing that might keep her sane.

She neatly changed the subject. "And speaking of Captain Marlowe and the navy, Mr. Tupper, I desire to meet the rest of the servants."

A look Lizzie could only characterize as wariness crept across Tupper's worn, brown face. "There are no other servants, ma'am. Surely Captain Marlowe explained that? He expected the house to be kept closed up."

She attempted to cajole his caution away. "Yes, yes. Captain Marlowe did inform me of his plans. He also informed me there were groundsmen. Jack-of-all-tradesmen, I believe he called them. Now, if we're to have any peace, we'll need everyone to keep a sharp lookout for unwanted visitors like the Wroxhams, don't you think? So what about that big, blond lad I saw about the other day? He looked as if he would be handy at warning people off." She tried to smile pleasantly to leaven her insistence.

"That'd be Hugh, ma'am."

"Hugh. Good. I should like to meet him. And the other?"

"The other what, ma'am?"

"Mr. Tupper, I do appreciate your loyalty to the Captain, I do, and I am well aware of the Captain's feelings regarding the house being unfit for occupation, but as I also told him and Mrs. Tupper, I'm here now and things are going to be different. And there is, by everyone's reckoning, a vast deal to do. I *can* make it better, I promise. You'll see."

Lizzie could feel, rather than hear, his sigh. "Yes, ma'am."

"Thank you. And the other groundsman? The Captain said there were two, I believe?"

"He's not here at the moment, Ma'am."

Mr. Tupper was hedging, she could tell. Every time he told an untruth he bobbed his chin down quick. Poor fellow. Obviously he was not a man accustomed to lying. It spoke well of his character, though it did make her wonder, and worry, why he was lying now.

"And pray, where is he, if he is not here?"

"Gone for supplies. Building materials and the like. Into Dartmouth." Three emphatic bobs of the head, confirming his statements. Not only curious but, to her mind, highly suspicious.

"Lovely. I'll see him when he gets back, but the first one, Hugh, you may send to me at your earliest convenience. In the meantime, I should like to have a look through all the ledgers."

"All the ledgers, ma'am?"

"All. I think it best, don't you? Hard work is best tackled straight off. You may bring in them to me directly."

"Yes, ma'am."

Lizzie found the exertion of closing her mind to the sorrow felt oddly like contentment. She looked at the neat rows of her books, stacked tidily on their dust-free shelves, and let the fragile beginnings of peace and contentment wash over her. Despite Jamie's death, this was what a home, her home, was meant to be. She began to believe, for the first time, that she might just survive. She might just succeed. She might, in time, be happy.

Until Mr. Tupper ushered in the groundsman—and every instinct began to prickle with unease.

They appeared a little after one o'clock, the former with another stack of canvas-bound ledgers under his one arm, and the latter looking something like a dog might have dragged in off the beach.

He was handsome enough; a big, strapping young man, wearing well-worn clothes of a nondescript dirt color and a tired, resigned expression that told her he was not best pleased to be there. That made two of them.

Oh, and there, at the bottom of the disreputable picture he presented, were the sea boots she'd seen worn by sailors all along the waterfronts of the South Devon Coast. So damnably curious on a groundsman.

"Ah, there you are. It's Hugh, isn't it? You may come in."

She hoped her smile wasn't as nervous and intimidated as she felt. But no doubt that was his intent, with his heavy scowl.

He stepped carefully into the room and pulled off the floppy-brimmed hat, revealing a shock of wheat-blond hair and light blue eyes the temperature of ice. The familiarity was instant. He was definitely the man Jamie had been talking to that afternoon down along the low cliffs, and the man whom Tupper had sent to find her when she had been wandering the estate. So he was a servant after all. Curiouser and curiouser.

"You are the under gardener?"

"Groundsman, ma'am," came the mumbled reply as he turned to toss a glance at Tupper.

A flash of something—the way he stood in profile and the fact that he was wearing a brown coat, clicked in Lizzie's mind. She had seen him before, somewhere else. Before Glass Cottage. Not quite so natty as the first, but just enough of the same color to recognize him, finally. He was the man she had seen with Jamie, that day in town.

Nearly a month ago, on the High Street. She'd been there with Celia, on their way to the Booksellers. Her eye had been caught by the sight of two such striking men walking together. Until she had realized one of them was Jamie, and her heart had jumped and tumbled somersaults in her chest. And this was the same man Jamie had been talking to so strangely on the path that first morning she'd come to Glass Cottage. The one who had said it would be better if the house were empty. It struck her again—the impression that he and Jamie had been talking, conversing, almost as equals.

Equals, or near to it. He must be another of Jamie's charity cases, but unlike Tupper, who was possessed of a bluff good humor, this Hugh seemed resentful, and perhaps even embarrassed, by his circumstances. What else but embarrassed pride could explain the raw hostility emanating from the man like steam from a teakettle?

But she should not forget her first impression, that the man was a smuggler. Oh, it was all so bloody curious.

"Your name please, Hugh?"

"Ma'am?"

"Your surname, please. Hugh what?"

"Hugh McAlden."

"Thank you. And just what is it you do, Hugh?"

"I, ah, work for the groundsman."

"That would make you the undergroundsman then, wouldn't it? Our own mole, as it were?" He didn't laugh at her little joke in the way a good servant would have, just to oblige his mistress. No, the man was clearly not a servant at all. Oh, this was dreadfully, marvelously curious. It would be a relief to puzzle this mystery, something to occupy her mind instead of incessant grief.

"And what is the groundsman's name, Hugh?"

"Uhh. Sir?" The man attempted to give all the appearance of a dim rush light. Oh, no. No matter what he wanted her to think, he was not stupid. Stupid men were like dumb animals, incapable of showing anger or disdain, both of which were evident in the cold blue of this man's sharp eyes.

"Yes," she carried on in what she hoped was still a pleasant tone of voice, "Mr. Tupper's had some difficulty with the matter as well. Which leaves me in a difficult position, you see. If an employee, a servant, is not around long enough for his employer to know his name, it suggests he is not doing his job properly, doesn't it?" It meant he, whoever he was, was most likely smuggling. As perhaps were these two, Tupper and McAlden. Just what had Jamie gotten himself mixed up in?

"Did Captain Marlowe employ you himself, Hugh, or did Mr. Tupper?"

"Captain Marlowe, ma'am."

"And are you a veteran of the navy, Hugh?"

"Ah, yes, ma'am." His eyes cut across to Mr. Tupper's.

Lizzie brought his attention back. "And may I ask, what was your rank, Hugh?"

He sharpened his gaze and, so very unlike a real servant, looked directly at her. "Mate, ma'am."

That was ambiguous enough. "A warrant officer. Might I also ask why you chose to leave your profession after you had achieved such a high rank?"

He took a long moment to answer. "I no longer liked getting shot at, ma'am."

This little unpleasant reminder knocked her curiosity back a step or two. She couldn't blame the man for not wanting to end up as Jamie had. She wouldn't wish that on anybody.

"Yes, one can hardly argue with that. As I said to Mr. Tupper, it does seem a particularly mortal occupation, doesn't it?" She nodded her apology and firmed her jaw to keep the sudden heat from pooling in her eyes.

"I am sorry for your loss, ma'am."

"I thank you, Hugh. You're very kind. Though I suspect I need to offer the same to you. And to the Tuppers. You all knew Captain Marlowe, too, and have felt his loss as well."

Another glance between the two men, this time uneasy, almost embarrassed. Well, she wouldn't dwell on something that obviously brought pain to them all.

"Am I to understand you're still handy with a boat? There seems to be a dory down in the cove."

"Yes, ma'am." Yet, another glance at Tupper, but different. This time it was sharp with communication. Oh Lord, they were definitely up to something together.

"And Mr. Tupper indicates there are eel pots and other—" she waved her hand vaguely, "fishing things. I thought supplying the table here and at the cottages would be a better, or more likeable, occupation for you."

"Ma'am."

"I hope to make Glass Cottage entirely self-sufficient. But that will demand we all do our jobs conscientiously and well."

"Ma'am."

"Oh and one other thing. I am not fond of company, so I would ask that in the course of your work you keep an eye out for, and discourage, uninvited visitors."

A ghost of a smile wafted across his lips, with just enough of a sneer to get her back up. Why was she tiptoeing around these men, with their significant looks and games? Why should she countenance their dabbling with the smugglers?

"I shall be keeping a sharp lookout as well, both for unwanted visitors and for anything . . ." She finally chose her father's word. It was the only one that suited. "For anything havey-cavey."

"Havey-cavey." His eye held the glimmer of a genuine, amused smile. "Yes, ma'am."

"Right. So, you may feel free to put that wonderfully intimidating scowl of yours to use immediately to warn off all visitors. You may tell them—and you'll be glad of this, Mr. Tupper—that the house is closed."

He seemed as pleased as Tupper. "Closed," he repeated with a nod.

"Yes, closed. Thank you. You may go. Now, Mr. Tupper about this other groundsman of yours? I have a list of tasks I should like to see accomplished in the kitchen gardens."

"You may just give that to me, ma'am. I'll know what to tell him."

"I have no doubt of that, Mr. Tupper. However, I should like to meet all the persons in my employ. Considering the estate employs only four people at present, I shouldn't think it was too much to ask." She smiled again to try and leaven the firmness of her request.

"Begging your pardon, ma'am, but are you planning on hiring more?"

"Of course. Eventually. As we see how well the estate does."

"Ma'am, I know it isn't my place, but the master, Cap'n Marlowe, did say as he didn't want you living out here."

"Yes, so you've told me. I do understand. And I do appreciate your loyalty, I do. But this is where I belong. I hope you can respect my wishes and square it with your loyalty to the Captain's memory. Now when can I expect the other groundsman?"

Tupper bobbed his chin down. "He's away, ma'am."

"Away? You said he had gone into Dartmouth for supplies. So when might I expect him back?"

"Now, missus . . ."

Oh Lord, now they were in for it. Her mother's servants only ever called her "missus" when they were prevaricating or placating. Maybe both. She had hoped for none of that from Tupper. But she needed to start as she meant to go on.

"Mr. Tupper, if you please." She made her voice as calm, unruffled, and sweetly commanding as ever her mother had done. "If the groundsman is not back on the premises, with his repairing supplies, and presenting himself to me with an explanation of his absence, I shall simply have to give him notice."

"Now, ma'am, I'm after seeing the fellow all the time. I give him the jobs and he gets on with it. There's no reason you need to worry yourself about that. I'll see to things."

"Yes, Mr. Tupper." Lizzie fought to keep her temper, never predictable at the best of times and lately wildly erratic, under control. She must resist the temptation to give into the hot clarity of anger. But she was getting damned tired of having this conversation. She made her tone quiet but firm. "But the point is I *want* to meet him. I do not seek to supervise him or his work, but I do intend to meet him and put an eye to his face. I'll thank you to *please*," she made her voice firm and not placating, "see that it's done without any further delay. Do I make myself clear?"

"As gin, ma'am."

She had to laugh. It was such a manlike, exasperated thing to say. And it was funny. She could just picture Mr. Tupper tossing back a dram of the cloudy spirit with his one good arm.

Her change of demeanor gave him an opening. "But if I may say, ma'am, this groundsman was hired by Captain Marlowe himself, and neither of us are in a position to be able to let him go."

"What?" So much for her attempt at a sunnier demeanor. "You're telling me I can't give my own servant notice?" She was flabbergasted. "Oh, good Lord. Don't tell me—another navy veteran, isn't he?" Lizzie began to laugh and laugh. "You'd think we were running a home for superannuated sailors and not a farming estate!"

CHAPTER 13

The Heart of Oak stank of stale, spilled beer, damp wool, and day-old fish, but it was close to hand and the patrons knew how to mind their own damn business.

"What the hell's going on?" The tall man threw his bag into the bar with obvious disgust.

"Keep your voice down. What do you mean?"

"What's this business about scaring the shite out of the bloody woman?"

"Which woman? The old housekeeper, Mrs. Tupper?"

"No. She's no problem. Keeps to her cottage."

"The place is supposed to be empty."

"Well, it bloody well ain't!"

He swore colorfully into the night. This was not a part of the plan. They would have to adapt. Quickly.

"So we're to go in and put a fright into her?"

"I guess. I don't like the idea. Could get dicey. Always does with women. Unpredictable, that's what they are."

"Don't be such a flaming puss. We've run this ken before to empty the place out. You go in disguised and armed. She's not like to say boo to a pair of pistols."

"Pistols? Since when have we taken to threatening women with guns?"

"Since that house became occupied, that's when."

"I don't like it."

"You don't have to like it. You just have to do it. There's plans made can't be changed. They might be asea already."

The tall man shook his head. "There's things and then there's things. I don't want any part of going after that woman, pistols or no."

"Orders is orders. We need to see this done. So shut your gob and drink your beer."

Lizzie got up to poke up the fire and then retreated to the warmth of the wide bed. Though it was the beginning of summer, and the days could be warm and lovely, the nights were still apt to have a chill. A damp, sea-borne chill.

Somewhere in the house below, a door groaned open, and then creaked closed. At least she thought it was a door. Directly below, in the library.

Had Mr. Tupper finally relented and come back to restock the wood for the fire? Lizzie had been used to coal fires at Hightop, and indeed there was a grate for coal in the fireplace, but she suspected the wood, or the lack thereof, was just one more way for Mr. Tupper to discourage her residence. But a glance told her the copper bucket next to the fireplace was already stocked full of seasoned wood. How strange.

She glanced up at the clock on the mantel. Well past one o'clock in the morning. Mr. Tupper would never be up so late.

The upstairs corridor was dark and empty and she was, of a sudden, reluctant to leave the warm glow of heat and light in the bedroom. How ridiculous. Since when was she such a faint heart? And in her own house?

She would have gone out into the hall but a sound, rising up the stair and echoing through the empty halls, raised the hairs at the back of her neck.

A long, low moan. And then again, louder, as if the noise,

the person, whatever it was, was moving through the house. Searching for something. For her.

Her lungs filled with the hot acid of panic. She stared blindly into the darkness and strained to hear in deafening silence, but the pounding of her blood in her ears drowned out all other noise. Lizzie could only sort out two thoughts—this was what it was like to be frightened, and how stupid she was to be so alone.

Everyone, from Jamie to her parents, had told her, over and over again, it was not safe for her to be living in the house alone. Why hadn't she listened? Jamie had begged her, had made her promise him. She should have listened, damn her ears. She should have kept that promise.

Then the eerie sound came again, rising out of the darkness below to lift the fine hairs on her arms. But the ghostly moan was rapidly followed by a sharp grunt, a muffled curse, and a sound that was very much like the scrape of furniture along the floor.

Lizzie's brain latched on to the distinct noises. Whoever it was—and it was a person—had bumped into a piece of furniture. A person who was unaccustomed to moving about the house with new furniture in place.

A sharp sliver of relief pumped air back into her lungs. Someone was trying to frighten her. And was doing a damnably good job of it, at that. But God damn, she'd have none of it. She'd be damned before she hid sniveling with fear in her own home.

Lizzie darted across to the dressing room and quickly found the long rectangular leather case that held her fowling piece. Technically, it was her father's fowling piece, but since she had pinched it, as Jamie had said, more than ten years ago, and had kept possession of it ever since, it was now hers. She felt better once she had her hands around the reassuring, smooth metal barrel and polished stock. No one was going to frighten her out of her own home. No one.

Her hands moved through the well-practiced motions of loading with easy efficiency even though her fingers shook from nerves.

She slipped out of her chamber and out into the hallway quietly, staying along the wall, letting her eyes adjust to the dark, trying not to broadcast her movements by casting shadows. She stopped at the end of the corridor, just at the turn of the corner to the balustrade. Her hands still shook a little with tension where she gripped the gun, but she clamped her jaw down hard to steady herself.

Lizzie crouched down and peered over the edge of the balustrade. She searched, squinting hard into every dark corner, reaching out with her ears into the silence, ready for any flicker of movement, any vestige of sound.

And it came again. She wasn't sure whether she had sensed it or heard it first, but the effect was the same; her ears pricked and distinguished both a stronger moan and the swish of clothing from directly below her.

Moonlight filtered fitfully through the windows, dappling the stairwell with the shifting shadows of the trees outside. And there he was.

The hooded figure was all in black, covered head to toe in a long, flowing robe. A ghostly form rather than a defined shape. But the man was too tall for Mr. Tupper, as tall as Jamie, and he had two very long and very large arms. At the end of which, the barrels of two very old pistols gleamed in the moonlight.

Sweat broke out along her lip and down her the back of her neck. She swallowed the dry knot of panic and reminded herself—it was only a man. She had not imagined him. He had grunted in pain. She had heard him. And it was a him. She drew another slow breath, to try and quiet the horrible hammering of her heart and let the panic recede.

Yes, a man. It could not have been Mrs. Tupper. Too large. More likely that other one, McAlden, the rude, antagonistic undergroundsman. The mole. He and Tupper were up to something. And she was going to God-damned well find out what it was.

The footsteps continued across the entry hall and began to tread up the stairs. She let him take another ten or eleven steps upward, until he was in the middle of the curving stairway. Until she had a clear shot.

Her heart pounded riotously against her rib cage. She stilled it with her anger. Damn their interference. This was her house! And no sea boot–wearing, smuggling excuse for a groundsman was going to cheat her out of her independence. No one.

In the space between two heartbeats, Lizzie stepped out clear of the corner, raised the fowling piece to her shoulder, sighted, and squeezed the trigger. The gun spat its thunder and retribution straight into the tall figure on the stair.

The heat and flash from the pan blinded her for a moment, but Lizzie could see the figure crumple backwards and fall in noisy thumps back down the turning length of the stairs, his pistols clattering down along with him.

He moaned again, this time from pain. He was real. He was only human, and he could not hurt her now. But she stayed where she was, safely hidden behind the corner and reloaded as swiftly as her shaking hands would allow before she crept cautiously down the steps towards him. He was a big, brawny lad, even peppered with shot, and she was taking no chances.

He lay at the bottom, a long dark smear of blood marking the trail of his passage down the steps. As she approached, she kept the fowling piece raised, ready to fire again should the damned mole attempt to rise.

He didn't move, so she took another cautious step closer.

The sudden sound of a heavy fist pounding against the wide front door made her jump back. Lizzie realigned her aim on the door when she recognized Mr. Tupper's voice. "Mrs. Marlowe? Ma'am, are you all right?"

And then the clatter of keys working the lock. Lizzie kept sighted on the door and waited.

The front door burst open and banged against the wall behind with a loud crash. Dark figures spilled moonlight into the foyer. Mr. Tupper rushed across the threshold, brandishing a saber or cutlass of some kind with a wicked smile of a blade that grinned in the moonlight.

She kept her piece up as he ran forward.

"Madame! Are you all right?" His eyes ran over her and then he turned to search the room.

Lizzie never let her grip waver. "Yes, thank you, Mr. Tupper. I appear to have an uninvited guest."

And then a circle of light from a lantern was carried through the door. It was held in the firm grasp of the big blond groundsman. The mole held the light.

Oh, Lord. Lizzie cut her glance back to the man in the widening puddle of blood on the step at her feet. Holy Christ Jesus.

Tupper thrust his blade in the direction of the man's throat, straight to business. "Who is he?"

"I don't know who he is." Her voice had gone all thready and weak. She was not going to be ill. She was not. Even if the cavernous room began to move around her.

Mr. Tupper made a descriptive little flick with his sword. "Is he dead?"

Lizzie took refuge again in anger. "No, damn it. I only winged him. I must be out of practice." She only said it for show, of course. It was pure bravado, but she couldn't be shaking like a palsied old woman in front of the servants, who still might be smugglers, especially the sharp-eyed and quietly sneering mole, McAlden. Lizzie lowered the muzzle of the gun, but still held it carefully at the ready. "Bring the lantern closer."

Mrs. Tupper, armed with a wicked kitchen knife, and another figure crowded behind into the doorway. So much for all her self-pitying thoughts of being alone. She had her own little army of defenders clustered around, bristling with anger and outrage. At least Mr. and Mrs. Tupper were. Big blond McAlden stood back, keeping a respectfully watchful eye on her gun. Good.

Another servant, who she supposed must be the missing gardener or groundsman, or whatever it was they were calling him this day, lurked with his guns in the doorway, just beyond the circle of lantern light.

Tupper knelt down on the stair next to the injured man and stripped back the hood and cloth mask.

"Do you recognize him?" Tupper asked the assembly in general.

Lizzie answered. "Lord, I think he might be Dicky Pike's brother." She bent down to take a closer look. "I think he must be Dan. Dan Pike. Dicky's the barman at the Heart of Oak Tavern down on Warfleet Row. We need another lamp."

Mrs. Tupper bustled forward from the door to light tapers, but the other lad shifted backwards into the gloom, away from the bloody body.

"Our stalwart lads." It was so much easier to replace the shock and horror with anger, especially aimed at someone else. "If you can't stomach the blood, then go fetch the doctor and the magistrate. Though God knows it won't do much good."

"You don't think he'll live?" Mrs. Tupper brought another lantern, and a fully lit candle branch closer to the prone figure.

"Oh, no. I mean, yes, he should live. It's just a fowling piece." She handed the gun down to Mr. Tupper, while she peered down to have a second look and muster her bravado. The mole was still standing there, silent as the grave, listening. She'd give him an earful. "It's meant for felling ducks, not a great, big slab of stupidity like Dan Pike. I reckon he's taken lead balls aplenty that weigh more than I do. He'll live, damn it. Which is rather infuriating after all the trouble I've been to to shoot the poxy big bastard, but there you have it." She looked back at the tall lad still hanging back in the doorway. "See if you can get Dr. Craig from Stoke Flemming."

McAlden spoke up. "Isn't that the other way from the magistrate? Begging your pardon, ma'am," he added as an afterthought.

"An extra hour or so won't matter to the magistrate. Not for Dan Pike. And with luck he might come around before then, so I might get at least some of my questions answered. Like why in the hell has the likes of Dan Pike resorted to housebreaking?"

The big slab of stupidity never did come round, though they did him a kindness and poured whisky down his throat to dull the pain. Or at least he was canny enough to pretend he was still out cold, even when the doctor pressed and probed and fetched birdshot out of his great big, dirty hide. Good Lord, how could someone live so close to water and be so vastly unwashed?

The magistrate's carriage fetched up in the stable yard right after ten.

Sir Ralston Cawdier slid his girth to the ground with a hearty sigh. *Sir* Ralston. Lizzie could feel the sneer build behind her lips. He'd only been elevated to his baronetcy on the strength of his excellent cellar. All smuggled brandy and claret.

Portly, florid, and easing comfortably into his middle age, Sir Ralston had the well-fed, complacent look of a man who was pleased with where he was in life. A rich, country fellow like him was bound to be up to his neck in the smuggling. He'd be absolutely no use to her.

"And what have you got here?" Sir Ralston cast a rheumy eye around the place.

"Dan Pike, full of birdshot."

The magistrate pulled a face as he looked skeptically at Mr. Tupper, his gaze resting on the empty sleeve.

"I shot him," Lizzie clarified. "He was in my upper hallway. Near two o'clock this morning."

"Ah, Miss Paxton."

Since he didn't bow, she didn't bother to curtsey. "Mrs. Marlowe, sir. I am lately married."

"Mrs. Marlowe." And now he made a handsome enough bow. "My congratulations on your recent marriage. No idea you'd taken this house."

"It has been my husband's property these four years. We have but lately set up housekeeping."

"I had not heard, but that would account for it. Four years you say? And your husband, madam?" He looked around the yard at the various occupants.

"Captain Marlowe is deceased." And suddenly she could feel the hot, useless tears prickle behind her eyes.

"Lately married and deceased?" Sir Ralston's hoary eyebrows flew up with unabashed curiosity. "My condolences, of course. Sorry business, this. His Majesty's Royal Navy, did you say?"

She hadn't. But Sir Ralston had had his ears to the ground, it seemed. Such an embarrassment of rogues to choose from.

"Yes, now I recall," he answered for himself. "Marlowe. Rector's son. Wasn't he friends with that other Navy fellow, what was his name? Palmer?"

The heat of tears was instantly banished as Lizzie felt cold creep along the ladder of her spine. Francis Palmer. Jamie had mentioned Frankie that first night, and said he was dead.

"I am not acquainted."

"Ah. Yes." He exhaled another heavy sigh and scratched his head through his wiry, gray wig. "Well then." He cast an assessing glance at Dan Pike's prone form. "Sorry you were troubled for a lark."

Lizzie's eyebrow rose all by itself. Lark? But such obvious flummery hardly mattered—let him spout his bouncers. She was quite determined to find the truth in the puddle of lies and half-truths pooling wherever Sir Ralston, and the rest of her staff for that matter, walked. But she couldn't let such a bold-faced piece of bluster pass without remark.

"Lark?" She couldn't have made her tone any more sarcastically incredulous.

"Nothing more than a lark, I'm sure." He gave her a smile meant to be reassuring. "A harmless prank by high-spirited boys."

Boys? In a hen's eye. Dan and Dicky Pike would never see the sunny side of thirty again.

"Not exactly harmless, sir. I might have killed the man. As I said, he was found standing in my home in the small hours of the morning armed with a brace of pistols."

"Hmph," Ralston grunted away her application of logic. "Ain't you got locks?"

Patronizing bastard. Thought she was an imbecile.

"As a matter of fact I do—they are new. But come to think of it, the locks had not been disturbed. My steward needed his key to come to my assistance. The doors were locked, and still Pike got in. That's no lark."

"Yes, but as you say, you're the one that shot at him, not the other way round. He's harmless enough."

"He was carrying pistols, sir. And masked. And robed. A masked, robed man doesn't housebreak in the dead of night unless he is bearing more than a load of mischief."

"Yes, well . . ." Sir Ralston's voice trailed off for a moment before he resumed in an overly cheerful, avuncular tone. "You leave it to me then. I'll see to everything. No need to bother you again. You can put it from your mind."

He wouldn't have been so infuriatingly condescending if Jamie were the one standing before him, but then again, would the whole incident have even happened if Jamie were here? It was something to think about.

A quarter of an hour later, Sir Ralston's carriage trailed the farm cart bearing the restless figure of Dan Pike up the lane and out of sight.

Lizzie was pleased to note, in the moment that came after, everyone turned to her. Everyone being the three of them, the Tuppers and the mole. Who still exuded antagonism the way a flower continuously gave off scent. Lizzie wasn't sure whether she was glad she hadn't shot him or not. Another thing to think about.

"Well, that's the end of that. Breakfast, I think, Mrs. Tupper. It will be all the satisfaction we'll get for this morning's work."

They retreated into the house. At least the women did. The two men disappeared somewhere together the moment Lizzie's back was turned. Just as well. It would give her what Jamie would have called "sea room" to maneuver.

Mrs. Tupper bustled about brewing up a pot of blissfully hot coffee and milk, and set out a loaf of bread, jam, and the remains of a cold meat pie. "There's ham as well, if you've a mind for it."

"That would do nicely, Mrs. Tupper. Just the thing to counter a 'lark.' "

"Lark, mine Aunt Fanny," Mrs. Tupper growled.

"Why, Mrs. Tupper." Lizzie could not stop her smile. She'd never expected such a piece of cant out of straitlaced Mrs. Tupper. But here the dear lady was fair bristling with indignation. And after all, she was married to Mr. Tupper.

"Not right that a man of the law shouldn't do something about a man breaking into a house in the dead of night and threatening a lady like that. Not right. It's one thing for these men . . . here, dear." She passed Lizzie a wet cloth. "You've got a big smudge of black powder all along your cheek."

From firing the gun, no doubt. No wonder Sir Ralston had looked so askance at her. She must look a pirate with her strange combination of clothes and her blackened face.

"Yes, well, you are correct, of course. It's *not* right, but I'm afraid it's the way of things here on the south coast. I daresay you haven't been here long enough to understand."

"I understand a defenseless woman shouldn't be attacked in her own home—"

"Hardly defenseless, Mrs. Tupper," Lizzie interjected mildly.

"Well, just because you've the good sense God gave you to know the business end of that gun from the other, doesn't excuse his mischief."

"And 'mischief' is all the explanation we're like to get. Free traders' mischief."

Mrs. Tupper ceased being indignant. "Free traders?"

"Smuggling," Lizzie added for clarity's sake. "I'm sorry if I shock you, but everyone within three counties must know Dan Pike and his brother Dicky are up to their red eyeballs in the smuggling, and I'd wager this house that our Lord Magistrate, Sir Ralston is as well."

"Sir Ralston?"

"I shouldn't be at all surprised. The coast's riddled with smuggling gangs, but what I want to know is why they were inside my house and how they got in, with all the doors locked. Of course I do reckon now it was for the smuggling. They've probably used the house for years as it's been sitting here conveniently vacant—at least for most of Captain Marlowe's tenure." Lizzie let her brain ramble over the questions in her mind. "But why they couldn't just ask me to come to some sort of civilized gentlemen's agreement about the matter, in the usual manner, is beyond me."

Lizzie got up and began to stroll back and forth before the great stone hearth. It was always so much easier to think when she was moving. And her agitation, she hoped, might inspire Mrs. Tupper's confidence. If it didn't, there was always brandy.

"Well, Mr. Tupper does say that the house is meant to be closed. Perhaps they thought so too?"

"Mmm," Lizzie agreed. "Or perhaps there was a prior agreement? Do you know, Mrs. Tupper, if anyone tried to contact Captain Marlowe, or any of the other men, here at the house? Did anyone come to Glass Cottage or perhaps try to tip the wink to Mr. Tupper at a public house with a discreet word about the free trade?"

"No, ma'am." Mrs. Tupper looked acutely uncomfortable, but firm in her denial. Curious.

"Would you check with Mr. Tupper just to be sure, please? Although perhaps this incident has more to do with Captain Marlowe's former profession. I can only imagine His Majesty's Royal Navy doesn't exactly see eye to eye with the Free Trade on most matters."

"No, ma'am." There was some vehemence in that statement. Very heartfelt. Again, curious. Just what part exactly did the Tuppers play in this little drama?

And then there was that mole, McAlden. The one who might or might not be a smuggler himself. The one Jamie had been so cozy with. The one every instinct she possessed told her to be wary of. But he had also been in the Navy, like Jamie and Mr. Tupper.

"I say, Mrs. Tupper, is it generally known in the neighborhood Mr. Tupper was a sailor in the Navy before he came here? Is it generally known that he and Captain Marlowe sailed together?"

"Well, no, I don't rightly . . ." Mrs. Tupper pulled back visibly, her face tightening and closing as if she were battening down for a gale.

"Oh, it's quite all right, Mrs. Tupper. I'm just puzzling things out. You see, if it were well known that Mr. Tupper came from one of Captain Marlowe's ships, it might explain their, the free traders', reluctance to parlay with us, as it were. Do you see?"

Lizzie took the opportunity of Mrs. Tupper's shocked silence and resolutely turned back to liberally lash the coffee with brandy. Her mother would have called it "French cream."

But it would do her, as well as Mrs. Tupper, the world of good. It might help to rid her of the last of the cold knot of fear still firmly lodged in her throat.

The brew went down a treat. And a few unguarded sips were warming Mrs. Tupper as well. Her face was beginning to take on a decidedly rosy cast.

"Jamie, Captain Marlowe, told me they served together, in the navy, he and Mr. Tupper?"

"He did, ma'am. That he did. The *Resolute* it were and then *Swallow*. Captain Marlowe's first command."

"Of course." Lizzie smiled to herself. "And how long were they together? It seems it must have been a great friendship for Captain Marlowe to offer him a home and a position after his injury."

Mrs. Tupper, that bastion of straitlaced morality, was rapidly loosening her stays. Lizzie kept the brandy to hand and would have poured her a deep dish without the coffee to keep the flow of words, but as Mrs. Tupper warmed to her subject, it became apparent that any more would be extraneous. The laced brew was doing its job quite well, without need of any further assistance.

"Lost his fin at Toulon. Bloody mess that were, but the Captain, he were First Lieutenant then, pulled Tupper out right and tight. Eight years we sailed together with the Captain, all in all."

"We?"

"Oh, aye. My man and me. Ne'er been apart in all of six and twenty years of marriage."

"And you lived on his ships, the whole time?" Lizzie thought her eyes must be round as saucers. She did know her mouth was gaping open like a seal's.

"Bless me, yes. Nowhere else for me to live."

"I'd no idea." She had no idea women went off to war at sea with their men. It did account for Mrs. Tupper being as stout-hearted as any tar. Lizzie wondered if the Navy itself knew.

Or admitted it. "Well, we'll canvass that entire topic, for I'm sure I've a hundred questions to ask of you, at another time. But, to get back to my point, does anyone else hereabouts know that Mr. Tupper is, or was, navy?"

"Well . . ."

Mrs. Tupper was hedging.

"Have you kept it a secret?"

"Not a secret exactly. Just keep our business to ourselves. No need for anyone to know or care about our business. Tupper knows what he's doing—raised on a farm out to the west. No one can say he doesn't know how to manage things for Captain Marlowe."

"Oh, I've no doubt." Lizzie only wanted information, not retribution. But it just might account for why the free traders would try such a hamfisted approach the way they did. "Well, there's nothing for it. We shall have to get in touch with them."

"With the free traders? The smugglers? Hadn't you best let the authorities deal with all that?"

"The authorities? Come, Mrs. Tupper. What happened to 'Lark, mine Aunt Fanny'? You heard Sir Ralston. The magistrate won't do a damned thing. It's all my eye and Betty Martin. No, if we're to get any answers we'll have to ask the questions ourselves."

Mrs. Tupper looked decidedly uneasy. As if she had suddenly become seasick.

"Don't you worry. I know exactly what to do." Lizzie smiled. "I'll make a call to Old Maguire."

CHAPTER 14

"**Y**ou're awfully tetchy this morning."

Marlowe shot a venomous, if weary, look at his companion. He was too tired for a proper sneer. "Dan Pike bloody well shot at my wife last night."

"No, I believe it was the other way round. Your wife shot at Dan Pike. And hit him. Almost makes me want to admire her."

"Don't." Marlowe grunted in response and gave the dory another shove across the sand towards the water.

McAlden continued along as if Marlowe hadn't said a word. "Don't admire her, or don't tell you I admire her? In fact, I think I'm beginning to like her. I begin to see why you married her. Apart from the obvious."

"Shut your bloody mouth before I shut it for you, Lieutenant," he grunted.

McAlden grinned into the gunwale and put his back into it. The dory slid the last few feet until it was suddenly weightless and riding gently on the water. The two of them jumped fluidly over the rail and fell quickly to work, Marlowe at the tiller and McAlden in the sheets, hauling up the sail. Another moment, a push of ocean air, a turn across the wind, and the potbellied canvas billowed out before them.

They worked in perfect silence and harmony until they were comfortably under way for Plymouth, riding west on the tide.

"Well, you did say the house needed to be empty," McAlden commented casually as he squinted up at the sail, checking its trim.

He just couldn't leave well enough alone. "I did, damn your eyes." His tone was enough to halt all conversation for an hour or so.

In time, McAlden spoke again. "Did you hear what the magistrate said?"

Like him, McAlden had been going over all the evidence, working it all out in his mind.

"Not all. But I got the general impression he's in it up to his neck."

"Only about his stomach, I should think."

That raised a little smile out of him. The magistrate's involvement was definitely suspect. But so was his own wife. Lizzie and her devilishly quick trigger finger. "And Lizzie's got it all figured near as sixpence, Mrs. Tupper reports."

"I told you—nothing but trouble."

"Not nothing but, but trouble all the same. God damn, but she's got an unholy talent for mucking things up. Though she may possibly do us some good if we play her right. Mrs. Tupper said she was going to get in touch with someone named Maguire."

"Ring any bells?"

"There used to be an old fisherman of that name. Saved Lizzie from near drowning once, if I recall, but that was at least fifteen years ago. He'd have to be elderly by now, if he's still alive."

"I gather he must be a free trader of some sort. But I think we should see what kind of information she can get. At least she'll lead us to this Maguire. Mrs. Tupper going to stick on her?"

"I hope so." No one knew better than he just how damn slippery Lizzie could be. "If Lizzie can figure out half of what's going on at the first whiff of trouble, how long is it going to be before she's figured out the rest and sussed us out?" The thought made him acutely uncomfortable. The image of Lizzie with her bloody fowling piece all but smoking rose like a specter before him. She also seemed to have an unholy talent for retribution. It didn't bear thinking.

"And how long do you think it'll take the traders to figure out as much as she has?"

"I've got to get her out of there before she gets herself killed. They won't keep their sticks in their pockets next time."

"They'll take a page from her book and fire first and ask questions later." McAlden looked as though the idea amused him.

"We have to get her out of there first."

"What do you propose? Nothing else seems to have worked."

"Blast and damn. Maybe I have to go to her, show myself to her, and make her see reason."

"Don't like it, Captain. You could end up like Pike. Or worse, like Palmer. We both could. And where would your fine house be then?"

"Lizzie'll still have it. And they'll still be after her." God, he hated to even leave her at all. Marlowe stared back at the retreating coastline. Redlap Cove had long since disappeared astern.

"I still don't see why you had to involve a woman. She was just bound to muck things up."

"I wanted to keep the house secure—legally I mean. As you said, it was hard-earned prize money. And the house was supposed to be security for when all these God-damned wars are over and done with. But in the meantime, Lizzie's my best bet. And we can't have some other miscreant get it and move in—we've got to keep it vacant so the trade will continue."

And truth was, he couldn't envision a future for them together without the house as a stage, a backdrop, to her understanding and forgiving him. But if Lizzie could puzzle out the Navy connection, so could those bastards. The magistrate had been near enough to it with his comment about Frank Palmer.

McAlden's thoughts had been moving just as rapidly along the same lines.

"Did you hear him speak about Frank? Wanted to rip the bastard's throat out. I near did. But she didn't give much away though, your wife."

"No, but they've connected Frank to me and then me to Lizzie. . . ."

McAlden nodded. "We don't have any more time to lose."

"Once we get to Plymouth and get the sloop, it may behoove us to split our efforts. You stay aboard the ship, and I'll continue to try to infiltrate the smugglers."

"It'd be best if I stayed. She's already accepted me as one of her staff."

Marlowe shrugged away the suggestion. He knew it made sense, but he felt compelled to stay near, to keep an eye on her. He changed the subject as he let the boat fall off the wind as they neared the entrance to Plymouth harbor.

"You will appreciate the fact that the Admiralty has given us the sloop we cut out at Toulon." It was a marvelous joke of fate. The sloop had saved their necks that night, sailing them out of the conflagration. And they had saved it as well, from being burned to a cinder in the harbor. It was much too beautiful, too sleek and yachtlike, to have burned.

Damn their eyes, but they had been lucky that night. Lucky to have made it out alive.

"God, what a night," McAlden mused morosely. "You'll tempt fate just to talk about it." He rubbed his face absently, as if he could still feel the heat and searing flames of that fateful night.

"Who knows, maybe the sloop will be lucky for us again.

There she lies." The vessel was snugged up against the wharf, riding high on the incoming tide.

McAlden let out a low whistle of admiration.

"Yes," Marlowe agreed. "We'll have to take her out to a mooring to take on crew, and guns, away from curious eyes."

"I'll see if I can arrange it with the harbormaster by the time the tide turns."

"Very good. They've let us pick a few men of our own— Wills and Davies, as well as the Gypsy."

"Good men." McAlden walked farther forward to assess her lines. "Things will change once we're on board." He spoke in an offhand manner, and without looking at his friend and superior, but Marlowe understood.

"Will they? Do you think you can manage to call me Sir without choking?"

"No." But he smiled. "I'll keep a slop bucket at the ready."

"And I'll make sure you have to say it at least twelve times a day."

That got a laugh out of McAlden, and seemed to dispel his air of gloom.

"They had me rename her." Marlowe gestured to the painter working below the bow in a dory. "Something not Navy. No H.M.S."

"*Defiant?*" McAlden read the bow carving. "Isn't that a bit obvious?"

"Is it?" Marlowe smiled at the saucy, bare-breasted figurehead the painter was giving a coat of red hair.

"Oh, Jesus." McAlden passed his hands over his eyes. "You've named it after the ginger-hackled witch. Why do I have a horrible feeling our luck is about to change?"

"Come along, Mrs. Tupper. You'll need to pack yourself a bag. We're going back to town."

"London, ma'am?"

"Sorry, no, only Dartmouth. And only Hightop House, but I think this is a propitious time for a visit."

Mrs. Tupper heaved a massive sigh of relief. "Now that's the first sensible thing you had to say since you got here. I'll see to packing your trunk."

Lizzie did not quibble with her. Nor did she feel the need to mention the visit was not permanent, and she would be using the opportunity to hire suitable servants to populate Glass House properly. Servants who knew how to use guns. And replace plaster. Surely there could be no shortage of such along the south coast.

Because now they, whoever *they* might be, knew she was armed, they weren't likely to be as ghostly and circumspect in using their weapons next time. A show of greater force, and greater occupancy, was necessary if she didn't want to blow holes in every run of plaster in the house.

And with a visit to her mother she could finish her order at the drapers. Check on the progress of the upholsterer. Order some new linens. Get some answers to her questions.

And search out Phineas Maguire.

Lizzie drew the line at visiting public houses by herself. She had at least that much care for her reputation. But she asked every shopgirl and errand boy, every ostler and stevedore she encountered. No one knew. Or would say.

Maguire was finally found, of all places, at the kitchen door to Hightop Manor. He simply presented himself there two afternoons after she had arrived.

Mrs. Tupper, whom she had kept with her as her personal servant on this short trip, because she knew not to fuss, bustled across the terrace to rouse Lizzie from her contemplation of French-style chairs for the music room.

"Big fellow to see you, ma'am. He looks respectable enough and had a civil tongue in his head, but he does seem . . . a bit rough."

That might have been any number of her acquaintances along the south coast. But there he was at last, the grizzled old specimen.

"Mr. Maguire, to what do I owe the honor of this visit?"

"Nice to see you, missus. I give you my gratulations on your wedding. And my most true condolences."

"Thank you, Mr. Maguire, you are very kind. I wonder if I might have a word." Lizzie closed the kitchen door on Mrs. Tupper and led Maguire back down through the gardens for a stroll, much like she'd taken Jamie. And for the same reason. Out in the shrubbery, their talk could be entirely private. It seemed such a long time ago, that last walk.

"What could you want with old Maguire?"

Maguire didn't seem particularly old to Lizzie, but he wasn't young either. He had looked exactly the same since the first time she had met him, well over fifteen years ago, when he had plucked her out of the Dart and into his dory. She had been seven and attempting the great feat of swimming all the way across the river. Maguire had most likely saved her from drowning.

He had the look of an aging prizefighter. Tall build, broad shoulders, enormous, capable hands, wide broken nose. His skin was bronzed to the color of mahogany. The difference was in his eyes: they were clear and bright blue, once one got close enough to see them.

His hair had always been a short, salty mixture of gray and white, his teeth (and he still had his teeth) had always been crooked, and his warm blue eyes had always twinkled when he was amused. And he often was. Little whiskers of lines etched out from the corners of his eyes, but they always made him seem merry, rather than old.

And he always knew what was what.

Lizzie lowered her voice. "Answers. About the free traders."

"Now, missus, I been out of that ken for more than a score of years. Game's changed, it has."

"But you still have an ear to the sand. You still know more than any three men in this county about what's going on."

"I might know a thing or three."

"Then you know about the house at Redlap Cove? How it's come to me in my marriage settlement?"

"There's been some talk. High and low."

"How flattering. And what do you make of it?"

Maguire gave her a squinty-eyed assessment.

"Come Maguire, I'm past being shocked. Putting a barrel full of birdshot into Dan Pike rather put paid to any delicate sensibilities I might have had left."

His pale blue eyes twinkled merrily. "Been some talk about that as well."

"And how does it go?"

"You're a cool mort, they'll give you that."

"I'm flattered, but how will it all play out?"

"Well then, the way I see it, missus, you got two lays."

"Yes?"

"You can either abandon this ken—Redlap—or you can try to parlay with the gang running out of Redlap and take your cut."

"Simple enough. What's the rub?"

His face cracked into a smile. "Clever girl, you always were. Aye, there's a rub. Don't know as you'll want to parlay with them lot. Don't know as you can. T'weren't like the old days. These fellows aren't the usual run. Near as I can reckon, the Redlap gang are part of a sort of clearinghouse ken. Someone's running two, three large gangs at the same time, see. Powerful they are. Don't mind a gratuitous application of force, like. But then, from what I've heard, neither do you."

"Ah, but mine wasn't gratuitous. Dan Pike was housebreaking. I had ample justification."

"But now, they ain't so very likely to make a parlay, or offer you a cut, if you see what I mean."

"I'm afraid I do." If only she hadn't been so sure the housebreaker was the mole, McAlden. She might have had the presence of mind to simply offer the man a drink and a parlay. No. She was only fooling herself. And forgetting Dan Pike's loaded pistols. "So now, what do you advise I do?"

His eyes were positively glowing now. "Well, depends on what you want."

He didn't like these morning visits. He had never been very good at explaining himself. Especially when he didn't have good news. And he didn't have good news.

Still, best to take it like a man and get it over with. He gave his coat one last tug at the hem and smoothed his hands over his waistcoat. Nervous gesture that.

He was shown in directly, without being announced.

"What are you doing here in town?" the figure on the chair asked testily without greeting. "You're meant to be elsewhere—at Redlap."

"Good morning. I'm afraid a difficulty has arisen."

"Difficulty?"

"Yes. The house is still occupied."

"By you, I should hope. That was my instruction."

"Yes, well, no."

A hissed sound of impatience urged him to clarify. "I have not been able to take up residence. Even with Marlowe dead, Elizabeth continues to live in the house."

"Still prostrate with grief, and can't be moved? Ridiculous. Self-indulgent nuisance. You must get rid of her."

"As I said, she's become rather more than a nuisance."

"Are you deficient in understanding? I said to get rid of her. It ought to be easy enough to move one flighty young woman."

"We tried. She shot Dan Pike last night."

"Shot him? How?"

"I sent them in to frighten her. I thought she'd go easily enough. But she shot him."

"Is he dead?"

"No."

The silence that followed was not pleasant.

"Then, all things considered, perhaps it is time you shot back."

"I don't—"

"Or is it in nerve that you're so lacking?"

"No, I . . ."

"Get rid of her."

"How do you mean?"

"I don't care. And I don't care to know how. Just get it done. Only do it yourself, carefully this time. Don't leave any trace of connection back to you. Or me. Do you understand?"

"Yes, I understand."

Lizzie heard the bell on the front door and looked out her sitting room window, down over the threshold. It was too late in the day for visitors—Mr. Tupper had collected her in to eat another hearty, healthy dinner Mrs. Tupper had prepared just to tempt a few pounds onto her thinned frame. And she had told them to turn away all visitors.

It was Sir Ralston Cawdier and a small company of men. Lizzie felt her surprise as if it happened somewhere outside her own head. How strange. She had not expected the magistrate to trouble himself on her behalf regarding Dan Pike.

"Elizabeth Paxton Marlowe, if you please."

"One moment, please, sir, I'll see if she's at home."

Lizzie could hear Sir Ralston's deep gravelly voice from the entryway as she made her way down the upper corridor. ". . . not here on a social visit. I'll see her whether she's receiving or not."

"Sir, Mrs. Marlowe is still in mourning . . ."

"It's all right Mrs. Tupper, thank you." Lizzie took her time coming down the stairs. "Sir Ralston. Do come in. To what do we owe the honor of your," she searched for the correct word, "visit?"

"No visit, I'm sorry to say. I've come on business, and I'll come right to it." He turned to face her, but focused his eyes on a spot somewhere above her head. "Mrs. Elizabeth Paxton Marlowe, as magistrate of this county, I am here to inform you that someone has laid information against you for the murder of your husband, Captain Jameson Marlowe, late of this parish. You'll need to come with me."

There was a very long, absurd moment of silence while Lizzie grappled to understand. She looked at Mrs. Tupper, whose mouth stood agape, and then back at Sir Ralston, who continued to look at the wall. "I do not have the pleasure of understanding you, sir. What do you mean, murder? My husband was killed on active duty in the navy."

"I am arresting you for . . ." He consulted a folded piece of foolscap from his large pocket. "For conspiring to murder, or have murdered, your husband."

"But that's preposterous. He died while aboard ship out of Portsmouth, or somewhere." She waved her hand in the direction of the Channel. She couldn't recall where the letter from the Admiralty had said he'd died, if it had mentioned it at all.

"Be that as it may, you'll have to come with me." He clamped a meaty fist around her upper arm.

She slid out of his grasp, more indignant than angry. "Sir Ralston. Unhand me this instant. This is preposterous."

"Information has been laid against you, and that's all there is to it. Now, you'll come along, Mrs. Marlowe, or the sheriff will cuff your hands." He reached for her again.

"No! God damn it. Let go of me. Tupper. Tupper! Do something!"

For a portly man, Sir Ralston's grip was surprisingly strong. He hauled her easily towards the front door, despite Mrs. Tupper clinging to his other arm like a terrier, pulling in the opposite direction.

"Damn it, woman," he shouted at the housekeeper while not letting Lizzie loose by so much as an inch. "Let go, or by God I'll haul you in as well, on a charge of disrupting the peace."

At his call, the men from outside entered and took her by the arms, one to a side, while Sir Ralston held off Mrs. Tupper. There was nothing either Mr. or Mrs. Tupper could do, though Lizzie was touched to note Mrs. Tupper had to be restrained by her husband from doing Sir Ralston any further harm. She had the impression of watching them from afar, at a great remove. It was unreal and all so thoroughly, entirely ridiculous. A very, very bad joke.

"Where are you taking her?" Tupper asked.

"Dartmouth Gaol. Murder is a capital offense."

"Sir," Tupper reasoned. "There must be some mistake. My mistress—"

"No mistake."

Cold reality descended with bruising speed. Lizzie began to feel a desperate pressure in her chest.

"Sir Ralston, you've known me all your life. Everyone knows me. Everyone knows I could never . . ."

"Aye, everyone knows you, and has heard your views on marriage often enough to wonder why you'd marry a man like Captain Marlowe, when it was clear you had no liking for the man. You stated publicly you should like to become a widow."

"How dare you! My affections for Captain Marlowe are none of your business, nor are they anyone else's business."

"They're my business right enough when someone lays information against you for conspiring to murder."

"Who would do such a thing? Who would tell you such lies that you'd believe them? Captain Marlowe was killed on duty— on his ship! How could I possibly be responsible for that? Did you check these ridiculous allegations with the Admiralty? Are you entirely mad?"

Sir Ralston ignored both her logic and her insult, and dragged her out the door. "You'll be held in Dartmouth Gaol until the Assizes, yours being a capital case. That'll be sometime after the Quarter Sessions at Midsummer."

"Midsummer isn't till the end of June," Mrs. Tupper blustered. "That's near a month away!"

"That's right. Doesn't matter when to me. But it will give you plenty of time and money to spend on your defense. Come along."

But her legs, which had gotten steadier from all the long hours of walking, refused to work. She couldn't have walked anywhere, much less to gaol.

No matter. They frog-marched her off to the wagon, where they bound her wrists together with iron handcuffs. Oh yes, the proper treatment for such an unrepentant, dangerous criminal such as herself.

God Almighty. First Jamie and now this. Surely the angels must hate her to serve her such abuse.

Chapter 15

Mrs. Tupper had taken to fussing like a duckling to water. "I've got you a warm meat pie and then a few other things from our larder, good cheese and fresh bread. Baked this morning for you. Is that warm enough?"

"It doesn't matter."

"You need to have good warm food, what with the damp, but the distance . . . And I don't half like that Mrs. Carter, down the Turks Head. Always asking after people's business, though she does make a decent eel pie."

Lizzie let the rest of the words wash over her like the warm ale Mrs. Tupper had also provided. Just as the housekeeper had each day at precisely four o'clock in the afternoon, without complaint. Every day Mrs. Tupper brought more and more food, and with every passing day Lizzie ate less and less of it.

The stouthearted housekeeper kept up a constant stream of chatter, too, as if her bright words and bright, determinedly optimistic attitude could lighten the hideous darkness of the gaol. Or the hideous darkness inside Lizzie's heart.

At night it was so dark she could see nothing, only hear the incessant sound of dripping water and small scurrying feet. She'd never felt so close and utterly confined. Her fingertips were nearly raw from the way she scratched compulsively and futilely against the stone. That was one of the things she had liked at home, at Glass Cottage. The house was so open: there were no curtains to cut off the light and the view. In almost every room in the house she could look out over the sea in the moonlight. Lizzie shut her eyes and tried to see the image. The moon making a trail of gold across the water to the shore.

It had been fifteen days now. Fifteen days and fifteen even longer nights of being closed up in this tomb. The air was somehow stale, rank, and damp all at the same time. Only the pests were fresh and lively. They made her skin crawl, but at night the constant discomfort of their bites kept her awake and from slipping into the nightmare world of sleep.

Aside from the turnkey and Mrs. Tupper, the vermin were the most reliable company she had. Mama, poor Mama, had come eleven days ago, her eyes red with weeping and agonized frustration.

"We are doing everything we can. I have engaged solicitors, but the magistrate says the evidence is incontrovertible, though he will not tell us what it is! I am out of my mind with worry for you, child."

If the county magistrate would not answer the questions of Squire Paxton and Lady Theodora, there was obviously little that could be done. And it was too distressing, both for Mama, and for herself, to see the mutual confirmation of hopelessness in their eyes.

Papa did not come. Instead, Mama had brought dear Celia as her aide and comfort. Poor, appalled Celia grasped Lizzie's hands through the bars as she apologized over and over again for her inadvertent part in this horrible mess.

"They made me tell them, Lizzie." Celia's distress was so acute, her eyes were shining wet with tears. "Sir Ralston said they knew what you had said to me about wanting to be a widow and that I had best cooperate, lest I find myself charged with conspiracy with you."

After she had sent Mama and Celia away, with entreaties not to return to this ghastly place, she had no more visitors.

The turnkey had put her in a "private" cell, away from the other unfortunate guests. Whether this was due to her being a lady, Mama or Mrs. Tupper's ability to pay bribes, or her elevated status as the only alleged murderer in gaol, she had no idea.

She could hear the other prisoners sometimes, their voices echoing down the dank corridor with their raucous calls when the turnkey gave them her uneaten food. After he had first taken his fill, of course. At least her unintended beneficence saw that Mrs. Tupper was treated kindly and with respect.

The private cell was undoubtedly cleaner than the communal one—she had only her own filth to deal with, but it was isolated. No one to talk to, no one to watch, no one to help take one's mind off one's own seemingly insurmountable problems. No one to ask the questions that careened around in her mind unanswered.

No one had an answer. And slowly, it seemed to matter less and less. A sort of peaceful numbness was finally taking over. It helped when she stopped eating any of the food. But unfortunately, that's when Mrs. Tupper had taken to fussing.

Poor woman. She was simply indefatigable. She wouldn't give up.

"And here's a fresh dress and also fresh smallclothes." She pushed a bundle of material into Lizzie's hands. "I've had more stays made that lace in the front, the way you like. And I thought to bring another blanket. I'll just hold it up now so you can change into fresh things."

Poor woman. She must stink, though Mrs. Tupper brought clean clothes and took away the dirty every other day. Probably burned them once she'd cleared the walls. But Mrs. Tupper kept on, even though Lizzie told her it didn't matter. None of it would matter soon.

How cruelly ironic she had fought so hard for independence. Her death would certainly achieve that now. She'd be dead but then she'd be with Jamie. She clung hard to that thought, willing the questions, the doubts away.

She would be with Jamie.

"Now, miss. I'm not going to stand for this. I'm not. You need a change. Here." And Mrs. Tupper went to work, bullying and shoving through the bars to get her out and into her clothes, despite her indifference. But it was better than being alone.

"I want you to try and perk up now, Mrs. Marlowe."

So no-nonsense was Mrs. Tupper, amidst such incredible nonsense. Nothing could ever make sense again.

"We've seen to a solicitor, your mama, Lady Theodora, and I, though it was difficult to get one who wasn't in the magistrate's pockets. And such awfully large pockets they do seem to have around here. But he's to come, the solicitor, and we'll get this sorted out. You just have to be strong. And eat. And use the comb a little more regularly." She began to yank a comb through the tangles.

The sharp tugs of pain were slipping under the numbness.

"Leave it go, Mrs. Tupper. I'll do it. Just leave it go."

Marlowe and his crew had a fine few weeks of it, bringing *Defiant* up channel from Plymouth. They taken the sloop down to the Channel Islands on a sort of shakedown cruise, but also to advertise themselves there to the smuggling confraternity. The weather held fair, and the sail had become a pleasure, the way it had been when he was a boy and had hours of summer to spend exploring the river and surrounding shoreline. Lizzie would have loved it. Maybe when all this was over, he could find a bit of time to take her out.

And now they'd brought *Defiant* up right and tight into the Dart, and snugged up against the quay, to do the same advertising of themselves in Dartmouth, where the waterfront was always abuzz with the latest smuggling gossip.

And soon enough a conversation came to his ear.

"Ho, there, Bob, how you bin keeping? They 'ad a rum doing up to the magistrates a while back. Should 'a seen it, Bob. You see it lad? The old beak Ralston Cawd'yer come wif a company o' men. Marched over the hill to Redlap, well o'er a fortnight ago it were now."

"What'd the magistrate want with the business up to Redlap? Thought he were in the game?"

"Nothin' to do with the trade. Murder it were. A lady."

Bob sent a long, low whistle through his teeth. "Someone kilt a lady? Who?"

"No, t'other way round. Fingered the lady for the drop, they 'ave. They do say she were a rum mort—a game one, cool as water—ne'er a pucker tho' they gave 'er the sheriff's bracelets. Offed her 'usband they do say, for his money."

"They'll have some Scragg'em Fair with 'er. Ain't off'n they hang a Lady."

"I'd pay money to see a hanging like that."

Marlowe grabbed Hugh and shoved him back aboard *Defiant* and down the companionway to the cabin.

"Captain?"

"Jesus God, damn it all to hell! Lieutenant, we have an abrupt change of our plans."

"Sir? But why?"

"For fuck's sake! Didn't you hear?"

"The story? They've taken someone up, if I understand correctly. These rogues are worse than sailors with their lingo."

"Not someone, you jackass. Lizzie. They've taken up my wife."

"For what? Sarcasm?"

"Murder. They've clapped her in irons and taken her off. They've arrested her for murdering me!"

In the morning the turnkey took Lizzie to a small room with a table and two chairs. And a window. The light was nearly blinding, making her cover her eyes after the constant half dark of the cell. She groped her way closer, anxious for even the smallest trace of fresh air. My God, it was so clean and warm. She drank in a grateful lungful.

She grasped the bars set over the window, set deep into the whitewashed stone walls, a reminder she was still imprisoned.

"What goes on here?" she asked the turnkey. Perhaps Mama really had managed to hire a solicitor.

"Priest is here for you, miss."

"A priest?" Good Lord. Had he come for her final absolution? Her hand rose of its own volition to her throat. She could feel the pulse as it beat under her fingers, strong and hectic. She hadn't even been to trial yet. Why on earth should they be sending her a priest?

As her heartbeat accelerated, she realized this was going to be harder than she thought. The pleasant numbness was rapidly eroding in the face of the harsh reality. It was one thing to decide to die, but it was quite another to have the killing actually begin.

No. She was panicking. She closed her eyes and took a deep breath. Her heart hammered away in her throat, every beat, every breath reminding her she was still very much alive. This strange visit was likely just part of the whole infernally slow, stately progress of the law.

The priest came into the room alone. His long black robes swirled about his feet as he turned to make sure the door was shut behind him. His head was bowed and his face shadowed by the wide, flat brim of his hat. He was wearing the short, old-fashioned bob wig of his profession. She could see skin tanned pink at the nape of his neck.

She looked away from the intimacy of her observation and tried to refocus on the absurdity of a priest being sent to her. Anyone who knew her knew she didn't care a fig for preaching and all that. God was one thing, but she had never been a regular churchgoer. Rector Marlowe was all right, she supposed, but the rest was all a load of priggish rubbish, the lot of it.

So she was completely unprepared when the priest stepped close and whispered, "Lizzie."

She nearly screamed, in fright and relief and joy, but his hand was already there, pressing hard and strong and alive, so alive, against her mouth.

"Hush," he hissed fiercely as he pressed his lips to her ear. His eyes skated in warning to the closed door.

Jamie. Her Jamie. Her eyes strained to look at him, to cover each and every last inch of his dear face. He wasn't dead. The deep ocean-wide gray eyes she'd thought she would never see again were here, now, in front of her.

Her hands were on his face, touching him, sliding along the smooth skin of his freshly shaved cheeks, delving back into the newly shorn, bristly hairs of his head beneath the wig. She pushed the hideous thing off.

"Jamie."

"It's all right Lizzie, I'm here. I've got you. Hush. I've got you." As if he needed as much reassurance as she. As if he needed to hold her as much as she needed to hold him. Desperately.

She clung to him like a barnacle, holding him ever so tight. As if she could never again let him go.

And then his mouth was on hers, covering her lips, and nothing else mattered. Nothing but the heat and light that his kiss brought. Nothing but the bruising pleasure of his body pressed hard against her.

He nuzzled her neck and held her close against his body. She could feel the hectic beating of both their hearts. "Tears, Lizzie? For me?"

"You're alive."

"So I am."

A strangled little hiccup burbled out of her, and she gave

him what must have been a watery smile. She wiped her face hastily on her sleeve.

"Oh, Jamie." It was better than anything to be held against his warm, solid body. "I don't suppose this would be an opportune time to tell you, I missed you a great deal more than I had planned."

He kissed her forehead. "I heartily return the sentiment."

"Oh, Jamie. What have you done to your hair?"

"I cut it." His mouth turned down in apology.

"It looks awful. If this is what happens to you when you die, God needs a new barber." She wasn't making any sense, she knew, because all she could think about was running her hands against the ragged edges of his hair. It looked like it had been done with hedge shears.

He tried to hold her still before him with his eyes. "Everything's changed."

"Yes. Thank God. You're alive." She ran her hands over his face, across the strong plains of his cheekbones and down his smooth shaven cheeks. She couldn't stop touching him. She ran her hands over his shoulders, down his arms, hugging and letting go, but never stopping. She couldn't overcome her need to feel his long, taut body warm and alive under her hands.

Her mouth followed, kissing him and sliding down his neck to put her lips against the strong pulse at the base of his throat. To seek out his scent—bay rum. And it was there: a base note covered by unfamiliar layers of wool and salt and fish. And liquor. How impossibly strange that he should smell of fish oil and cognac. How curious.

It made her wonder what *she* smelled like. Good heavens. "I'm sorry. I shouldn't stand so close. I'll probably give you lice." Her forced laugh sounded rusty to her ears.

He smiled but didn't step away. "Mrs. Tupper said she feared you were being bitten to pieces. She's had to boil your clothes in lye soap."

"Mrs. Tupper? Then she knows you're alive. She'll be so relieved. When, how did she find you?"

"I can't explain. I came because . . . because I had to and because Mrs. Tupper was certain you'd gone . . . well, she was very concerned for you. She said you were wasting away and had awful dark circles under your eyes." He cradled her face in his hands and frowned into her eyes. "As though you'd gotten used to staring at death."

"Mrs. Tupper said that? To you? When?"

"Lizzie, you must listen to me. I can't explain everything. I'm sorry, but you must hang on. You must bear it for just a little while longer. We're working to have you freed. We're working very hard, so you must not despair. Do you understand?"

"No. You must tell me everything. What happened to you? Where have you been?"

"Love, I'm sorry. I can't explain."

Something was wrong. Something was awfully terribly wrong. Her fingers snatched at him to catch a fistful of his coat.

"What do you mean? How did you survive? How did you get here, how did you get in? Why in the world are you disguised? Especially like this? You don't know, or you won't tell me?"

"Lizzie, please." He held her hands between his own and spoke quietly. "You must understand. You must bear it for a little while longer."

Her heart went cold inside her chest, as if it had been torn and all the heat was leaking out of her.

"No! You can't mean that. You can't. I can't bear it. I won't. Not even for another hour. You can't ask me to. You must take me out of here. You must."

"Lizzie." He held her hands steady, warming her suddenly clammy palms between his own. He spoke very quietly. Too quietly. His voice was unsteady. "You must stay."

She wrenched her hands away. No. She wouldn't listen.

This was all very, very wrong. She had to move. She had to get out of here. Jamie had to take her out of here. She bolted towards the door.

He engulfed her in his arms, trying to hold her still. "Lizzie. Please."

She couldn't make sense of it all, but now she fought him, nearly clawing at him in her need to get out of the room. Get away from this awful, awful feeling. This newly unbearable pain.

"Please," she begged, "you have to get me out. You're alive. Tell them. Tell them and get me out!" She could hear the hysteria, the sharp wounded edge of her voice.

"I won't let them touch you, Lizzie. I promise. I promise," Jamie whispered into her ear, his voice harsh and raw. His arms were iron bands holding her tight, making her crave the comfort and warmth of his body even as she fought to get away.

"How can you promise that? You have to let me out. You can't leave me here." She was shouting now. That was it. She should make so much noise the turnkey would come, and he would see that Jamie was alive, and they would have to let her out. "Let me out."

"I can't. Jesus, Lizzie. I can't." His face, his eyes were nearly black with anguish. His voice was cracked with it.

"But how could I kill you when you're here, alive and well? You're not dead. You're not dead."

Footsteps sounded in the corridor, and then the jangling of keys could be heard on the other side of the door.

Jamie crushed her hard against his chest and whispered into her ear. "I can't explain. And you can't tell anyone you've seen me."

"No. How can you ask me that? No!"

"Jesus, Lizzie, I can't. I can't. There's too much at stake. You must be patient. You must trust me. Soon. I promise. I swear it."

But nothing he said in such a tormented voice could reassure her.

"You can't mean to leave me here. You can't." He was pulling back, trying to set her away. She held tight to his coat with desperate, clutching fingers. He was forced to pry them away and hold her hands together at the wrists.

"Lizzie, listen to me! Listen. It's only for now. I promise. I promise. Guard!"

She twisted helplessly in his relentless grasp, her frantic strength ebbing away. "No, Jamie, no. Please, please don't leave me. Please. I'm begging you. Don't leave me."

"I'm sorry, Lizzie." He eased her down as her legs gave out, and she collapsed onto the cold stone floor. He pressed his lips to hers one last time. "Forgive me. I'm sorry. I'm so bloody sorry."

And then the door opened, and he was gone.

"Jamie. Jamie!" She could only say his name and pound her fists into the floor. Over and over, until her throat was raw and her hands bled.

Marlowe's hands were shaking by the time he made the gatehouse. He all but staggered out of the stone building and around the corner until he could lean his back against a wall and scrape some air back into his lungs. Thank God, he had told McAlden not to accompany him.

He, and he alone, had done that to Lizzie. She was utterly damaged, perhaps almost destroyed from being shut up in that place. He could not have caused her any more or less pain if he had taken a stick and beaten her.

How on earth had he allowed this to happen?

He never imagined, not in a million years, this would, or could, have come to pass. The stench, the filth, the waste. And Lizzie, in the midst of it. Damn his eyes. She was the wreck of herself, like a fallen building with only the outline of a few walls standing.

She would have been better off if he had not given in to his damned tormenting guilt and gone to see her. She might have carried on well enough without his bloody interference. But now he had destroyed every shred of trust she had ever had in him. He had chosen his country and career over his family, and Lizzie was paying the price, the very high cost of his duty. She would never forgive him.

And he never told her what he had gone in there to say.

That help was coming. Through the diligence of Lady Theodora and Mrs. Tupper, and the belated influence of the Admiralty, he had managed to secure the offices of a barrister of high repute. It helped to alleviate his crushing guilt at having done this to her, however inadvertently. It assuaged his conscience, but it did nothing to silence it.

And he had not told her he loved her. It had been there, on the tip of his tongue, but her obvious pain, her obvious feeling of betrayal, combined with his own overwhelming regret, had shut up his mouth. He had no right to love her, if this is what his love did to her.

He got himself under control, found a hack a few blocks away, and met McAlden in a little-used back lane he knew near his father's church.

"Nice togs," was all McAlden said, as he climbed aboard.

"Please, Hugh." He felt too wretched to even joke.

"Oh, aye, sir," he answered easily enough. "I got us a job. Unfortunately, things seemed to have livened up now, with her in gaol."

"Bloody rotten bastards."

"Well, now we're in with them. We're to sail to Guernsey on the morrow, pick up a little something or two, and sail back under cover of night." McAlden shook his head. "It'll be a queer feeling to pray our own navy won't blast us out of the water as we sail by."

"Be a devilish way to die, wouldn't it?" Marlowe agreed with vicious humor. "Poor Lizzie'll have to bury me twice."

McAlden frowned. "Was it that bad?"

"Worse." Marlowe scrubbed a hand through his hair. "I . . . I never thought I would have to choose between them. Between my wife and my mission. It's all very well to think of orders, to say I can't get you out, but you'll be fine, and then leave. You didn't see her." Marlowe closed his eyes, but he couldn't blot out the image of Lizzie in that wretched place. "She's not a sailor or a soldier. She didn't sign up for this. She wasn't trained for this. But the only reason she's locked up is because I haven't finished this bloody godforsaken mission and blown these smuggling bastards out of the water yet. We can't even find them properly!"

"Well, they've a network, haven't they?"

"Such a network they can have my wife arrested and charged for murder, and I have to sit back and watch! And I have to leave her in a louse-ridden gaol, exposed to typhus fevers and God knows what other putrid diseases, so I can use her just as mercilessly until I can give the Admiralty and the Prime Minister what they want."

McAlden stared grimly back. "Stands to reason. After all, they've already done murder itself, so what's a trumped-up charge on a woman? Or had you forgotten they killed Frank?"

"No," Marlowe growled. "I bloody well have not." But all he could think of was Lizzie. And all he could do was regret.

By the time they had ridden back to the Redlap he was in a foul mood, which was not helped at all by Mrs. Tupper's news.

"You saw her, then?" the housekeeper asked. "Did she promise to eat the food? I can't like you taking a chance like that, going in there, but if she'll eat the food, and get stronger, then it'll have been worth it."

"I hope so, Mrs. Tupper. I hope so. We'll have her out." His words were spoken with his typical captain-like confidence, but the words sounded hollow to his ears. Because Lizzie hadn't believed him.

The thought of her was like shrapnel in his chest—an omnipresent pain.

"Well, thank God for that. But another problem has arisen. Someone else has arrived."

"Who?'

"That cousin of yours, Mr. Wroxham, moved into the big house. Came this afternoon, valet and all, said he was to watch over the place for you. I felt I had to let him in as Mr. Tupper was out, over at the Dawson Farm, about the leaking roof tiles."

"Damn his eyes. Bloody fucking idiot. We'll kick his skinny arse out at first light."

It had seemed simple enough in the beginning, to keep the house empty, damn it, but instead there seemed to be a continuous procession of potential tenants. First poor Lizzie and now bloody Wroxham. They'd be doing his cousin a favor by kicking him out. If he stayed who knew when he'd end up in gaol on a trumped-up charge of conspiring with Lizzie to murder his cousin.

"Mr. Tupper's compliments, sir," the housekeeper interrupted his thoughts. "But Tupper did say it's not the first time Mr. Wroxham's been to live in the house."

"Tupper said that?"

"Ejected him once before. Right after you first left, moved right in like he owned the place, Tupper said. But he came back again twice: once to visit Mrs. Marlowe, and then again today."

What possible use could his impecunious cousin have for squatting at Glass Cottage? Of course, it was entirely possible his pockets were completely to let and he had nowhere else to go. But surely he could have stayed at his parents' house in town? They had a beautiful town house in the fashionable section of Dartmouth. Surely he would have been more comfortable there than in an empty remote seaside cottage?

It didn't make much sense, and so it bore watching. Nearly everything at Glass Cottage bore careful watching.

"We'll let him stay," he decided. "But we'll want to keep a very close eye on my cousin, shall we? Very close."

"Aye, sir," Mrs. Tupper responded. "I'll see to it, sir."

Marlowe rubbed his chest absently and went back to worrying about Lizzie.

CHAPTER 16

Lizzie ate her food with a vengeance, stuffing her mouth with every last crumb, though it nearly made her sick. She did everything now with a vengeance. It seemed to have become her new reason for being. Morning, noon, and night, she had one and one thought only—revenge.

Anger snaked through her lungs and kept her breath tight and hard. She was such a fool. And she had thought *him* the foolish, trusting one. And all the while he had been a liar and a swindler. And somehow he had gotten her mixed up in murder and set her up to take the bloody four-foot fall for it all.

If she ever saw him again she'd kill him. Such wretched irony.

Bloody bastard.

But she wasn't going to die. Because he wasn't dead.

She pinched her eyes shut to stave off the headache that came every time she tried to sort it all out. It was so hard not to believe the evidence of her memory—the coffin, the funeral, the bloody letter from the Admiralty.

The Admiralty. Sir Edward Foster's assertion that a trip to the Antipodes was unlikely in such a time of war came flooding back, ringing in her ear as if he were next to her repeating the words. Jamie had lied about that as well, no doubt. Bastard.

"Mrs. Marlowe?"

It was the turnkey with the local solicitor, Mr. Benchley.

Lizzie stood up and brushed off her skirts as best she could as the turnkey opened the lock to let her out. Mrs. Tupper still brought a freshly cleaned skirt and chemisette or gown every day, even though Lizzie had refused to see her, but the garment always grew soiled with the grime and damp of Dartmouth Gaol's less than salubrious accommodations.

"Mrs. Marlowe," Mr. Benchley began, indicating the tall, dignified man behind him. "I have brought to you my Lord Edwin deHavilland, Serjeant of King's Bench, London. He will argue your case before the court at the Assizes."

"My Lord." Lizzie sloughed off the slattern and executed a gracious curtsey. This man was to save her life.

He didn't speak to her, but to the air around himself, as if it would naturally leap to his bidding.

"I require a room with a table and chair, preferably two, and good light."

And of course, both the turnkey and the warden were delighted to show so august a visitor a private chamber. It wasn't often that a Serjeant of the King's Bench in London came to Dartmouth Gaol. He must have deep pockets. Or perhaps, somehow, she still did.

"Now, then, Mrs. Marlowe. I am deHavilland, and I shall be arguing your case." He consulted a leather folio in front of him. "Mr. Benchley has done a thorough job of acquainting me with the particulars, but I should like to speak to you directly. This is a capital case, Mrs. Marlowe, and while I shall, of course, argue that you are not guilty of this crime, I should very much like to be apprised of the truth. Did you kill your husband, or conspire with person or persons unknown to have him killed?"

She had not expected such bluntness.

"No." The word was awkward and forced.

"I ask, Mrs. Marlowe, not because I care either way, but because if I know all the circumstances, then I am prepared and can argue a stronger case. I do not like to be surprised by inconvenient facts."

"Well then, my lord, you may be astonished to know you are the first person in this entire benighted, corrupt exercise who is even remotely interested in the facts. And I have some facts of my own to seek. How was it that I was charged with conspiring to murder in the first place?"

Lord deHavilland's nostrils tightened as if he had encountered a very unpleasant odor. Doubtless it was her, but she had to give him points for gentlemanly stoicism.

"The misunderstanding seems to rest with the magistrate."

"Sir Ralston?"

"Indeed. He indicates that a person, a gentleman, gave evidence against you. We are not entitled to know who that gentleman is, nor what evidence he gave. However, when your apparently well-known views on the marriage were made known, well . . . You became suspect."

"A gentleman? This would mean someone influential."

"Yes."

"It seems I have a made a very powerful enemy."

"Indeed, ma'am. But I am sure this can be laid to some minor property dispute. Such vindictive actions always turn out to have so little basis in fact. People out to make some money."

She hadn't thought of that—this whole misunderstanding might have come from her plans for Glass Cottage and the Redlap farm estate. In her quest to make changes and improvements, she might have stepped on someone's toes. But her plans for the Redlap estate stepped on the free traders' toes as well. And perhaps even the very long toes of the Admiralty. And then there was Jamie. Such a lot of injured feet from which to choose.

"And as to my first question, madam?"

"My lord, you should know I definitely did not kill, nor did I conspire to kill, my husband, for the simple reason and inconvenient fact that he is still very much alive."

Lord deHavilland cut his eyes swiftly to Mr. Benchley, who shook his head sadly.

"Mrs. Marlowe has not lately been herself, sir. The effects of her incarceration, you understand. Captain Marlowe's body was brought home and buried by his own father, the Reverend Doctor Marlowe, in the churchyard on May the twenty-fourth."

"Is she mad?" The Serjeant returned his sharp gaze to Lizzie as if she were a scientific specimen, but something in his dry tone gave Lizzie pause.

"I'm not mad," she articulated very clearly, "I'm livid."

"Mrs. Marlowe, please . . . ," the solicitor began to cajole.

"No. I am not mad. I know my husband," she spat the word out, "is not dead because he came here, to this room, in this prison not three days past. He was not a figment of my imagination. He came here disguised as a priest, and there must be a record of his passing through the gates. There must be, and if he bribed them to have his name omitted, then you can bribe them into revealing it. And you will find that no parish or church in the district sent out a priest to the prison to comfort and succor me, because it was in fact not a priest, but my husband, who is alive and very clearly up to no good. And I want some answers from him, or barring him, the Admiralty, who are the ones who told me he was dead."

DeHavilland let the echoes of Lizzie's raised voice subside off the walls before he spoke.

"That is an extraordinary story, Mrs. Marlowe."

"The truth often is quite extraordinary, my lord."

DeHavilland looked at her for a very long while before he

spoke. "Call the warden." He instructed the solicitor. "And you," he ordered Lizzie, "will stand there, next to the window, quietly. Amuse yourself with this little glimpse of the outside. I believe the dogwood tree is in bloom."

The warden came and the question was put to him. He professed his ignorance on the subject and, in turn, called the greasy turnkey.

"Aye, sirs. He come Tuesday last. Said he come to hear her confession, her being a papist and all.

"What a bouncer. I am not a papist."

"Mrs. Marlowe, you will refrain from interjecting, please." Lord deHavilland readdressed the turnkey. "What was this priest's name?"

"Dunno."

The barrister spoke with the patience of a panther. "Have you no record?"

The book from the front gate was finally brought in and consulted. Impatience and rage roiled around inside her while they looked. And looked.

Finally they decided—there was no signature. No name. No record.

And strangely, Lord deHavilland did not seem at all surprised. How damnably, bloody curious.

Lord deHavilland dismissed the men and turned back to Lizzie.

"Let us assume, Mrs. Marlowe, for the sake of argument, as there is no evidence to the contrary, that your supposition is true. That Captain Marlowe is alive. How do you think I might prove the existence of a man who clearly wants to leave no record, and who, if I may make another assumption, is patently not willing to have his identity revealed in order to free you?"

Lizzie swallowed the bitter tonic of humiliation. "Your assumption, my lord, is correct. Which is why I would start with the body."

"You have a very agile mind, Mrs. Marlowe," he said by way of a compliment. "Mr. Benchley indicated the body of your late husband was buried in the local churchyard?"

"Saint Savior's, milord."

"Thank you, Benchley." He leveled his dark stare at Lizzie. "You yourself were there, I understand."

"Yes, but if he had really died at sea, the way they told me in that letter, they never would have sent a body. They would have pitched him over the side as he deserved."

"Mrs. Marlowe! Such unguarded words can only hurt your case." The solicitor was shocked.

She waved his niceness away with a flick of her hand. "My point being, whoever is in that grave is not my husband, and I want you to prove it. If I were a Serjeant of King's Bench, I should start asking questions of the Admiralty."

They came back at dawn. Lizzie was awake. She was always awake well before dawn, staring up through the darkness, waiting for the first glimpses of daylight to filter through the tiny, bar-covered window set high in the wall above her head.

The barrister, Lord deHavilland, came with his servant.

"Come along then, Mrs. Marlowe."

"Where are we going?"

"Out of here, to begin with. You've been set free."

Lizzie stumbled on the smooth stone floor. How could it have been that easy? "Free? From gaol?"

"Yes. Here, put this on." He took a dark woolen cloak from the servant and passed it to her. "There's a chill fog this morning."

And then they were outside, in the damp air and walking through the high iron gates and across the empty stone courtyard to an unmarked carriage. Lizzie had to resist the urge to run, in case there was some mistake, in case they should try to force her back, but the yard remained deserted. They were completely alone. No one, not her parents or even Mr. and Mrs. Tupper, awaited her release.

Well, she could hardly blame Mrs. Tupper. Not after the way Lizzie had refused to see her in the wake of Jamie's visit. She oughtn't have done so. Mrs. Tupper was the one person who had been entirely steadfast and loyal, and Lizzie had spurned her help. She ought to be grateful Lord deHavilland had come at all. And she was grateful, immensely so, but her overwhelming emotion was a sort of numb relief.

But she was wrong. The carriage door was opened by one of Lord deHavilland's impeccable servants, and there was Mama, drawing Lizzie into her lily-of-the-valley-scented embrace.

"Oh, my child."

It was heaven to release herself from thought for just one fleeting moment and give herself over to her mother's care as she if she still were a child. But Lizzie would not give herself more than a moment. Any more and she might give her mother lice.

"Oh, goodness, just look at you." Mama peered at Lizzie's borrowed cloak and bedraggled clothing, and fluttered a lace handkerchief up to her nose. "You poor thing. We'll have a bath prepared, straightaway."

Lord deHavilland joined them and they pulled away just as a light drizzle began to fall, muffling the sounds of the city and wrapping them in a sort of benign anonymity. The carriage was a comfortable, well-appointed barouche with glass windows in front. It was light and airy, and for the first time, Lizzie did not seem to mind the closed carriage. After the weeks without sunlight, it seemed positively expansive.

But there were still unanswered questions. Lizzie hoped that deHavilland would finally have some answers. "How did this all come about?"

"A simple visit to the Admiralty offices at Portsmouth. The report was there for anyone to see. Killed by a falling spar whilst aboard his ship. His head hit the deck, and that was an end to it. Witnessed by several officers and seamen. All very aboveboard."

Exactly as she had expected, but still a lie. "And the coffin they sent to Saint Savior's?"

"A simple mixup, I'm afraid. The Admiralty wished to offer their most humble apologies for the unfortunate error. And they . . . well I'm afraid they don't know where the body is. Officer in charge, Lieutenant . . ." He consulted his notes. "Here it is, Lieutenant McAlden's correspondence indicated they're not used to having bodies brought ashore. Common practice is to bury their dead at sea, so they've little practice in sending bodies home for burial. A simple error."

"Lieutenant McAlden?" Here was something that could not be coincidence. "Did you meet him in person? Tall, ruddy-faced blond man. Blue eyes, handsome?"

"I did not meet him. We communicated through correspondence. Are you acquainted?"

"Lieutenant Hugh McAlden? Is he currently with the navy?" Her mind boggled. The lies—they were all around her, everywhere she turned. No one could be trusted. She looked again at deHavilland as he consulted some paper from his valise. How much did *he* know, with all his correspondence with the Admiralty? It was bound to be more than he was letting on.

"I believe that's correct. And are you acquainted?"

"Oh, yes. Lieutenant McAlden and I are well acquainted. It was very good of him to assist in this way. I shall have to thank him personally." The audacity of Jamie and his men was astounding. Bloody lying, conniving bastards. But it was at least a beginning, to understand the Admiralty was complicit in this entire mess.

Her suspicions must have shown on her face.

"Now, I must ask you, Mrs. Marlowe, for the sake of your health, not to persist in this dangerous belief that your husband still lives."

"My Lord, I *know* . . ."

"Please, Mrs. Marlowe. I beg you, no more." He passed a blue-veined hand over his face. "I have seen you freed from gaol, with all charges withdrawn. You are restored to your family. What more could a sensible woman want?"

Answers, damn his aristocratic nose. And no one had ever been foolish enough to call her sensible.

"Lizzie, darling, let it be."

"I daresay you are right." For now. Questioning Lord de-Havilland further, after all her had done to secure her release, would appear churlish. The carriage turned up the hill. "Where are we going?"

"I thought it best to take you home."

Lizzie peered through the rain. They weren't headed home. They were headed to Hightop Manor. When the carriage rolled to a stop in front of the portico, Lizzie was shaken by the remembrance of the last such carriage ride she had taken, to Mr. Harris's offices, with Jamie.

That bastard.

And just as Jamie had made to see her to the door, so too did Lord deHavilland.

"No, please, don't get up. Thank you, my lord, for all your assistance." She offered him her hand to shake. "I can't thank you enough. I'll see that the cloak is returned to you."

It must have been a foolish statement, for he gave her the first smile she had seen from him. "Oh, no, I insist."

Of course. Why would anyone want a cloak back from a vermin-infested woman? "Thank you again."

The butler, Cushing, having seen Lady Theodora inside, awaited Lizzie with his ubiquitous black taffeta umbrella.

"Miss Lizzie."

"Hello, Cushie. Thank you." She ducked up under the cover and then into the house.

"May I say, I'm pleased to see you, miss."

"Thanks, Cushie, you're a brick. Tell me, how bad is it? The smell?"

"Hardly noticeable, Miss Lizzie. We'll have you to rights in no time." Cushing's nostrils were pinched flat against his nose, though he strove manfully not to show it as he escorted her in through the door.

"That bad? Then don't stand too close. I'm sure I've bugs."

Cushing paused outside the drawing room. "Would you care to refresh yourself first?

"No, Cushie, I thank you. I'm afraid I've some business that can no longer be postponed. I can't stay."

"But, miss, we've had a bath prepared . . ."

"Lizzie, darling, what are you thinking? You cannot leave. You must stay. I told your father so. You must. People have been saying the most dreadful things."

"We know none of them are true, Mama. That's why I've been released, because I'm innocent. But you do understand it hardly matters whether I'm innocent. I'm sure my reputation has been ruined."

"Don't say that. I won't have it."

"I am sorry, Mama. But I think it best, for all of us, for your reputation as well as mine, that I leave." Lizzie kissed her mother's soft, scented cheek and turned to walk toward the back of the house.

"Darling, where are you going? Elizabeth?"

"To the stables."

"Yes, but where will you go?"

"To Glass Cottage. I'm going home."

There was, however, one other place she needed to visit. She needed to know how bad it really was. If she could even expect to be let into Glass Cottage. If she had a *right* to.

The cozy offices of Harris, Harris, and Harris enfolded her with all the warmth the brokerage could manage. Probably frightened she'd collapse in a fit of sobs again.

"Mrs. Marlowe. You honor me." Mr. Harris greeted her himself, and brought her in close to the fire laid in his private office. "I did not expect you so soon. What a delightful surprise."

"As I still have the stink of Dartmouth Gaol about me, I'm sure I'm less than delightful, but I find myself in the unhappy state of not understanding my present finances and . . . I've come to hear the bad facts, as it were. I need to know if I have any money left. Enough to get me a room, a bath, and a decent meal for the night."

"My dear Mrs. Marlowe." Mr. Harris's pale face registered deep concern as he offered her a chair. "It is all quite secure. Just as it should be. I made sure of that while you were pressed with this unfortunate business. Mr. Benchley indicated you were to be set free of all charges. I must say on behalf of Harris, Harris, and Harris, we are most pleased by your triumph. Such a dreadful business. Indeed, I think your husband must have had a premonition about his death. He most especially wanted to make sure, as his relic, you would be left quite secure."

"So I do have money?"

"Yes, of course, madam."

A vague feeling of relief lightened the tense set of her shoulders. "May I see the figures?"

"Certainly." He went to one of the honeycombed cabinets, opened one of the locked little doors, and drew out a ledger. "Murchison, fetch Mrs. Marlowe a dish of tea."

She looked at the books. It was all as Jamie had promised her. All of it, every last penny was accounted for. She looked again and again. To convince herself it was no sham.

It was so hard to conceive. Jamie was not actually dead. But legally he was dead, and this money, all of it, was hers. Still. The file held a number of copies of his will and of the legal transfer of all Jameson Marlowe's worldly goods and chattels to his relic, Elizabeth Genevieve Paxton Marlowe. There it was on ink and paper.

Remarkable. Alarming. And so . . . contradictory.

No other man of her acquaintance, no husband of any of her friends or relations, no father she'd ever come across, would have let her have complete and total control over so much money. And yet Jamie had.

Why? Why did he do this one thing, when all the rest were lies? He wasn't dead and yet he wanted everyone to think so. And he must have had help. Lieutenant McAlden and certainly the Tuppers. And perhaps the Admiralty.

She hated being a pawn. Hated the feeling of being used without her consent or understanding. The way men always treated women. As if they were all especially stupid children.

Well, if he wanted to be dead, then let him be.

"It is all my money?" She wanted to be very sure.

"Yes, Mrs. Marlowe. All quite secure." He smiled in encouragement.

"And the house?"

"The deed is quite secure, madam. I have a copy right here. Is there a difficulty?"

"No. No, it's just. I am rather in shock."

"How so?"

Because her husband was a liar. A bloody, charming, accomplished liar. That's what Jamie was. She'd bought everything he'd said without for a moment doubting his word. And all the while he'd been a faithless blackguard. And she was a stupid, gullible idiot.

Except, he had left her all his money.

Her mind boggled.

"Madame? If I may broach a rather delicate subject, I would advise you to make out your own will. Your husband was very particular about the disposal of his estate to you and I should so hate for anything to . . . go awry."

"Yes, one would so hate that." And things were, to her certain knowledge, bound to go very much further awry, once she'd sorted Jamie out. But in the meantime, there was no need to take it out of the helpful Mr. Harris's hide. "I couldn't agree more, Mr. Harris. Let us commence at once in preparing a draft."

Phineas Maguire was waiting for her at the back entrance to the brokers, lounging under the eaves as dry as a toad.

"Why, Mr. Maguire. How do you do?" She wasn't sure why she used the formal address with Maguire, especially as they were clearly alone in the alleyway. Perhaps it had to do with her newfound descent in society. She needed to treat any friends she still had with as much care as she could muster.

"Ma'am." He doffed his cap.

"What might I do for you?"

"Got it arsy-varsy, you have, ma'am. I come to do for you."

He made no sense. "For me?"

He crossed to the mews and led out two horses, Serendipity and a respectable but much less flashy black mare. "I'm going with ye. I've a mind to see what it's like out there at Redlap."

Lizzie didn't argue. However astonished she might be, she was grateful. It would be nice to have someone watching her back. In reality, she had no one else left to trust.

Even with the rain pouring down, they walked the horses. Lizzie wanted to go slowly and let the cold, clean rain wash over her, rinsing away the worst of the stench and grime before she made it back to her house. It seemed somehow important.

The house looked just as inviting, just as peaceful and embracing as it always had. It was the clouds beyond, gray and roiling at the edge of the sea, that made it look sinister and foreboding. And she was worried about her welcome.

The stables were more populated. The hunter Jamie had

ridden out to Glass Cottage so many weeks ago was still there. And Mr. Tupper's horse, a decent sturdy mount—no bloodlines to speak of, but still a good-looking, steady animal. And another pair, a matched set of high-blooded horses. A carriage pair. Curious.

"Do you think perhaps you could see to the stable, Mr. Maguire? There are rooms above. I could arrange it with my steward, if the job's to your liking."

"Right. There's a lad I know, right good with horses. I'll have him to help. You leave it to me."

Lizzie knew she was going to have to question it all later, but for now, she was too weary, wet, and cold to care to think about anything but the prospect of a hot, hot bath and some peace and quiet.

She walked around to the front door of Glass Cottage, just as she had that first day with Jamie. It seemed so long ago.

She let herself in, and the scent of lemon and beeswax flowed over her like a balm, a benediction. She stood still in the entry hall, marveling at the beauty built into the lines of the stairwell and walls. She may have come to hate him, but she still had this beautiful house because of Jamie.

There was a sound from the music room, well lit by all the long windows even with the gray drizzle. Good Lord. Wroxham was there. Reading the London newspaper, lounging sideways with his feet over the arm of one of the lovely bergère armchairs she had ordered with the lemony silk cushions.

"Get off my armchair with your boots!" She slapped his legs off. "What are you doing here?"

"Gad," he exclaimed. "How did . . . When did you arrive? You've been released?"

"As you see." She rubbed her temples, but it brought no relief, only the smell of her filthy hands closer to her nostrils. Here in this lovely, clean, fresh house the amalgamation of her grime overpowered her.

"Why have you come? Go away. Take yourself home." She shooed him away as she headed for the stairs. "I'm not at home to anyone right now."

She went immediately upstairs, completely out of charity with everyone, especially Mrs. Tupper. Had she been entertaining guests while Lizzie was in gaol?

And it was worse when she opened the door to her bedchamber.

She looked around the room. It was scattered with the evidence of masculine attire and living: a bootjack near the dressing room, a shaving stand nearer to the windows. For a long moment she was too confused. Had Jamie come back to live here? Without her?

But then the smell of a different eau de cologne drifted out from the dressing room. Sandalwood. Wroxham's scent. The bastard had taken up residence. In her bedroom.

"Mrs. Tupper!" she bawled at the top of her lungs. She was behaving like a fishwife, but she hardly cared. She yanked viciously on the bellpull.

A man appeared from the dressing room.

"Oh, I beg your pardon."

"Get out!" Another screech that left her throat feeling raw.

One look at her and he fled, just as Mrs. Tupper came bustling in.

"Mrs. Tupper, what is that bounder doing in my room?"

"Mr. Wroxham's valet?"

"Neither Mr. Wroxham nor his valet is welcome to move into my home. And into my chamber. How long has he been here?"

"Since you were taken, ma'am. Mr. Tupper thought it best to keep an eye on him. I'm sorry he's upset you."

As she had said to Lord deHavilland, she wasn't mad, she was livid. "Well, he is to leave. Now." She stormed into her dressing room. The evidence of his residence was everywhere. "I'd like a bath brought in here, while my bedchamber is cleaned and all of Lord Wroxham's possessions packed up. A very hot bath, Mrs. Tupper. And a metal comb. I have any number of stowaways from Dartmouth Gaol." She grimaced and scratched her head.

"Yes of course, ma'am. Right away. I have just the preparation. Something I brought back from the Antipodes. I'll get everything prepared right away."

Even tired, her brain latched on to the words.

"Antipodes, really? Did you actually sail there during your tenure at sea? With Captain Marlowe?"

"Yes, ma'am. Only he was Lieutenant then."

"Ah, so he'd already been to the Antipodes. How nice he was able to give his lies some flavor of truth."

"Ma'am?"

"Your master Captain Marlowe is a liar. But I'm sure you were well aware of that, as you've been in personal contact with him. Now, I've had a rather trying day, a trying month if you will, which was rather capped off by Mr. Wroxham's unwelcome presence downstairs upon my arrival. But I find myself in very great need of that bath."

Mrs. Tupper pursed her mouth up tight. "I am sorry, ma'am. Mr. Wroxham, said he was here at your, or rather Captain Marlowe's, behest. I . . . I am very glad you're back with us, ma'am."

Lizzie wasn't sure she believed her, but she kept her civility anyway. "Thank you, Mrs. Tupper. The bath, if you will. I'll also need a fire. A wood fire, a roaring one. I mean to burn these clothes. To save you the trouble of soaking them in lye. I do believe I mean to purchase new ones anyway."

It took over an hour to convincingly wash off the accumulated filth of several weeks of incarceration. Mrs. Tupper had to change the bathwater twice.

The worst was her hair. Lizzie washed it over and over, and then combed it relentlessly, until Mrs. Tupper stopped her.

"You'll wear it to shreds like that, ma'am. It's clean. You can leave it be."

And since Lizzie had tolerated her assistance, the house-keeper must have felt herself safe to fuss. "Let me bring you something to eat, ma'am. A proper hot meal. A nice lobster soup. And then you can rest."

"Thank you, Mrs. Tupper," Lizzie relented, if only to stop her fussing. Despite her divided loyalties, Mrs. Tupper had always treated her with respect and even affection. And Lizzie would catch more flies, and learn more information, with honey than with vinegar. "I do appreciate all you've done for me. Really I do. But you can stop fussing now."

When she was finally alone, after Mrs. Tupper had retreated with the empty plates, Lizzie could feel herself break down like a worn-out racehorse she had seen once. She made it as far as the bed, sat down, and was confronted by the stars on her ceiling, when her chest began to feel hot and achy. Her throat closed like a fist and her knees crumpled. She fell sideways back onto the bed and lay in a huddled heap.

Tears, the tears she had ruthlessly hidden away the whole time she spent in gaol, began to plummet down her cheeks.

It was awful, this tight, poisonous feeling of betrayal. It was worse than thinking he was dead. At least then she had been able to think of him as she wished, with a sort of rosy fondness. But now, the joy of finding him alive had faded into the cold steel gray of his betrayal.

CHAPTER 17

It was worse than the last time he had abandoned her, when he'd gone off to sea all those years ago, without so much as a word or a note. He had been there one day and gone the next. He had been her best friend, the only one she'd trusted implicitly, and she had been entirely unprepared to be without him. She had been bereft. As she was now.

But this was worse. Because she knew this time, he'd abandoned her on purpose. He had kissed her mouth, looked her in the eye, and abandoned her to her fate.

Jamie was like a stone she had swallowed. A painful lump she could not dislodge from her throat no matter how she tried. Her only hope was that in time she could grow accustomed to the pain.

And she would, by God. She would get over him. She would recover from his betrayal. She would become herself again.

And she would begin immediately, with an end to her widowhood.

There was no fire laid in her bedchamber or sitting room— the day was too mild. So Lizzie collected up her widow's weeds in bundles and threw them down over the balustrade to the floor of the foyer below. Perhaps a bonfire in the yard was the order of the day.

"Ma'am?" Mrs. Tupper's brow was puckered with anxiety as she watched Lizzie descend. "Is something amiss?"

"Mrs. Tupper, is there a fire laid anywhere today?"

"In the kitchen, ma'am."

Not as dramatic as a bonfire perhaps, but just as functional. "Lovely. Let's have this lot into the kitchen, then."

"Ma'am, is there a problem with the laundry? I've taken great care to launder all the clothes you wore when—"

"No, not at all," Lizzie cut her off. "I am simply done with widowhood." She took the first offending garment, the beautiful black silk she had worn to Jamie's burial, and cast it onto the fire. The flames danced and changed color and consumed the fabric greedily.

And on she went with all of them. Yards and yards of hideously dark cotton and silk. All tossed into the flames. Gone.

"There. And you can take down the crepe from the windows and the knocker, as well, Mrs. Tupper. We all know he's not dead. We've all spoken to him. Perhaps you even spoke to him right here, in this kitchen, and so I, for one, have absolutely no interest in continuing the strange fiction of his death."

Mrs. Tupper kept her face carefully blank. "Yes, ma'am. I'll see to it."

"Now then, have you and the others made the acquaintance of our new stable master, Mr. Maguire? No? Hasn't he been in for a meal? I wonder what the poor man's been eating? Well, he's resourceful," she reasoned. "Why don't you get Mr. Tupper and the rest of the staff, so I can make introductions all around."

The walk across the west lawn and through the shrubbery to the stables did her good. She felt purposeful and independent. She would get over him. She would be herself again.

Every day, with every accomplishment, with each decision, she would recover more and more.

All was quiet and serene as she walked across the yard and into the stable. The pungent odor of horse, hay, and leather rose around her like a balm. She'd always loved that smell.

"Maguire?"

"Yes, miss?" Maguire appeared from one of the box stalls she had just passed. He was as silent as water. She'd have to remember that.

"I wanted to see how you were faring."

"Well enough, thank you." He called over his shoulder, "Here now, boy. This is my grandnephew, my sister's daughter's boy, Jims. Jims, make your respects to your lady."

The boy tugged his cap and said what was right.

"Pleased to meet you, Jims. You've settled in then? I rather felt I had neglected you."

"Not to worry, missus."

"Good. And what do you think of the place so far?"

"It's a fair setup, miss. I can see why someone would want this for their ken."

"Yes, it is everything a smuggler could want, especially when it was empty. But do you think, once the house is properly filled, that they'll give it up?"

"Don't know. It might be too sweet to give up."

"Hmm. And what about the staff here? I'm not sure what to make of them or if I can trust them."

"Can't rightly say, yet. But they're up to something. Especially that lank-sleeved fellow. I can practically smell it."

"Mr. Tupper. I fear you're right. They certainly know more about my husband than they're letting on. But if I simply let them go, I may never find out. They are my one connection to him."

Maguire nodded, but said no more.

"Well, why don't you come down to the house now? I'd like

to introduce you to the rest of the staff. And you can tell me what you think."

"Right then, missus. Let's have a look."

Mr. and Mrs. Tupper were waiting in the kitchens, entirely Friday-faced. Tupper started right in, without waiting for the introduction.

"Ma'am, Captain Marlowe did not give leave for the hiring of any extra staff. In fact, he gave specific orders that the house was to be closed up and be opened only to work on repairs."

"Yes, he may have done. But as he has chosen to absent himself from his responsibilities here for whatever reason, his words no longer have any sway." Lizzie waited a moment for the words to settle in. "I'm here now, and I think it might be too much for just the two of you and those unreliable groundsmen, so I've got Maguire here, and his nephew Jims, along to take care of the stables. And speaking of the groundsmen, where is that big blond boy, McAlden? Does he never do a lick of work?"

"Ma'am, he's out in the dory this morning, checking the pots. I've asked him to do that for your supper." He gave her that little nod of his chin, in confirmation. Which meant he was lying.

"Out sailing. How fitting. Well then, what about the other one, the one who's groundsman proper? I don't think I've ever even seen him." She looked down at the leeks stacked up on the table. "Well, at least he seems to know his business gardening. Unless you're the one keeping us in turnips, Mrs. Tupper?"

"No, ma'am." Mrs. Tupper kept her eyes downcast as she fiddled with her keys. Another liar. Oh, they were really going to have to get much, much better at this if they had any hope of succeeding. It was almost insulting, how gullible they must think her.

"And the stables are just a start. Now the whole household

is up to six, plus me. That will be too many mouths for Mrs. Tupper to feed by herself as well as see to her other duties, so I'll be interviewing with an agency of employment in town about a cook and a kitchen maid. And possibly a footman, to actually be around. Perhaps you'd like to suggest someone else from the Navy, Mr. Tupper? No? Perhaps not. These Navy lads do have a regrettable tendency to be off in boats and whatnot, and I should like some indoor staff I can count on to be present, on the off chance we have another rash of housebreaking." She gave the Tuppers her sunniest stare. "Any questions? Protestations on behalf of the Captain? Good. Mr. Maguire will be accompanying me to Dartmouth. I expect to be back for tea, and I shall want dinner for eight o'clock."

Lizzie pulled on her riding gloves and moved towards the door. "Though I will have to see about purchasing a dining table straightaway so I might have somewhere to eat."

The trip through the principal mercantile establishments of Dartmouth town was productive, if not amusing. While the shopkeepers, warehousers, and employment agents were happy to engage her trade, her fellow shoppers were not.

She was being cut. Everywhere she went, with Maguire a silent shadow behind, Dartmouth's residents pulled in their skirts and turned their backs. Remarkable how the taint of the gaol lasted. She may have escaped the prison and the charges against her, but people had their own ways of enacting a kind of bitter justice.

It stung. But it could not turn her from her purpose. She would see Glass House transformed. And she would do it her own way.

Early the next morning, Lizzie headed through the east vestibule with her fowling piece. Mrs. Tupper would be engaged throughout the morning with all the deliveries she had arranged and in greeting the new staff scheduled to arrive.

Maguire was meant to poke about in his useful, cunning way down towards Stoke Fleming to see what he could find. The Naval crew, as Lizzie has taken to thinking of the men, were most likely off on their own secret agenda. Maguire was meant to be keeping loose tabs on them as well.

Which left her alone. Despite her current state of bravado, Lizzie was still not confident enough to venture forth by herself. Or unarmed.

Pistols were probably the most ladylike, as they could be concealed in one's pockets, but she was comfortable and well used to the fowling piece. She'd been firing it successfully since the day more than ten years ago when she had absconded with it from her father's gunroom.

"Ma'am." Mr. Tupper appeared in the doorway, tugging at his hat.

"Ah, Mr. Tupper. Are you engaged at present? I wondered if we might speak later this morning about the vacant tenant farm over towards Swannaton? I think we might want to consider a dairy. The grazing up along Jawbone Hill is very good, but I have an imperfect understanding of the buildings there. I'm going out shooting now, but I should like to ride over there this afternoon."

"Perhaps you might put that off until tomorrow, ma'am."

"Why might I want to do that, Mr. Tupper?"

Lizzie waited, but when an explanation was not offered, she felt her temper and patience snap.

"And am I really to expect no explanation, no elaboration on your plans? Mr. Tupper, perhaps, given the nature of your employment by Captain Marlowe, God rot his soul," she muttered as an aside before continuing, "you are not aware that as steward, your employment rests solely on my pleasure. Your job is to accommodate me and the business of this estate. And while I should like to honor your employment agreement with Captain Marlowe, as both you, and Mrs. Tupper especially, have been very good to me, and have served me faithfully in an extremely trying time, I do not feel bound to do so. And until such time as Captain Marlowe decides to walk back through that door and see to this estate, the task will fall to me, and I shall run this estate as I see fit."

Mr. Tupper worked his jaw, but after a long moment, he nodded grimly.

"Thank you. I value your advice and assistance, Mr. Tupper, but I should value it more if I knew you were always telling me the truth."

He couldn't even meet her eyes. She took up the gun to move off.

"I don't like the idea of your going shooting alone, ma'am, if I may be so bold. It isn't safe. If you want birds for your table, you can safely leave the shooting to me."

"I daresay I could. And I will concede you are a fine shot for a one-armed man. Indeed, you could bring down more birds with a pistol than any ten men with shotguns, but I do think the birds deserve a sporting chance. And besides, I like to shoot. I find I rather want to keep my hand in. One never knows when gun skills might come in handy."

But she really didn't want to kill birds. She really just wanted to be able to walk out of doors, in the fresh, clean air, and think. And she needed the gun to feel safe doing so.

Lord, but it was a hard thing, feeling afraid. And not knowing exactly what, or whom, to be afraid of.

There were so many choices, so many unanswered questions. Why was Jamie not dead? Why were naval men, or former naval men, who may or may not be working for the smugglers, working as staff in her house, and why were free traders breaking into her house in the middle of the night, armed with pistols? But she *didn't* know who the smugglers were, apart from Dan Pike and Sir Ralston, and she *did* know who was Navy, or had been. Mr. and Mrs. Tupper. Hugh McAlden. Francis Palmer. And Jamie. Wherever he was.

Lieutenant McAlden, Lord deHavilland had called him.

There must be some way to find out if McAlden was still considered an officer of His Majesty's Navy, or if he was just forging documents willy-nilly and turning smuggler. Perhaps Maguire knew a way. He would at the very least know someone who would know someone else, who would know. Much like Lord deHavilland.

There was another cunning fellow. How much else did *he* really know? He had been very canny about his contact and knowledge of the Admiralty. And as far as she knew, she had never paid his fee through the solicitor, Benchley. If she hadn't, who *had* paid his honorarium? That was another avenue she would need to pursue. So bloody much to do.

Lizzie leaned her elbows on the low stone wall edging the cliff path. Bother. She hadn't even gotten around to the part where she hated Jamie and would never forgive him. After she found him, of course.

She threw a loose rock out over the cliff towards the sea, but she was still so weak, it didn't go very far. Bloody bother.

It fell into the underbrush at the base of the cliff. As she looked down, her eyes picked out a slight pattern. There, below to the right. A ribbon of sandy brown. Not a ribbon—a path. A path straight into the cliff side.

Lizzie was enough of a child of the south coast to know exactly what that meant. Hadn't she and Jamie explored countless limestone caves along the river cliffs as children? Everybody knew the seacoast was riddled with them, too. And everybody wanted to use this house and these cliffs and the private, protected, secluded waters at Redlap cove.

She scrambled down the path and around onto the beach of the cove. The cliff grew in height as it jutted out into the water, away from the sandy beach. It took her some little while to get her bearings and pick it out. Farther right, behind one of the large shed-sized boulders. The path, a thin sandy trail through the scrubby underbrush, led to the small round entrance to a cave.

She had to duck down on all fours to get through the entrance. Lizzie was glad for her leather gloves and boots as she crawled her way in, only so far as was still illuminated by the sunlight from the opening. She went slowly, letting her eyes adjust to the diminishing light. About eight to ten feet into the hillside the tunnel opened up to a larger earthen room, a cavern with a higher ceiling—she could stand up. The cavern was empty, but there were marks in the sand. Footprints and wheel marks from a narrow-axle handcart, leading ahead to the left, following the line of the cliff face around a dark corner.

What an astonishing discovery.

Odds were the cave, or more likely the series of caves, were connected to the house. There was another dark passageway at the back corner, leading straight back, north under the land. There were holes halfway up the walls surrounded by large dark, greasy patches of soot. Places for torches. And here and there, between the torch holes, were empty hooks, for hanging lanterns. This cave had been used for a very long time. This cave was where her answers would lie.

It all made perfect sense. She should have known, or at least suspected. Stories of caves and smugglers' haunts were the stock-in-trade of the Devon coast. Every child from Dartmouth to St. Ives had grown up on such tales.

But who else knew about this cave? The smugglers, certainly. Dan Pike could have used the caves to gain access to the house if they were connected. That could have been why the doors had still been locked when she'd shot him.

But she wasn't in the least bit equipped to follow his trail, whichever way that might be, through the passageways. She needed to get the proper equipment for an exploration. A lantern and replacement candles, a long spool of heavy twine to mark her way, and a compass to keep track of her direction and distance.

It was just like the old days, when she and Jamie had explored the caves along the river cliffs when they were children. Except this time she was working against Jamie and all of his lies.

Lizzie inched herself back out of the passage and out onto the beach. The tide was fairly low, about three quarters ebb. How deep was the water in the cove at high tide? How large a ship could come in, and how close to the cliff could it come? And how tall a ship could be concealed by the cliffs and trees above?

She'd have to come back later, possibly tomorrow, since she had already engaged herself for the afternoon with Mr. Tupper. She could hardly disappoint him and change her mind. Not after that haughty dressing-down she'd delivered. He might just remember he was a bosun and toss her out on her ear with his one brawny arm.

She took the path east off the beach. It would give her a longer walk back to the house and more time to think. Did the old-timers, like Maguire, know about this cave? Most likely. And she should certainly get his help. She really oughtn't go exploring the cave on her own.

Strange. After her recent stint in Dartmouth Gaol, one would think she would have had a reaction to the closed confined spaces of the cave and tunnels. The thought brought her up short. She always said it, didn't she—she couldn't abide a closed space. And yet she had just crawled in and out of a confined tunnel and into a cave without the least bit of trepidation. The whole time, the thought, the feeling of overwhelming panic, had never occurred to her.

She smiled to herself, for the first time in what felt like forever. A genuine smile of happiness. It was a true accomplishment, conquering her fear and her panic. She was becoming independent. Even if she had to surround herself with people to do so.

It was then she saw movement ahead on the path. The flare of a coattail. A man. Was someone watching her? Had he seen her under the cliff? And suddenly her heart was pounding and her hands were shaking, just as they had the night she shot Dan Pike. And just as she had the night she shot Dan Pike, she look a deep breath, and pulled back the lock on the gun.

She edged forward along the side of the path cautiously, close to the trees and undergrowth, trying to get a better look.

It was a man, dressed in plain work clothes of the country, walking down the lane towards the cottages and the house. His back was silhouetted by the sun, and his walk was a bit careless, what she might have described as jaunty and optimistic.

Familiar.

And there was that same strange feeling of tight pain in her chest, the one where she could feel the hole open up in her heart and the blood leak out into her body. She felt it when they'd told her he was dead. And now, she felt it because Jamie was alive and he was walking, cocksure as you please, up her lane.

God damn him.

She tore after him.

She wanted to call out his name but somehow she couldn't, like in a dream when one opens one's mouth to scream and nothing ever comes out. But she could run, as fast as her feet would carry her, moving as silently as she could manage, but when she turned the corner near the orchard, he was gone. Then another flash—the flare of his coattail again as he turned around the corner of the kitchen garden. Just a glimpse of his dun brown coat before he disappeared behind the wall.

She went pelting into the garden after him.

And straight into Hugh McAlden. Just as she reached the corner and would have gone through the gate, the big, blond groundsman came loping along in the opposite direction, blocking her way with his sheer bulk.

"Ma'am." He tugged respectfully at his knit cap, but remained lodged firmly in the center of the path. "Were you looking for me, ma'am?"

"No. Damn your eyes. Get out of my way. Allow me to pass." She darted under his elbow, into the walled garden and down the nearest path between the desultory rows of vegetables. The garden was empty. She wheeled back on McAlden. "Where did he go?"

"Who, ma'am?" McAlden showed her a carefully blank, bland face.

"The man who just came in here. My husband. Where is he?"

"No one here but I, ma'am." He shrugged.

"Good Lord. Just how stupid do you think I am, *Lieutenant* McAlden? I saw him. He was here! And I wonder how your superiors at the Admiralty will feel when they learn about the sneaking little smuggling ken their veterans have got going here."

Oh, that got his attention, the use of his rank. He may have been a useful, successful naval officer, but he was no card player. His absolute horror at her discovery showed clearly in his face.

And then it hit her. Another powerful, painful thought slammed into her brain. My God. The elusive groundsman. Jamie. His tall silhouette, walking down the lane. And the tall silhouette of the groundsman, lurking at the shadows of the doorway the night she'd shot Dan Pike. Lizzie turned to look back down the lane and picture him again in her mind's eye.

Jamie. He'd been there the whole time. The whole time, when he'd kissed her good-bye and said he was off to sail to the other end of the world, he'd stayed here. He'd never left. The whole time he was supposed to be dead, he'd been here. The whole time she'd been in gaol, threatened with hanging for his death, he'd been larking about the lanes of Glass Cottage. Right bloody here.

When she turned back, McAlden had disappeared as quickly as Jamie.

"Oh bloody, holy, damned . . . son of a bitch!" She didn't even have adequate vocabulary to express the rancid thoughts and anger towards her husband. "No account, low-down dog of a sneaking, lying, bloody bastard!"

She *was* going to kill him.

CHAPTER 18

"**I**s she gone?" Marlowe had caught a glimpse of Lizzie on the beach and turned back to avoid her, as he'd done every time he'd spotted her over the past week. It was growing tiresome. And frustrating, in more ways than one. She kept popping up in the damnedest places—and always with that gun of her father's. He'd recognized it straight off. But he didn't know she'd followed him until he'd heard the rapid footsteps behind him in the lane.

"Yes. For now." McAlden didn't look pleased.

"That was close. What the hell was she doing down on the beach? She just came out of nowhere."

"She knows."

"Knows what?"

"She *knows*. She called me Lieutenant McAlden, and she said she knew you. That you were her husband."

Marlowe let fly a colorful invective. His day of reckoning with Lizzie had finally come. And frankly, it was a relief. It had been killing him, having her back at Glass Cottage, wanting and needing to protect her and being reduced to watching from a distance. He didn't know how much longer he could hold out, peering up at her windows, waiting into the wee small hours for her candle to go out and for her to fall asleep, so he could lie himself down on the floor of her hallway, guarding her door. Her presence, so close and yet always out of reach, had become his well-deserved, continual penance.

McAlden let out a mirthless chuckle. "You have similar taste in oaths, you and your wife. She let loose some remarkable Billingsgate language. Almost have to admire her for it."

Marlowe nodded wearily. "Oh, yes. I'm familiar with it."

"I saw her from the house, running up the lane, just after you went by. I thought she was still just being bloody-minded about the 'groundsman.' And then she called me Lieutenant."

Marlowe swore again. "Points to Lizzie for accuracy."

"How much do you think she knows?"

"Enough. But the more pertinent point is, how did she find out, and with whom is she sharing her information? That Maguire chap she's installed in the stables *was* running a gang out of this coast when I was a kid, as we suspected. Everyone knows him. But everything Palmer found out, and everything I've heard, indicates he's been out of the game for years. Or was, until he got hired on by Lizzie."

"And maybe he wants back into the game?"

"He's definitely a possibility."

"And what about your wife?"

"What do you mean? What about her?"

"It seems everyone on this coast, from the fishmonger to the magistrate, is running with a gang. Why not her? How well do you really know her? By your own account, before you married her, you hadn't seen her in years. Ten years. She's what, three and twenty, maybe four?"

"Two. Two and twenty."

"Old enough. And who's to say she isn't part of or even the one heading this gang? She's certainly clever enough. And she's been remarkably stubborn about the house. Insisting on staying here in the face of all opposition. Bloody-minded, even."

"Then why was Dan Pike shooting at her?"

"She shot Dan Pike, not the other way round. Because she and Maguire are expanding their lay? Because the free traders think Maguire wants back into the game? Because she's one of the Corresponding Society members who's working with the smugglers to move the weapons, and the locals want out? You tell me."

Every single question, Marlowe had already asked himself. And dismissed.

No, Lizzie still had no idea she was nearly up to her neck in this business. A lovely, white neck the Prime Minister would have no qualms about seeing stretched on a gibbet, hanged until dead. And Marlowe was not going to allow that to happen. Absolutely not. No matter what else happened on this mission, he would see to her safety. Whether she wanted him to or not. His girl might think she was independent and worldly, but she was only idealistic. She had too little practical experience of the world, and certainly not nearly enough to coolly fool all of Dartmouth and run a gang of cutthroat thieves out of her house. She was clever enough, but her fright and her devastation had been all too real.

"She's not."

"You're sure?"

"Positive, Lieutenant. Get a move on. We still need to get the dory out to *Defiant* and make for the islands. Maybe this will be the shipment we need, and we can finally pin something on somebody other than bloody Dan Pike and his minders."

Whoever they were.

She waited for hours. She'd come to check on the height of the tide as she'd planned, seen the dory was gone, and drawn her own conclusions. It had been difficult to try and track them in the dark, but now that she knew where they'd gone, she also knew they would be back. Jamie had done too much, told too many lies to keep himself at Redlap to abandon it just because she had chased him down the lane.

Lizzie settled herself in the underbrush, schooled her eyes upon the beach, and waited for them to reappear.

As the hours stretched on, she fell into fitful dozes, awakening suddenly a half dozen times before she finally saw them: two men rowing silently and smoothly across the dark, glassy water. They stashed their empty dory high on the beach, above the tidemark, and then moved back up the lane towards her, their dark, worn clothing absorbing the play of moonlight flickering off the water of the cove.

They looked exactly like what they must be. Bloody smugglers. And traitors.

She stepped into the lane behind them and cocked the hammer on her gun.

The two men froze. One of them began to slowly turn. Only one.

McAlden, his arms out at his side, palms open and up. At the sight of her, he swore beneath his breath.

"It's only McAlden, ma'am. No need for the gun."

"Turn around, completely. Both of you."

It was a long moment as McAlden looked at the other man and shook his head.

And then the other one spoke.

"Hello, Lizzie. You ought to get more sleep."

His voice was deep and rough, and poured over her like lye, stinging and burning. She'd expected it, of course. It wasn't a shock. Her breath wasn't locked inside her chest. Her hands weren't trembling. She gripped the stock tighter, forced a deep breath, and sighted the gun on Jamie's heart.

McAlden made an exasperated sound.

"Your friend—or perhaps the word I'm searching for is *accomplice*—is correct in his assumption." Her voice was firm and clear, even a little sarcastic. Good. "I do have half a mind to shoot you."

"What does the other half say, Lizzie?"

God damn, but it was pure Jamie. Slow and cocky enough to warm her from the inside out. Damn him.

"To shoot both of you. Although I'd prefer to shoot just you. I can't be tried twice for the same murder, can I?"

He acknowledged her point with a rueful nod of his head. "To be fair, you weren't tried the first time, Lizzie."

Was he trying to tease her? "No thanks to you. Now, tell me what you and your loblolly boy here are up to."

He made that sideways wince he always made when he was embarrassed. And even though he tried to smile, his eyes never left hers. They pored over her, searching out all her secrets.

"Do you even know what a loblolly boy is? No, don't answer. I'm sure your association with Phineas Maguire has furnished you with your colorful vocabulary. Not to mention your stint in . . ." He shook his head again. "You need to go home and get some sleep. You have bruises under your eyes."

Lizzie was not about to let Jamie coddle her out of her well-earned anger with his belated concern. She resighted the fowling piece on a spot between his eyes. "Try again."

"Lizzie, please put that blasted thing down. You'll be the death of me."

"Yes, that was the plan, wasn't it? But if you insist." She smiled and leveled the weapon at his crotch.

She was satisfied to note his hand flinched down to cover his cods before he got ahold of himself and relaxed into his usual loose-limbed stance.

"This isn't a game, Lizzie. We have to talk. But this isn't the time."

"Oh, and here I was having so much fun playing at going to prison."

"Lizzie. I am sorry. But please, go home. It's very late and you'll catch your death in this damp."

"I'm not twelve anymore, Jamie. You can't just send me home when you don't want to play."

"And I'm not the rector's son you can tell off and dismiss as if I were nothing more than a bloody servant." There was an edge of anger, as sharp as a blade, in his voice before he sheathed it. "Please. This is deadly serious. And I don't want you hurt any further."

She was not going to be taken in by him. Nor intimidated. He could be a traitor. She already knew he was a liar. "Then I suggest you give me a deadly serious explanation."

"Would you two mind," McAlden asked carefully, "if I opted out of this little family discussion?"

"No," Jamie growled.

"Yes," Lizzie countered. "Stay where you are."

"Go," Jamie ordered curtly.

McAlden obeyed. He started slowly on towards the cottage. "I'm going to bed. You know where you can find me."

Jamie watched him walk off before he turned his darkened eyes back to her. "We can't talk here." He looked around for a moment before he began to follow McAlden up the lane, checking constantly over his shoulder to see if she followed.

She did, keeping a safe distance, and holding the fowling piece carefully in front of her, aimed in his general direction. His hand kept clenching and opening by his side. It was unsettling. But she followed him cautiously through the fallow walled garden and into a long glass plant shed set against the far sidewall. Moonlight filtered through the dirty slanted panes of the roof glass.

Jamie went down the aisle between empty tables and turned. "Close the door, so we won't be overheard."

"There's no one here but you and I. And the Navy Pensioners Guild you've employed to help you with your smuggling game."

"Lizzie," Jamie repeated in a quietly stern voice, "I am not a smuggler and this is not a game."

"Then what is it?" When he didn't immediately answer she pressed. "Shall I tell you what it looks like? It looks like you faked your death to be rid of me, so you and your navy mates could play house in my garden, Jamie. I hate to break up your 'cozy moment,' but you're trespassing." She gestured back towards the door with the muzzle of the gun. "Get off my estate."

"It's not yours."

"Oh, yes it is. You're dead! You'll have to go to Chancery Court to take it back."

"Lizzie." He reached out his hand towards her and then let it drop. He was tense with stillness. "I won't have to go to the Court of Chancery. I made sure of all the legalities before I undertook this."

It felt as though he had slapped her. The pain of the phantom blow ricocheted through her, rocking her on her feet. "How flattering," she said, as breathlessness made her voice too soft, "to know you considered all the 'legalities' as you were planning to use and defraud me."

He colored, two spots high on his cheekbones as he realized just what he'd said.

"I haven't defrauded you, Lizzie. I have done more than enough other harm to you, however inadvertently. And I have apologized for that. But I have not defrauded you. I invited you to take a chance. And that's what you did. And so did I. I gave you control of all that money. And you still have it. I haven't interfered."

"I did not take a chance on being thrown in gaol and being potentially hanged. But to be fair, I do still have the money. And you haven't interfered. Which leaves me to wonder why?" When he made no answer, she continued. "Is it because you can't? Hmm. For whatever reason it is you won't tell me, you can't. How interesting."

"Lizzie." His voice was sore with regret. "I know you're hurt and angry. You have every right to be. I'm sorry."

He had no right to feel such anguish. He had caused it.

"I'm not hurt." Nothing so paltry as hurt could describe what he had done to her and how he had made her feel. Still made her feel. She spat her anger and pain at him. "I'm livid."

More angry than when they'd hauled her off to the gaol. At least then she'd thought there'd been some mistake. She had been so sure there had been a mistake. Now, she knew there had been one. Her own. She had trusted him.

Never again.

The bitterness and bottomless anger still roiled endlessly in her belly. She couldn't keep it in. "You left me there to die, or be killed!" The tears she refused to shed ate at her throat like acid.

"Stop, Lizzie, please." He reached for her. "I couldn't. I didn't. I sent help."

She batted his hand away. "What help? The only reason I got out of that hell was because my mother braved my father's disapproval and found a decent solicitor and barrister."

He shoved his hands deep into his pockets. "I know. She was a wonder, your mother. Lord deHavilland was magnificent. But Lady Theodora did not act alone. You were never alone."

"I have never been so alone in all my life. And I intend to keep it that way. So you and your sodding, traitorous smugglers should clear out of my house while you have the chance."

"My God," he pinched the bridge of his nose, "your language. Remind me to throttle Maguire."

"You'd do better to sit down at his knee and take some advice. Maguire knows more about the business along the south coast than either of you two greenhorns can ever hope to figure out."

He moved an involuntary step closer. "What do you know, Lizzie?"

She took a step forward herself. "What do *you* know, Jamie?"

His eyes, always the indicator of his scruples, slid away. Whatever it was he knew, he wasn't going to tell her. Or trust her.

Bastard.

But she would find out all of Glass Cottage's secrets anyway. Tomorrow, when she and Maguire would follow the cave and trace its likely connection back to the house.

Icy hot silence stretched between them until Jamie broke it with an exasperated expulsion of breath.

"I know that look in your eye, Lizzie. For the love of God, please, stay out of this. Let me handle this."

"Handle what? The smugglers? This estate? You can't. You're dead."

"Listen to me!" he ground out, moving closer. She could see the tension, feel it coming off his body in heated waves. "We are determined, *I* am determined to prevail here. Do you understand me? For your own good, put your gun away and do as you are asked. Everything depends upon it."

Jamie took a long moment to look at her face. A long, searching moment, with those pale, piercing eyes moving slowly across her like a touch. Lizzie looked away. Damn him. She would not weaken. She would not give in to those damned eyes of his.

She held her ground. "Not to me. Your plans, the plans you were willing to sacrifice me, and my freedom, for, can go to hell. The only thing that matters to me is whether you live or die, and I'm sure you can guess my preference."

"God damn you, Lizzie." With a suicidal disregard for the gun, he grabbed the barrel and pushed it away. "Why won't you let me protect you? I may have been forced into my career by your overprotective father and his aristocratic notions of what was good enough, or more importantly *not* good enough, for his daughter, but it's my bloody career, and I have never, never once forsworn my duty or failed to accomplish what I set out to do! Everything I am, everything I value, is at stake here, including you. I won't have it. I can't."

Lizzie gripped the edge of the potting table and held herself entirely still, to keep her body from swirling as precipitously as her thoughts. When she finally spoke, her whisper seemed to cleave the silence. "What did you say?"

"I said, everything I value—"

"No. *My* father forced you?" It made no sense. How could her father have had anything to do with Jamie's chosen profession?

But he must have. She saw the truth of it in Jamie's eyes, pale and cold as he stepped back, away from her. Bitter bile rose in her throat even as the bottom dropped out of her stomach.

"And you didn't know? You expect me to believe that, you who knew everything that happened in Dartmouth? You who had your nose in every corner it didn't belong?"

She had not known, because from the moment he was gone, she had ceased to care. There was nothing she wanted to know if she did not have him to share it with. Stupid, willful child. "How?"

"In the usual, time-honored method. Blackmail."

"How could he force *you*?" The words were hot and raw, as if they were being torn in half at the back of her throat.

He stared at her silently for a long moment. When he spoke, his voice was weary with bitterness. "He arranged it. Bought my midshipman's berth with his influence and dangled it in front of my father, much like a noose. Either I took it and went away quietly or he'd ruin me, and ruin my father, too, no doubt, though he never said so in front of me. Nor did my father. It was just agreed upon between 'gentlemen.'"

"And that's when you left. That summer."

He didn't answer. He didn't need to. The answer was in his insistent eyes.

"You were only fourteen." Even she could hear the useless regret in her voice.

"A good age for a midshipman." His voice remained flat and emotionless. But she couldn't imagine he'd felt so sanguine ten years ago. He had been only fourteen. She had been twelve. They had been children.

"And that's why you just left?"

"Just left? I didn't have a bloody choice, did I?"

"I thought . . . I thought I'd done something wrong."

He stepped closer now, and she had to tip her head up to see his face. He was so close, she could feel the heat from his body. "Of course you had. You'd taken your bloody shirt off, hadn't you? Showed me your . . . You were brazen as the day was long. Asking for it. But *I'm* the one who had to pay for it. Not you."

"I was twelve. I don't think I knew what I was asking for. And you took yours off, too." But she felt as if the wind had been knocked out of her. He was right—she ought to have known. She ought to have realized. "Christ. What a horrible mess this is."

"I don't know. It got us both what we wanted."

"What we wanted?" She had wanted independence. And he? "Oh my God. I've been so blind, so stupid, haven't I? You just wanted revenge. I've gone and given you your revenge."

A brief flare of heat and triumph shone from his eyes before he masked it. "It wasn't revenge. I didn't plan for any of this to happen to you. I was . . ."

But he didn't finish. He didn't have an answer. He wouldn't say it, but it was true. And it had worked. Beautifully. Everything she had worked for, everything she had loved, even the house, had been an illusion.

She, who always said what she thought and always thought she knew best, had been a complete and utter fool over this man. A complete, hopeless fool.

Lord, but it was wearying, all this anger.

"So you can just take it all back, whenever you're ready?"

"Yes. When I'm ready."

She didn't want to know when that would be. Lizzie took a long breath. The cold night air stung her lungs and shocked her into awareness. "But in the meantime, I've still got control of it?"

"Yes, I'm not . . . vindictive. I don't want you do have to do without. I won't—"

"Good. I'll spend it."

He looked at her blankly.

"I *am* vindictive. Or rather, I plan to be. I'll spend as much as possible. You've had your revenge and now I'll have mine. I'll bankrupt you." She gave him a dazzling smile to accompany her defiance. "I'll spend every last groat."

"And leave yourself destitute in the process? Really, Lizzie. Don't be spiteful. It doesn't suit you. You're no gamester, and you clearly don't run up dressmaker's bills." He waved his hand at her old, plain cotton work dress. "But somehow you look lovely anyway, although you ought to sleep more. And eat more."

She wouldn't listen to the almost wistful concern in his voice. He had used her. Not only since he had left her in gaol, but from the beginning, from the very first time he had seen her, he had been planning his revenge.

"No. You're right, but I thank you for the excellent suggestions. Mother is always after me to dress more fashionably. And I suddenly feel a great ambition to become a great patroness. Of the arts. Yes, musicians, artists, poets, and painters are always looking for someone to finance their genius. To buy them well-made instruments. I'll fill the house with them. Bound to be terribly expensive to keep, artists. Bottles and bottles of champagne, for inspiration you know. I'll have Mrs. Tupper order some laid in. Yes, and they'll all be suitably grateful, won't they? Bound to want to do me all sorts of kindnesses."

She felt a savage burst of satisfaction at the look on his face. It was murderous. Good. Now he knew how she felt.

"Don't interfere with this mission, Lizzie." He didn't bother to veil the threat in his low tone.

"Or what? You'll have me thrown in gaol? Again?" She tossed her scorn at him like an old shoe.

"Damn your eyes," he growled. "I told you, I didn't have anything to do with that."

"And I'm supposed to believe that? I'm supposed to believe you? When everything out of your mouth has been a lie? You expect *this* pathetic ruse to work? Look at yourself. Creeping about in the dark dressed like the roughest sort of fisherman. Do you honestly think you're going to fool people into thinking you're my groundsman? You can't even pot a tulip."

"No, I don't expect people to believe I'm your groundsman. I expect them to believe I'm a free trader, with a ship at my command, and that I'm masquerading as your groundsman because of your charming little cove."

She caught the filthy, suggestive intonation of the last. "You bastard."

"I have been a bastard, my dear, but I'm still your husband." He stepped forward and snatched the gun out of her hand so hard and so fast she flinched. And then he had her, hauled up tight against his chest, his heat and his power surrounding her, making her feel helpless. And wanting.

CHAPTER 19

That was bloody besides enough.

Marlowe had taken more than enough of Lizzie's spleen and now his patience was at a bitter end. He had tried to explain, he had apologized, he had taken every bit of her well-deserved anger when all he wanted to do, from the moment he saw her in the lane, was take her into his arms and hold her. Keep her. Safe. Show her with the protection of his body what he never could manage to put into words.

Her sinewy little body wriggled furiously, and futilely, against his. He forced himself to disregard the fact that she felt too light: fragile, almost crushable. He wouldn't notice his rough hands could span her tiny waist. He wouldn't feel any tenderness. Tenderness wouldn't scare her. And she needed to be scared. Scared so badly she'd finally listen to what he needed to tell her about his mission. So badly she'd pack up and leave Glass Cottage and Redlap and Dartmouth directly. And be safe.

What he couldn't disregard was how impossibly good it felt to have her in his arms again, after what had seemed a tedious eternity of watching and keeping his distance. He couldn't disregard the jagged jolt of arousal at holding her pressed against him with nothing more than a few thin layers of fabric between them.

A moment ago, he had thought he felt nothing but disappointment and frustration, but now, all he felt was the febrile heat flowing from her body and the aching want flooding his skin. His need was like the roaring of the sea in his ears, drowning out all other senses. He couldn't sustain disappointment when she was in his arms.

God, he wanted her.

He'd been consumed by need the moment he had turned to see her standing in the lane with her gun, so provoking, so defiant. So fragile, held together by nothing more than grit and willpower. He'd wanted to take her and hold her tight within the protective circle of his arms and never, ever let her go again. He needed to feel the fragile strength of her body against his. He'd been wanting and waiting to hold her, to take her, to possess her, for weeks. Forever. Always.

She might never trust him again, but she might be seduced into listening to him long enough to explain fully and honestly what he had to do. And God knew he wanted to seduce her.

He ached to plunder the tart sweetness of her pliant mouth. To see the soft white skin of her face and body washed pale by the moonlight. To feel the tight pulse of her quim as he opened her flesh and to experience the moist heat of her slick passage when he finally, finally slid his aching cock home inside her.

He couldn't stifle the groan of longing that crawled out of this chest as he buried his face in the soft hair at the nape of her neck. The scent of citrus, of light and heat, filled his head. "God, Lizzie, I've missed you. How I've wanted you. Needed you. You smell like sunshine."

"You smell like fish."

He leveraged away for the barest moment and stripped off his woolen sweater and cotton shirt in one smooth motion, throwing it on the damp slate floor. Then he took her by the wrist and placed her cool palm flat against the skin of his chest, just to catch the icy electrical heat of her touch.

"I've been fishing, haven't I?" He dropped his voice to a rough whisper. "That's why I smell of the ocean and sand and fish. But now, whenever you smell that, you'll remember this moment and how much I wanted you. You'll remember the way I kissed you. You'll remember the way I touched you. You'll remember how I lifted your skirts," he fitted his actions to his words, fisting up the material, "until I could see your soft, beautiful pussy and how I put my hands between your legs. And how I told you to open your legs, Lizzie, so I could touch you. You'll remember how much I wanted you. How much I needed you."

She was trying to back away from him, looking sideways for the door, but he wouldn't let her leave his arms. He couldn't. And her breath was growing shallow, with fear perhaps—he was rapidly losing all restraint—but also with excitement. He hadn't forgotten how much his words could arouse her. So all the while he stalked her, crowding her back against the wall.

"There's nowhere to run, Lizzie." He kept her tethered by the fabric of her skirts, his words a harsh murmur next to her ear. "I've missed you. God, how I've needed you."

"No. You haven't missed me. You left me." Her words were a breathless rush as she burrowed and twisted her arms between them to push against his chest, to push him away. But it only brought her soft belly squirming against the growing length of his arousal. And gave him a better view of her ripe little breasts.

His mind's eye instantly conjured the way she had looked that summer day so long ago, the dappled sun on her bare skin, her nipples like wild strawberries, tight and pink. He'd always wondered what she would have tasted like.

But she had been worth the wait, hadn't she? He held her still against the unyielding brick and set his lips to the hollow of her throat. He could feel the hectic beat of the blood in her veins and smell the intoxicating lemony tang of her warm skin. He plied his teeth along that lovely, sensitive tendon on the side of her neck, nipping his way up to her ear.

"No," she panted. "I won't let you. I won't let you try to seduce me out of—"

She broke off with a gasp as he bit down just a little, just enough to raise a mark. Marking her as his. Only his.

"Then what will you let me try, Lizzie?" He dragged his lips off her skin to look directly into the depths of her green eyes. "If you don't care for seduction, how about a subtle application of . . . restraint? Just enough so you can let go? I haven't forgotten how much you liked it when I sailed you across your desire like a nimble sloop, all battened down tight and close-hauled. It's been a long time, Lizzie, but I haven't forgotten. And I've wanted you. I want you. I want my wife."

"I'm not your wife. I'm no man's wife. You're dead. I'm a widow." She repeated the words, more for her own benefit than his.

"Am I?" He purred low into her ear. "If I'm dead, then tell me, would you, what this is?" He put his palms flat against the wall to either side of her head, leaned his considerable weight and height into her and carefully, and oh, so slowly, rubbed the length of his ruthlessly erect cock against her mound. "I have ached for you, Lizzie. And God help me, you feel so good."

Her breathing fractured, and her eyes slid shut. Her breasts rose and fell against his chest in shallow gasps, the blistery friction of each breath shooting a prick of want deep into his bones. He let his hand follow his eyes, running a firm palm along the rounded underside of her breast and up across the needy, beading peak. Her answering gasp of pleasure decided his course.

"Ah. Restraint it is then." And God knew he needed all the restraint he could muster. His hands were nearly shaking with the effort to go slow, to hold his clawing need at bay.

It gave Marlowe a deep-seated shot of pleasure to watch her silent complicity as he slowly gathered her porcelain wrists in his hands. With exquisite care, he slowly, inexorably pulled her arms behind her back until he could band their fragile strength in one hand. He tugged down slightly, to pull back her shoulders so he could bend his head to her breasts, wetting her and sucking her through the fabric of her dress, giving her pleasure, until she began to arch away from the wall and small, needy sounds began to wing out of her throat. He let his mouth slide up the sweet gloss of her neck to skim the edge of her jaw as his fingers loosened the neckline of the gown.

"Open your mouth, Lizzie. I want to taste you." He didn't bother to hide the anguished need in his voice.

She closed her eyes even as her lips parted on a shallow breath. He covered her open mouth with a deep kiss, stroking her with his tongue and stoking the carnal heat in his belly.

"Show me your breasts, Lizzie," he pleaded, though it was he who loosened and pulled the neckline of both her gown and shift down over her arms, leaving the material to trap her arms tight to her sides. "Let me . . ."

Let me give you what you need. Let me touch you, let me need you, let me lose myself inside you.

He covered her breasts with his hands, drawing lightly over the sensitive peaks, and then not so lightly, letting the rough calluses on his fingers drag over and rasp against her nipples. As she arched helplessly into his palms, he wedged his knee between her thighs and raised her up until she was lifted off her feet, and he could feel the enticing heat of her cunny through the coarse wool of his trousers. He continued to stroke and tongue her perfect breasts, hungry for the taste, the smell, the feel of her, as she rode his leg, her thighs clamped tight around him in search of her own pleasure, until her breath was coming in great panting gulps, and he couldn't wait another moment to be inside her.

He dropped his leg and she made a sound of desperate

protest. He answered her plea with a rough, possessive kiss, as he bore his weight into her and rucked up her skirts with more speed than finesse.

And then his hand found the folds of her quim, slick with moisture, hot and waiting for him. He slipped a finger into her opulent silkiness, opening her to his touch, readying her for his possession. He swallowed the groan tunneling out of his chest and closed his eyes to shut out everything but the blinding pleasure of touching her.

She ground down into his hand, wanting the pressure, needing more.

Marlowe let go of her to rip open the buttons of his close. "You like it when I take you like this, don't you, Lizzie? When you can't make a choice, when all you can do is feel." He freed his cock and guided the broad head to the very edge of her opening. "Feel the way your cunny responds to my touch, and comes to do my bidding. How do you feel now, knowing you're wet from my touch and ready to be fucked?"

Her response was a keening gasp. He felt a fierce moment of possessive, predatory triumph. She was his. His to take. His to love.

"Open your legs for me. Lizzie. Wider. Take me inside you."

All she could do was tilt her hips forward, but it was more than enough. Marlowe pushed into her and slid home with one swift thrust.

"Yes," she gasped into his ear. "Yes, Jamie."

Yes. Finally.

And then there was nothing else but her. Everything else: the brick of the walls, the glass of the ceiling, the earth, the stars, and the moon fell away and there was only her. Only her heat and her passion. Her body pressing into him, taking him inside her warmth and her light. He was lost inside her silkiness: her hair, her skin, and her gloriously tight cunny, pulsing and whirling around him. He was drunk on her essence. He could never get enough.

He held her tight against his chest, and when her open mouth slid over the muscles of his shoulder and she bit him, he careened headlong over the edge.

His orgasm, as he pumped his seed into her clinging cunny, ripped through him with enough force that his knees buckled into the wall. If he hadn't been holding tight to her neck, his face pressed into the glorious riot of her hair, he would have fallen.

He pushed himself, and his bruised knees, off her and leaned his forehead against the wall, waiting for his breathing to return to some semblance of normal.

Marlowe reached out to cup her cheek and brush the tumbled hair off her forehead. He liked her like this. Soft and exhausted, her claws sheathed. Beautifully, thoroughly fucked. God, how he had missed her.

She sighed, a weary exhalation from deep in her bones, as she tentatively moved cramped arms and shoulders. He reached down to help her collect her clothes about her.

"No." She surprised him by shaking her head. "You can go now." Her voice was low and clear. "And please don't come back."

She shrugged her bodice back up onto her shoulders and moved away. She wouldn't look at him, just collected her gun and made for the door.

She was dismissing him. From her arms. From her life.

He couldn't lose her again. He couldn't possibly endure it.

Lizzie damned herself as two kinds of fool. She headed out of the garden and across the lawn towards the relative sanctuary of the house, keeping her mind a careful, incurious blank. She wouldn't think about what had just passed between them. How she had been unable to resist the lure of his body. How she had responded exactly as he had known she would. How she was right back where she started, stupidly enthralled. Damn his fine eyes.

She couldn't think about it, or even acknowledge it. Not just now. If she did, she'd fall apart.

Better to ride the numbing, but temporary tide of physical satiation for as long as it lasted. There would be time enough for contemplation, and recrimination, later.

"Where the hell do you think you're going?" Jamie came out of nowhere to grab her elbow and haul her to a stop on the damp, dew-slick lawn.

She only just managed to keep her footing. How dare he? *He* had no right be furious.

"I'm going to bed. You can go to hell."

"No." He took a steaming breath of night air. "You're not going anywhere. We've still got unfinished business between us, you and I. You can't pretend to me you didn't feel anything, Lizzie. You can't. And you can't walk away without any explanation. You owe me that much." The words sounded as if he'd gnashed them between his teeth.

"I owe you nothing." She was weary to her soul from the ache of loving him.

"You do, damn your eyes." He was grimly adamant. "You promised. You promised to honor and obey, Lizzie. Upon your *honor*. And you never go back on your word."

Oh, he was a clever bastard. The urge to hit him, to make him feel even a fraction of the pain he inflicted, was monstrous. "My word, is it? What about yours? The only person I have ever promised to obey is dead to me. I owe you nothing. You're not my husband, because a husband wouldn't lie to his wife. A husband wouldn't desert his wife. A husband wouldn't leave his wife rotting in gaol! The minute you start acting like a husband, I'll start acting like a wife."

"Fine. We can begin right now."

"Bugger off."

The flinty spark in his eye told her she had finally pushed him too far. He growled into her ear, his voice a velvet threat.

"Such filthy, unmannerly language, Lizzie. So that's how you want it to be, is it? My God, why can't you ever learn?"

"Really? And here I thought I'd learnt to be well-fucked, or wasn't that what you had in mind?"

His head snapped back in recoil at her purposefully vulgar language. Good. Turnabout was fair play: she was glad *she'd* finally shocked *him*.

His immediate response was to tighten his grip on her arm. "My God." He was stunned into momentary silence. When he spoke, he chose his words carefully, as if he were picking out weapons. "Well, it seems another kind of more advanced lesson in fucking is in order. But you were always a fast learner, Lizzie, an eager student. I'm sure you'll like it. Because, if it's the last thing I do on this earth, I will show you that you need me just as much as I need you."

His intent gaze slammed into her like a slap, his words just as blunt and forceful.

"No. I don't need anybody. I—" But she had no air in her lungs.

He turned her around and lowered her belly-first into the grass, with his big hand hard against the small of her back, just above the rising curve of her buttocks. He came down atop her, his long, lean body fully covering hers, giving her no time to think, or even breathe.

"I've regretted many things, Lizzie. I've regretted not telling you the truth. I've regretted every single hour of every day it cost you in that God-forsaken gaol, but I will never, ever regret loving you. And I won't allow you to regret it either." His voice in her ear was low and gritty, an agony of tortured need. He could light a bonfire with the inferno he contained. She could feel his passion smolder off him in waves.

She twisted around to catch a glimpse of his face: he looked lethal. And very, very intent. And so powerful. His body was carved by moonlight and shadow—his muscles stark with straining to control the force of his hunger.

"You need me, Lizzie. You need my body. And you want me."

Lizzie was stunned to feel the first unwelcome stirring of her newly familiar desires. No matter her wishes or her feelings, her body awakened to his dark words and barely leashed passions. Heat began to collect and unfurl from between her legs, deep inside her belly, as she looked at him, half-naked, holding himself above her. He looked relentless, dangerous, and exciting.

"I will make you ache for me, the way I ache for you. It's past time you had a quiet lesson in admitting your desire, I think. A nice," he wedged his knee between her tightly clamped legs, "hard lesson in grown-up desire. On the proper way one fucks one's husband."

For all his force, his knee came against her precisely, touching her with the exact amount of pressure needed and in exactly the right place to send shivers of want cascading down the backs of her legs. That was his real power, the precision with which he could scale her defenses, and the ease with which he demolished her resistance. Clever, clever bastard. He knew exactly what he was doing.

She tried to wriggle away, uncomfortable with the turbulence of her conflicting feelings.

"No. Hold still." He whispered it as if he knew she wouldn't. Knew she couldn't possibly obey. Knew she was already moving, trying to put her arms out and push up.

He was waiting as soon as she so foolishly obliged him: he grabbed her wrists and held them pinioned above her head, stretched out flat before him. His to control.

Her heart was pounding with exertion: a hammer inside her chest. Her own uneven breath was roaring in her ears. She was definitely, entirely out of her depth, treading on very dangerous ground.

"Can you feel how much I want you, Lizzie?" He pushed the full weight of his long, sculpted body atop her and breathed the words into her ear. "I'm bigger, I'm stronger, and I can make you *want*. I can make you *need*. I might even make you beg. Beg me to have you raining your honey down over my hand and my cock."

She would have gasped if she had any air in her lungs. Even his quiet threat was full of erotic promise.

She fought the urge to cry in frustration and confusion. She swallowed the hot tears pressing at the back of her throat. How could she hate him and want him at the same time? Want to let him do such things?

"All right, go ahead, make me, you swiving bastard." She wanted to enrage and arouse him the same way he enraged, aroused, and confused her. "See if you can make me."

Oh, but he was subtle, her Jamie. While he held her completely and exactly still, he let her feel the harsh rasp of his breath against her ear, as he pushed aside her hair to tease the sensitive side of her neck with his open mouth. He gave her no choice but to experience the unrelenting domination of his big, masculine body surrounding hers and to feel the tensile heat of his chest against her back. He invited her to discover the careful, powerful strength of his hand holding her wrists.

He left her no option but to suffer the bitter truth of the want curling slowly through her bones. He plucked her strings like an instrument attuned to his touch. He had only to move his hand slightly to the downward slide of her rib cage and she was moaning with need, aching to experience the intimate touch of his mouth and his hands on her breasts.

She could not see him. He was a dark shadow behind her, a constant unyielding presence. Under the adamant onslaught of his arousal, Lizzie felt the ties that tethered her to herself loosen and fall away. "Yes, take me. Take me with you."

Behind her, Jamie let out a low rasp of surprise. But still, his rough hands sent tendrils of anticipation trailing down the backs of her legs as he dragged up her skirts and bared her to the cool night air. And then his strong, purposeful fingers were kneading into her bottom, arranging her for his pleasure. Longing spiraled through her belly, and she moved, undulating into him to ease the terrible tension coiled at her center.

She could hear the harsh cadence of his breath as he worked to position the wide head of his cock against her and to push the length of his engorged flesh into her. She shut her eyes and opened her body to welcome him, to take him in and let him fill her.

His groan of pleasure shuddered through her chest, and he began to stroke in and out of her: long, hard thrusts she felt from the pebbled, sensitized tips of her breasts all the way down the tender inside of her thighs and on to her toes. It was too much and not enough. Not nearly enough.

Yes, more. She was becoming ravenous. She wanted to consume him and be consumed by him, swallowed whole and taken away from all the pain of this truth he forced upon her. But she had the strangest urge to tell him he was wrong. She couldn't beg. She couldn't even ask. She could only demand.

"I need more. Give me more. You promised."

A growl echoed out of his chest as she tightened her muscles on him again and again, greedy for the sweet friction of his cock. She arched her back and tilted her hips, desperate to take him deeper inside her.

"Damn you, Jamie Marlowe. Damn you."

He wrapped his free hand across her lips and put his mouth next to her ear, his words a low, gravelly rush. "Shut up, Lizzie. Hold your tongue or I won't fuck you anymore."

He sounded wounded, in pain. But how could that be, when nothing but pleasure surrounded them? When they had nothing to do but give in to the insistent demands of their bodies?

She turned her head into his palm and, with her tongue, found the tip of his finger to pull into her mouth to suck and worry and bite. His chest was heaving with the effort to breathe, crushing her into the grass, but still he rocked into her, lunging now with erratic strokes, desperate to find his release.

He finally let go of her hands, and when she pushed herself up just that fraction of an inch, his hand reached around her hip to flick a finger at the very center of her being.

"There. Touch me there. Yes."

"Lizzie. Lizzie!" He jerked hard against her back, a mixture of pleasure and pain she welcomed. And then, she felt his release roar through his body and hurl her over the edge, and she lost herself in him again.

It was savage, and it wasn't pretty, this dark roiling need within him, but he didn't care. He was long past caring. She was still wet and pulsating with the last vestiges of her orgasm, and he felt something bound up inside him fall free.

He was still somewhat stunned, unsure of exactly what had happened. Of exactly who had taught whom. The only thing he did know was Lizzie was like opium: debilitating in small doses and damn near fatal at any greater strength.

And still she would not go. And, it seemed he could not make her.

He was hopelessly in love with her, his maddening, defiant little wife. She was too clever to struggle fruitlessly, too alive, too much of a natural hedonist to fight pleasure when she could grasp it with both hands. He had used every ounce of power and control at his disposal to bring her to a shattering, explosive climax.

He would happily make himself old trying.

He had only been furious at her, at her dismissal, because he wanted her. Wanted more than just the sweet friction of her body. He wanted her to need him and want him, because he needed her. Because he wanted her to love him.

He wasn't going to accomplish that by shoving her face into the damp grass and dirt. God, what an unmitigated cad he was.

"Lizzie, are you all right? Come here, love." When he rolled his weight off her, he brought her with him, cradling her snug against his chest as he lay sprawled on his back, filling his lungs with air and gazing in stupid awe at the stars. His breath was still crashing in and out of his chest like waves against a hull, and it was a long while before either of them could account for themselves.

Lizzie roused herself first. She sat up slowly, and then stood, brushing her hair back out of her face and then bits of grass and twigs from her damp skirts.

"Lizzie." He reached out to take her hand, sure of the words he needed to say, knowing honesty was the only place to begin.

"I never want to see you again," she said.

The words carved a hollow place inside his chest. It would kill him never to see her again. It was impossible. The truth of what was between them was too big to simply dismiss. It was too strong to walk away from. They had both already tried, and failed.

"Lizzie. Please. You can't mean that. No matter what, we mean too much . . ."

She flicked that wrist to stop him. He watched as she collected the parts of herself he hadn't ever really noticed, dignity and restraint and even regret, like flotsam on the beach she'd somehow overlooked, forgotten and adrift until this moment of rediscovery.

When she spoke it was unlike her, quiet and low and devoid of any inflection. He could see the quiet, painful determination on her face.

"I don't want to need you," she said. "It hurts too much. And I don't want to see you again. You of all people, Jamie, should know I always mean it. Always."

CHAPTER 20

Lizzie hadn't slept. How could she? It was ludicrous to think she could after what had happened in the lane. As a result she was inordinately tired. And incredibly sad.

She wandered out of the breakfast room into the little octagonal room at the southeast corner of the house. Perhaps it had originally been intended as a small conservatory or orangerie, with its tall, arched windows looking out over the circular drive and east lawns. It almost felt as if she were out of doors. She could see all the way across to the woodland, over across the riot of color blooming in the disorderly perennial borders, and beyond, to the walls of the kitchen garden. And the gardener's cottage.

No. She would not do this. She would not concern herself every minute of the day with Jamie and his whereabouts. She would concern herself with the caves and their access to the house. She would meet with Maguire this morning and they would go to the caves. Afterwards, they would decide what to do and how to proceed to protect Glass Cottage and its growing number of inhabitants.

So she wasn't prepared for the sight of the beautiful curricle that bowled around the drive and drew to a smart stop under the shade of the porte cochère.

It was Wroxham. Dressed for visiting and, oh, good Lord, he was carrying a nosegay of flowers.

Lizzie didn't know whether to laugh or stamp her foot in indignation. When they had last met, it had not been under the best circumstances.

She had screamed like a fishwife. He had been intolerably obtuse.

Yet here he was, leaving his equipage to his tiger and walking around, right past her windows, to call at the front door, very correctly.

Well. Wasn't that curious?

Lizzie waited in a state of suspicious expectation until Mrs. Tupper finally found her. "Mr. Wroxham, ma'am, has come to call."

"Has he now? And where have you put him?"

"The music room, ma'am. As it was closest to the door. And I've had the new boy, the footman, Stephen, take a place in the foyer, just in case."

Mrs. Tupper's memory was just as long as hers.

"Very sensible precautions, Mrs. Tupper. But I do believe I'm prepared to extend Mr. Wroxham the benefit of my doubt. At least for the time being. Let's see what he wants, shall we?"

Wroxham stood with one hand behind his back and the other resting against the fireplace mantle. He straightened as Lizzie approached, and Mrs. Tupper, sticking to her proprieties, announced her.

"Mrs. Marlowe, sir."

"Mrs. Marlowe." Wroxham bowed and smiled charmingly, and Lizzie was again struck by how much he looked like Jamie. And how much Jamie hated him. How this visit would vex him.

Lord, but all this strategizing, all this keeping in and releasing of anger, was so infernally wearying.

She rallied herself anew and gave her guest a careful smile. "Mr. Wroxham, to what do I owe the honor?"

"An apology." He brought out his blossoms from behind his back, a bouquet of roses and hothouse flowers. "I fear I was greatly imposing upon you and your hospitality at our last meeting."

"Imposing" was a decided euphemism, but Lizzie decided to let it pass. Wroxham was on his best behavior, and so would she be. She determined not to be awkward.

"You've had a long drive out here. May I offer you some re-freshment? Tea?"

"Yes, please, I thank you."

Weren't they just the most civilized things? Lizzie was so amused at the pretty picture they were painting, she almost laughed. As it was, she gave Wroxham quite the sunniest smile she'd worn in quite some time.

"You look lovely. Quite well, I'm happy to see." He smiled back, perhaps even a bit surprised by the observation.

"As do you." And it was true. The caramel-colored coat, im-maculate fawn breeches, and brilliantly polished top boots gave him an aura of easy elegance that suited him better than the dark austerity and elaborate waistcoats of his more formal attire. The very picture of an elegant, tamed wolf.

"Will you sit?" She took her seat in one of the yellow em-broidered silk bergère chairs flanking the fire.

"I thank you. I must say the house looks beautiful. You've done it up superbly. I always thought it could turn into a proper home with the right care and attention."

He stopped then, perhaps remembering his part in its ne-glect and inattention, or perhaps because he had at one time fancied himself the person who would one day provide that care and attention. And money.

But no matter the reasons, she took the compliment grace-fully.

"Thank you. You are very kind."

"You seem to have done a prodigious amount of work. The change is remarkable."

"Yes. Would you care to see the other principal rooms while we wait for tea?"

They wandered out into the foyer, examining and exclaiming over the new circular table with its vase of blooms from their garden, past the watchful eyes of Stephen the footman, and into the dining room. It held only a table and sideboard, as the chairs as well as the drapery were still on order from the draper and upholsterer.

Wroxham said charming and appropriate things, and Lizzie almost began to relax and enjoy his company. Almost. She reminded herself a wolf didn't often come to the door unless he was very, very hungry. And she seemed to have such an embarrassment of wolves.

They moved on to the drawing room and its sunny north-facing windows, commenting on how agreeable and cool it would be in the summer not to have direct sun. All so uncharacteristically civilized, Lizzie was nearly beside herself with impatience and curiosity by the time they wandered back to the music room to find their tea.

Wroxham took it with milk and sugar and stood by the mantelpiece to drink, his gaze roaming the room.

"Do you play?" he asked when his look came to rest on the pianoforte.

"Yes, but I haven't in a long time. I'm only just starting back." Something in his gaze prompted her. It was a beautiful instrument. "And you?"

"As a matter of fact, I do."

"And would you, please? I've only heard it answer to my own poor efforts."

He put down the teacup and complied, playing a lyrical sonata. He played it beautifully, his long fingers moving smoothly and powerfully along the keys.

It was as pleasant and lovely a time as she had ever spent with any man who had come to call, let alone Wroxham. And when he had finished the piece, she rose and came to him and said simply, "Thank you," and meant it.

He smiled, a little ruefully, she thought, before he spoke. "Why is it, do you think, we've never gotten along?"

Because I always fancied your cousin.

But she said instead, "I daresay it's because we're too much alike."

"How candid. You surprise me. I had not expected such generosity."

Lizzie smiled but did not respond. She still wanted to know what all this flattery was in service of.

"But this not the first time recently you've surprised me, either."

Lizzie couldn't imagine; there was too much to choose from—her marriage, her husband's death, her recent incarceration.

"I was talking to a friend in town, in London, not Dartmouth, a friend who happens to be a fellow member of the London Corresponding Society, and he mentioned your name."

It was Lizzie's turn to be surprised. More than surprised. Astonished into wariness. Jamie had warned her against the London Corresponding Society. Quite specifically. This could not be coincidental. "Are you a member of the London Corresponding Society?"

"Yes, I am. And my mother as well. How improbable is that? That we should have such a thing in common."

"Very improbable, but true." She searched for polite conversation while the greater part of her brain blared out alarm bells. "I feel more inclined now to show you my library and my collection of books. I have as well a great many pamphlets and tracts from the society."

"Do you really? Well done. I should like to see them someday." He paused, and then shook his head. "No."

"No?"

"Just another improbable thought. I couldn't . . . It's impossible, really."

Lizzie gave him what she hoped was an encouraging smile and waited.

"Its just that we're meant to have a meeting of the society, here in Dartmouth. Some of the principal, important members are traveling, trying to build up support for the cause. But Mother's house is so small, and . . ." He let the thought trail out there, waiting for her to take the bait.

So this was why he had come all this way and lavished so many compliments upon her. It ought to have been farcical. But here it was suddenly before her: the key to everything that had gone on, and was going on, around Glass Cottage.

If the Society, as Jamie had so strongly warned her, was involved with treason, and they wanted to come here, to the Devon Coast, to a house with smuggling caves and a deepwater cove beneath it, then Jamie had been right. All along. Right from the beginning.

He had warned her, hadn't he?

And now, it seemed she held that key: the ability to bring the Society and the smugglers together here, where Jamie and his Royal Navy could see what they did and could find out once and for all what was really going on.

"I should be happy to have the honor of hosting the Society, if that is what you wish."

"Would you really?" He looked so relieved. So hopeful. "But it's so soon. Could you really do it, do you think? In three days' time?"

Lizzie smiled ruefully. "At Glass Cottage, you'll find, Mr. Wroxham, almost anything is possible."

She abandoned all her other plans. The caves could wait. And as she was the only one who knew of them, and with the expected commotion focusing attention solely on the house, her secret seemed safe enough for the time being. Nothing else mattered but proving to Jamie that she *had listened*. And she knew now he was right.

She threw herself into preparations. There was so much to do. So many furnishings to still be delivered, the drapers and upholsterers to chivvy along and the butcher to seduce into his best joints. Extra staff to be hired, rooms to be finished, beds to be made and freshly aired. The list was endless. It was hard work, but she had the satisfaction of seeing Glass Cottage shine the way it was always meant.

The only dissatisfaction was Jamie. He didn't bother to hide now, but still he wouldn't speak to her, wouldn't come near her. She was reduced to sending oblique messages through the Tuppers.

She told Mr. Tupper he was to have free rein in hiring the additional staff needed, knowing Jamie would fill the house with navy men. She told both Tuppers each and every rooming assignment of every guest, made a chart, and gave it to Mrs. Tupper, knowing she would give it to Jamie. She asked the Tuppers for their suggestions and changes to the planned entertainments, knowing they had come from Jamie. She would give him every opportunity to prove that he was right.

But still he kept his distance, only now and again looking at her, shading his eyes. Letting her get on with life without him.

The festivities began with a supper and soiree, an evening gathering for conversation. The first of the guests to arrive were Wroxham and his mother, Lady Mary Wroxham.

"I always felt we should become fast friends," Lady Mary told her in greeting, before she was forced by the press of other arrivals to give herself over to Mrs. Tupper's care.

Lizzie had dressed with great care to look her part, wearing one of her new high-waisted gowns in the French revolutionary style. It was a dark peacock blue silk, low cut and showing what was for her an inordinate amount of bosom. To counter the expanse of skin, she dressed her hair flowing loose in a bandeau style. And of course, she wore her jeweled shoes.

The ones she'd been wearing when Jamie proposed. Just for luck. She was going to need it.

The evening was a parody of what she had always dreamed her independent life would be. She was the hostess, moving amongst her intellectual and artistic company, greeting and being greeted, enjoying the witty repartee and intelligent conversation. She moved from room to room, seeing to the comfort of her guests, conferring with Mrs. Tupper, directing the new servants and keeping things running smoothly.

Lizzie was aware behind her brittle smile, she was tense as a bow. Almost frightened, even. So much was riding on this house party. Everything. When she stepped back into the drawing room, she suddenly realized all of the men, all of the players in her little personal farce, were arrayed around the edges, most of them in full footman's livery.

She had suggested the idea of the rented livery to the Tuppers with the thought that the Navy men were bound to look too rough for footmen, and would give themselves away were they not sufficiently camouflaged behind gold braid and powdered bag wigs. And here they were. The real footman Stephen, as well as Tupper, McAlden, Maguire, and Jamie, stood with their backs to the wall, silent and as unseeing as statues as they held out trays of drinks.

At least they were *supposed* to be unseeing and unhearing, but McAlden and Jamie looked as sharp as razors. How anyone was supposed to believe they were footmen was beyond belief. It was incredibly risky.

Lizzie cast her eyes across the room to find Lady Wroxham, seated on a chaise near the fire conversing with another woman from Bath or somewhere. Her back was to her nephew, but all she had to do was turn around to be able to see his face.

Lord, Jamie was playing out his game with very, very long odds. Wroxham was about, too, mostly in the music room, where he had stationed himself by the pianoforte, making himself entertaining and agreeable to any guests of a musical bent. She'd have to warn Jamie to stay out of there.

Maguire sidled up with a tray of champagne. "Best have a drink, miss, before you crack yourself in two smiling away like that."

She kept her face glued to its happy smile as she and Maguire slipped into the doorway of the butler's pantry. "How goes it?"

"Right enough, miss, with such a gang of rum-gaggers. Plenty of men for the job, though. And none of the swells have made a move, yet."

"They are all Admiralty, still in the Navy, under orders? Captain Marlowe and the rest?" She wanted to be very sure.

Maguire nodded. "Near as I can tell, ma'am. Only thing that makes sense."

"Do the free traders know who they are?"

"Not like. They've only dealt with the lower-downs, not the higher-ups. Trips back and forth to Jersey and Guernsey to establish their bona fides. They've been very canny. If you h'ant told me, I'd a never knowed."

"And what's your opinion of the other one, not his compatriot, but this one, who only comes calling when he seems to want something?" She indicated Wroxham, who waved back with a genial smile on his handsome face.

Maguire made a sound of sneering dismissal. "That one? I shouldn't trust his arse with a fart."

Well! Lizzie fought to suppress her laugh. Who would have thought Maguire and Mr. Tupper would ever have such a thing in common?

By one o'clock in the morning, many of the guests were leaving, and a few that were staying were beginning to make their way upstairs to their beds. And the "footmen" were disappearing just as fast, presumably to keep watch on the guests from the Society, which was everyone except her.

Including her. With the way Jamie had been keeping a constant watch on her, she knew she was still a suspect, no matter what information she had given to the Tuppers, and through the Tuppers, to Jamie. No matter she had arranged this whole extravagant house party for him, so he could finally do . . . whatever it was he was going to do. Arrest somebody. Prove treason.

And then, when he was done, they could finally figure out what they were going to do about them and their marriage. She didn't have very high hopes for that. Depressing, exasperating thought.

Lizzie stepped out of the drawing room and into the service corridor outside the kitchens looking for Mrs. Tupper, and he was there, pulling her back against his chest and covering her hand with his mouth before she could do or say anything.

Lizzie knew not to struggle. She waited calmly until his arms relaxed and then turned to face him. He looked awful. Tired. There were purplish hollows under his eyes. The Admiralty was working him too hard. Not that she cared.

"You look awful. It suits you."

He ran a hand through his tousled, cropped hair. He was still dressed in livery, but his white footman's wig had disappeared. He carried the damp but clean smell of the ocean, all salt and cold air, on his body. The scent that had surrounded her four nights ago. Bother. Damn him even. She was determined not to let her weakness for him distract her. Or goad her into anger.

"Lizzie, what do you think you're doing?"

She tried for witty. "I'm glad you asked. I'm meant to be having a salon, but there are still scads of people, all chatting away and drinking champagne and having far too good a time for a mere salon. Do you think I've got it wrong?"

Jamie let out an expletive so foul, she wasn't sure she understood it.

"You'll have to explain that bit about the goat. I'm afraid I can't quite comprehend your meaning."

He grabbed her and shook her once before dragging her up close. "My God, Lizzie, what am I to do with you? Every time I try to help you, to keep you safe, you end up doing something else twice as foolish."

"I can't see what is so especially foolish about hosting a salon. All the best people do it."

"Lizzie, this is intolerably dangerous. I've told you, it's treason."

"I know."

"Do you? Do you really?" His voice was low and harsh. "Do you understand that someone here, in this house—and perhaps many more than one someone—some members of the London Correspondence Society are smuggling weapons into France and French spies out? Do you understand that at least one of them and possibly more killed Lieutenant Francis Palmer, and if you don't bloody well watch your scrawny little arse, they may, if they find it convenient or necessary, kill you? If the government doesn't stretch your pretty little neck first."

He stepped back and moved towards the east door.

Lizzie put a hand to his sleeve to stay him. "Where are you going?"

"Go back to your guests, Lizzie. But keep Mrs. Tupper with you at all times. I have to leave. There are too many men to watch, too many potential avenues of escape. Be careful, damn it."

He kissed her, hard and stern, pressing his will, his warning upon her. But when his hand came up to tangle in her hair, his lips, his soft beautiful lips, turned tender and tentative.

He drew back and rested his head for a quiet moment against her forehead. Then he made a sad, incredulous sound. "What have you done?"

Lizzie had trouble placing his tone. He was talking about

treason, and she hadn't done anything treasonous. She had done all this to help him. She shook her head. "I don't take your mean—"

"Your ears." He stretched his fingers out and turned her chin aside. "They're . . ."

"Pierced." She had done it earlier that night as an attempt to play her part, to make herself appear more sophisticated and worldly. But now, with Jamie looking at her with sad, weary eyes, she felt foolish and childish, as if she'd dressed up in her mother's clothes.

"Who did this for you?"

She shrugged away any importance. "I did it myself."

"You would, wouldn't you?" He fingered the swollen, tender lobes, and she couldn't keep from scrunching up her eyes at the hot lick of pain sliding over the dull ache. "Oh, Lizzie," he chided. "Does it hurt?"

"Stop it, Jamie. I'm well aware you think I'm a child playing dangerous games. But I know what I'm doing. So it's no matter if it was painful. It's done. You once encouraged me to be fashionable, and to care about my dress, so that's what I've done. I look the way the hostess of such an assemblage should look. I look fashionable and gay. No one should have any reason to be suspicious about the real reasons for this house party. And I will keep this fashionable appearance up for as long as is necessary to convince the Society I am fully committed to the cause. In fact, I'm thinking of cutting off my hair. Several gentlemen here have told me the fashion now is all for cropped—"

"Please, Lizzie, stop. Please." He put a finger across her lips in supplication. "I don't think I could bear it." And then his hand was back at her chin, holding her still so he could look into her eyes. His clear gray gaze appraised her, open and unclouded by the lies they had become so fond of spouting. He looked at her face as if he was trying to memorize her and his eyes, full of unhappiness and disappointment, pierced her armor of indifference and left her bleeding. She pulled away, blundering out of reach. He let her go, dropping his hand to his side as a footman came through the side door.

"They're looking for you, sir."

"Coming." He took a careful, measured breath. "Stay with Mrs. Tupper, Lizzie. Have her sleep in your room tonight. And if anything should happen, come to me. Do you understand? And for God's sake, don't bloody cut your hair."

And it was only after he had gone that Lizzie realized they were finally telling each other the truth.

CHAPTER 21

Lizzie hadn't even known where she was going until she was there, at the door to the small, darkened cottage at the end of the lane. Come to him, he had said. It was all the invitation she needed.

Nothing had happened, not in the way he thought, but it was nearly three o'clock in the morning, and she hadn't been able to sleep. Mrs. Tupper snored.

She'd never been to the gardener's cottage before, and didn't know what, or who, she might encounter. The house had seemed still and quiet, but once she had slipped out the kitchen door and gained the lane, the traffic was astounding.

The putative "footmen," some still in, and others out of, livery, came and went at a scalding rate. What very busy spies they all seemed to be.

There was a light coming from the kitchen door, and she tried the knob. It opened easily, and she stepped into the tidy little kitchen. A low lantern was set on the wooden table, which was covered in charts of some kind and surrounded by people. By men. Navy men, who all stopped talking and stood to silent attention the moment she walked through the door.

Well, then. That answered her questions as to whether she was still under suspicion. Clearly, the answer was yes.

Jamie's eyes seemed flat and closed, not giving anything away. "Yes?" Yet, there was a note of urgency to his voice. He had said to come only if anything was amiss.

"Yes, might I have a moment to speak to you?"

He backed away from the table with one final glance at the men surrounding it, and said in a very noncommittal tone. "We can speak in here. Gentlemen, if you will excuse me?"

He led the way through the dark passage to the front of the house, past the narrow staircase and into an even darker room at the front of the house. Lizzie followed slowly, trailing her hands along the walls to find her way in the low light. She paused at the bottom of the stairwell, peering upwards in the dim interior, waiting for her eyes to adjust to the dark.

"What are you doing here? What has happened?"

His voice came from what must have been the front parlor.

"Might we have some light?"

"No." He was slouched in a straight-backed chair, his long booted legs sprawled out in front of him. Moonlight and the spill from the candlelight from the house across the lawns bathed him in a wash of golden white. "It's easier for us to see out if the lights are doused. For us to keep track of things. Why have you come?" His voice was a weary growl. The hour had not improved his strange mood. He was in good company. She didn't know why she'd come either. "You've really complicated things for us, Lizzie."

"I'm sorry. I'd rather hoped to simplify them."

He rose slowly, unfolding his tall form from the chair. He had changed into his rough work attire. He still looked tired, but at her words, all signs of weariness had dropped from him like a cloak. "Simplify? Do you mean to say you haven't come with your attempts to torment me with talk of cutting your hair and other acts of defiance?"

Torment him? She hadn't thought herself capable.

But he went on, misinterpreting her hesitation as some sort of answer.

"I do understand it's all the rage in Paris, where they crop off ladies' hair before they crop off their heads. *À la guillotine*, I believe they call it." He turned away and gestured her into the room. "Do come in, Lizzie, so I might oblige you."

She took a few cautious steps into the moonlit parlor. A greater portion of the little gardener's cottage sat behind the kitchen garden wall, but this corner room looked out over the east lawn towards the house. Glass Cottage glowed like a lamp across the wide velvet greens.

She jumped at the sound of metal sliding across metal and turned to find Jamie standing behind a desk, holding up a pair of wickedly sharp shears.

"Do you want to sit, or do you want to stand and let me cut away?"

"No! I didn't come here to do that."

She had come, she realized with belated clarity, because she wanted him to sound and to look at her the way he had two hours ago in the kitchen at Glass Cottage. She wanted him to look at her again, as if *something*, anything, about her mattered to him. As if *she* mattered to him.

He walked to her, crossing the room in steady strides, but Lizzie felt as if she were being stalked by a wolf. She could already feel the probe of his clear, almost luminous, gray eyes as he sought her face. She fought the urge to step back, to turn and run as fast and as far as her legs could carry her.

"Then why did you come here, Lizzie?" He was so close she could feel the heat of his breath against her neck and smell the scent of his body. Bay rum.

She smiled to herself. Footmen would never smell of bay rum. Silly, nonsensical thought, but that was it. She loved the way he smelled. She loved him. And this might be her last chance to tell him.

"There are caves under the house. They lead in from the cliff face down at the cove."

He went still, searching her face. "I know," he said finally.

"Oh. Well good. I found them, myself. The day I found . . .
you." It seemed somehow important to tell him this, so he
might credit her with the accomplishment. How foolish. "I
haven't had a chance to explore or map them yet, but I think
it's where the free traders, where your smugglers, have hidden
their cache. I think that's how Dan Pike got into the house.
And why he got into the house."

Again, there was a pause before he answered. He was
weighing her out, deciding if he was going to trust her with
the truth. "We've mapped them, McAlden and I. And so had
Francis Palmer. They're empty. And they don't lead to the
house."

"Really?" Lizzie was disappointed. "I was so sure they
would go up to the house. But if they don't connect, how did
Dan Pike get in while the doors were still barred?"

"Don't you think we've asked ourselves the same questions?"

Oh, good Lord. She hadn't. She hadn't thought so at all. She
had thought she and Maguire were the only ones who knew
anything. What had Wroxham said to her about thinking she
was the cleverest girl in the room? She certainly didn't feel
that way now.

"Don't you think we've been over every inch of that house?
Searched every cellar and attic looking for the shipments of
guns? Don't you understand why McAlden and my crew have
taken every stupid, dirty job, every workday run possible between here and the Channel Islands to try and find out who is
running the Pikes' organization? Who wants to use Glass Cottage so badly they were willing to kill Frank Palmer and even
perhaps you?"

"I didn't know. I . . ." It hit her—a low blow behind her
knees. They had been trying to kill her. She worked hard to
stay upright. To think. "I think you should tell Mr. Maguire.
Or let me tell him."

"Ah, yes, Maguire. Why do you trust this Maguire, Lizzie?

Did it never occur to you *he* might be the one? The one running this gang of cutthroats, the one who sent Dan Pike and
his pistols, the one who killed Frank Palmer, carried his body
across the hill and threw him into the Dart?"

"No! I've known him all my life. He saved my life."

There was a little moment of quiet before he inserted his
words like a knife thrust between her ribs, silent and close.

"You've known me all your life as well."

That was what it all boiled down to between them: trust.
The root source of all their problems, of all their disagreements. For all their love, they had never fully trusted one another.

Lizzie took a first tentative step into trust.

"I used to trust you just as implicitly. And I desperately want
to again."

"Really? You didn't trust me three days ago."

"No. That was a mistake. I should have done."

He stepped so close she could see the sheen of moonlight
in his luminous eyes. "Do you trust me now?"

"No," she whispered and saw his eyes sharpen with a pain
so keen she felt its cut herself. "No, Jamie. I don't entirely
trust you, not only because you've still got those wicked, sharp
scissors in your hand, but because you've got that look in your
eye." She leaned in close and raised her lips to his ear. "The
one that tells me you'd very much like to take all my clothes
off and take me, naked, right here in the middle of your car-
pet."

His body stiffened and he might have held his breath, so
she continued. "And I rather hoped you might have seen I
had a look in my eyes that tells you I'd very much like to take
off all my clothes and lie down and fuck you right here, in the
middle of your front parlor."

She heard the slice of air as the scissors dropped, but he
stepped away. She felt the enormous gulf those scant inches
opened up between them. Felt the chilling loss of his heat.

"No," he said quietly, but firmly. "Not in the middle of the floor. Not naked in the front parlor. You're my wife and I mean to make love to you properly, in a proper bed."

He took her by the hand and led her, quietly and slowly, up the steep, narrow stairs and into his small, steeply pitched room and next to his narrow, soft bed.

"Handsomely now, Lizzie," was all he said.

They undressed each other slowly and carefully, like an old married couple. Like a couple who had all the time in the world together, every day, and never had to rush and fumble. Like a couple whose love and devotion and respect were made manifest in long languid strokes and quiet, low words. Who took the time to savor and appreciate each other. Who knew by heart the things to do and say to make the other sigh in bliss, and offer their bodies to each other in pleasure.

And when they had done, and were sated with the physical pleasure, they held each other close and were still, with nowhere to go, and nothing left to hide from one another.

Marlowe tightened his arms to hold her closer. "Lizzie." He said it like an incantation, as if he could bind her to his soul. As if he could keep her next to him like this, quiet and soft, forever. But with Lizzie, the storm clouds were never far off.

She sighed, a long shiver of breath, and he braced for her dismissal. "This is how I always imagined it would be."

He answered cautiously. "How what would be?"

"Between us."

"Quietly erotic?" He let his hand shape her lovely little breast in encouragement.

"No, I mean yes, but that's not what I meant."

"What did you mean?" He caught some of her quiet gravity, her wistfulness.

"I meant this was how I had always imagined our first time together would be. In your narrow bed, in a small cottage somewhere. Somewhere cozy, just the two of us, and that after you made love to me for the first time I would feel . . ."

He rolled up on his elbow so he could see her face. He let the silence lengthen for a long moment, until he quietly prompted, "You would feel?"

"Complete."

Marlowe felt a welling of tenderness. Oh, yes, this he understood. Completely. He brushed a loose strand of hair off her face. "And do you?"

"Yes, I suppose, now."

The breath he didn't realize he'd been holding relaxed. He thought about her answer for another moment as he stroked her hair and then asked, "And did you not before?"

"No. I didn't understand. I thought it was something you could give me. But I never thought we would be at odds with each other the way we have been."

That was an extraordinarily polite description of what had occurred between them, but it was important to show her he understood. "Yes, we have been at odds, haven't we?"

"Yes." She was quiet again for along time. He gathered her to him, so her head could rest against his chest, to encourage this extraordinary rush of confidences. "Did you mean what you said, really? About the government and treason, and my," she swallowed hard, "neck?"

"Yes. I'm sorry." He tightened his arms around her, trying to temper his fierce possessiveness. "But I'll do everything in my power to see it doesn't happen. That you're safe. I'll protect you."

Not even an extraordinary rush of confidences could change her personality. "I don't need you to protect me," she began with predictable bravado. "I can take care—"

He cut her off. He wasn't going to stand for such a ludicrous fiction any more. "Lizzie, do you honestly think what you've been doing has been either prudent or effective? You've taken care of yourself by what? By carrying around that fowling piece like a third arm? By shooting Dan Pike and bringing the rest of the smuggling confederation down on your head? By ignoring every piece of sane advice to go back to town and leave this godforsaken house behind?"

She shook her head stubbornly. "No. I can't leave the house, it would—"

"Why is that bloody house so God-damned important to you?"

"Because it was yours, you ass! Because you gave it to me. Because you gave me everything I had ever dreamed I had wanted, all covered with roses and windows and stars, God damn it. Stars! You made me see stars." Lizzie punctuated her speech with vehement little pokes to his chest. But she wasn't trying to move away.

His smile started deep in his chest and by the time it made it all the way up to his mouth, he was almost laughing.

"Why, my darling, Lizzie, that is completely and hopelessly sentimental."

They might have both laughed if there were enough room between them to draw sufficient breath, but he could feel her smile. And hear it in her voice.

"I've missed you." It was a quiet admission, but he would have heard it in a room full of noise. He'd been waiting and longing to hear it.

"I have missed you, too, Lizzie."

But all this emotion, all this sentiment was too much for her. "How can you miss me when you haven't gone away?"

But this time he caught the self-mockery in her languid humor. He did laugh then and kissed the top of her head. He picked up a strand of her silky hair and ran it through his fingers. It was rather extraordinary, talking to her, being with her like this.

She glanced cautiously at his face before she asked, "What are you going to do now?"

"Tonight? Or rather today? My duty." He thought she had

finally come to understand this, but he had to be sure. "Figure out which one of your guests is our smuggler. Which one of them killed Frank."

"And when this particular duty is over?" Another careful probe.

"I'll receive another posting from the Admiralty. Hopefully, a more straightforward posting to a frigate or any ship in one of the fleets seeing action."

"And what about me? Are we even really married?" This time he could feel the quiet tension of her body.

"I suppose that depends on you, Lizzie. I thought—" he hesitated. "I hoped you loved me."

"Perhaps I did." Her voice was quiet and small. "But that was before you lied to me. No, that's not right, is it? That was only before I found out you'd lied to me. You'd been lying all along. I just didn't know it."

"I don't suppose you might forgive me?" The tightness in his chest grew unbearable. He supposed he really ought to breathe.

"Is that what you thought I'd do?"

"Don't know. I suppose I thought you'd shrug your elegant little shoulder and tell me you didn't give a royal damn what I did so long as I said I loved you."

But she remained quiet. He could feel her eyelashes against his chest, fluttering back and forth as she blinked. Trying to find an answer. Or hold back tears.

"Can you forgive me?" The tightness grew into a sharp, steady pain.

"You left me in gaol," she whispered, her voice thin and haunted. "Your plan, or mission, or whatever it is, landed me in Dartmouth Gaol, for weeks. Endless weeks," her voice cracked. "I don't like being in my house, my own house, for longer than a few hours. I hate being shut up. You know I can't even abide a carriage ride, and you left me there, locked up for days and days, and I got infested with vermin, and I've never been so dirty or so humiliated in my entire life. And you just left me there." She was crying now. He felt the warm wash of her tears against his skin.

"I'm sorry, Lizzie. So sorry." And he was. Deeply. And he would make it right. He would give her the future she wanted, even if it didn't include him. "I'll make it up to you. I promise. I'll buy you another house all your own. One made entirely of glass so you'll never feel closed in."

"But that's this house. Glass Cottage. That's why I love it. Why I can't leave."

But she was still holding on to him, her arms latched around his neck. It occurred to him that she was not letting go. That she was staying with him. So he continued to hold her carefully and reverently, and stroked her hair and her back and kissed away her tears until she settled back against his chest. She wasn't leaving him.

"But the house is just a building. Suppose we could, or need to, live elsewhere? What if I asked you to come live aboard a ship? My ship."

"Would you really? I would say yes." Sweet, emphatic Lizzie.

"And you wouldn't need this house?" He wanted to be sure. He remembered how he'd wanted her to admire the house, so she'd admire him.

"It's not just the building. The house was the answer, I suppose. My answer to my discontent."

"Lizzie, how could you be discontented? You had everything—family, fortune, education placed in your hands."

"*I* didn't have them, not truly. My father did. And once I grew up, all of those things I had were to be denied me, just because I am a woman."

"I don't understand? How could he deny you what he'd already given?

"By simply removing them. I had no further education, and no choice about the manner of making my fortune. And for no other reason than that I was a female. My only choice, other than—I don't know, becoming a starving, ill-thought-of old maid—was to marry." She rolled onto his chest, poking it with a stiff little finger as she made each of her points. "By the simple fact of your birth, you have, by right, everything—education, affluence, and influence. How can you wonder when some portion of that comes our way, we should not grasp it with both hands? That is what this house was—my opportunity."

"Your opportunity for independence?"

"Yes. Do you see? The only real way for a woman to make her way in this world, in this society, is to marry. I was never inclined towards that state, but I needed to be 'got rid of,' hadn't I? My father gave me a fine dowry, but that money wasn't ever to be mine. It was for my husband to control, and would never have been given to me for my own use if I did not marry. Though he has never spoken of it to me, I know he has left his estate entirely, less my mother's jointure, to his nephew."

"But that is life. That is simply the way of the world, Lizzie. You should be glad of what he did do for you. I had only education from my father. Affluence and influence I have had to make for myself."

"So you of all people should understand. My education was cut off, just as it would have made me capable of making my own affluence. Such a thing is feared above all else: that a woman, at least a woman of my class, should use her mind to make her way in the world. They had much rather she use her body, for all their moralistic talk."

"Don't say bad things about what happens with our bodies—I hold that rather sacred."

She rolled over onto her back and stared up at the low ceiling.

"I had never realized how dependent I was. I had taken it all for granted. I never dreamed it could all go away. That he could take it away. And all I could do was marry, but I don't possess the happy faculty of making men feel pleased with themselves."

"I beg to differ. You make me very happy. When you're not making me unbearably sad. But can you forgive me?"

She didn't answer right away. She shut her eyes for the longest time before she spoke. "That all depends on you, Jamie. The other day you reminded me of our vows. To love and honor. Why couldn't you do that? Why did you choose to use me, and place your mission before me?"

Marlowe didn't hesitate. "I was committed to this mission before I ever thought of you. No, that's not right. When I was assigned to come back to Dartmouth all I could think of was you. How I could use my position to my advantage to get you. To get you back. You were all I ever wanted. All I had ever loved. And it seemed at first that we would both get what we wanted. I just hadn't weighed the cost, to you or to my family. I thought it would all come right in the end. But then you were taken." He rolled away and scrubbed his hand over his face. "Nothing in my life, no assignment, no battle, no loss, has ever been so hard as seeing you in Dartmouth Gaol. Nothing on this earth has ever tested my resolve that much. Nothing. Because I never expected you to fall in love with me."

Lizzie's eyes grew bright with tears. He thumbed them carefully away.

"And I can't swear to you that something like that will never happen again. Because you're you and I'm me, and we seem to have an unholy talent for getting ourselves in trouble together. But I am sorry for what happened, and I'll spend the rest of my life doing whatever it takes to make it up to you. I will care for you. I will protect you. I will never leave you alone again if you can forgive me, and let me stay."

CHAPTER 22

Jamie walked Lizzie back across the lawn in the cool night air, his arm thrown around her shoulder. They walked all the way around to the library, where she'd left open the latch before she'd slipped out of the house to be with him. When they reached the terrace, she turned and he kissed her softly on the lips. She leaned back against the wide casements and pulled him against her, absorbing the last vestiges if his heat and warmth. His love.

"Try to get some sleep," he said, before he kissed her one last time on the forehead and moved off into the dark to relieve McAlden.

She stayed, pressed back against the casement of the door, and watched him move off through the first faint glimmer of dawn. When she couldn't see him anymore, she opened the wide French doors and slipped inside, stifling a large yawn. She could possibly catch a few hours of sleep before she had to put in an appearance. And she was the hostess—she could set the tone. Most women of her acquaintance who were on the social whirl never rose before noon.

"I must say, I am disappointed. Consorting with the footmen? Really, Mrs. Marlowe, that really is too vulgar. It shows

the morals of a she-cat. Even for a widow so young and newly
bereaved as you."

Lizzie's absolute fright and horror dissipated quickly under
Wroxham's scorn. At the first sound of his voice, her hand had
flown to her chest, but her heart was already regaining its normal, steady beat. Indeed, such sniping was the normal order of
the day with Wroxham. It was their getting along that had
been so unusual.

"Wroxham. I didn't see you there."

"Evidently not. And why would you, with your arms all
over your footman?"

"He was the groundsman, really." Lizzie was feeling wonderfully perverse. "I prefer that hearty, out-of-doors type."

"Really? Dirt under the fingernails? How gauche."

"As you noted, I'm a widow, Mr. Wroxham. My preferences
are nobody's business but my own."

"True, but I have to wonder if your tastes have deteriorated
because you live so far out from town and have become, shall
we say, countrified. Or if you choose to live so far from town to
satisfy your deplorable taste."

"Is there a point to all this elegant abuse, Mr. Wroxham? I
really am quite tired."

"Yes." He drew himself up before her. "I'd actually come to
seek you out earlier and I waited. I waited a long time actually.
Because I thought . . ." He paused, and shook his head, weighing his words carefully. "I had thought you and I shared . . . a
certain sensibility. But you're a newly bereaved widow and
very young. And in such a circumstance I suppose a certain
amount of . . . allowance needs to be made. I had hoped you
might give some thought to allowing yourself to be guided by
an older and wiser, more experienced hand. My hand."

There was a very awkward silence, during which Lizzie
tried desperately to misunderstand his words.

"Mr. Wroxham, I am . . . confused." She tried to keep her

tone as polite as possible. A gentleman who made dramatic, break-of-dawn proposals was bound to have delicate sensibilities. Especially a gentleman who had all but called the woman to whom he was proposing a whore. It was bound to be difficult. And she was far too tired for a fuss. "Are you by any chance offering to make me your mistress?"

He pursed his lips together tightly and then said, "I said my hand, cousin Elizabeth. My hand."

He must be very, very hard up for money. Lizzie raised her eyes heavenward to contemplate the beamed ceiling, as she thought of what on earth to say. The wooden molding was covered with beautifully carved scrolls of flowers and flower faces, and there, in the corner, near the casement for the French doors, was the carved leaf-face of a Green Man, the pagan god of the forest, of whom she was particularly fond. But the little green gentleman had nothing to say and no advice to give in the present circumstance.

There was really nothing she could say besides "no thank you." There was no explanation she could give. *Sorry, but your cousin, my husband, isn't really dead, and I've spent the night being well* . . . would only make everything, *absolutely* everything, so much worse.

But a thwarted proposal *would* give her a very convenient and plausible excuse for vacating the premises and taking herself off to Hightop Manor, or London, or Manchester. Some place suitably remote where she couldn't be accused of fomenting treason.

And still she had her delicate refusal to give. By now, the first warm glimmers of dawn had already crept over the cliffs and swept over the lawns. She could begin to see Wroxham more clearly. He stood, stiff and still, with his hands clasped behind his back, waiting. Waiting for her answer.

How had she ever thought he was anything like Jamie?

"Mr. Wroxham, you do me a great, undeserved honor by

your proposal. I am only too sorry to be unable to accept it. Now, if you'll pray excuse me, I must be alone."

He did not take the hint and retreat in haughty dignity as he was meant to. He didn't do anything. He just stood there and let the silence build.

Oh, Lord. This was going to be terribly awkward, and he was no doubt going to say all sorts of things unbecoming to a gentleman, and she was going to say all sorts of things she would never have the scruples to regret. But she ought to try.

"I am sorry, Mr. Wroxham. And I am very tired. It has been a very trying night. It's been a very trying month, don't you know?"

The sun continued its slow climb to the treetops, and even though they were on the north side of the house, the golden light of morning was warming the rich wood tones of the paneling. It really was a very pretty room. She was going to miss Glass Cottage desperately. She was going to miss Jamie desperately. But she was going to do as he asked and leave the rest of the entire business to him. For the time being. It was as much as she could promise.

But there was still Mr. Wroxham, who would not go. The faintest poundings of a headache began at the back of her neck near the base of her skull. She straightened her shoulders to shake it off. And changed the subject.

"It really is a very pretty room, isn't it? And the rest of the house. It all came together quite nicely, don't you think?"

"The house is magnificent."

A lovely concession. It was something. And it was so much better than the part when he had called her a whore. They would simply have to stick to architecture. But she would do it on the move. If he would not retreat, she would.

Lizzie stepped away from the wide French doors and across to the open door to the hallway. The lime-washed, paneled casement surrounding the door was just as wide as the others.

In fact, there was another little face, which she had never noticed before, in the carving.

"How pretty," she prattled. "I have never noticed this one before. Such beautiful carvings, such detail. I have always admired it, and no doubt you have too?"

"Are you . . . are you refusing me?"

"I am but newly bereaved, Mr. Wroxham, and a good deal of that time I have spent unjustly imprisoned."

He colored, two vivid spots high on his cheeks. Yes, perhaps he'd forgotten that little blight on his potential wife's character.

"It is simply too soon for me to make any sort of decision regarding my future. I need time to recover."

"You didn't need time when you married my cousin."

"No. You are correct. We didn't take any time. And that was a decision I came to regret." She had since, in fact as recently as last night, gotten over that regret, but that was nothing Wroxham need to know. She only needed to extricate herself delicately from this ridiculous situation. "Please, Mr. Wroxham, I beg you would understand. I bid you good morning." And she closed the door in his face.

Well, she thought as she hurried, lest Wroxham decide to follow, up the stairs and down the hall to hallway to her bedchamber, she certainly hadn't seen that coming. Such an extraordinary proposal.

He must be very hard up for money. Maguire had confirmed that his pockets were completely empty. And the way she had lavished so much spending on Glass Cottage, she had practically advertised herself to the county's gamesters: *rich widow to let.*

Lizzie threw herself on the top of the bed. She couldn't possibly get to sleep now, even though she was almost shaky from fatigue. What a night.

She turned to see if Mrs. Tupper had been so kind enough to leave a glass of water the previous night, and there it was, a small decanter and glass resting on its usual tray in the corner cabinet.

Lizzie heaved a long-suffering sigh and slid her feet off the bed. She hoped a long drink of cool water would help her pounding head. It must be the fatigue. She had been too busy last night to drink more than a few sips of wine or champagne, so she couldn't be cup-shot.

She reached to refill her glass and she saw it, another small face carved into the decoration, this time in mother of pearl. Lizzie stooped down to contemplate this laughing, impish face.

Why, they must be all over the house. Whoever had originally built the place must have had a marvelously puckish sense of humor to place these delightful imps throughout the place. It was almost as if the spirit of the place were laughing at her.

A strange feeling, like floating in cold water, came over her. She felt suspended, staring at the carving, repeating her own words in her head. The house was laughing at her.

Could it be so simple?

She looked around. The casements on the windows. The depth they gave the walls. And here in this room, she was directly above the library. Directly above the wide casement she had leaned back against this morning. Directly above the first carving she had noticed. The Green Man.

Lizzie clasped the little mother-of-pearl face with fingers suddenly slippery with nerves and pushed. Nothing happened. She pushed up, down and to each side. Nothing. Perhaps she was wrong and the house was laughing at her in more ways than one. But then she pinched the delicate little creature's nose between her fingers and turned.

There was an audible click, and slowly, carefully, Lizzie pulled the whole cabinet away from the wall. It squeaked and creaked loudly on its hinges. The mechanisms hadn't been oiled in ages.

That was the sound: the hinges creaking. That was the sound she had heard from the library that night, the night Dan Pike had broken in. He must have tripped a noisy panel in the library casement.

Lizzie peered into the dark and dusty space behind the wall. What a discovery! A tight, dirty passageway led to a hole in the floor. No, not a hole, but an opening with a ladder built into the far end of the wall. It led both upwards to the floor above and down.

She checked the back of the cabinet to see if she could discover how the panels opened from the inside. She was nearly beside herself with excitement, but she hadn't become so foolish as to lock herself into her own walls. The thought of being trapped inside *this* enclosed space made her heart start to tighten and pound.

She left the first cabinet open and went over to the other corner, found the elaborately carved flower face in the same spot, and twisted. It popped open as well. Good Lord, it was just like the caves in the cliff face—the house must be riddled with them. This one didn't appear to lead anywhere. Just a safe hiding place—a priest's hole.

But the other, she would lay odds, led down to the library— the room where all her troubles with Dan Pike and the smuggling confraternity had begun.

She ran back down the stairs and tore straight back into the library until she was face-to-face with the Green Man. She reached for his long, pointy nose and gave the Green Man a tweak.

The lime-washed wood panel beneath the bookcase popped open with a loud creak. Lizzie ducked down and peered in, and this time she could see it clearly—the metal latch mechanism. She moved into the space and touched it, and a second door panel swung open to the outside. She crawled out onto the library terrace. She'd found Dan Pike's most likely entrance route.

It was a very promising start.

"Mrs. Marlowe?"

She screeched. And jumped. And then dissolved into nervous laughter. It was only Wroxham, where she had left him, sitting woebegone in a chair, nursing a brandy.

"Mr. Wroxham, you will forgive me. But I've just made the most astonishing discovery."

He rose and came towards her, peering in astonishment through the open panels. Bloody persistent man. He had to be got rid of. Immediately.

"Mr. Wroxham, yes. I need your help. I need you to call Mr.—" She almost said Mr. Marlowe. Lord. "Mr. Maguire," she finished. "No. Don't bother." She could see Jims trudging across the lawn, coming to the kitchens for his breakfast.

"Jims," she called across the lawn and waved her arms to get his attention. "Get Mr. Maguire."

The boy stopped, turned back to look towards the stables and then turned back toward Lizzie. "Don't know where he is, ma'am," he called back.

"Just find him," she shouted.

Lizzie reentered the library through the French doors and found the carving on the opposite panel. When it swung open, she could see this was the passage connected to the ladder and corner cabinet in her bedchamber. But this passage was larger, slightly wider, running behind the bookshelf. And it had a narrow stairway that led down. She couldn't possibly go in there. Certainly not alone.

Wroxham was still standing there, still as a statue, gawping at her.

"Mr. Wroxham, if you would be so kind as to fetch the steward, Mr. Tupper. You know the house. He'll most likely be in the kitchens. Tell him. He'll know what to do."

Wroxham looked strangely undecided.

"Mr. Wroxham. I must insist you find Mr. Tupper for me. I need to wait here for Mr. Maguire."

"What goes on here? Jeremy?" Of all people, Lady Mary Wroxham had risen supremely early from her bed to join them.

Lovely. This was not good. If this kept up, she'd be leading guided tours of Glass Cottage's subterranean passages. Like the Catacombs in Rome, full of delightfully horrified pilgrims. Only these guests were all suspects.

This was a very bad idea.

"She's found the passageway."

Lady Wroxham brushed by her son for a closer look. "How?"

"Some carving on the wall."

Lady Wroxham was close to Lizzie now, crowding up to her, peering her birdlike face into the dusty gloom. Her look was not one of idle fascination.

"Fascinating isn't it?" Lizzie edged back towards the doors to the lawn.

Lady Wroxham ignored her. "Who else knows?" she asked her son.

"No one. Yet."

"Get a light. There, the branch on the table. Light it with the taper on the mantle. Hurry."

"Lady Wroxham, I do understand your excitement, really, I share it, but we must not be hasty." Another moment and she'd be out the door, and onto the lawn where she could get help.

"Shut up," the lady snapped over her shoulder. "Bring it quick. Here." She took the candles from her son. "Now get her in there."

And before Lizzie had a chance to tell the stupid old bat to shut up herself and go to hell while she was at it, Wroxham was obeying his mother and bundling her roughly through the larger opening. He was faster than she had expected. She'd underestimated him. She'd underestimated them both. Lady Wroxham stepped in behind them and shut the door.

Lizzie's heart began to pound. Oh, Lord, it was just like

Dartmouth Gaol. Only worse. Here the walls were much closer; she could touch them on each side. The air was dank and still and unused. And the only light was from Lady Wroxham's candles.

"Here," and the lady passed the larger of the two branches over her head to Wroxham.

Tall, Jamie-like Wroxham. There were certainly bastards enough to go around in that family, weren't there? He still held her arms in a tight, painful grasp.

"Take her down. Move."

Wroxham complied, pulling Lizzie behind him towards the stairs as Mary Wroxham shoved at her back from behind. Lizzie decided this was as good a place as any to make a stand, now that she had been so foolish as to let them get her in here. And she had had just about enough of Lady Wroxham's rude behavior. Really. It was hard to believe she was the rector's wife's sister.

"Don't shove me," she hissed, and even though Wroxham still had her arms, she kicked back viciously with her foot. She caught Lady Wroxham in the gut, and the older woman went back hard against the wall.

"Don't hurt my mother." Now it was Wroxham's turn to yank hard on Lizzie and send her shoulder into the wall. Lizzie gave him a nasty, fierce jab with her elbow and heard him stumble on the top steps of the stairs.

Quite a pathetic little scuffle they were having within the walls—like huge rats arguing over a crumb of cheese. They'd have the whole house awake in no time. Speaking of which. Lizzie opened her mouth and let out a bloodcurdling scream.

"Shut up," Lady Wroxham hissed from behind. And then there was the distinctive metallic snick of a gun hammer being cocked back. Lady Wroxham had pulled out a pistol. The deadly bore winked at Lizzie in the dim, wavering light.

"Down. Now."

And so they went. Lizzie kept her hands out to either side, touching the wall to keep her balance and bearings as they went.

It was a very long way down. She counted sixty-two steps in all. The first twenty-eight had been in a straight line down wooden steps, putting them, she thought somewhere deep under the music room. But then the passage walls had given way to stone and they had taken a flight of twisting stone steps, curving down to the right. Then another close passageway carved out of the rock and another shorter left-handed stair. Which brought them to a stop in front of a thick door made of oak and covered with metal studs.

"It stops," Wroxham called over his shoulder. "There's a door, but no handle."

"It's broken," Lady Wroxham stated.

"Broken?" her son echoed. "Then how do we go on?"

"We don't."

"Then why did we come, if we can't get out?"

"We can get out, back the way we came. But first you need to kill her."

Lizzie's mind had been busy gleaning information, such as the fact that while Lady Mary was well familiar with the passages, her son was not. He had not been down here before. But such a command snapped Lizzie's attention back to Lady Wroxham.

"Kill her?" Wroxham looked at Lizzie, standing caught between them, with genuine horror. Lizzie doubted Lady Wroxham had been brought up to date on Wroxham's latest matrimonial plan to keep himself in money. "I don't want to kill her."

"You don't think I'm going to do it? You killed the last one."

"By accident, damn it. He cracked his skull on the stone floor."

"Yes, before he could tell us what he'd done to break the mechanism. Well done."

Wroxham's face was pinched down hard. Oh, he surely was navigating his treacherous way between a rock and a whirlpool. And his mother was done with her explanations. She handed him the pistol and took the large branch, then lighted the single candle that had snuffed out when Lizzie had shoved her. She handed the single flame to Wroxham.

"Shoot her. No one will hear it this far down. We'll get the body when we can get Pike and the others down here to open that door."

"Don't you think someone will miss me?"

Lady Wroxham turned the full force of her icy gaze upon her. "I really don't give a damn."

Lizzie was about to say that Maguire and Jamie and every servant in the place likely knew about the passageway by now, and they were probably on their way to save her, but maybe that would give Lady Wroxham too much information, give her an edge. No, best to take her chances with Wroxham. At least he liked her well enough to have asked to marry her. And he did seem sincere about his desire not to shoot her.

So she let Lady Wroxham go without another word. She would try her gambit on Wroxham.

"I think I know how to open it." She turned and gave him her back, moving, making herself not a target, and thinking of the right thing to say while she searched. "It's like a puzzle, all these catches. In the house they were all the same, but different. They were all up on the right."

And then she saw it. A smooth pebble, seemingly stuck to a little ledge on the wall. "There." She pointed. It was out of her reach. That made two things she knew about the man who had built Glass Cottage and all these caves—he had a funny sense of humor and he was tall. No wonder tiny Lady Wroxham was in such a bad state. "You get it. I can't reach it. I'll hold the candle."

But Wroxham was cautious. "Move back."

"Oh, come Wroxham, you don't think I'm going to try anything? I know you won't shoot me, no matter what your mother says." But she backed away, easing past him. If she got on the other side of him, she could douse the light and make a run for it. Sixty-two steps. First two—up to the right. She could do it.

But it must have shown in her face.

"No. Come here." He reached out and pulled her back against his chest, with the gun tightly pressed against her temple.

Lizzie felt all the breath leave her chest. Oh, Lord. He just might do it after all.

He reached up and grasped the pebble, and then had to readjust his grip as he realized the pebble was just the placeholder for a long chain that disappeared into the wall. The heavy door began to creak upwards like a drawn portcullis. That's exactly what it was, a miniature portcullis.

It stopped. The bottom edge was only about five inches off the dirt floor. Wroxham pulled again on the chain, yanking hard. Something on the left flashed. A tiny piece of light winked at her. Wroxham let the chain out and then pulled hard. The light winked again.

"I think . . ." Lizzie stopped herself. Something was jammed into the tiny crack between the portcullis and the stonewall. She saw it now. A pen—a thin brass pen tip. The expensive kind one got at a stationer's shop, with the metal nib. It must have been Palmer's. This must have been what Lady Wroxham meant when she said Palmer deliberately disabled the mechanism.

But if she told Wroxham about it, then they would open the door and go to the other side and he might shoot her. Or she could push the lit candle into his arm and try to wriggle under the gap at the bottom. But then she'd be on the other side of the door, trapped. She didn't know what to do.

Wroxham pressed the muzzle more firmly into her temple. "How does it open?"

"You do realize I've only just discovered this place and I

don't know a thing about it? But I think it's jammed." She was babbling.

"Very good." His tone was sarcastic, but Lizzie could tell, could practically feel, he was thinking too.

"Wroxham, why did you ask me to marry you?"

"Flattered, were you? Don't be. Because you're rich, with all of my bastard cousin's money, and you're in possession of this house, the house that should have been mine, and it seemed marriage to you would solve two problems, my mother's and mine."

"Oh," Lizzie nodded her understanding. "That makes sense. But I also thought you might feel something . . ." She turned slightly against him so the side of her breast, rather magnificently displayed in her low cut blue gown, would slide against his arm.

She felt him stiffen, both, as Maguire would say, high and low. She shifted her weight in the other direction, so the front of her breasts might brush against the arm raised to hold the chain.

"Perhaps we might . . . come to an understanding?"

He still seemed undecided, holding himself as stiff and still as he had this morning. But he wasn't holding her as tightly any more, so she turned fully, so her breasts brushed right across the front of his coat and his view, as he looked down at her, was filled with a creamy expanse of flesh.

"You really do have the morals of a she-cat." His words were full of contempt, but his body was an entirely different proposition. He was hard.

"I really do. And you're hard. And if all this," she leaned in close and whispered, "is about a thwarted fuck, then why don't you open those breeches and show me what you've got to bargain with?"

CHAPTER 23

Wroxham let go of the chain and reached down for the close on his breeches. Lizzie shifted back, leaning against the portcullis door with half-closed eyes. And when he looked down to free his cock, she kicked him right between the legs as hard and mean and angry as she possibly could. As he collapsed in on himself, she hit his wrist hard with the candle-holder until he dropped the gun. The candle dropped out and rolled, still lit, behind him. She kicked him again, this time in the head, and although he wavered, he still did not go down. She was too small—she'd never get by him. There was no time for anything else. She dropped to the dirt, grabbed up the gun, and scrabbled her way under the jammed door.

The first thing to hit her was the darkness. The second was the stench. It was gut-wrenchingly horrible, a dank metallic miasma that clogged up her nose and lodged in her throat. She felt as if she'd already been sick.

She moved up against the wall beside the door, out of Wroxham's line of sight should he choose to look under the gate, and waited for her eyes to adjust to the thin light still coming from the single candle in the dirt on the other side of the door.

It was too thin, and the darkness too dense. And Wroxham

was stirring. She could hear his deep breaths as he struggled to regain himself. And then he must have picked up the candle, because the light waned.

She edged along the wall to the right. It was stone, carved out of the living rock. She reached her hand up the wall, over her head, and could feel it curve inward slightly. So the ceiling was about six feet. She pressed on, inching jerkily to the right.

Wroxham was doing something, searching for the jam in the mechanism. He must have been moving the candle up and down along the seam, because the light kept disappearing.

Her foot hit something and she bent down to search out a hard, cloth-covered bundle with her fingers. They came to a button, then another. Oh, sweet Lord above. It was a body. The stench. It was a deteriorating body.

Not Frankie Palmer's, she was at least glad to remember. They'd fished him out of the Dart. Someone else then. She was nearly jumping out of her skin, involuntarily jerking herself up and over the body so she could continue along the wall. And then wooden boxes stacked high on her right. She followed the line of the crates. Five of them, at least, one in front of the other and stacked, she searched with her fingers, five tall. At least twenty-five crates. Of guns. Had to be. She felt around the front. Long crates. As long as a gun, yes.

The door creaked. Wroxham was moving it slightly, up and down, gaining an inch or so at a time. In another moment he'd have it open.

She could hide behind the crates, if she could find the edge of them. But they had been stacked up tight against the wall. He'd come around eventually and find her.

And she'd have to shoot him.

She'd done it before. She could do it again. It might not be her fowling piece, but it would do. She crouched at the corner of the crates and pulled the hammer back. Or would have, if the hammer mechanism hadn't been jammed. The sand, when she'd crawled through.

Shite and damn. Of all the bloody bad luck.

She'd have to hit him. Hit him hard and get by him to go up the passage, and hope to God that Jamie or Maguire or someone had dealt with Lady Wroxham and she wasn't lying in wait at the other end.

She scurried across the sand, low and careful lest she trip on any more bodies, and came up against the right side of the door. No, the left. His right side would be stronger, and he would most likely put the candle in his left. It would make him a little blind on his left side. And everything, all the mechanisms, everything had been to the right. He would look to his right.

She skirted around and pressed her back into the wall.

There it was again. That strange feeling of floating in icy water. Her hands were cold but slippery with nervous sweat. She wiped them on her skirts and closed them tight around the barrel of the pistol.

The door gave one more heave, and then it rolled up. Wroxham was still holding the chain, unsure. He held the candle forward, in his left hand, but didn't step through. And then she heard the rustle of the chain as he released it. She pressed back, caving into herself, willing herself into the indentations in the rock, and making herself as small as possible.

It took forever. He moved so slowly, so cautiously, reaching out with his left hand high in front. His wrist appeared, then his elbow, followed by the long length of his upper arm, his shoulder and then, finally his upper back and his head. And just as she brought the gun butt down on the back of his skull, he swung left, his arm crashing her into the wall. But she had hit him and he was going down.

She hit him again and again, even as she fell with him, the skirts of her gown tangled with his legs. She kept her arm free and hit and hit.

A gunshot roared from down the passage past her head. She

could hear the unearthly whiz of the bullet and feel the belch of sulfurous smoke as it passed.

Lady Wroxham had returned. She stood in the passage, holding up the branch, a tiny, hideous Medusa.

Lizzie was pinned under Wroxham's heavy, unconscious form. She pushed at him, but her skirts were hopelessly tangled. She grabbed at the fabric pulling, tugging.

Lady Wroxham threw her spent weapon on the ground in disgust and advanced down the passage like a vengeful fury. Lizzie kept on pulling but it was useless. Lady Wroxham was already there, standing over her, breathing hard. Wax dripped off her candle and splashed onto Lizzie's face, burning her.

She flinched away, but Lady Wroxham's face lit with the genius of an idea.

"A Lady," she spat, "doesn't like to have to do for herself, but for you, I'll make an exception."

She reached down, and would have thrust the burning candles into Lizzie's face, but Lizzie let go of her own skirts, grabbed the hem of Lady Wroxham's, and yanked as strongly as she could.

Lady Wroxham went down hard. The candle branch fell back and hit the sand behind her.

"Lizzie! Lizzie!" The call came from far away, somewhere in the passage. Jamie, Jamie was coming. Thank God, Jamie was coming.

But Lizzie didn't stop. She groped out through the sand, trying to find something, anything to use as a weapon. There was nothing. She kicked and wriggled and still, she lay trapped under Wroxham, her hands empty, full of nothing. But sand.

She fisted up a handful, and just as Lady Wroxham began to regain her wind, she pitched it in her face.

It gave her time, a few precious seconds, to pull again, and the exquisite watered peacock silk gave with a wonderful rending of fabric. She kicked her legs free.

And then there was light, and the passage was filled with people—Jamie and Mr. Tupper and even the footman, Stephen. But all she could see was Jamie. Jamie as he rushed straight over to her side.

"Lizzie." His eyes, poring over her.

"I'm fine. Watch *her*." Lizzie pointed at Lady Wroxham.

Jamie gathered Lizzie into his chest as the other men surrounded Lady Wroxham, who groped slowly to her feet. The light from their lanterns lit the room.

The small cavern carved into the rock held a large stack of crates, all stamped with the British Broad Arrow. British Army guns. And three dead bodies. Smugglers by the look of them. Most likely killed by Lieutenant Francis Palmer. But there was time enough to tell Jamie that later.

At the moment the only thing Lizzie wanted was to feel his arm around her waist and the weight of a fowling piece in her hand. And for some reason, Jamie was carrying it. "You left this," was all he said.

"Thank you," she mumbled into his chest. Only Jamie would give her a gun as if it were a jewel.

"Steady, Lizzie. Handsomely now. It's over." Jamie again, knowing just what to say.

The others were turning their attention to the large portcullis door on the other side of the room. It was much the same construction as the smaller one. Tupper walked over to it.

"How does it open?"

They all looked at her. "How should I know?" Just because it was her house. She scanned the walls. "Everything else was up to the right. The rings probably. The rings there, for torches or lanterns. Try them. Twist or pull. It's bound to be one of them."

It was. The second on the left this time, instead of the right. The iron ring, when twisted and then pulled, ran a pulley mechanism, which lifted the heavy gated door to reveal McAlden, Maguire, and young Jims, carrying three lanterns. Their boots were wet. It must be high tide. She'd been so busy last night, she'd forgotten about the tides.

"Aunt Mary." Jamie was speaking to his aunt.

Lady Wroxham gave him no answer. She didn't even bother to share her contempt.

But Jamie persisted anyway. "Why? Why would you put everything you had in jeopardy?"

Her voice was incredulous with scorn. "Stupid man. Everything I had, I had because I had the brains to put it in jeopardy, to risk everything. Maguire had only a small paltry gang. They only worked when they wanted, only made a run when they thought they could sell. They needed to be led and to be told what to do. To orchestrate the shipments of the entire coast so they weren't competing against each other. To control the market, instead of merely supplying it. Why?" She hissed her answer. "Because I *wanted* it. Because someone could be the one to take all that money from the smuggling, and I decided it should be me."

"And you decided to betray your country for money?"

She snorted. "I'd hardly be foolish enough to do so for ideals."

There was nothing more to be said. Maguire and McAlden took her by the arms and led her out towards the mouth of the cave.

"Don't underestimate her," Lizzie called. "Keep a firm hold."

Jamie was standing over Wroxham's crumpled, bloody form. "Is he . . . ?"

"Still breathing. What happened?" He reached out to take her gun, but thought better of it. He satisfied himself by leveling his own gun at Wroxham.

"Overpowered the brute," she said with some vindictive satisfaction.

"Lizzie, are you run mad? He must weigh fourteen stone."

"That's why I kicked him in the cods. Hard. I didn't care for the way he spoke to me."

"My God, woman. Have you no idea you're just a little bird of a woman?"

"That's ridiculous. I'm no bird. I'm as angry as a cat. Odious man. He called me names. Bloody Oxford men, think they own the world."

"Ah. Poor stupid bastard." Jamie came closer and put his hand carefully along her cheek. "Made a fatal error, then, didn't he? He underestimated you."

"But you didn't." Was it hope that made her voice thready?

"I did once. An error I do not plan on ever repeating."

She felt a small wave of relief. But they still had, as Jamie had said, unfinished business between them. "What do you plan on doing? Now that you've solved this?"

"Well, strictly speaking, I did not solve this—you did. But with your permission, I should like to get credit for it with the Admiralty anyway."

"I've no particular regard for the Admiralty, so you must get most of the credit, though you must say extremely flattering things about my help."

"Thank you. And will you be my wife?"

"Is that another proposal? I have one of my own this time. Are you going to be my husband?"

"If you'll let me, Lizzie."

And of a moment, she could no longer joke. "Why should I let you? I'm still not sure I can trust you."

"Because I love you."

"You lied to me. You used me. You left me in prison. And you said it might happen again."

"I'm sorry. Deeply sorry. When this whole scheme began I . . . I just didn't plan on falling in love with you. And I know you had no intention of falling in love with me. But it happened. I did fall in love with you and I do love you. And I think perhaps you love me, at least a little bit. Or else you wouldn't be so angry. The opposite of love is indifference, and you're still mostly furious at me. And I know I'd have liked to throttle you a time or two, but as it happens I always find I'd much rather kiss you."

She scrunched up her face tight and closed. "That's not love, that's just lust."

"Well, it's a very good place to start. It's an important part of love."

"What if . . . love is not enough?"

"Of course it is. Love is enough. It's the only thing that matters. If I were to die tomorrow the only thing that would matter in my life is that I loved and was loved. All the medals, accolades, the victories will be nothing if I cannot say that I loved and was loved by an extraordinary young woman. By you, Lizzie."

"Well. There is that. I'd hate for your life to amount to nothing because of me."

He looked at her, pressing for the truth with those relentlessly honest gray eyes. The eyes that never let her lie to him and which had never lied to her.

"And you? You never did say, Lizzie."

"Of course I love you. What do you think I've been about?" She flung her arms out in exasperation. "Stupid man."

"Your stupid man. The man you love."

"Oh, don't bother turning your wolf eyes on me. I've become immune."

"Wolf eyes?" He laughed. "But if you're so immune, why have you got your eyes scrunched up tight?"

She smiled and let her eyebrows arch away, but she kept her eyes closed.

"I'll tell you what, Lizzie. I promise, if you open your eyes, I'll make it very much worth your while."

"Really?" She peeked one open.

"Yes, so open them. There's a big brawling world out there, Mrs. Marlowe. Didn't you know?"

She did.

Take your pick of the LORDS OF PASSION,
a steamy anthology featuring Virginia Henley,
Kate Pearce, and Maggie Robinson . . .

The Hague, Holland
November 28, 1719

"**D**amnation, Cadogan, you've the devil's own luck. You've won every hand we've played for the last sennight." Charles Lennox, Duke of Richmond, pushed his chair back from the games table and wiped his brow. "Stap me! I'm wiped out—you've had the lot!"

General William Cadogan glanced at his darkly handsome opponent. He was the illegitimate son of the late King Charles, who in his old age had impregnated his mistress, Louise de Kerouaille. "Would you like me to tally up, your grace?"

Richmond waved a negligent hand. "By all means, let me know the damage."

The dashing Irish general didn't take long. He had a damn good idea of what the duke had wagered and lost in their endless games of *écarté*. The duke was a heavy drinker, which was the main reason for his losses. The general set the seven scorecards down on the table, one for each night they had played. "I tot it up to a little over ten thousand guineas."

"*What?*" Richmond howled. "Are you jesting?" By the benign look on Cadogan's face, Charles Lennox knew he was serious. He downed the glass of gin sitting before him. "I don't have it. You'll have to accept my marker."

The men sitting at the table, who had been observing their deep play, began to murmur. Richmond flushed darkly. A gentleman always paid his gambling debts. His shrewd mind quickly inventoried his assets. Land was out of the question— the aristocracy accumulated property; it never relinquished it. Besides, the Earl of Cadogan already owned the hundred-acre Caversham estate on the outskirts of Reading.

Horses were the next things Richmond thought of. His family seat, Goodwood, at the foot of the South Downs, had a racing stable of Thoroughbreds. The thought of parting with his horses made him feel physically ill.

He looked across at General Cadogan. "You have a daughter, I believe."

"I do, your grace. Her name is Sarah."

"How would you like to make Sarah a countess? My son, the Earl of March, is without a wife." Lennox believed no man could resist such a magnanimous offer.

But the Earl of Cadogan, who was Marlborough's top general, and largely responsible for Britain's victories in the wars of Spanish Succession, was a shrewd negotiator. That was the reason he had been given the diplomatic duties concerned with resettlements among Great Britain, France, Holland, and Spain.

"My daughter, Lady Sarah, has a dowry of ten thousand pounds. If I gave you my daughter and her marriage settlement, I would have to pay you ten thousand instead of *you* paying *me* ten thousand." He raised his hands in appeal. "It doesn't fly, your grace."

"Charles is heir to my dukedom of Richmond and all the estates that encompasses," Lennox pointed out. "Lady Sarah could become a duchess." *Surely it's not necessary to remind you that we have royal blood?*

"A marriage between my daughter and your son, and heir, could be the solution."

Cadogan paused for emphasis. "Without the marriage settlement, of course."

"Curse you, general. You're not negotiating with the enemy here!"

"Since we are civilized gentlemen, I propose a compromise, your grace."

"Let's split the difference," Richmond suggested. "Your daughter's hand in marriage along with a dowry of *five thousand*."

The other men at the table leaned forward in anticipation of Cadogan's answer.

"Done!" The general's reply was heartfelt. He raised his hand to a servant. "Drinks all around. We must toast this historic union."

The Duke of Richmond raised his glass. "Here's to you and here's to me, and if someday we disagree, fuck you, here's to me!"

All the gentlemen roared with laughter and drained their glasses.

"I shall send for my daughter immediately."

"And I shall summon my heir," the duke declared.

"The *Green Lion* is a lovely name for a ship," Sarah exclaimed as they boarded at the Port of London.

"I only hope our cabin is warm. This is a dreadful season to be crossing to the Netherlands," Lady Cadogan said with a shiver.

"I'm glad I'm wearing my woolen dress and cloak. This is so exciting!"

The pair was shown below to their cabin, and when their trunk arrived, it took up most of the space between the two bunks.

"Such cramped quarters," the countess complained. "It's a good thing we will be arriving before dark tomorrow. But at least the cabin is warm."

"Oh, I think we are under way." Sarah grabbed hold of the bunk rail as the vessel swayed. She was bursting with excitement. "May I please go up on deck and watch as the *Green Lion* navigates through the Thames?"

"If you must, Sarah. But when the ship approaches Gravesend, you must come below decks immediately. Daylight will soon be gone, and the wind will be so fierce, it could easily blow you overboard," her mother cautioned.

The grave warning did not deter Sarah; it made her more eager to go up on deck.

"Thank you, Mother. I'll be careful."

Sarah climbed the stairs that led onto the deck and pulled her cloak tightly about her. She watched the docks recede slowly, but soon lost interest in looking back. She much preferred to look ahead and made her way to the very front of the vessel. She stood in wonder as the banks of the river widened. She breathed deeply, filling her lungs with sea air, as if the smell of tide wrack were the elixir of life.

She lifted her face to the cold breeze as she heard the gulls and terns screaming overhead. *What an exciting life to be a sailor!* Sarah stood enraptured as the ship reached the estuary and headed out to sea. She became aware that the light was fast fading from the day, and the moment the ship sailed into the North Sea, the wind whipped her cloak about and she remembered that she must go below.

The fierce wind was against her as she lowered her head and began to run. Suddenly she collided with someone, and the impact knocked the breath out of her.

"You clumsy, idiot girl! Watch what you're about, for Christ's sake."

Sarah paled as she stared up into the furious face of a young man. "I'm . . . I'm sorry, sir," she gasped.

"Sorry, be damned!" He blocked her way. "You haven't the brains of a bloody baboon, barreling down the deck like a loose cannon."

"I have to get below—I promised Mother."

"We all want to get belowdecks to a warm cabin, damn your eyes."

"You are frightening the girl, Charles. Let her pass," Henry Grey said quietly.

Charles Lennox grudgingly stepped aside. "The witless girl needed a lesson. I hope you remembered to bring that bottle of rum. It's colder than a whore's heart tonight."

When the Countess of Cadogan and Sarah stepped from their carriage at the Court of Holland, a liveried attendant ushered them inside. Margaret's father had been Chancellor of the Court before he retired, and the servants showed her great deference.

When they arrived at the suite of rooms that had been assigned to General Cadogan, he flung open the door and welcomed them warmly.

"Margaret, my dear, I hope your voyage wasn't a rough one."

"It was tolerable. December is no month to be at sea."

"It was an absolute necessity, my dear. We couldn't let an opportunity like this slip away." He looked at his young daughter and gave her a hug. "Were you seasick?"

"No, Father," she said breathlessly.

"That's my girl. Take off your cloak and let's have a look at you."

Sarah removed her cloak and bonnet. She smoothed her hands over her flattened hair. "I must look a fright."

"Nay, child. The wind has put roses in your cheeks."

Sarah blushed with pleasure at the compliment.

William raised his eyes to his wife. His daughter's figure was slight and her face extremely pale. "I hope you've brought her a decent dress to wear tomorrow."

"You gave me such short notice, there was no time to have a new gown made. In any case, it's cold. A woolen dress will suffice."

"Have you told her?" William asked.

"I thought it best to wait until we arrived. You may have that pleasure, my lord."

Told me what? Sarah went very still. She had an ominous feeling that her mother was being sarcastic. She doubted that *pleasure* would be involved. She couldn't find the words to ask, but the apprehensive look in her eyes questioned her father.

"We'll wait until after dinner," he said heartily. "Sarah looks like she could use some food. There's nothing like a thick broth to warm the cockles of your heart. After dinner, Sarah and I will have a private chat."

"I'll go and unpack." She sensed that her parents had something to discuss that concerned her. Something was in the air, and she took refuge in the short reprieve.

When she lifted the lid of the trunk that had been delivered to the bedchamber, she stroked her hand over the rich material of her mother's gowns. One was purple velvet, embroidered with gold, and another was black, quilted brocade decorated with crystals.

Sarah carefully lifted them from the trunk and hung them in the wardrobe, along with two other day dresses and the lovely whalebone panniers that went beneath. Her own clothes had been packed on the bottom, and as a result were slightly creased. As well as flannel petticoats and knitted stockings, she had brought only two dresses. One was oyster-colored wool with a cream frill around the high neck, and the other was gray with fitted sleeves that ended in white ruffles around the wrists. She wished that she had panniers to hold out her skirts. They would help disguise how thin she was, but her mother had decreed that she was still too young for grown-up fashions.

Sarah hung her dresses next to her mother's and sighed

with resignation at the contrast between the rich, fashionable gowns and her own plain attire.

Since the hour was late and the ladies had been traveling for the past two days, the trio ate dinner in Cadogan's suite. Tonight for some reason Sarah's appetite was nonexistent.

Her mother gave her a critical glance. "You must eat more. You will never fill out if all you do with food is push it about your plate."

Her father changed the subject. "What are you learning at school?"

"Latin," she said softly.

"Latin? What the devil good will Latin do you? Surely French would be better for a young lady of fashion."

I don't feel like a young lady of fashion. "We say our prayers in Latin."

"I wager you have some uncharitable names for the nuns."

Sarah's eyes sparkled with mischief. "We call them the *Sisters of the Black Plague.*"

Cadogan threw back his head and laughed. It tickled his Irish sense of humor. "By God, I warrant they teach you not to spit in church, and very little else." He bent close.

"I think a change of schools is in order. What d'you say, Sarah?"

"Oh, I would love it above all things."

When they finished eating, the earl gave a speaking nod to his wife and she excused herself so that her husband could have privacy for the chat with his daughter.

Cadogan led his daughter to a chair before the fire and sat down opposite her. "The time has come when we must think about your future, Sarah."

She nodded but made no reply, knowing there was more to come.

"I have no son, so I want the very best for my daughter." He paused to let his words sink in. "For some time now I have been searching for a suitable match for you. I would never consider any noble of a lower rank than my own."

Sarah's blue eyes widened. *You are talking about finding a future husband for me.*

"Not only must he be titled, he must be heir to wealth and property."

You married a lady from the Netherlands. I hope you don't look for a match for me here. She clasped her hands together tightly. *I want to live in England.*

"I have been offered a match for you that surpasses all my expectations. It is an undreamed-of opportunity that will raise you to the pinnacle of the aristocracy. A premier Duke of the Realm has asked for your hand in marriage for his son and heir."

Sarah sat silently as questions chased each other through her mind. *Who? Where?*

When? But most puzzling was *why?*

William Cadogan's face was beaming. "The Duke of Richmond is offering marriage with his son, Charles Lennox, the Earl of March." He leaned forward and patted her hand. "Sarah, my dear, you will be the Countess of March, and the future Duchess of Richmond."

"I . . . I can't believe it," she murmured. "Are we to be betrothed?"

Her father waved a dismissive hand. "You are to be *wed*, not betrothed!" He loosened his neckcloth. "Fortunately, Richmond and his son are here at The Hague."

"So we will be able to meet each other and see if we suit?" she asked shyly.

"Of course you will suit! The marriage contracts have already been drawn up. You will meet each other at your wedding . . . tomorrow."

Sarah was stunned as a sparrow flown into a wall. *"Tomorrow?"*

Don't miss ETERNAL FLAME,
the latest novel from from Cynthia Eden,
in stores now!

"You shouldn't go in there." The husky, *very female* voice stopped Zane cold just as he prepared to climb the steps leading up to Dusk.

The voice was laced with a soft drawl, edged with a breath of sex, and it crawled over his body like a caress.

A demon shoved past him, heading inside Dusk, and when the door opened, the beat of the music blasted Zane's ears and the scent of drugs burned his nostrils.

"Of course, you don't have to listen to me," she murmured. *Jana.* He turned his head a few inches to the right and saw her slide from the darkness. "It can be your funeral."

She looked vulnerable. Small, delicate. Almost helpless as she stood in the shadows with her arms crossed over her chest. Watching him with such big eyes.

But her words... "Ah... did you just threaten me?" He moved away from the door. Turned his back on the den and began to stalk her.

She crept once more toward the shadows and he followed her. His heart rate kicked up. *She's making it too easy.*

"You won't believe this," she told him, "but I'm not the threat tonight. Well, not the one you need to be worried about."

She was close enough to grab now.

A soft sigh slipped past her lips as her hands dropped to her sides. "You shouldn't have come here. You should've just taken the demon in and called it a day."

A shocked laugh broke from his lips, one without a drop of humor. "Lady, you *killed* someone in that alley."

She flinched. "The vampire would have killed me. I didn't have a choice." Her right hand lifted and rubbed against her chest. Thanks to his demon-enhanced senses, he saw the blood on her shirt, and he caught the coppery scent on the wind. "What did you want me to do?" she asked, and heat blasted through her words. "Just stand there and let him cut my heart out?"

A muscle jerked in his jaw.

"Or maybe I should have waited for you," she muttered, those sexy eyes narrowing, "like he wanted. I should have waited, and then I should have made sure you were the one who didn't walk out of that alley."

His hands flew out and he caught her, pulling her close and lifting her right off her toes. "Don't make the mistake of thinking I'm easy to kill."

Her chin inched up. "And you don't need to make the mistake of thinking you're immortal. Everyone can die. *Everyone.*"

"You'd know, wouldn't you, baby? You kill for the highest bidder."

She didn't blink. Those eyes stayed locked on him, still blue. The fire hadn't lit within her yet. If it had, her eyes would have been bloodred.

"Do you know what I did to the last Ignitor who came at me with fire in her eyes?" he demanded. Her mouth was temptingly close. He'd kissed that mouth before. Tasted her. Wanted more. *Fool.*

A guy's dick could get him into some serious trouble.

"Dumb ass," she said, and his eyes narrowed. "I'm not charging up. I'm trying to *warn* you."

"About what?"

"My . . . services." The right side of her mouth kicked up into a hard smile, and damn if a dimple didn't wink at him. *Deceptive package.* "Who do you think the number-one target is in this town? Who do you think the demons want taken out? The vamps?"

Shit.

"That's right. *You.* The vamp in that alley wanted you taken out, and he sure wasn't the only one to want a fried demon handed to him." Her gaze darted behind him to Dusk. "The demons sure don't like that you've been hunting your own kind."

Fuck 'em. "I don't hunt them all." What? Was he defending himself? To her? "Just the ones who cross the line." His fingers were digging too hard into her arms.

He took a breath and let her slide back to the ground, let her feet touch down, but he didn't free her. Wouldn't. He had plans for Jana Carter.

"What line?" she asked him, shaking her head. "The one *you* made up? The one that says some folks are bad, some are good, and smart, all-powerful you gets to punish the ones you *think* screwed up?"

He glared at her. Like she could judge him.

"Maybe I *should* let them rip you apart." Her tongue flashed out to lick her bottom lip.

He couldn't help it. His stare dipped and followed that fast lick. His body tightened. *Damn.* He took a breath and swore he tasted her. "If you'd been smart, you would've left town. After you killed the vamp, you should have run."

"Maybe." A shrug. "But you came into the fire for me."

Because he'd thought she needed him. Thought she was a human who'd needed rescuing. The truth was that the woman could have gotten out of that house without the flames even touching one inch of her perfect skin.

"No one's ever tried to save me before," she added. "I thought you were . . . sweet."

He growled.

"So I wanted to even the score."

And keep an eye out for Donna Kauffman's latest,
OFF KILTER, coming next month!

Turn the page for a fun, flirty preview . . .

"**M**an up, for God's sake, and drop the damn thing."

He supposed he should be thankful she could only turn his heart to stone.

"We're not sending in nude shots," Roan replied through an even smile, even as the chants and taunts escalated. "So, I don't understand the need to take things to such an extreme—"

"The contest rules state, very clearly and deliberately, that they're looking for provocative," Tessa responded, sounding every bit like a person who'd also been forced into a task she'd rather not have taken on. Which she had been.

Sadly, that fact had not brought them closer.

She shifted to yet another camera she'd mounted on yet another tripod, he supposed so the angle of the sun was more to her liking. "Okay, lean back against the stone wall, prop one leg, rest that . . . sword thing of yours—"

"'Tis a claymore. Belonged to the McAuleys for four centuries. Victorious in battle, 'tis an icon of our clan." And heavy as all hell to foist about.

"Lovely. Prop your icon in front of you, then. I'm fairly certain it will hide what needs hiding."

His eyebrows lifted at that, but rather than take offense, he merely grinned. "I wouldnae be so certain of it, lassie. We're a clan known for the size of our . . . swords."

"Yippee," she shot back, clearly unimpressed. "So, drop the plaid, position your . . . sword, and let's get on with it. It's the illusion of baring it all we're going for here. I'll make sure to preserve your fragile modesty."

She was no fun. No fun 'tall.

"The other guys did it," she added, resting folded hands on the top of the camera. "In fact," she went on, without even the merest hint of a smile or dry amusement, "they seemed quite happy to accommodate me."

He couldn't imagine any man wanting to bare his privates for Miss Vandergriff's pleasure. Not if he wanted to keep them intact, at any rate.

He was a bit thrown off by his complete inability to charm her. He charmed everyone. It was what he did. He admittedly enjoyed, quite unabashedly, being one of the clan favorites because of his affable, jovial nature. As far as he was concerned, the world would be a much better place if folks could get in touch with their happy parts, and stay there.

He didn't know much about her, but from what little time they'd spent together this afternoon, he didn't think Tessa Vandergriff had any happy parts. However, the reason behind her being rather happiness-challenged wasn't going to be his mystery to solve. She'd been on the island for less than a week now, and her stay on Kinloch was as a guest, and therefore temporary. Thank the Lord.

The island faced its fair share of ongoing trials and tribulations, and had the constant challenge of sustaining a fragile economic resource. Despite that, he'd always considered both the McAuley and MacLeod clans as being cheerful, welcoming hosts. But they had enough to deal with without adopting a surly recalcitrant into their midst.

"Well," he said, smiling broadly the more her scowl deepened. "'Tis true, the single men of this island have little enough to choose from." The crowd took a collective breath at that, but his attention was fully on her now. Gripping the claymore in one fist, he leaned against the stacked stone wall, well aware of the tableau created by the twin peaks that framed the MacLeod fortress, each of them towering behind him. He braced his legs, folded his arms across his bare chest, sword blade aloft . . . and looked her straight in the eye as he let a slow, knowing grin slide across his face. "Me, I'm no' so desperate as all that."

That got a collective gasp from the crowd. But rather than elicit so much as a snarl from Miss Vandergriff, or perhaps goading her so far as to pack up and walk away—which he'd have admittedly deserved—she shocked him instead. By smiling. Fully. He hadn't thought her face capable of arranging itself in such a manner. And so broadly, too, with such stunning gleam. He was further damned to discover it did things to his own happy parts that she had no business affecting.

"No worries," she stated, further captivating him with the transformative brilliance of her now knowing smile. She gave him a sizzling once over before easily meeting his eyes again. "You're not my type."

This was not how things usually went for him. He felt . . . frisked. "Then I'm certain you can be objective enough to find an angle that shows off all my best parts without requiring a more blatant, uninspired pose. I understand from Kira that you're considered to be quite good with that equipment."

The chants of the crowds shifted to a few whistles as the tension between photographer and subject grew to encompass even them.

"Given your reluctance to play show-and-tell, I'd hazard to guess I'm better with mine than you are with yours," she replied easily, but the spark remained in her eyes.

Goading him.

"Why don't you be the judge?" Holding her gaze in exclusive focus, the crowd long since forgotten now, he pushed away from the wall and, with sword in one hand, slowly unwrapped his kilt with the other.

He took far more pleasure than was absolutely necessary from watching her throat work as he unashamedly revealed thighs and ass. He wasn't particularly vain or egotistical, but he was well aware that a lifetime spent climbing all over this island had done its duty where his physical shape was concerned, as it had for most of the islanders. They were a hardy lot.

There was a collective gasp from the crowd as he held a fistful of unwrapped plaid in front of him, dangling precariously from one hand, just on the verge of—

That's it! Tessa all but leapt behind the camera and an instant later, the shutter started whirring. Less than thirty seconds later, she straightened and pushed her wayward curls out of her face, her no-nonsense business face back on track. "Got it. Good! We're all done here." She started dismantling her equipment. "You can go ahead and get dressed," she said, dismissively, not even looking at him now.

He held on to the plaid—and his pride—and tried not to look as annoyed as he felt. The shoot was blessedly over. That was all that mattered. No point in being irritated that he'd just been played by a pro.

She glanced up, the smile gone as she dismantled her second tripod with the casual grace of someone so used to the routine and rhythm of it she didn't have to think about it. "I'll let you know when I get the shots developed."

He supposed he should be thankful she had saved him the humiliation of publicly rubbing her smooth manipulation of him in his face. Except he wasn't feeling particularly gracious at the moment.